STALIN'S BARBER

STALIN'S BARBER

A NOVEL

★

PAUL M. LEVITT

TAYLOR TRADE PUBLISHING

LANHAM • NEW YORK • BOULDER • TORONTO • PLYMOUTH, UK

Published by Taylor Trade Publishing
An imprint of The Rowman & Littlefield Publishing Group, Inc.
4501 Forbes Boulevard, Suite 200, Lanham, Maryland 20706
www.rowman.com

10 Thornbury Road, Plymouth PL6 7PP, United Kingdom

Distributed by National Book Network

British Library Cataloguing in Publication Information Available

Library of Congress Cataloging-in-Publication Data
Levitt, Paul M.
Stalin's barber : a novel / Paul M. Levitt.
    p. cm.
ISBN 978-1-58979-771-0 (cloth : alk. paper) — ISBN 978-1-58979-772-7 (electronic)
1. Barbers—Russia—Fiction. 2. Albanians—Russia—Fiction. 3. Stalin, Joseph, 1879–1953—Fiction. 4. Soviet Union—History—1925-1953—Fiction. I. Title.
PS3612.E935S73 2012
813'.6—dc23

                                                                              2012027405

Printed in the United States of America

To Luther Wilson

STALIN'S MUSTACHE

in homage to Osip Mandelstam

In Warsaw near the Tomb
of the Unknown Soldier,
in a treeless square,
there used to scowl a statue

of Feliks Dzierżyński,
founder of the CheKa,
the Bolshevik Secret Police.
His nickname was "Bloody Felek."

Before the unveiling,
someone managed to paint
the statue's hands blood-red.
When the string was pulled,

the dignitaries gasped:
the blood of his victims
seemed to drip
from Bloody Felek's hands.

The speaker on the podium
began to stammer.
The military band
struck up, then stopped;

feebly began again.
To the stuttering tuba,
the string was pulled back.

Fifty years later, ten thousand
people jammed the square
to watch the demolition
of a monument to a mass murderer.

*

My cousin Ewa tells the tale
of yet another fallen icon:
a giant statue of Stalin,
the largest in the world.

Taller than the Statue of Liberty,
the dictator stained the sky
at the joining of two great rivers:
the Volga and the Don—

his "sneer of cold command"
staring down the starving
Ukraine. The ten-story
pedestal still stands.

Stalin was toppled into the water—
shallow enough, they say,
that from the cruise boats one can see
his colossal face.

Ewa was on one of those boats:
"From where I stood,
I only caught a glimpse
of Stalin's mustache."

She giggles. She must have told
this story countless times.
We sit around the table smiling,
sipping home-made hawthorn wine.

Stalin's mustache.
The empty
pedestal still stands.

—Ioanna Warwick

CONTENTS

Part II

ACKNOWLEDGMENTS

Like a nested doll, a novel masks the other figures in the finished form. So let the unmasking begin. I am particularly indebted to Kathryn Barth and Robert Hohlfelder, who hosted a Christmas party at which Bob described a visit to Istanbul and his first and only Turkish haircut. His own vivid storytelling planted the seed for a story about a barber and his tonsorial skills. For their suggestions, I thank Peter Kracht and the anonymous reader at Verso Books who read a first draft of the manuscript. My colleagues Elissa Guralnick and Tim Lyons split the chapters between them and, not surprisingly in light of their critical skills, advised revisions in organization. Michael Glueck, a professional writer, spent a day on the beach with the manuscript and returned with not only a sunburn but also several pointed observations that led to further revisions. But, of all the stylistic advice I received, none eclipsed that of my colleague Victoria Tuttle, a brilliant prose writer.

With any historical fiction, the author is always trying to balance fact and fancy. Not knowing to whom I could turn for an evaluation of historical accuracy, I asked my friend Alan Wald, an eminent professor at the University of Michigan. He recommended Susan Weissman, professor of politics at Saint Mary's College of California. Suzi, the author of several books, hosts a weekly radio program on KPFK in Los Angeles and writes on Left dissent. She read the manuscript and sent me a list of corrections, as well as a coruscating reader's report. Her personal help cannot be exaggerated. She is a gem beyond price.

All writers should be so fortunate as to enjoy the level of moral and technical support that I received. My daughter, Andrea Stein, and her husband, Stefan, were at my dinner table when I needed them. My son Scot, his wife, Erica, his daughter, Amy, and his son, Mathew, gave me invaluable assistance. My wife, Nancy, never once complained about my moodiness and absences from home. My sister, Sandra, years ago forgave me my reclusiveness.

Frank Delaney, the Irish novelist, deserves a paragraph to himself. Talk about the kindness of strangers! From a simple dinner to an exchange of e-mails to a reading of the manuscript has grown a lasting friendship. His advice, his untiring efforts to see this book published, and his enduring generosity have set a standard for kindness that I have never seen the equal of.

For their help in the production and preparation of this book, I am indebted to Jehanne Schweitzer, senior production editor for Rowman & Littlefield, for her meticulous work; and to Gene Margaritondo for his impeccable copyediting and creative insights. His command of English usage is daunting; hence, any grammatical errors or stylistic misadventures proceed from my own imperfections. For their careful proofreading, I thank Lillia Gajewski and A. J. Kazlouski.

Given the shrinking population of readers and the paucity of presses willing to publish literary fiction, albeit historical, writers increasingly need some form of financial support to offset printing costs. I am particularly lucky to have received such support from Philip DiStefano, chancellor, University of Colorado at Boulder; Russell Moore, provost, University of Colorado at Boulder; and the Kayden Research Grant Committee, University of Colorado at Boulder.

The courage to publish this book comes from one person, Rick Rinehart. To him, I say, thank you.

Although it has become a cliché to observe that all art is collaboration and that we stand on the shoulders of giants, I cannot leave until I acknowledge to which authors and works, in particular, I am especially indebted.

SOURCES

Anna Akhmatova, *Selected Poems*
Isaac Babel, *Short Stories*
Andrey Biely, *St. Petersburg*
T. J. Binyon, *Pushkin*
Bertolt Brecht, *Mother Courage*
Frederic Buechner, *Godric*

Mikhail Bugakov, *The Master and Margarita*; *The White Guard*; and *The Heart of a Dog*

Ivan Bunin, "The Gentleman from San Francisco"

Philip Cannistraro and Brian R. Sullivan, *Il Duce's Other Woman: The Untold Story of Margherita Sarfatti, Mussolini's Jewish Mistress*

Alfred Edward Chamot, trans., *Selected Russian Short Stories*

Anton Chekhov, "Gooseberries" and "Ward 6"

Robert Edwards, *The Winter War: Russia's Invasion of Finland, 1939–1940*

Nikolai Erdman, *The Suicide*

Merle Fainsod, *How Russia Is Ruled*

Orlando Figes, *A People's Tragedy*, *Natasha's Dance*, and *The Whisperers*

Sheila Fitzpatrick, *Everyday Life in Early Soviet Russia*

Varian Fry, *Surrender on Demand*

Vsevolod Garshin, *A Red Rose*

Evgenia Ginzburg, *Into the Whirlwind* and *Within the Whirlwind*

Nikolai Gogol, "The Overcoat"

Ivan Goncharov, *Oblomov*

Maxim Gorky, Avrahm Yarmolinsky, and Baroness Moura Budberg, *The Collected Short Stories of Maxim Gorky*

Vasily Grossman, *Life and Fate*

O. Henry (William Sydney Porter), "The Ransom of Red Chief"

Ilya Ilf and Eugene Petrov, *The Twelve Chairs*

Amy Knight, *Who Killed Kirov?*

Arthur Koestler, *Darkness at Noon*

Walter Krivitsky, *In Stalin's Secret Service*

Natalia Kuziakina, *Theatre in the Solovki Prison Camp*

Mikhail Lermontov, *A Hero of Our Time*

Nadezhda Mandelstam, *Hope against Hope* and *Hope Abandoned*

Osip Mandelstam, *Selected Poems*

Thomas Mann, *Mario and the Magician*

Vladimir Mayakovsky, *The Bedbug*

Simon Sebag Montefiore, *Stalin: The Court of the Red Tsar* and *The Young Stalin*

Alexander Orlov, *The Secret History of Stalin's Crimes*

Boris Pasternak, *Doctor Zhivago*

Ronald Ribman, *The Journey of the Fifth Horse*

Roy R. Robson, *Solovki: The Story of Russia Told through Its Most Remarkable Islands*

Joshua Rubenstein, *The Life and Times of Ilya Ehrenburg*

Anatoli Rybakov, *The Children of the Arbat*

Thomas Seltzer, ed., *Best Russian Short Stories*

Victor Serge, *The Case of Comrade Tulayev*

Varlam Shalamov, *Kolyma Tales*
Mikhail Sholokhov, *And Quiet Flows the Don*
Kirill (Konstantin) Simonov, *The Living and the Dead*
Isaac Bashevis Singer, "Gimpel the Fool"
C. P. Snow and Pamela Hanford Johnson, eds., *Stories from Modern Russia*
Aleksandr Solzhenitsyn, *One Day in the Life of Ivan Denisovich*; *The First Circle*;
and *The Gulag Archipelago*
Sophocles, *Antigone*
J. Swire, *King Zog's Albania*
Yuri Trifonov, *The House on the Embankment*
Marina Tsvetaeva, *Selected Poems*
Suzi Weissman, *Victor Serge: The Course Is Set on Hope*

PART I

EXILE

After sprinkling alcohol on the British sergeant's left ear to singe the unsightly sprouting hairs, the barber Avraham Bahar ignited the liquid just as two men in long overcoats and black fedoras burst into the shop, pulled out machine pistols, fired, and fled, but not before one of them shouted, "Death to foreigners!"

From the force of the shots, the barber's chair slowly turned, though the sergeant remained motionless. As the red spot on the barbering cape rapidly blossomed into blood, Avraham removed it and grew faint. A gaping hole exposed the man's slippery intestines, which slowly oozed, like eels, through the gore and down his legs. When the bloody snakes ran into the sergeant's shoes, Avraham puked.

Avraham, having never before witnessed death, staggered to the front door and cried into the rain for help. Minutes later, he heard the wailing siren of an ambulance. The gendarmerie and medical attendants pushed through a crowd of the curious. As the police interrogated him, an agitated Avraham walked backward and forward repeating, "*Vey iz mir*" (Woe is me). Could he identify the men? Why was the sergeant alone in the shop? Where were the other barbers?

"I can tell you," said the investigating officer, "it looks suspicious to me. You and Sergeant Jenkins by yourselves. Two unidentified men riddle the sergeant and leave you untouched. It smells like a setup."

By the time the police left, with the admonition that Avraham be available for further questioning, the barber had already begun his characteristic parsing of words. His mother, a literature teacher, had taught him that both letters and life require close reading. Had his aunt not read the meaning of a priest's muttering at a café, his family would not have escaped the Kishinev pogrom of 1903—a time when the clergy incited mobs to kill Jews. On her advice, Mr. Bahar had bribed a Greek tailor to hide them in the event of a riot. Avraham and his family had escaped harm and emigrated to Tirana, where they resettled and changed their name in the hope of living free of anti-Semitism. But that was twenty-eight years ago, when Avraham was eighteen.

But now Avraham had to face a new reality: "Death to foreigners." The absence of the word "the," as in "the foreigners," meant the assassins wanted all non-Albanians out of the country, not just the British. His parents had openly spoken Russian and readily admitted that they had emigrated from Kishinev. And what of the police officer's words, which all but accused him of engaging in a setup? "It looks more than a bit suspicious to me." And the initial phrase, "I can tell you," emphasized the point that the officer had no doubts about the killers' accomplice. And don't forget the accusatory diction, Avraham told himself. The word "riddled" he wouldn't even begin to fractionate.

The next day, as he followed his usual path to work through the bazaar, with its maze of cobbled, crooked streets, he was stopped at a roadblock by two Albanian soldiers in poorly fitting uniforms and unpolished leather boots. Groups of women dressed from head to toe in black burqas, with narrow eye slits, squatted by a wall, their embroideries spread out before them on inexpensive Turkish rugs, while across the way sat a chaos of other vendors, selling charcoal, vegetables, chickens, eggs, fruit, firewood, pots, trinkets, baskets, and rope. The only unveiled women were dark-skinned Gypsies, who were reading fortunes and using short-handled brooms to sweep up the market refuse. Off to one side, under a porch roof, moneylenders haggled over percentages. All across this city of thirty-two thousand people, the government, determined to catch the assassins, had posted descriptions of the killers and put up roadblocks.

"Your papers!" demanded one of the soldiers, folding his arms and slyly holding out a hand to indicate that baksheesh would do as well.

Avraham shook his head in despair. Reaching for his papers, he remarked, "I can remember when people doffed their caps at one another. Now they ask them for identification—or bribes."

"Idiot!" said the second soldier. "We are merely collecting for the poor."

"Preventing poverty with charity," Avraham remarked, "is as effective as making a bullet out of shit."

The blow to the nose happened so quickly that Avraham never saw the soldier swing the butt of his rifle. Kneeling on the ground, he wiped the blood from his face. In the distance, he could hear one of the soldiers laughing and repeating, "A bullet out of shit."

Two days later, he paid the groundskeeper of the Jewish cemetery a large sum to have his parents' plots cared for in perpetuity. In front of their marble stones, he silently spoke to them, occasionally reaching down to remove an offending weed. As he read the dates of their deaths, Esther Bahar, 1929, Isaac Bahar, 1927, he remembered attending one of his mother's classes in Tirana, where she taught both Russian and English, and his father giving Turkish haircuts to men of every nationality: Muslims, Christians, and Jews. He consoled himself knowing that in exile he would be taking with him sacred memories and, of course, his handsomely painted *matryoshka* doll, the one that his mother had given him on his sixth birthday, the one that told Pushkin's fairy tale of Ruslan and Liudmila. Avraham's mother had used the nested doll to teach him that most great writers, even the incomparable Shakespeare, root their tales in a family. By exploring how parents and children relate to one another and how their travails affect other family members, even outsiders, writers create a nested fiction.

On his way home from the cemetery, he felt the weight of his impending decision: whether to remain in Albania or leave for Russia. The comforts of his house would be hard to forsake—a bath and a kitchen range, a sitting room and a fireplace—even though a poor draft allowed smoke to befog the house and drive the scorpions from their hiding places. But at least he could afford the price of wood; these days, not many could. Best of all, the house had a large garden, enclosed by a high brick wall, and dozens of trees: walnut, cherry, plum, fig, and thorn. He likened gardening, his passion, to barbering. Both required pruning and trimming, clipping and cutting, and a sense of shape and design. Some trees leafed low, some high, just as he shaved some sideburns above the ears, some below.

In the Jewish quarter, Avraham had heard whispers that a single silver candlestick could buy passage to Skopje, where fellow congregants would hide a person until it was safe to cross into Rumania, then Moldavia, and finally Ukraine, where a new society, a democratic one, had begun to take shape. When he had first shared his thoughts of emigrating with Rubin Bélawitz, his rotund childhood confidant and a woodcarver, Rubin had cut him short.

"The Tsar may have been deposed, but Russia's no paradise. If you think so, you're dreaming. You know the adage: 'Ivan will always be Ivan.'"

Avraham had replied by mentioning some of the Jews in the new Soviet government: Kaganovich, Kamenev, Litvinov, Mekhlis, Pauker, Radek, Sverdlov, Trotsky, Uritsky, Yakolev, Zinoviev. Was their presence not a portent of a new order, one without religious hatred? At least in Russia, a Jew could live safely.

"If the country's so wonderful, why do all the different nationalities, including the Jews, want to speak their own language? They should all be glad to speak the same tongue. It's just lucky for you that you know how to speak it—and Yiddish."

"We are dying here, Rubin. Albania is dying."

For many days after the grisly murder, Avraham ruefully looked out the front window of his barbershop, the same one his father had opened in the shadow of a mosque. At that moment, the muezzin's voice sounded, calling the faithful to prayer, and Avraham recalled the old Muslim aristocracy demanding perfect pruning and perfume for their finely fashioned beards. But that was before the worldwide depression had put an end to silk robes and imported cigarettes and a costumed palace guard, a time before the Albanian government of King Ahmet Bey Zog was forced to import grain from Fascist Italy and dance to Mussolini's tunes. The fancy carriages and plumed horses that used to sound a merry tune as they passed down the streets had disappeared into the vortex of European bankruptcy. Handsome homes had fallen into disrepair, gardens gone to seed. Even the professors and poets who would sit in the barbershop quoting from journals and exchanging literary ideas had disappeared. So too the gazettes featuring serialized literary novels, now replaced with patriotic stories extolling the impoverished homeland. The barbershop no longer rang with the political arguments among Greeks, Russians, Armenians, Serbs, Mingrelians, Azerians, and Kurds who would huddle around the charcoal burner, sipping Turkish tea, and weigh the virtues of independence or confederation. All gone. Now the barber chairs and benches stood empty, gaunt auguries of the future.

Avraham had but one *naches* (joy) as he stared at the wind-tossed trash and watched two men fighting over the carcass of a dead cat. Thank god that his parents had not lived to witness these troubled times: Fascism in Italy, Nazis in Germany, the Balkans in turmoil, crushing debt in Albania, and the attempt the year before in Vienna on King Zog's life. Little wonder that people of all faiths were fleeing, the roads clogged with wagons and carts. The newspapers were saying that planes would no longer take bookings and that Greece and Macedonia, unable to handle the mass exodus, had sent troops to seal their borders. It could be only a matter of time until Albania stopped issuing emigration visas.

Should he leave or should he stay? Tirana was home to his parents' graves, to his friends, like dear Rubin Bélawitz, to his barbershop, his house and trees, his memories. King Zog was a liberal monarch, well aware of the danger Italy posed. Political disruptions were fugacious; they came and went. Perhaps this one would also blow over, in which case why quit the country? The familiar streets of Tirana were as much a part of him as his own limbs. Here he could see dancing dervishes, sheep slaughtered in the squares for the Bajram feast, turbaned Muslim priests, and bearded Christian bishops. Tirana had airmail and passenger service, electric lights, military and civil hospitals, and traditional bakeries that still prepared his favorite bread dough, Valya, in the old-fashioned way: thin, coated with paprika and olive oil, and then shaped into a circle and baked. He had often brought his neighbors Valya bread to repay their many kindnesses. To leave such people and this city was tantamount to amputating a limb.

On the other hand, Tirana had no sewer lines or water pipes, no buses or trams, no railways. Roads were generally deep-worn tracks that became muddy ditches in the rain. Half-naked beggars constantly pulled at one's sleeves; fanatical Sunni Turks conspired in cafés and swore allegiance to the sultan; corruption was rampant; eligible Jewish women were in short supply. And, perhaps worst of all, he feared that the freedoms he enjoyed as a Jew would be lost under Fascism.

Assiduously studying the newspapers and questioning his every customer, he worried that if he remained too long, he might lose the chance to leave. Like a spiritual accountant, he totted up and weighed all his outstanding moral debts and loans and collateral and promissory notes and good intentions, met and unmet. As so often happens, his decision came not from a careful reading of his human balance sheet, but from events beyond his control. When he saw Albanian brown shirts marching in the street and read Mussolini's demands that Albania pay for its debts to Italy by granting Il Duce control of the sugar, telegraph, and electrical monopolies, and that King Zog make the teaching of the Italian language compulsory in all schools, he lost all his parsing reservations and decided to flee before all the borders closed and checkpoints appeared on the roads leading in and out of major towns.

To purchase his escape, Avraham sold his barbering equipment at a loss to a competitor on the other side of Tirana. His shop was purchased by a Tajik barber who attended the neighboring mosque. Well known for his haggling, the man pursued a simple strategy: he stated his price and then fell silent. In the end, Avraham received half of what he had asked for. His last painful task was to say goodbye to Rubin. They agreed to have dinner at the Juvenilja restaurant on Avraham's last night in Tirana. Fortunately neither man, unlike their parents, observed the dietary laws, because Rubin suggested a main course of *kukurec*, stuffed sheep's intestines, dipped in yogurt and red wine, followed by a salad of roasted red peppers, onions, and toasted walnuts. At first, Avraham's broken nose sustained the conversation. But then Rubin, wishing to make light of that unfortunate subject, tried another tack. "Do you remember our camping trips in the Dajti Mountains? Such wonderful days!"

"When it didn't rain."

"Who noticed? We made a fire and played cards and talked about which girls we had and we hadn't. And no matter how many times you tried, you could never persuade Dominika."

"True," said Avraham, fondling the corner of his napkin.

"Such a dark-haired temptress. Now she's married to a farmer."

"Marta, remember her?" He paused. "I thought I loved her."

"Did she ever answer your letters?"

"Never," he sighed.

"Just as well. She was too religious for your tastes."

"My tastes?" He held up the palms of his hands. "What are they? How does anyone know himself? Our heads always get in the way."

Through the restaurant window, they observed in the distance fractured lightning marbling the darkness.

"Albania is black," Avraham remarked, "but in Russia a new day is dawning."

Scoffing, Rubin said, "I don't believe in omens."

"I'm no political philosopher, Rubin, but from the reading I've done, I really think the measure of a government is not how well it treats the powerful but rather the weak."

"Avraham, tell me. Who are these weak you cry over: thieving Gypsies and Muslims with four wives and fifteen children?"

"No," Avraham sadly replied, "most of the people."

Rubin shook his head skeptically. Avraham looked at Rubin's fat cheeks and thought that he had never wanted for a meal.

"You can't name a dozen."

"The crippled, the paralyzed, the limbless, the blind, the beggars, the hungry, the out of work, the stateless refugees, the dispossessed, the Christians, the Jews . . ."

"*Genug* (Enough)! That's twelve. In other words, you're mostly talking about the sick and the poor."

"Which is most of the world."

"No government can solve the problem of hunger."

"Socialism?"

"Even if you could persuade people to share—and I don't believe you can—there are only so many steaks, so many houses, so many jobs." He laughed censoriously. "Even just so much caviar."

Avraham studied the fading light. The lightning had ceased, and the moon sat on a ridge, as if resting before rising. To lighten the weight of parting, Rubin manufactured a chuckle and said:

"You mentioned our camping trips. Do you remember our lying on the ground and imagining that above us, somewhere in that starry plenitude, planets existed where people lived the Law?"

Rubin wiped his mouth with the napkin and slapped the table. "When Hillel said, 'What is hateful to you, do not do to your neighbor. This is the whole Torah; all the rest is commentary,' he was stating the Golden Rule. A dream it is. You notice, don't you, he left out all the difficult parts, the commentary."

With more hope than assurance, Avraham responded, "Where I'm going is a better world."

"Such a place exists only in words."

Eventually theirs faltered, a sign that it was time to part. Rubin insisted on paying for the meal, but before leaving the table, he touched his friend on the hand and said:

"I have a gift for you."

He handed Avraham a small package.

Rubin watched intently as Avraham untied the string and opened a teakwood box, revealing a hand-carved razor that Rubin had fashioned.

"It's a copy of my favorite . . ."

Rubin interjected, "Same color, same length, same turquoise facing." He added proudly, "A perfect replica, even to the raised edge that looks like a closed blade."

"It's a work of art."

"Feel the finish . . . like your own razor. See for yourself."

Avraham turned the carving over and over, admiring its exactitude. His smile indicated pleasure but also mystification.

"Yes, I know, you're thinking what can I do with this wood carving. I could say treat it as a knickknack or display it in your barbershop." He shyly looked at his hands. "I just wanted to give you something that would remind you of Tirana . . . and me."

"But I have nothing for you."

"You've given me years of friendship."

"If you keep talking this way, Rubin . . ." He choked on the words.

At the Lana River, where the bullfrogs filled the still darkness of summer nights, they embraced and parted. Rubin, sick with sorrow, slunk across the bridge, remembering how Avraham used to make loneliness strange with his presence. But Avraham was now persuaded that survival eclipsed friendship.

He unlocked his front door, packed two cane baskets, one with food, the other with his barbering equipment and personal items, like the nested doll he had removed from his shop. In his bathroom mirror, he studied his collapsed nose bridge. His was no longer the handsome face and Roman visage that an Italian client had once compared to Vatican canvases, perhaps because of his Mediterranean coloring and the sensuous full lips he had inherited from his mother. From his father he owed his soft-spokenness, strong hands, and long narrow fingers. His sharp facial features were accentuated by high cheekbones and a narrow chin. Having always wished to stand six feet tall, he had missed the mark by three inches. Besides his broken nose, he bore other signs of wear: a thinning hairline and legs with prominent varicose veins, a barber's bane.

He made it a point to leave his small house unlocked, for beggars to bed there. Wending his way along the cobblestone alleys in the wretched precincts of the Gypsy village, from which the government drew its *hamals* (blacksmiths) and Gypsy men to execute stray dogs and cart away rubbish, he was stopped by a woman who begged a penny to read his palm. A small charcoal brazier glowed in the dark, casting a copper light across her uneven features and dark eyes. With his future in mind, the barber dug out a coin and seated himself on her rug. In the cold night, the Gypsy's words left him bewildered.

"Beware the man who wants his face
Visible in every place.
The devil has just one intent,
To change the world to excrement.
Goodness has a thousand cares,
And can't escape the Hydra's stares."

When he entered the Dajti Mountains, east of Tirana, he wore on his back his whole store of clothes: three shirts, two pairs of pants, a heavy sheepskin jacket and mittens, a woolen cap with earflaps, and a muffler that his mother had knit. From his innumerable walks in these woods, many of the paths were as familiar as Tirana's streets and buildings, as were the mountain eagles and hawks, roosting in the trees, and the black woodpeckers, beating their recognizable rat-a-tat-tat. Here resided the real soul of Albania: the beech trees and Eve's Edenic song issuing from the rictuses of birds.

He had taken the precaution of wearing galoshes, knowing that underfoot the ground would be wet from the frequent rains. Soon the forest floor would be blanketed with snow, and each morning would reveal the footprints of hares and otters and wolves, to say nothing of the numerous bird tracks. As he walked, he looked behind him to see if he was leaving tracks. But the falling leaves and light rain erased the marks of his presence as soon as he passed. A life, he thought, was no different. As the religious texts say, we are only passing from one world to the next. Why, he mused, are some people remembered and others not? Through countless years of evolution, the different species had learned to survive by refining memory, remembering their enemies and avoiding pitfalls, like quicksand and sticky amber. And yet, he often heard people say that to survive, one must learn to forget; that the remembrance of pain past can kill. So who was right? He voted with those who celebrated memory, a form of bearing witness, without which he deemed progress impossible.

He had been told to move only at night and sleep during the day. More than once he was awakened by curious animals led to his scent. Eventually, he made his way southeast from Tirana to the rutted road leading to Bitola. From a hilly vantage point in the woods, he could see the border and guards turning back emigrants. The barber would have to bribe not only the Albanian sentries but also the Macedonian ones, whom he could see at a checkpoint down the road. His first impulse was to follow the barbed-wire border fence into the forest and crawl under the divide undetected; but he remembered that land mines had been planted to deter political adventurers. Several hours expired before he saw a means to escape. An itinerant cook, harnessed like a donkey, dragged behind him a two-wheeled cart. The cook had not yet reached a point at which he could be seen by the guards. Avraham scooted down the hill and asked the man if he might join him. The presence of a barber might prove especially profitable, one person preparing a meal for the soldiers, the other cutting their hair. When the cook paused, Avraham gave him a lek, worth a hundred qintars.

"Have you a government pass to be in the area?" asked the peddler. "It's off-limits to those without a license."

From one of his cane baskets, Avraham removed a framed photograph of himself and an aide of King Zog's, whom he'd barbered. "Will this do?"

The peddler stared at the picture, wiped his nose on his arm, and said. "Come on."

At the border, the two guards, awed by Avraham's picture bearing a flourishing signature, vied to be the first to have his ear hairs singed. Delighted with the results, they urged him to travel down the road to the Macedonian checkpoint, where their counterparts, friends from the old days of open borders, would have the pleasure of the barber's pyrotechnics. And so it was that Avraham passed from one group to the next on the wings of his wondrous barbering, waving goodbye to cook and country.

From Macedonia, he traveled to Moldavia or, to be exact, the Moldavian Autonomous Soviet Socialist Republic, where the local Jewish population advised him to continue east until he arrived in the pale. Moldavia, they said, harbored only criminals and corrupt government officials who would steal your toenails if they could market them. During his trek, he supported himself with stops in dozens of villages, exchanging barbering for a bed. In November 1931, still on the road, he arrived at a train station occupied by hundreds of Soviet military personnel. Here was an ideal place to pick up a few extra coins. Most of the men needed a shave, and with the train temporarily stalled on its way to northern Caucasia and Ukraine, a modest bribe to the stationmaster enabled Avraham to use the primus stove to boil water, and use the waiting room for his shop. When the train was ready to depart, the Soviet troops pressed him to join them, at least as far as Ukraine. His indecision moved them to describe the beautiful landscape, drawing on quotations from Lermontov and Tolstoy.

Through his train window he watched the great steppes, as the famed prairies of grain turned russet in the autumn light and gray in the morning fogs. Although his command of Russian diction and nuance fell short of his parents', he knew that the oft-repeated word "kulak" was being used pejoratively. What did it mean? By the end of the first day, he had made the acquaintance of a young Jewish soldier, with whom he conversed in Russian and Yiddish.

"Kulak," breathed the boy, "I doubt even Stalin could define it. Generally, the word refers to rich farmers who lend money, employ peasants for pennies, buy and sell, and refuse to let the government confiscate their grain and animals in exchange for foreign currency." The boy paused. Someone passed. "They hide or destroy their possessions, or even fight. But we know how to break their will." The soldier looked around and barely whispered. "We starve them. But you never heard me use that word. It is forbidden."

As the train lumbered along, it passed countless stations, all of them looking the same. Women and children, with distended bellies and bony limbs, stood with outstretched hands, begging for food. That first night, the train pulled off to a siding to replenish the steam engine's water supply. Most of the troops were asleep. Avraham slipped off the train to stretch and saw in the dark the outlines of a village that seemed utterly deserted. In the moonless night he stumbled down blue pestilential streets, past dozens of dark windows, past burned houses and barns, past dead animals, past strange wall posters, stamped "GPU." From days of rain, the ground had turned to mud. Taking a different path back to the train, he heard a rustling noise and stopped to listen. Nothing. At length, he detected a human whimper that came from a dilapidated pig shed. A woman and two children, a boy and a girl no older than five and seven, were huddled together under a threadbare blanket, eating leaves and tree bark. Next to them lay a dead dog that the woman, with a pile of twigs at her feet, was preparing to cook. The skeletons of cats, frogs, mice, and birds lay scattered about, all of them devoured to the bone. Catching sight of Avraham, the woman scooped the starving boy into her arms. She handed the barber the living corpse, hairless and wrinkled, with greenish stumps for arms. Her mumbled dialect was unintelligible to Avraham, who held up the palms of his hands and shrugged to signify that he could not understand. Pointing a bony finger, she indicated that she wanted Avraham to take the boy and feed him. The emaciated child felt like a skin stuffed with feathers. Avraham would have given the boy back to his mother had he not suddenly spied in the corner of the shed, peeking out from a thin layer of straw, the skeletal remains of a man. His genitals lay rotting to one side. He had been cannibalized.

Avraham took the boy, ran to the train, and laid him in the baggage car, which always stood open waiting for whatever farm equipment the eager young troops could requisition from those villages targeted for collectivization. The baggage master, asleep on a sack of corn, awoke and shook his head disapprovingly. "Too late," he said. "Bury him."

"But he's still alive!" a shocked Avraham exclaimed.

"Technically speaking but actually not," said the baggage master, picking up the child and throwing him off the train as carelessly as one would dispose of a cigarette.

Back in his own car, Avraham awakened the Jewish soldier and told him what had just happened. "Is all of Ukraine this way?"

"It's especially bad in those villages that refuse to give up their private property for the greater good of the collectives."

"Is any part of Russia untouched by this . . ." he wanted to say "madness," but instead he said "policy?"

"One place, Birobidzhan. Although it's not been officially established, Jews from the pale are moving there."

"Where is this place?"

"Thousands of miles away on the Chinese border."

The reason Avraham changed his Albanian names was owed to one man, Gimpel, who recommended that they bear some resemblance to his trade. Hence, Avraham Bahar became Razeer Shtube.

How Razeer met Gimpel is a story in itself. The night before reaching Birobidzhan, Razeer had stayed in a small village, where the local butcher, Mr.

Cleves, had offered him a hot meal and a night's lodging to cut the hair of his daughter, Anne, whom the butcher hoped to marry off to "the Yid baker, Gimpel." So great was Anne's body odor and bad breath that Razeer could barely cut her hair. When the barber was introduced to Gimpel and learned that a marriage broker had arranged for the baker to marry Anne, Razeer told him that the family was not *frum* (pious), ate *traif* (non-kosher food), and never bathed. She smelled of urine and feces. Her foul breath brought to mind the sulfuric fumes of a sty. Gimpel, who could not think poorly of any soul, man or woman, sighed and remarked:

"A bath and a toothbrush can cure many ills."

"Not a limp and a squint."

"That too?"

"More." He shook his finger. "She's twice your age, flat-chested, and has four grown children, all penniless."

Gimpel's face fell. "You know this for sure?"

"From my own eyes and nose."

"But the go-between promised . . ."

"Never trust a marriage broker. They are liars by trade."

From this encounter dated the friendship of Razeer Shtube and Gimpel, who traveled together to the shtetl of Birobidzhan, where it was said that a Jew need never fear religious persecution. Living among two hundred Israelites and a few Sabbath goys, Razeer would have been happy in his new home, even though the land resembled a desert, but for the fact that the Orthodox don't barber their beards. Taught to cut hair in the Turkish manner by his father, who in turn had learned his craft from Albanian Muslims, Razeer had little opportunity in Birobidzhan to show, with scissors, hand clippers, and Damascene razor, the range of his art. The women shaved their heads and wore wigs, and the men grew side locks and beards and long hair, which Leviticus prohibited them from trimming. Some of those Hasidic men, in their broad-brimmed beaver hats, had actually taken to heart the story of Samson and believed that hair loss would result in enervation and impotence. Baldness, akin to nakedness, diminished a man's holiness, forcing him to wear his side locks down to his waist. But as Razeer told Gimpel, it took a *mensch* to cut another man's hair, to say nothing of rounding his beard so that the whiskers did not strain the evening borscht. To shave with a razor? Virtually unheard of among the Orthodox. If not for the few secular Jews, most of them young and lacking a full face of hair, the Damascene razor, a bar-mitzvah gift from his father, would never have been removed from its finely grained teakwood box, lined with blue flannel.

Mr. Bahar would have preferred that Avraham attend university, but the young man had seemed bent from an early age on becoming a barber, and had commanded the second chair in the family barbershop from the time of its opening in Tirana. In those days, expert barbers, always refined and well dressed, never regarded a haircut and shave as complete until they had flossed the patron's face with two thin strings to eliminate any cheek fuzz, singed the hairs in and around the ears, massaged the person's neck, popped his cervical vertebrae, and applied a cologne made from attar of roses. As an apprentice, he cut the hair of children and the lower classes; as well, he swept up the locks that fell on the floor, lit the samovar, served the customers coffee and tea, and, in his free moments, learned the craft by attentively observing his father. So quickly did Avraham master the trade that before long, some of his father's own regulars requested that the son attend to their barbering, shaving, flossing, and flambéing of ear hairs. Avraham's father took pride in his son's dexterous hands, one clipping, the other gently guiding the movement of the client's head, but he could see that soon he would not brook competition from any barber. A kindly man, Mr. Bahar, at the moment of Avraham's ripeness, quit the first chair in favor of his son. In his new position, Avraham would occasionally step across to the second chair and whisper corrections to his father. "You need to cut more off the left side" or "The goatee is uneven." His father never argued but smiled inwardly, knowing that his son would one day learn that even perfection perishes.

To stave off starvation, Razeer had to travel once a week to Brovensk, where the town's barber had recently died. At first, the local population worried about his place of residence, Birobidzhan.

"Are you a Jew?" they inquired.

"Do I look like one?" he said, pointing to his nose.

"You live in Birobidzhan."

"A bitter joke."

"Who?"

"Ah," he said, piously clasping his hands. "If I told, you'd hear about the treachery of mortals, but since I don't want you to doubt the goodness of men, which leads to despair, I'll spare you my story."

"The Lord bless your kindness."

If not for his flattened nose, the townspeople might have thought him a Jew. Instead, they treated him as a man of faith, cruelly used. Even so, they came to him cautiously. The previous barber's palsied hand had pulled their beards; he had also used a bowl to cut their hair. Razeer's first customer, an elderly widower who walked with a stick, had decided that if the haircut turned out badly, he could always say that he had cut his own hair, as most people did. But the old man came away so handsomely barbered that several unmarried women urged him to come to their homes for a meal. With Razeer's artistry now proved, both men and women—healthy, crippled, one-eyed, blind, beggars, hawkers, priests, and prostitutes—eagerly sought his artful hands. They put aside every Thursday for "the barber" and seated themselves on a low wall, waiting for Razeer to cut their dark wild hair. Given the harshness of winter, the widower let Razeer use his barn, though the Arctic winds whistled through the cracks in the boards. He would have been the first to admit that even with woolen knuckle gloves, he could not do his best when his hands burned from cold and hair froze.

His winter ordeals—as well as his life—radically changed when death came to Brovensk for Pyotr Lipnoskii, the blacksmith. His wife, Anna, invited Razeer to set up a chair next to the forge, which one of her three sons had inherited at her unfaithful husband's death from an excess of vodka. After a night of reveling at the tavern, he had stumbled on his way home and fallen into the creek, where his body lay face down until her oldest boy had discovered him at dawn. Out of respect for Mr. Lipnoskii, a regular customer, Razeer had made it a point to attend the church service. At Anna's request, he trimmed Pyotr's bushy mustache before the dead man, twenty years his wife's senior, lay in an open coffin in the municipal hall and joined his ancestors in the local cemetery.

After the interment, Anna asked Razeer to share a meal with the family: three sons, ages twenty-nine, twenty-seven, and twenty-five, and one daughter, turning eighteen. He gladly accepted. As they passed under the roofed walkway that connected the house and the forge, Razeer saw the rows of meticulously stacked firewood. Behind the house stood a vegetable garden planted with radishes, carrots, beetroot, turnips, and small onions, but no potatoes. Like many peasants, Anna considered potatoes the forbidden fruit that Eve had used to tempt Adam. Those who eat them, it was said, disobey God, violate the holy testament, and deny themselves the kingdom of heaven. Beyond the fenced garden were rows of fruit trees: plum, apple, and pear. On entering the house, Razeer discovered rooms without wallpaper, each wall painted a different bright color: red, blue, and yellow. Anna and her daughter laid the table with bowls of cabbage soup, sweet pea porridge, baked mushrooms, a bottle of *kvas*, and a prodigiously large pike, which had been packed in ice and shipped from the Volga region. One of the sons held up three fingers, and the family bowed their heads to say grace. Looking around the table, Razeer saw all the children peeking at him. He could read distrust in their eyes. It was not until much later that Anna, seeing him undressed, discovered his secret.

MAKING THE FAMILY
SKELETONS DANCE

All of Anna's children had inherited her talent for survival. That three sons—
Pavel, Dimitri, and Gregori—came first led the peasants to say that their births
were a sign of the blessed Trinity, and that having a beautiful daughter, Natasha, was a further sign of God's love. Pavel, the oldest, was now the new blacksmith, and he looked the part with his expansive chest and muscular arms.
Having managed his father's forge for the last several years during Pyotr's
drunken absences, he knew well how to shoe a horse, hammer an axe head
into shape, and repair metal plows. In addition, he had an artistic flare for
wrought-iron furniture, which he fashioned whenever traffic was slow. The
handsomest pieces in Anna's house had come from Pavel's sensitive fingers,
including a table with a glass top and metal legs that looked like delicate flowering vines rooted to the floor. The mirror frames were all his own design, and
so too were the handsome metal fence and gate in front of the house. He had
one other skill that attracted notice: horseshoe playing. Crowned the Brovensk
champion, he had traveled to other towns where he likewise won acclaim. As
every horseshoe player knows, the clay that fills the pit must be just the right
consistency to hold the horseshoes fast once they land. To stay in practice,
Pavel built a professional pit in Brovensk, and with the mayor's help imported
blue clay from the Maloarkhangel'skoe deposit in the Far North, making
Brovensk a center for horseshoe pitching, and Pavel, with his curly black hair
and long eyelashes, a local hero and heartthrob.

Dimitri, the second son, seemed impervious to feeling, but his mother knew that his stony exterior concealed a great gentleness. From an early age, he had been a serious student, a fact that appealed to the GPU, the secret police, for whom he worked. A handsome man, sturdily built and always freshly shaven, his intelligence and Praetorian bearing led the GPU to bring him to Moscow for training in the black arts of spying. Like most of his colleagues, he had sworn to live a sober life, devoted to leader and country, and never to compromise the organization. Impeccably groomed, he made it a point to have his hair cut every Thursday at Paul's Hairdressers, popular with Moscow's beau monde. Despite the interminable wait that tempted him to exercise his right as a GPU agent to jump the line, he judiciously refrained from disclosing his government status and his attraction to Paul's assistant, Yuri Suzdal. Hoping that the two men might meet in the park one night and secretly exchange loving touches, Dimitri had never so much as hinted at his secret wish—and did not until he felt safe.

To dispel his homoerotic feelings, Dimitri frequently studied his signed photograph of Iosif Vissarionovich Dzhugashvili, who had taken the revolutionary code name "Stalin," which combined the Russian word *stal* (steel) with Lenin; and he kept on the nightstand of his cramped room a picture of Feliks (the Iron Felix) Edmundovich Dzerzhinsky, the well-groomed founder of Cheka, the first Soviet secret police, and a copy of *Antigone* to remind him of Creon's predicament. Dimitri's devotion to the state was evident in his worshipful letters home about Stalin, whom he also affectionately called "Vozhd," "Supreme Leader," "Soso," "Koba," and "the Boss." His mother kept those letters, which eventually caught Razeer's eye. In Birobidzhan, he had heard it said that the secret police, taking for their model Dzerhzinsky, prided themselves in their grooming. Perhaps, thought Razeer, a splendid Turkish haircut could make a friend of Dimitri, who might one day prove a valuable ally, as he eventually did.

Gregori, the third son, a seminarian in Leningrad, was a stooped, sweaty-palmed, pensive, pale, knock-kneed, pervious seeker. In prophetic tutors and tomes, he tried to discover the Word, the one Truth, by which to live—and for which to die. On his twelfth birthday, Gregori had accompanied his father to Kiev Pechersk Lavra, the eleventh-century Kiev Monastery of the Caves, the source of his faith. A center of Orthodox Christianity, the monastery sheltered rock caves that had been the original churches when Christians had been persecuted for practicing their religion. The walls of the dimly lit passageways and stairs had been fitted with glass cases that shelved thousands of skulls and skeletal remains. A number of open coffins contained the mummified remains of ancient Christians, their bodies covered with a faded fabric, their faces hidden under an ornate cloth. Some wore crowns to signify their church eminence. Only their parched hands, resembling tight-fitting brown leather gloves, lay uncovered, petrified by the porous rock that, like desert sands, had absorbed the moisture.

For hundreds of years, the Orthodox Church had said that the stuffy rooms were the place where saints rose from the dead. But when the Soviets came to power, they discovered that the monks had rigged several of the mummified saints with springs. As the ignorant peasants passed through the shadowy caves, the monks pressed levers to make the skeletons slowly rise and recline. The faithful regarded these movements as a miracle and gave what little money they had to the church. The Soviets, of course, hoped that by debunking these frauds they would turn people away from Russian Orthodoxy or to atheism. But at twelve, Gregori paid no heed to deception and tricks. He was moved by the fact that people had once cared enough to hew caves from the rocks to practice their faith. At that moment, in the heavy air, thick with incense and candle smoke, peering into the glass cases, he felt his soul swoon, and he knew his calling: He would study for the priesthood and serve the Higher Authority.

Natasha, an alabaster-skinned, blond, bountiful beauty—physically perfect but for one deviant eye that occasionally led to double vision—had the instincts of a magpie, always gathering to herself loose items. Her hands were never idle, picking up one object and purloining another. The items she kept for herself had, in fact, little or no financial value. Sensitive, she had a weakness for tales of woe, especially romantic stories of abandoned women, for whom she always cried. Like most girls her age, she wanted to look pretty and be desired by the most eligible young men. She rouged her cheeks and reddened her lips and kept her nails, both fingers and toes, pared and clean. For the most part, she sewed her own clothes, which she always designed with an eye to showing off her bulging bosom. The local shoemaker, whom she had bewitched with her fluttering eyes, had made her two pairs of handsome shoes and had charged her for one. Because numerous boys sought her, she came to believe that to attract flies all one needed was honey. Good looks and an attractive figure were a poor girl's best friend. She therefore, like many young women, traded on her beauty and drove her suitors to distraction with her practiced blushes, winks, wiggles, sighs, and coquetry. But from her mother she learned that what is obtained cheaply is valued lightly, and that what we regard as most rare is what we consider most dear. Alas, no one had ever told her that her greatest chance for success lay in the schooling that came to her easily and that she passed off so lightly.

★

Razeer had long wished to marry, but had never found a woman to his liking, neither in person nor in religion nor in politics. A practical man, he saw in Anna the same balance between order and aspiration that he embraced. In her movements, he detected a feral heat, and in her role as the village storyteller, he heard echoes of his mother's tales. She was only the second woman who had ever truly arrested his attention. The first, a Tirana widow with plump cheeks, full lips, and an ample derrière had regularly brought her young son to him for a haircut. Razeer had courted her briefly, and he had once even accompanied her to church. On the appointed Sunday, he waited on the porch steps under the rose window. She arrived, as always, with a babushka covering her head and dressed in black. He listened intently to the priest but could not bring his rational mind to accept the miracles that lay at the heart of her faith. Her obedience to the church finally overruled the pleasure he took in her company; so he let the friendship languish.

Again, Anna asked him to dinner. She hoped that before Gregori and Dimitri left Brovensk, they would feel, as she did, that Razeer was a good man who felt kindly toward their mother and wished them no harm. After hot soup and a buttered roll, Razeer *kvelled* and shivered with pleasure as Anna Lipnoskaya served him a river trout, skillfully boned and perfectly seasoned. But the four children remained unreconciled to this man who came from Birobidzhan.

The townspeople, however, liked the barber and treated him as a Gentile, a characterization that the Lipnoskii children found hard to accept. So when Anna suggested that Razeer sleep on a straw mattress with new ticking that she had placed next to the forge, where he could escape winter's chill, her children mumbled that first she had invited the devil to dine with the family and now to sleep in their midst. Did she wish to have the nonbeliever slit her throat—and theirs—or poison the family well, the best in Brovensk? What could she possibly be thinking?

Her husband, Pyotr, had virtually abandoned her bed shortly after Natasha's birth. He preferred wenching to wiving, and drink to domesticity. Even if Razeer were an apostate Jew, how could he not make a good husband? A shrewd hot-blooded woman, Anna could see the twinkle in Razeer's eyes and knew from local gossip that Jews eschewed drunkenness and wife beating. She in turn could offer him ample breasts in which to bury his face; full thighs, thin ankles, and small feet to envelop his body; a generous, though not ungainly, backside; hands hardened by labor but gentle in bed; a thick head of black hair braided across the back; a wide light-skinned face, distinguished by dark eyes, broad cheekbones, and healthy teeth. An enterprising woman, driven by boundless energy, she was fearless. Razeer had no doubt that she could assuage his perturbations with passionate lovemaking. Just sitting in her presence excited him, and he could foresee a sensual life of physical pleasures, to say nothing of the joys of gardening. By the time the blossoms of spring had transformed the bleak steppes into cascades of color, Anna and Razeer had declared their intentions and, when Pavel was off playing horseshoes, had already been naughty, which is when Anna saw Razeer's circumcision and told him that his being Jewish mattered not a straw.

A dismayed Gimpel repeatedly told his friend that Gentiles had but one word for Jews: "vermin." When Razeer registered to marry, Gimpel persuaded the local rabbi, Lev Kanoff, to share with Razeer his Talmudic wisdom. The old rabbi, leaning on a crutch to ease the pain of his arthritic back, walked the entire distance because the shtetl donkey had cut a forepaw on a barbed-wire fence. As the rabbi sat next to the forge in colloquy with the apostate, he employed the time-honored method of telling a story to instruct.

"I once knew a Jew from Frampol," the Rabbi patiently explained, "who married a Gentile woman reputed to be as pure as a mountain stream. Six months after the marriage, she presented him with a son. 'Who is the father?' asked the man. 'You, of course. Are you a fool and so addled that you do not remember when we lay together?' The Jew counted on his fingers and said, 'But that was six months ago, and here already you have a child.' The woman shook her head in despair. 'Do you not believe in miracles, you who believe the Messiah will return riding a white horse?' The Jew thought a moment and replied, 'Yes, you are right.' To which she said, 'Of course I am right. You have often told me that behind this world lies another, the real one, and it is there, in that other realm, that the real truth resides. Here, in this place, we see only shadows.' The Jew nodded in agreement and apologized to his wife, who never again lay with him and yet gave birth to eleven children. Is this the life you wish to live? The Gentile takes our own beliefs and turns them against us." The Rabbi spat. "And of all the twisters of truth, the worst are women. Think of Eve, think of Delilah, think of any number of women who have misled their husbands. Bad enough a whining Jewish wife, but a Gentile one is worse. She turns your head and makes you think horseradish is honey. Marriage at best is a mixed blessing. So why start out with all the odds against you? Stick to your own. At least with a Jewish wife you'll be familiar with her *shtiklech*; a Gentile wife will use tricks you've never seen before."

Razeer nodded and gave the rabbi a few coins for the needy, but remained steadfast in his decision to marry Anna Lipnoskaya. He had often savored Anna's apple pie and told Lev Kanoff that if she was imprudent enough to marry a barber, he felt confident that he could support her with a good garden. Lev shook his head, grumbled "nonsense," took Gimpel's arm, and hobbled back to the shtetl, where Razeer's name was struck the next day from the synagogue rolls.

So upsetting did Gimpel find this excommunication that he tried one last time to persuade Razeer to marry in the faith. He said that for the Jews to survive they had to remain one people and not dilute the culture, and that the religion was greater and more important than any one person.

Razeer complained, "Now you sound like a Bolshevik zealot. They say the party matters more than the individual and that, in fact, the individual—the 'new man'—finds his identity in the party."

"An army cannot go to war if everyone is pursuing his own self-interest," said Gimpel, chewing a cuticle. "Jews, like soldiers, must observe the same values and rules. Otherwise, chaos ensues. If we mix with barbarians, we lose our identity."

"Aristotle," said the barber proudly, "have you ever read him?"

Gimpel shook his head no.

"Me neither. But according to our rabbi in Tirana, the age-old conflict between the individual and the state—and its consequences—even appears in his work. Let me tell you what I know."

The baker anxious to return to his oven, which he had left in charge of an apprentice, ran his hand through his hair and asked Razeer "to make it brief."

"The great Aristotle says there is a difference between what is just according to the law and what is just according to the person. He says that sometimes it is just to act contrary to the law, such as when religious rites are at odds with the decrees of the state. In other words, Gimpel, there is no right answer, only the one that issues from each individual soul."

Not until Gimpel had tasted Anna's pirogies and blintzes did he agree to serve as best man, a service he proudly rendered when the couple were wed by a minor official. Her deceased husband's relatives could not believe the news and thought the barber must have given her a potion. Similarly, her children found it hard to accept their mother's new married name, Shtuba, but slowly resigned themselves. Razeer, after all, never struck her, nor even cuffed her with his open hand, never drank himself into a stupor, never in fact scolded Anna for buying hens high and selling fryers low. Pyotr would have whipped her for such poor husbandry. Did she not to this day bear welts on her back from his belt?

With the ease of a native-born Russian, Razeer fell in with the flow of the seasons and events. In autumn, when thick clusters of mushrooms sprang up in the woods and fields, he and Anna, armed with baskets and buckets, scoured the countryside for the many varieties of edible fungi, and especially *beliy grib*, which they took home either to eat raw or to add to one of Anna's incomparable soups or to dry for future use. Those forays took on a special meaning because on warm days they would put aside their baskets and make love in the grass, even though the evening frosts had stiffened the stalks, which scratched his backside. After coitus, he would hold her close, and she would thank him for his kindness. He in turn appreciated her physical generosity and spirited independence. Razeer often wished that the fall would never end. But when the dark winter closed in around them, they played dominoes and chess in front of a potbellied stove, while a puffing samovar, heated by a central tube filled with pines and kindled by charcoal, stood at the ready for their weak black tea. On those days when the winter snows abated, he and Anna took pleasure in skating on the frozen ponds that the locals swept clean of snow. Cross-country skiing, a favorite sport of the locals, never appealed to Razeer, but he did enjoy ice fishing. He and the like-minded anglers built rough shacks around the holes they bore with drills and built fires for warmth. Although the ponds froze entirely from top to bottom, the lake ice stopped a few feet from the bottom, where the fish, thick with fat, pooled to feed. The spring, every poet's delight, brought wild flowers and migratory birds, drawing hikers and ornithologists. Summers they swam and picnicked next to a favorite stream, from which they drank the clear, pure water.

Yes, Razeer indeed treated Anna with kindness. He had even changed his name at her request to "Razan"—to honor a deceased friend—and plied his barbering trade professionally, never objecting when ignorant peasants refused to pay on the pretext that Razan had given them the evil eye. What Razan didn't know was that Anna used Dimitri as her collection agent. From his desk in the secret police office, Dimitri wrote more than one letter to the local party secretary, at his mother's behest.

The Brovensk Communist Party secretary, Basil von Fresser, thought himself superior to the locals because his family had immigrated to Russia under Peter the Great, who had brought thousands of Germans into the country to help westernize it. Initially, Basil moderated his aristocratic pretensions, a ruse that made possible his election as party secretary. But the day after the vote was counted, he appeared in lederhosen and a green alpine hat topped with a white feather, and he strutted with such airs that one would have thought he was the kaiser's cousin. As Razan trimmed his beard and, in the Turkish manner, flambéed the hairs in his ears, a part of the haircutting ceremony that the party secretary always requested and that never failed to give him a start, he would talk about his noble German family, whose roots went back to the Middle Ages in Freiburg. These peasants—they were lucky to have a party secretary who spoke German and whose ancestors had worn armor and had been granted from the king a coat of arms, which to this day could be seen in a flag on the bedroom wall behind his bed. The Communist Party members, in fact, had elected him secretary in the late 1920s when reconciliation of the different social classes was still a hope and one's past forgiven. His comrades, most of whom were illiterate, looked to him to attract the attention of the many traders, some nomadic and Asian, some familiar and European, who passed through the city. And indeed he had arranged for one of the collective farms to be equipped with an electric generator that would have been the envy of Brovensk had the town been wired for electricity. But sadly, kerosene, coal, and candles provided the only available energy.

Every three days, the secretary came to the "Forge," as the barbershop came to be called, to have "the usual." Natasha's Botticellian beauty, not surprisingly, caught his attention. A corpulent, married man, with a neck as wide as his head, who had long ago discontinued marital cohabitation and comity, although he kept his wife on the party payroll, Basil always asked about Natasha. Whenever she appeared, he could not prevent his left foot from tapping rapidly, his right hand from smoothing his beard, and his chest from swelling as he recited some official state poem extolling tractors or trains or the Five-Year Plan. Sweet Natasha would blush and make some excuse allowing her to exit quickly. The secretary would sigh and repeat the same statement, "Such a paragon!" On this particular day, upon seeing Natasha, he blurted, "Miss Lipnoskaya, I have need of . . ." He paused for effect. "An amanuensis." Neither Natasha nor Razan had ever heard the word. "Well?" asked Basil?

Now it was true that Natasha seemed unfit for any kind of work except sewing and cooking, crafts that made her eminently suitable for marriage. But her stepfather was not about to see her deflowered by a married man, no matter what his title. Anna, on the other hand, knew that a pregnant girl could command a large dowry from a wealthy wrongdoer, lest she bring shame on his house. And with a proper sum, a great many handsome young men could be induced to marry her. Unlike myriad country lasses of her age, she could read and write, two of the benefits bestowed by the state, and she had once seen a typewriter in a government office in Minsk, where she had gone to inquire about a boyfriend garrisoned there. She later learned that the young man had married a Belorussian lass whose father was an officer in the People's Army. To repay the cost of that trip, she had taken odd jobs that included swabbing out pigeon roosts and slopping hogs.

Natasha found Secretary von Fresser's attentions flattering and finally summoned enough courage to ask about the word "amanuensis." She then volunteered that she could both print and write in cursive. Typewrite? No, but she was certainly willing to learn. Could the secretary or one of his party functionaries teach her? He said that his wife had always typed his papers. Perhaps she could be prevailed upon to teach Miss Lipnoskaya to at least hunt and peck. He therefore proposed that Natasha come to his residence on Wednesday morning, a suggestion that Natasha keenly accepted, until Razan asked wasn't that the day Mrs. von Fresser took the train to Bira to visit her mother, and Basil smacked his forehead and said, "How stupid of me to have forgotten. Make it Tuesday instead." But Razan knew that Mrs. von Fresser, embarrassed by the heavy hair growth on her upper lip, went on those mornings to a woman bristle dealer who specialized in hog depilation.

To overcome Razan's calendric memory, the secretary said that his family needed a housekeeper and a cook, and that Natasha could live in the bunkhouse, which had once been the playroom of his only child, Alexei, now a medical student in Leningrad. With the party secretary's offer to assume Natasha's entire support, Razan could not overcome Anna's insistence that only good could come from Basil's proposal. Would she not be given, Anna knowingly asked Razan, her own quarters, light work, and a modest fee to pay for her hygienic needs? And what of the secretarial skills she would learn? How could a sensible person say no!

More important, she had long ago surmised that Alexei, the von Fressers' son, had a yen for her daughter, yet another reason for letting the girl work in their home. Before sending her off, Anna told her how to prevent unwanted intercourse—a linen cloth cut in lengths to fill the aperture—how to promise, delay, and never deliver, and how to snatch the golden ring. When Alexei, unaware of Natasha's hiring, returned home on a school holiday, he found a delightful surprise: Natasha working in the von Fresser house. Unable to hide his affection for this young woman, whom he had long admired, he knew that even though the country had officially banned class differences, the disparity in their social positions, as well as her eye troubles, would make her unacceptable to his parents.

Indeed, the party secretary and his wife used every subterfuge to keep their son from being alone with Natasha. They never let him out of their sight and took every opportunity to criticize her provincial habits and modest schooling, and to rail about her mother, "the conniving harlot," and her stepfather, "that sneaky Albanian." But Alexei found the most compelling argument to be Natasha's physical charms, and the greatest obstacle his father's lust. To keep the first unsullied meant keeping the second at bay. Alexei therefore counseled Natasha that in his absence, she should flatter his mother and request that Mrs. von Fresser teach Natasha all that she'd learned during her commercial training in Moscow, before her marriage to Basil. And to get around Mrs. von Fresser's fierce temper, Alexei advised Natasha to appeal to her voracious appetite. Given Mrs. von Fresser's culinary ineptness, Natasha could win her affection by preparing a honey-glazed duck, red cabbage with walnuts, and a blueberry pie. To no one's surprise, Mrs. von Fresser soon found that she liked having both a tidy house and a tasty meal. The surprise was that Mrs. von Fresser actually enjoyed tutoring Natasha. Not since her marriage had she found an opportunity to use her few skills. Teaching came naturally to her, and Natasha proved an able student, learning to type in both Cyrillic and roman.

The principles of bookkeeping Natasha easily mastered, but the demand on the part of the new Soviet government that separate accounts be kept for two groups—poor farmers and prosperous ones, labeled kulaks—taxed her talents. This additional work caused Mrs. von Fresser to throw up her arms in despair. Poor Natasha was even worse off; her double vision caused her to confuse the accounts. But in the end, her diplopia proved a great asset because she always halved the production numbers as a precaution against doubling them, which she had previously done. The Brovensk farmers were therefore credited with half as much grain as they had actually harvested and half the livestock that they actually owned. But balancing debits and credits was not the same as confronting marauding soldiers.

When Stalin's death trains began to eviscerate landholdings, causing farmers to flee from their ruined villages, the people rightly called the troops harbingers of famine. In Brovensk, as the Soviets prodded their balking horses out of the freight cars, the thud of their hoofs on the wooden gangways and the clanging of their shoes on the stone platform sounded like a funereal knell. People silently watched as the horses were led, rearing, across the tracks, saddled, and mounted. Their riders, soldiers trained to find hidden stores of food and farm animals, arrested or shot anyone hoarding supplies.

Anticipating the arrival of these Communist locusts, the farmers hid their grain in mattresses, under floorboards, in furrowed fields, at the bottom of wells, in hollow trees, under haystacks, in pits dug beneath pig sties, behind false facades, in forests, and in forges. Their animals they either butchered and ate or tethered deep in the woods. The soldiers, convinced that the fat-faced people of Brovensk would lead them to a cornucopia, had some success but less than expected. With the help of an informer, they unearthed the grain sacks of those who had foolishly hidden them under their floors. Amidst keening and cursing, they drove the hoarders into a cattle car and bolted the door. A special freight car, painted bright red, had been equipped to show films, short agitprop stories with an unmistakable moral about the evil of kulaks and the goodness of workers. But even after the awed peasants saw these marvelous moving pictures, they still insisted that Brovensk had no natural riches for the Soviets to remove and sell to the west for hard cash. In frustration, the chief officer asked to see the books of the party secretary. Enter Natasha.

Her entries indicated that whatever crops and livestock the farmers had raised had gone toward feeding the farmers. Nothing remained. Suspicious but lacking proof, the soldiers boarded the train, pulled out of Brovensk, and moved to the next town. Party secretary von Fresser counseled his constituents to wait a week before recovering their stores, lest the soldiers double back and catch them red-handed. The week that they waited was the only time that the village felt the pinch of want. When asked what could be done for the arrested farmers, Secretary von Fresser swore that he would buy them back from the Soviets, a promise that he kept with his own kopeks.

The informer, never having ridden on a train and fearing for his life, had asked the soldiers to take him along on their forays. But the marauders left him behind to be dealt with by a mob intent on revenge. At the urging of a former priest, the crowd let him go in peace, albeit with only the clothes on his back and galoshes made of old rubber tires.

With Natasha settled, at least for the nonce, Razan concentrated on increasing his business. Pavel built him a room, attached to the forge, with a heating conduit. The barber had cards printed that Anna and her friends liberally distributed when they traveled outside the town. A few advertisements in the provincial papers brought curious men wishing to experience this thing called a Turkish haircut. Word spread, particularly about the barber's skill at dipping cotton sticks in alcohol, swabbing the ears, lighting the alcohol, and burning the ear hairs without the client suffering injury. Enterprising Anna served Turkish coffee or strong tea, and hired a young girl, an émigré from Anatolia, to make Turkish pastries to serve with the drinks, earning a few extra kopeks. Soon the cash register rang with rising profits, to the delight of Razan, Anna, Pavel, Natasha, and, strangely, Dimitri, who wrote to his mother that good tidings would shortly arrive for her and her husband.

Only Gregori remained unreconciled to his stepfather, whom he had tried, without success, to convert. On a recent trip to Brovensk, Gregori had insisted on showing his humility by washing Razan's feet, and had even soaped them with a loofah sponge. In return, Gregori asked his stepfather to pray with him in the cellar pantry, which Gregori had converted into a small chapel. A framed picture of Stalin hung above a low altar that supported an icon of the crucified Jesus. A votary candle flickered in the darkness, as Gregori and Razan knelt on a Bukharan rug to give thanks for the family's good fortune.

In the dancing flame, with the gold and silver paint of the icon shimmering like magical motes, Gregori tearfully begged Razan to see the light and truth of Christianity. Razan thanked him but declined. The two men then rose from their genuflections on the finely crafted red rug and repaired to the kitchen for *chai*. Razan felt uneasy. After the revolution, religion had fallen into disfavor, and yet to everyone's surprise, Gregori had not only joined the Renovationist Church, but also thrived as one of the *obnovlentsy*: those who lent themselves to a reduced liturgy and the curtailment of priests.

Sipping his black tea, Gregori said, "The faithful will live in a land of milk and honey." He then spooned two helpings of sugar into his cup.

"From your mouth to God's ear," said Razan, not wishing to be captious. "But tell me, in your religion, who comes first, God or the state? Both promise paradise." Pause. "Please pass the honey."

Caught off guard by the question, Gregori wished to appear neither anti-Orthodox nor counterrevolutionary. He mulled over the question, slowly stirring his tea. "Cannot a man believe in paradise on earth as well as in heaven?"

"So you equate Stalin and God?" asked Razan with raised eyebrows.

Crossing himself, Gregori replied, "Christ is our heavenly Savior, and the Vozhd our earthly one. Both love the people, and the people love them."

But Razan had heard the disquieting rumors that the priesthood was co-operating with the government. "The Soviets, like the Tsar, want priests to report the secrets of the confessional. Are you not troubled?"

"Can the state peer into a man's soul?" he asked evasively.

The barber used Gregori's defensive reply to probe into the Renovationist Church. "I see. Like the Marranos, you practice your faith in secret."

Gregori knew the allusion: Spanish Jews who had outwardly professed Christianity and secretly clung to Judaism as a means to stay alive during the Inquisition. "How can we know," shrugged Gregori, "what people will store up in their ghostly hearts?"

Razan concluded that Gregori was a catacomb Christian, one of those who practiced in secret a creed they could not publicly profess. Taking a dish of sugared yeast cakes, Gregori nibbled them cautiously, as if expecting to bite into a stone. Razan only then realized that Gregori had a dental plate with false teeth. His poor diet in the seminary had no doubt introduced gum disease. Unlike Stalin, who reputedly wore a dental plate because of the rancid effects of tobacco and alcohol, Gregori eschewed both. He stared at Razan and slowly rocked in his chair, as if mimicking a davening Jew. "You're a clever man, Razan, so tell me: Do you love God and Stalin?"

"Who doesn't?"

"Mensheviks, socialist revolutionaries, monarchists, Trotskyites, Zino-vievites, Kadets, anarchists, foreigners, saboteurs, spies."

Oddly, the group missing from Gregori's list was priests, and their children, few of whom, branded pariahs, could ever find work.

"Those who hate the proletariat," continued Gregori, pushing his teacup aside, "hate Comrade Stalin, just as the money changers hated Christ." He stood and started to pace, clearly agitated. "For hundreds of years church councils argued. Instead of bringing harmony, the church introduced schisms and hatred. Now we have the Renovationist Church, endorsed by the Vozhd, so all may embrace it."

Razan, imbued with a barber's truth that the proof was in the cut of the hair, retorted, "And for those who wish to have their mustache shaped differently . . . what of them?"

Gregori explained that religious sects should yield to the state for the greater good of the nation; and the state had approved of the Renovationists. "Since we have no infallible way of knowing which church is right, what's the harm, Citizen Shtube, in your believing in mine? If your belief proves right, you will spend eternity in paradise. If it proves wrong . . ." Gregori fell silent.

Razan wondered whether it could cost him his life or a place in heaven if he made the wrong choice. Gregori had joined a church that was on the right side of Stalin. But of God?

"In such hard times," asked Razan, "why seek ordination?"

"When I kneel before the altar . . . the candles illuminating the gold of the icons . . . I feel exalted, ecstatic." Sliding a hand across the table, Gregori murmured, "Perhaps if you followed a different faith . . . to believe is to know."

"I was always taught that to know is to believe."

Gregori withdrew his hand. "You are playing with words."

"My mother, a teacher, told me to beware of all beliefs not amenable to proof."

"The presence of the world is proof of God's greatest creation. To doubt is to put your mortal soul in peril."

"Whenever I burn the hairs in a Cossack's ears, I run that risk."

"Have you never felt yourself spiritually transported?"

"Yes, from your mother's love."

"Surely you believe in powers higher than yourself and causes worthy of martyrdom."

"Communism?"

"The Holy Spirit."

"Razan!" Anna called from another room. "The mayor wishes a shave."

Gregori, without clearing his dishes, started for the door, stopped, and remarked cryptically, "The higher cause is what we feel."

PURGING THE PARTY

Fortunately, Regional Secretary Basil von Fresser received the official letter ordering him to screen the ranks of the Communist Party membership before the envoy from Moscow arrived. No doubt the *chistka* (purge) had come to Brovensk because the town had been elevated to the status of a territorial seat. The letter ordered him to think like a *tovarishch* (comrade) in ridding the local party of undesirables. Secretary von Fresser, whose own preening behavior could have landed him in trouble, reminded the party faithful how he had protected them against the "death trains" and had gladly issued them membership cards, albeit for a price, a fact he preferred to ignore. As he spread the word of the official visit, he made a point of extolling the value of membership in the party and the privileges that belonging bestowed, like keeping one safe from purges.

"It allows you all manner of liberties," he harangued his listeners, "and provides special food rations and clothing. Even now, as collective farms promise a bright new future, we still need the protection of a party card. It provides immunity from arrest by the civil authorities, and the guarantee of a good job, as well as the respect of the community." He held up his card. "This marks me as a trusted tovarishch, wherever I go. Therefore, we must be ever vigilant to keep the party card from those who have been disbarred from holding it: terrorists, White Army officers, Tsarist officials, Old Believers, Trotskyites, and Mensheviks. And we must, as Comrade Zhdanov in Moscow orders, strip the card from those unworthy of it." He paused. "We will be examining party members as soon as the GPU men arrive."

But only one person stepped from the train, Irina Vostoyeva. The two policemen accompanying her had left the train when diagnosed with whooping cough. A stalwart party member, proud of the brave new Communist world that treated men and women equally, she had come from a long line of priests; in fact, her father had held a prominent place in the church before he stood up and renounced the cloth. His public renunciation had won favor for his daughter because it reinforced the Soviet position that religion was a superstitious habit that had been discredited by modern science. Her father had claimed that religion deceived the gullible and that he no longer wished to serve enemies of the people. At that point, he had thrown off his vestment, passed down the aisle, and left the church, accompanied by the wails and lamentations of the fanatical old women in the congregation.

Tall and bony, with closely cropped red curly hair and black-rimmed eyes that peered out of caves, Irina had honed her ripsaw cross-examining skills in Tashkent, prosecuting Islamic separatists. In Uzbekistan, her great talent was to make defendants think that she was a kindred spirit. Wearing a head scarf in court to give the impression of female modesty, she removed it when pulling off her mask and closing in for the kill. Her insomniac habits included the dangerous pastime of translating into German, under the assumed name of Katerina Tershina, the banned and self-exiled Russian writer Ivan Bunin, a critic of the Soviet system. To smuggle her translations into Germany—the Soviet postal system routinely opened the mails—she used couriers who moved translations of forbidden books between Odessa and Istanbul. Although a devoted Communist, her love of Bunin's work transcended her political convictions, even though she was risking her freedom and perhaps even her life.

Irina Vostoyeva requested a private meeting with Secretary Basil von Fresser. She came to his office dressed austerely in black with a high collar, white and starched, that accurately reflected her pinched moral views, except of course for her translations. Basil tried to make light of her visit, though he knew from her demeanor that she had come bearing complaints. "You've probably discovered," he said laughingly, "that our party membership has been swelled by dead souls."

"That and worse." She seemed to rise on her toes. "I have unearthed treachery." Basil looked at her uncomprehendingly. "Hundreds hold party membership cards that have been bought or stolen or forged. Children use the cards of deceased relatives. In the provinces, I learned that people routinely carry the card of a father, uncle, or brother. You know the conditions of membership: sobriety, familiarity with socialism, activism, probity. Among the peasants I have seen anything but." She clicked her heels. "We will have to institute a chistka and rid the party of all those who do not meet our high standards. Call your typist!"

Boris summoned Natasha, whose loveliness even Irina paused to appreciate. Looking at the girl and the party secretary, Irina immediately began to spin webs. Surely, here was a conspiracy unlike any other. In return for favors rendered to the party secretary, what did the girl receive? No doubt, all of her relatives owned party cards and received untold benefits.

"You do take shorthand?" asked Irina curtly.

"N-n-no," she stuttered, "but I can type."

Before a dumbstruck Irina could respond, Natasha had wheeled the portable table with its typewriter next to the prosecutor's chair.

"I can type over a hundred words a minute, so please start."

"*Incroyable!*" said Irina.

"How do you spell that? It's not a word that the secretary uses."

"Never mind. Just take down the following."

The typewriter sounded.

"What are you writing?"

Again it sounded.

"Stop!"

And again.

Irina leaned over and pulled the sheet of paper from the typewriter and read out loud: "Never mind. Just take down the following. What are you writing? Stop." Irina sighed. "My dear child, put a new piece of paper in the machine and type only when I say go. But you needn't type the word 'go.'"

Natasha shook her head in agreement at this frightening woman.

"To all party members."

Natasha's hands didn't move.

"Well, why aren't you typing?"

"You didn't say go."

Irina chafed at Basil's chuckling. "You ass, leave us alone." Quickly turning to Natasha, she said, "Don't take that down." Once Boris had left the room, Irina composed herself with a cigarette; in fact, she smoked three. Finally, extinguishing the last cigarette and taking a deep breath, she laid a hand on the typewriter and said softly, "Go."

Natasha smiled and readied her hands like a pianist poised to begin her concerto.

"Dear Members of Our Beloved Communist Party, I hail you, comrades, for your tireless work on behalf of the motherland. We have before us yet another task, one that may prove far greater than any previous work we have undertaken. Saboteurs, spies, foreigners, and counterrevolutionaries have insinuated themselves into the party and must be purged. We will therefore, two days from now, be reviewing party membership cards. You who live at a distance from Brovensk need not worry. The period of review will take place for a week.

"Please come to party headquarters with your membership card and any documentation that will prove that you are the person whose name appears on the card. Your local registrar or Communist manager can give you a letter certifying your identity, if you have no documents.

"To guarantee the purity of the party, this purge is necessary, though not punitive." Irina smiled at her alliteration, knowing that few party members had the literary sophistication to appreciate its effect. "Comradely yours, Irina Vostoyeva, Moscow Prosecutor for the Tenth District, USSR." She lit a cigarette and inhaled deeply.

Natasha handed Irina the piece of paper. After looking it over, Irina complimented the comely young woman on her flawless typing, eliciting a blush from the amanuensis.

Natasha hazarded, "If I may be so forward . . ."

"Yes?"

"Most of the people in this area, including the party members, are illiterate. They can't read or even sign their names. No one will read it. Secretary von Fresser has often complained about the difficulty of reaching the masses." She would have continued, but Irina slumped in her chair, her posture signaling defeat. Lighting another cigarette, she said, "*Govnaw* (shit)!"

The woman from Moscow, determined to clean up the Brovensk Party, announced she would be staying in town until every family in the province knew her mission. To her question, "Is there a boardinghouse nearby?" the party secretary told her no but she was welcome to stay at his home. Not wishing to incur the taint of compromise, she thanked Basil and inquired if another family would be kind enough to board her. Natasha volunteered the Lipnoskii house, to the chagrin of her mother, who regarded all authority with suspicion. Irina readily accepted, convinced that by keeping an eye on "Miss Prettiness" she would be led to all manner of official mischief.

Over dinner the first night, Irina met the family still resident in Brovensk: Anna, Razan, and Pavel. From the oldest boy, she learned that his father, Pyotr, had died from a surfeit of drink and that Razan had moved in with the mother shortly before they had married. Her nose for wrongdoing at first made her think that perhaps Razan and Anna had plotted Pyotr's demise; after all, Razan had almost immediately found accommodation in the house and a bed that Pyotr had ruled. So Irina, who foraged for fault, plied Anna for details of Pyotr's drowning. Anna repeated the story that she had pitifully shared with her neighbors and the local officials. When Pyotr failed to return, she had taken her coat and looked for him along the footpath that he normally followed. But though she crossed the icy stream in which he had drowned, she never saw him. Irina condoled with her hostess, smiled at Natasha, and asked, "How late does the local tavern stay open?" She lit a cigarette.

"It's not really a tavern," said Pavel, "so much as a roadside inn for travelers heading east."

"So they serve at all hours?" she said, exhaling smoke.

Pavel knew in fact that one could purchase a drink at any hour of the day but did not wish to make trouble for his fellow townsmen. "By midnight the inn is usually dark."

"Usually?"

"I'd say almost always."

"Then your poor father had to make his way home in the early hours. Did no one help him?" she asked with alarm.

"Not that we know of," replied Natasha.

"What are comrades for?" Irina said loudly, but to no one in particular.

Razan sat sipping his tea, fascinated by Irina's probing of the dunghill that was Pyotr. Anna, though, felt the air charged with suspicion, and took care not to fall into some Bolshevik trap designed to catch the unwary. She knew these officials for prigs, and wondered whether her having shared her bed with Razan before marriage would render her morally unfit in the eyes of the party, which paid lip service to proper behavior.

"You must have been worried to death when he didn't return," Irina continued, "especially when the inn closed at midnight and at one o'clock he still wasn't home. You did say that it was shortly after one that you put on your coat to look for him along the road?"

"Yes," Anna said, volunteering no more than a syllable.

"The creek, I gather, isn't very deep. But how does one cross it? There's no footbridge." She extinguished her cigarette.

Pavel answered, "We step on the rocks."

"In spring, when the water is high, are the rocks covered?"

"No," Pavel said, as Irina watched Anna's face, "but they are slippery when wet."

"Presumably a slick rock caused the accident."

"It was winter," Pavel replied. "The rocks were icy."

"And you, Mrs. Shtuba, do you agree?" She lit another cigarette.

"Yes."

As Natasha began removing the dishes, her mother rose to help.

"Permit me, Mrs. Shtuba, to ask your opinion about one point." Anna resumed her seat. "Might the poor man have been alive but unconscious for some length of time?" Smoke issued from her nose.

While Anna pondered the question, Pavel rushed in to dispel the silence. "Not with his head face down in the freezing water."

Losing patience, Irina asked, "And if his head had originally been face up, is it possible that someone turned him over?"

"Why in the world," Anna said heatedly, standing up, "would anyone do *that*?"

"Ah! The very question I've been asking myself."

Razan, fondly devoted to his wife, finally spoke. "Are you suggesting a murder was committed?"

"Your use of the passive voice suggests your unwillingness to give the murderer a name."

"Murderer!" several people said in unison.

Spreading her hands and stroking the air, Irina tried to indicate that she had no family member in mind. "I am still concerned that a comrade would let this man leave drunk without accompanying him home. And if a tovarishch was at his side, which one, and why did he not extricate the poor man from the creek? Comrades do not let other comrades suffer." She paused, clearly struck by an idea. "Perhaps then that explains what happened. The drunken man was so badly hurt that his fellows could not stand to see him suffer, and turned him over so that he would die without pain."

"Is this the way prosecutors split hairs and shave facts?" asked Razan. "Because if it is, then no man is safe from the law."

"Charles Dickens said the same thing," Irina observed, with a knowing smirk, and put out her cigarette.

That night, as Razan and Anna lay in bed, neither could sleep. He kindly tried to comfort his wife by assuring her that just as a barber wants a face to shave, a prosecutor wants a case to solve. But Anna kept returning to the fact that for some reason, Irina Vostoyeva refused to use Pyotr's name.

"She must have a reason," said Anna, rolling over to face her husband, "and I can't get to sleep until I've worked it out."

The chistka took place on the second floor of a storehouse, smelling of grain dust and exhibiting a large picture of Stalin. No one had thought to remove the cobwebs or to sweep the floor. In the stifling air, the light from the one window illuminated the millions of motes and admitted from outside the constant sound of chatter and animal noises, reminiscent of a scene from the Middle Ages. A long table covered with a green felt cloth that Basil supplied—he thought it gave the provincial proceedings an air of authority—rested in the center of the room. Three chairs stood behind the table, for Irina, for Party Secretary von Fresser, and for Natasha, who was present to record the proceedings on her typewriter. Two chairs faced the table: one for the party member and, if needed, one for his witness. The party secretary had arranged for the hammer and sickle, like the sword of Damocles, to hang from the ceiling, while another flag fluttered outside the building.

In the front yard, dozens of people waited to be called. Some had come with their families, some with witnesses, some with a faithful pet, like a dog or goat or pony or pig. Dressed in khaki green, Irina evinced austerity, while Natasha wore a flaming red dress and colorful babushka. For the occasion, Basil had brushed his brown gabardine suit, polished his black shoes, and oiled his hair.

Irina had looked over the list of party members the night before, noting the absence of last names. How was the party to tell one Ivan from another? When she asked Basil this question, he had replied: by their village, their street, or their occupation. Ivan the mason, with his immense hands, now stood before them, tipping his cap and waiting for his superiors to tell him to sit.

"We are all comrades here," said Irina, striking a note of equality. "Sit and relax. I have just a few questions to ask you."

Ivan perched on a chair, twisting his cap in his hands.

"May I see your party card?" she asked, as the typewriter began its interminable clicking.

"Which one?"

"Yours."

"I have several. From my dead father and uncle and brother."

"Your own."

"Why do I need my own when I have three others?"

"Please give me all three cards." Ivan passed them across the table. "Thank you." Turning to Basil, she said peremptorily, "Strike his name from your membership list." Straightening her back, she said to Ivan, "As you leave, please send in the next person."

The tanner, Jury Stas, smelling of some chemical, explained that he had lost his party card and had been too busy to request a new one.

"Comrade Stas, tell us," said Irina, "who was Karl Marx?"

"Sounds German to me."

"He was."

"Maybe a friend of the kaiser. Yeah, I think I heard that from my wife. He was the kaiser's friend."

Disgusted, Irina baited him. "Which one, Wilhelm the first or second?"

Basil held up two fingers on the side of his cheek farthest from Irina and mouthed the word "second."

"The second."

"Good. To have your membership card restored, you will have to take classes in socialism. Please take note, Secretary von Fresser."

"Right. We will offer courses starting next month."

Stas exited dispirited but not completely discouraged. In no time, word spread that to pass the purge a person would have to identify Karl Marx and answer questions about socialism. Outside, the few literate peasants shared what they could with the others, as fear gripped the group.

"What was your father's occupation?" Irina asked the next man, Ivan Merski, who had lost his left thumb in a sawmill.

"A farmer."

"Did he own his own farm?"

He laughed. "Peasants don't own anything."

Irina shuffled some papers in front of her and replied, "According to local land deeds, your father owned sixty acres."

"My father? He never told me."

"He was a kulak."

"What's that? I never heard the word."

"A landowner, a moneylender, a parasite, an enemy of the people."

"If he owned land, how come I have to work in a sawmill?"

"The government confiscated his property. Hand over your card."

Natasha couldn't keep up, though she kept typing as rapidly as her fingers could cover the keys. Taking one sheet of paper from the machine, she quickly replaced it with another, dropping the finished sheet in a wooden box, bearing an official seal.

Bogdan, a drunkard with a long-suffering wife, asked Irina to repeat her question, as he slouched in his chair.

"You are accused of passivity. How do you plead?"

"My papers are all in order," answered the red-faced and bulbous-nosed former shoemaker, passively ignorant of the word.

"Yes, I can see that for myself, but the party secretary tells me that you show no enthusiasm for party activities and, in fact, you have never attended a party meeting. Slackers and shirkers forfeit their rights, unless of course . . . you can identify any Trotskyites, Mensheviks, White Army officers, or Tsarist police among the local population."

Bogdan sneezed, held a forefinger to his nostril, blew the mucus on the floor, and considered Irina's offer. "I can point out some drunks and womanizers, but those other kinds I don't know."

"Give us the names of the drunks and womanizers, and don't fail to include yourself."

Bogdan reeled off several names and rose to leave.

"Your card, please," said Irina.

"You said I would get to keep my card!"

"Only if you become active in the affairs of the party."

He handed her his card and spat on the floor.

"Basil," Irina ordered loudly for Bogdan's sake, "I want that man punished for a lack of hygiene. Understand?"

"By all means," said Basil, putting a black mark next to Bogdan's name. "For starters, I'll require him to sweep out this warehouse."

Before Arkady Ivanovich entered the cavernous room, Basil said, to the surprise of Natasha, who looked up from her typewriter and gaped, that Arkady's membership card was probably forged.

"How do I know?" he asked rhetorically, troubled by Irina's comment in private that the books failed to balance. "Isn't the man a printer, with ink-stained hands, and didn't you imply, Comrade Vostoyeva, that the local membership rolls were padded?"

When confronted by Secretary von Fresser's accusation, Arkady Ivanovich stared at him incredulously. But when Irina pressed him with questions, Basil repeatedly winked at Arkady behind her back.

A moment later, Arkady admitted his forgery and added, "Now that I got that off my chest, I feel much better."

"How many cards have you forged?" asked Irina.

Behind her back, Basil held up both hands and opened and closed them three times.

"About thirty or so," Arkady said.

"I want the names," Irina ordered, nearly touching him as she reached across the table with an extended arm and pointed finger.

Basil interrupted. "Arkady, get someone to record them tonight, and I'll collect them in the morning."

"Your card!" Irina demanded.

Arkady passed it to her, apologized, and bowed out of the room.

"Thirty forgeries still doesn't account for the discrepancy between members and dues."

"Brovensk," said the secretary, "is not without thieves. Though I am reluctant to admit it, we have our fair share."

"How many people have keys to the files?"

He could have implicated his wife and Natasha, but he chose to limit the damage. "I have the only key."

That evening at dinner, Irina Vostoyeva imbibed plum brandy far more potent than her usual glass of white wine. In a slightly tipsy state, she told the family that she loved them and asked Anna and Razan to join the Communist Party.

"I'll spoon . . . sor you. No one would drear . . . dare doubt my word." Her eyelids drooped, and her jaw sagged.

Razan pleaded that he was a foreigner, and Anna said she would think it over.

"What's to wink over, what with all the prib . . . ledges you'll . . . an-joy." She would have continued had she not slipped from her chair to the floor and passed out.

Pavel lifted her onto his huge shoulders, as a child might a rag doll, and put her to bed. A short time later, Anna crept into her room and removed her briefcase, which she searched and then returned to its former place. In the morning, Irina complained of a migraine, but she managed nonetheless to take her briefcase and stagger off to the warehouse.

Party Secretary Basil von Fresser had spent the evening in the company of Arkady Ivanovich, the two of them composing fictitious names in faraway villages and hamlets. Basil also assured his good friend that after the woman from Moscow had left, Arkady would be given a real membership card, one from the dozens stacked neatly on his desk.

Irina's foul mood colored her questioning. Poor Petrovich, the tailor, had the misfortune of facing her first. Fingering a thimble, his constant companion and, until then, unfailing talisman, he faced Irina's withering interrogatives.

Previously, he had counted his worst moments as those coming from Razan, who had hounded him for months to make an overcoat that would be the envy of all. Money, the barber had said, was no object, and insisted that the coat be fashioned from sable and reach his knees, with a fur collar of marten, a hood lined with velvet, and a thick padding of calico wool sewn with fine double seams of heavy silk thread. The tailor could hardly believe his ears. In front of him stood a Jewish barber who had taken up with Anna Lipnoskaya and was now requesting an overcoat fit for a Tsar. When the tailor tried to dissuade him, Razan had answered, "I found it in a book." Although Razan was Albanian, he believed, like most literate Russians, that the ideas found in books enjoyed a divinity not found anywhere else.

Agreeing to make such a coat, Petrovich had opened the door to the very devil. Hardly a day passed that Razan did not stop to ask about the progress of the great creation or insist on yet another fitting. The coat, after all, had to be perfect. Nothing less would satisfy this crazy barber. What could explain Razan's obsession?

How could Petrovich have known that as a young boy, Razan had been given a blue snowsuit—the talk of his friends—made from the skin of a bear, with a zipper running from neck to knee? But one day, after the school bell had sounded, when he slid back the door of the cloakroom, he discovered that his coat had been stolen. So distraught was the little boy that he swore to himself that someday he would own the grandest overcoat in Kishinev. But living now in Brovensk, he would settle for the handsomest work that Petrovich the master tailor could make. And so it was that Razan hounded the poor man until he had produced what Petrovich himself admitted was his masterpiece.

"Identify Karl Marx, Friedrich Engels, V. I. Ulyanov . . ." Two other names, forbidden names, flowed from Irina's lips, though she couldn't remember summoning them forth: "Ivan Bunin and Osip Mandelstam." She attributed this slip to the plum brandy. To protect herself, she said, "Forget the names and tell me about the socialist theory of value. Is it the labor that goes into the manufacture of an object that determines its worth, or supply and demand?"

At a complete loss, Petrovich started to explain patiently how he fashioned trousers and dresses. "After measuring the person, I make a pattern, which I lay on the cloth and copy with chalk. Then I take my scissors . . ."

Irina interrupted. "Answer the question!"

A terrified Petrovich replied weakly, "I don't always get what I think I deserve, but then the customer is always right."

"So you believe that the buyer and not the worker determines the worth of a thing?"

"I know only what I know. If I ask for too much, I don't get paid." He shrugged. "So I take what's given to me."

"Under socialism a worker should be paid a fair exchange for his labor. If you are not, you should complain to the party, which will act on your behalf. That is one of the glories of socialism."

"If I complained, no one would come to my shop. You see . . ." He paused. "What you say sounds good, but in practice . . ."

Irina rounded on Basil, wanting an explanation. "How could you allow any man or woman to be exploited?" She lit a cigarette. "In addition to having inaccurate records, you permit capitalism to flourish here in Brovensk. The Central Committee shall hear of this!"

A cowed Basil said that Irina's presence would serve as a prod to purge from the party double-dealers, moral degenerates, exploiters, the undisciplined, and party officials who had been turning a blind eye to malfeasance and worse.

"Thank you for the wake-up call," Basil said.

She studied him for several seconds, particularly his bull-like neck, which brought to mind fragments from Ivan Bunin: "The stud pinched the sagging skin under his chin, strangling him . . . his eyes shone from exertion . . . his face was livid . . . he saw his ridiculous self in the mirror."

"Comrade, have you ever looked at yourself? Have you ever honestly assessed your behavior? I ask because I may have to recommend that you be removed as party secretary."

Natasha stole a glance at Basil, who was shaking his head sadly and looking like a beaten dog. Even with all his posturing, he had tried to improve the lot of his town. She felt sorry for him. No one should have to suffer public humiliation. Couldn't Irina have told him in private about her reservations? Why speak in front of others?

Kirill the baker had about him the sweet smell of cinnamon. His buns were a delicacy in Brovensk and carried by horse cart to nearby villages. Wisely, he came prepared, offering a sweet roll to each of the three people seated at the table. At first, Irina resisted, but the aroma finally drove her to enjoy the tastiest pastry she had ever eaten. Her mood immediately brightened.

"Tell us about your origins: your parents, their occupation, their house. According to the land records, a wealthy family, a noble one, owned thousands of acres not far from here. The family had six children, one of whom was christened Kirill. Kirill Glebovich Antsyforov, to be exact. You wouldn't be the same person?"

The baker knew that the party had access to the church registry of births and deaths. He would just make matters worse if he denied coming from a noble family. To the shock of Basil and Natasha, he declared, "I am a bastard son, who has renounced his family. I even paid to have a personal statement printed in the newspapers."

"So you have denounced your family?"

He pretended to wipe a tear from his eye. "I have."

Irina found herself at a loss. The children of nobility, legitimate or not, were always denied party membership. But the taste of the cinnamon bun lingered, so she boldly, and illegally, declared that a bastard son couldn't be held responsible for the behavior of his father. Kirill was therefore entitled to party membership, and could he, by the end of the day, please drop off a few cinnamon buns for the hardworking committee? He agreed and departed.

Several women then appeared before Irina; all but two of them, Mary and Oksana, were fieldworkers, deeply tanned, with calloused hands and muscular bodies. The daughter of a priest, Mary explained that because she was unable to support herself, she had gambled that by becoming pregnant, the young man would have to support her. Instead, he abandoned her and the baby. She bravely admitted that she had been reduced to prostitution "to make ends meet."

This explanation actually brought a rare smile to Irina's face as she considered the pun. "Where do you . . ." Irina paused out of tact.

"Do it? In a room behind the Borodins' barn. Either there or in the barn itself."

"And the baby . . . while you . . ." Again she interrupted herself.

"He's still in a cradle. I just tuck him in. I'm only gone a few minutes."

Irina gave this comment some thought. The few times that she had slept with a man, she had resented when he quickly came and went. She thought them unmanly, anti-Bolshevik, not to be more considerate of the woman. Now sitting in front of her was a woman who contributed to the diminishment of love, in both senses, feeling and time.

"How did you earn a party card when you're a . . . um, a woman of no visible means of support?"

Mary bit her lip, but said nothing. Her paleness made her look ghostly, and her gauntness, a skeleton. Irina wondered why men paid her for sex. There was so little of her.

"Please answer the question!" she said, pounding the table. "It bears on my trip to Brovensk and this chistka."

"I can't," she wept.

"And why not? Is the card forged or stolen?"

"No."

"Let me see it."

Mary handed over the card and wiped her eyes.

"It looks perfectly in order. So how did you obtain it?"

Mary just shook her head.

"Did Party Secretary von Fresser give it to you?"

"No."

"Then who did? Perhaps it's the young man who got you in trouble. He's the one, isn't he? He wanted to make it up to you."

"No, I haven't seen him since I told him I was pregnant, and he was the father."

"Then you refuse to tell me how you got the card?"

"I can't," she said and wept anew.

Irina scribbled a note and stamped the membership card invalid. "You can leave."

"Even with the card I was barely able to clothe the baby."

"Tell me who gave you the card, and you can keep it."

Mary slowly rose from her chair and like a holy penitent, with bent back, shuffled from the room.

A seething Irina couldn't quite locate the source of her anger, though she vaguely knew that it had something to do with herself.

Oksana, whose name indicated that she came from Ukraine, caught Irina's attention because of her golden braids, looped lyrically over her ears, and because she had lived in Kiev during the Civil War.

"You have only in the past ten years come into this part of the country," Irina observed, "so you must have been a teenager when the White Army occupied Kiev."

"Yes."

"Were you employed or in school?"

"Employed."

"Where?"

"In a Jewish home."

"As what?"

"A Sabbath goy."

"Religious imbeciles."

"They treated me well."

"No doubt they reeked with money."

"They never went barefoot."

"Why did you leave?"

"Jews were dragged into the street and shot when General Kornilov's White soldiers overran the city."

"Who is your current employer?"

"I work for Kirill the baker."

The last to leave the warehouse, Irina sorted through her briefcase and discovered one missing sheet: the first page of the introduction to her current Bunin translation. She would have to ask the family members if they had seen it.

After dinner, Irina declined the offer of peach brandy. She had enjoyed two glasses of Chardonnay and had no desire to repeat the previous night's misadventure.

"You didn't by any chance come across a sheet of paper that I left in my room?"

Anna shrugged, and the men said they had seen nothing.

"Strange, I could have sworn that I saw it in my briefcase. Perhaps I set it aside and you took it for rubbish." She cast her eyes on the trash bin. "The writing was not in Cyrillic script."

Irina stayed up late, studying every piece of paper she had brought, including those secreted behind her small portrait of Stalin. No luck. Shortly after 1:00 a.m., she heard the backdoor softly open and close. On previous nights, she thought she had heard footsteps on the back stairs. Turning off her light and drawing back the window curtain, she saw Natasha leaving the house. Did Natasha regularly go out and, if so, for what reason? Irina's investigative instincts led her to dress and follow "Miss Prettiness" through the dark streets, fully expecting the girl to rendezvous with some handsome lad. But Natasha made directly for the warehouse, unlocked the door, and disappeared. Irina stood outside the building, brooding from behind a hay wagon.

When a light appeared on the second floor, her suspicious nature drove her to follow. Knowing that the stairs creaked, she removed her shoes and picked her way to the top, where she paused and gently turned the door handle. Natasha was seated at her typewriter. On seeing Irina, she ripped a sheet of paper from the typewriter and tried to stuff it down her dress. Irina intercepted her, asking, "And what is our dear Natasha typing?" As she read it, her black look boded ill for "Miss Prettiness."

"Arkady never said these things!" Irina thundered. She opened a folder and read the contents. "Nor did Bogdan or Dimitri or Ivan or any of the others. You are forging transcripts. I see it all clearly. You intended to replace the official transcripts with these, and I wouldn't know until reaching my desk in Red Square. Well, your treachery has been exposed, and I can assure you that you will lose your lovely looks in a work camp. Why this deceit?"

Natasha rested her head on the typewriter and cried so copiously that she ruined the ribbon. "I have changed the transcripts," she sobbed, "because I was incapable of not changing them."

"The Communist Party is no place for bleeding hearts. You must be strong. No compromises, no wavering, no favors." She removed a cigarette. "I cannot bring myself to believe that you acted on your own. Who asked you to falsify the records?"

Natasha arrested her convulsive shaking and replied through her tears, "It was my own idea. I swear!"

"Socialism has put an end to *blat*. No more pull. Connections with black marketeers and speculators will no longer get you special treatment. Thieves, cheats, toadies . . . they are all wreckers. Bolsheviks proudly look truth in the eye and act accordingly!"

"These people have large families," Natasha pleaded, "and depend on their membership cards for rations and clothing."

"If we are to create a world in which people aren't always dreaming of a better future, we have to perfect our current state."

"What will you do?"

"When I board the train for Moscow, you will as well." She fiercely pulled back her shoulders. "Brovensk lacks the judicial apparatus to hear your case properly. My guess is that you will be found guilty and sent to a camp near Lake Baikal or to one outside of Voronezh, for ten years. With good behavior, perhaps five."

Natasha's tears increased. But Irina ignored her, gathered up the incriminating documents, and left the warehouse.

The next morning, as the family sipped tea and nibbled on the cinnamon rolls that Kirill's assistant had left on the doorstep, no one spoke. Natasha had staggered home after 3:00 a.m., awakened her family, and confessed her forgeries. Pavel, hearing his sister's crying, joined the others in the bedroom. His first instinct was to suffocate Irina. Normally gentle, Razan raged and volunteered to slit her throat with his razor. But Anna persuaded them to wait until she had spoken to the party secretary, Basil von Fresser.

"He excels at only one thing," Pavel objected, "womanizing."

"What you say is true, but I know the man to have a heart."

"If he won't help . . ." threatened Pavel, "I'll . . ."

"He'll help," Anna assured him.

Natasha clung to her mother like a needy child, while Anna gently stroked her hair.

"Should all else fail," Anna said, "we will hide you in a hayloft and, when the time is right, move you to another town. I promise, you will not be leaving for Moscow with Irina!"

Anna put on a freshly starched apron and babushka. Opening the bottom drawer of her dresser, she removed the icon of Saint Julianna. She kissed the icon in its imitation-gold frame and whispered:

"Most Pure Julianna, You are of the righteous, and are therefore worthy of glorification by Christ God. You trample underfoot the destroying passions of evil, bringing health to the faithful." She knelt. "Protect my daughter, Natasha. Blessed be your name. Amen."

Returning the icon to its hiding place, she left the house.

Basil answered the door in a foul mood. Who could be ringing his bell at five in the morning? He wished for a servant, but to have one would have cost him his party membership. Damn those busybodies! But once Irina had left

Brovensk to torment other towns, he would adopt a child as a way of showing his concern for the dispossessed and downtrodden. He knew a twelve-year-old girl whose father had been a Menshevik, thus making employment for her virtually impossible. By doctoring her papers, he would give her a different past. And then, in the future, she could answer the door and run errands and bring him his tea.

"Shh," said Basil, as Anna entered the house, "Mrs. von Fresser is still sleeping and doesn't take kindly to rising before nine."

Anna followed him to the door of his study, which he unlocked with a key that he fumbled out of his pocket.

"Important papers," he said grandly. "I have to safeguard everything, especially with our friend from Moscow in town." Exhausted, he sank into his overstuffed chair, behind his enormous walnut desk, made to order for the effect. He even lacked the strength to rest his feet on the green blotter, a habit that he employed to intimidate underlings. "Sit, sit!"

Anna chose the straight-backed chair with a wicker seat because it invoked India and Burma, places that teased her imagination. She had never before entered Basil's study, and found his wall decorations captivating: family photographs, reproductions of famous paintings, a child's drawings, a medieval leather helmet, framed certificates, and, hanging on the wall behind his desk, a large photograph of Stalin. Although she had seen dozens of the Supreme Leader's portraits, none of them looked quite like this one. The face was undoubtedly Stalin's, but his eyes seemed to peer in every direction. Perhaps what hung before her was an artist's interpretation. She stared at the face, when suddenly the Stalin smiling out of the frame above Basil's head seemed to move. For a moment, she thought the portrait, like a cancer, was infiltrating the other wall hangings and engulfing the room.

"Now tell me what brings you here in the middle of the night. It's not about Natasha, I hope."

"As a matter of fact it is."

Basil rose from his chair and stood as stiff as a Prussian diplomat. "I never touched her. If she said I did, she is lying."

"Sit down, Basil. If anyone touches her it will be Alexei, and for both our sakes, I hope he does."

"Madam, I have plans for my son, and they do not include marriage to the daughter of a . . ."

Anna interrupted. "All those party membership cards you've sold for a handsome profit: Natasha knows all about them."

"I have sold only a few during my term in office, even though the countryside seems to be rife with them."

"Perhaps," she volunteered, "because of Igor the forger."

He held up a hand. "The name means nothing to me."

"Bribery buys blindness."

He sighed, "Natasha must have told you."

"Yes. I even know about Mary, the priest's daughter."

"Ma-ry," he sputtered. "She wouldn't!"

"She didn't. Mary rents her hovel from Jury Stas, and Stas and my son Pavel are friends. You want to know more."

He sank back into the chair defeated. "I think I've heard enough. What do you want?"

"As you know, Natasha's been changing the transcripts."

Basil tried to object. "It was her idea!"

"But you," she pointed at him, "agreed not to notice."

"All those people ruined. How could I not?"

"Good, then we can get down to business."

"About what?"

From her apron pocket, she removed a neatly folded piece of paper and handed it to Basil.

Reaching for his glasses, he asked, "What does it say?"

"I don't know. The language is foreign. But I have the feeling it may be important."

He glanced at the paper. "It's in German." After reading the page carefully, he dropped it on the desk, clearly confused. "Where are the other pages?"

Anna told him that she had removed the paper from Irina's briefcase, leaving the others untouched. "If it will help, I can probably take those, as well."

"Not necessary," said Basil, gnawing on the end of his pencil and lapsing into a brown study.

Anna waited for Basil to gather his thoughts. Well aware of his reputation for posturing, she chose to believe that for all his preening—yes, he was a popinjay—he was not a cruel or stupid man.

"Unless I'm mistaken, this is the first page of an introduction that our friend Irina has written for one of Ivan Bunin's novels."

"And who is Ivan Bunin?"

"A writer on the forbidden list."

"Nowadays everything is forbidden. What does it mean?"

"If you are found with one of his books or if you speak his name in the wrong circles, you can be sent to a work camp."

"Just for reading a book?"

"Russians care more about the written word than the spoken, and you know how Russians love to talk." He wiped the perspiration from his brow. "In this country, we take literature so seriously that we'll kill a writer for any ideological deviations."

"And those who write about forbidden writers?"

Basil drew a finger across his throat.

Anna smiled broadly. "Saint Julianna be praised!"

The party secretary and Anna remained in colloquy the rest of the morning, causing Basil to arrive late at the warehouse. A red-eyed Natasha sat at her typewriter, and a silent Irina pored over her papers. As Basil took his place, Natasha whimpered. The party secretary tried to comfort her.

"No need to fret, child. Today is the last day of the chistka."

Irina said sourly, "For some, but not for our gorgeous Natasha."

Basil sympathetically patted Natasha's shoulder. "We'll see, we'll see," he said, and received in return a grateful smile.

Once again, the interviews discovered numerous false membership cards, which Irina confiscated. When the last person had left, she requested a meeting with Basil, in his study, to discuss the implications of the last few days. Her severe expression told him, like storm clouds, that he would have to endure some heavy weather. They exited with a softly weeping Natasha stooped over her typewriter.

Basil made a show of taking the office key from his pocket and commenting that he always locked up his valuable documents. Irina, as if wishing to emphasize the seriousness of their business, hastily seated herself. Basil plopped into his padded desk chair and put his feet on the blotter. Irina sniffed at his poor manners, crossed her arms over her chest, and, with the authority of Moscow behind her, began.

"Let us not fence with one another, Comrade von Fresser. We both know that in Brovensk and other towns in this oblast, skullduggery is not the exception but the rule. Am I not right?" Before he could answer, she thundered, "Of course, I am right!"

Basil took an expensive cigar from a humidor. Clipping the end, he lit it and expelled a stream of smoke toward Irina. "Do you see this cigar and clipper?" he asked. "They come from a *nepman* who wanted a favor. In the provinces, like the city, blat greases the wheels."

"Aha!" She pulled out a pad. "Then you admit to engaging in capitalist commerce with a merchant and taking a bribe?"

"Yes," said Basil, seeming to enjoy his role as the devil, while Irina took notes. "Frankly, my position gives me influence."

"Natasha has been falsifying transcripts, and you confess to doing business with a nepman. I am overcome by the degree of corruption that thrives here."

She scribbled more notes. "Both of you will be boarding the train with me to Moscow when I leave tomorrow!"

Basil said nothing and kept puffing on his cigar.

"Did you hear me?" she said.

"I heard."

"Call your telegraph operator. I want to send a message to my superiors at once. We will be met at the station by armed guards. Perhaps then you will remove that smirk from your face."

Inhaling deeply and exhaling the smoke slowly, Basil replied, "I think you'll be making the train trip alone. I also think that you will be telling your superiors that Brovensk is a model of party discipline and order."

"Are you mad, Comrade von Fresser?" Irina put aside the pad and opened the folder on her lap. "I have the evidence here." She tapped the papers in the folder. "You will be convicted as an enemy of the people and given twenty years at hard labor."

Basil cleared his throat, admired the long ash on his cigar, removed his feet from the desk, and sat upright. "Comrade Vostoyeva," he said, "do you know the name Ivan Bunin, the man who wrote that most wonderful story, 'The Gentleman from San Francisco,' the story in which a man oblivious to nature and the suffering of others dies on holiday. Surely you know this Bunin I speak of."

Irina's face flushed, and she closed her folder. "Only by name."

"Is he not on the forbidden list?"

"I believe so."

"Believe so," he chuckled, and then said sternly, "You know very well he is."

"What of it?"

He placed his cigar in an ashtray and removed a sheet of paper from a desk drawer. "Do you know the name Katerina Tershina?"

Her folded arms dropped limply to her lap, and her hands shook. "I never heard of this person."

"And yet her name appears at the top of this page."

"What does that piece of paper have to do with me?"

"Come, come, comrade, you said we should not fence. You are writing an essay under an assumed name about Ivan Bunin. Worse, you are writing it for a western audience. Doubly worse, you are writing it for a German audience— in German. If your treachery is not to leave this room, I trust that we can come to some understanding."

Irina's silence seemed to Basil like a thousand years. At last, she put her hands to her head and, with all the self-chastisement that she could summon, asked rhetorically, "What have I done?"

"Indeed, comrade, you have asked a critical question. I will answer you. With this document, which no doubt bears your fingerprints, you have put yourself in grave danger. But I am a merciful man, a forgiving citizen, as all party members should be. So tomorrow you will board the train for Moscow—alone. You will, as I said, give Brovensk a clean bill of health, perhaps even adding that the party secretary is a particularly effective leader. In return, no one in Brovensk shall ever repeat the name Katerina Tershina. If you wish, I can have this page copied so your work may proceed without interruption, and I can accommodate you to the train."

"The bitch! No doubt she stole the paper from my briefcase."

"Now, now, comrade, I thought we had agreed on a peace. Let us part with smiles on our faces and sealed lips."

"I agreed to nothing. I merely upbraided myself for stupidity."

Basil mulled over her mulishness and decided that like so many other Communist officials, she parroted a party line without the ability or strength to defend it.

"Then you wish, Comrade Vostoyeva, to proceed with your charges?" Irina studied one of her fingers and viciously bit off a nail, but said nothing. "The one consolation, Comrade Vostoyeva, is that we may be able to share a work camp and toil side by side cutting down trees for the motherland."

Basil could see her eyes moisten, and, though she remained mute, she rose from her chair as stiff as a ferule and nodded agreement. Coming from behind the desk, he extended his hand; she responded by clicking the heels of her ugly shoes. A moment later, a door could be heard opening and closing, but no one could actually say that he saw Irina disappear into the dark.

Her hosts, in fact, never heard her enter the house, or pack, or leave for the station. According to rumor, that night she had slept on a platform bench at the railroad, perhaps dreaming of a dead gentleman in a tarred box stored at the bottom of a steamship. She was last seen angrily shoving her bags on the train and pulling down the shades next to her soft upholstered armchair.

At dinner that evening, Comrade von Fresser sat at the head of the Shtube table for the celebration. He and his wife enjoyed mineral water, wine, and more than one box of chocolates. Before leaving, Basil requested that Natasha assist him in the office the next afternoon. "No need to get up with the sun now that the Moscow witch has taken her leave." When the von Fressers exited the Shtube house and arrived at their own, the hour was late. Closing the front door behind him, Basil lit a cigar and said to his wife, "Now that's what I call a pleasant evening."

By the time Natasha arrived at Basil's office, a line of people stretched from his desk, out the door, and round the corner. Their faces were familiar. And why not? The very people who had been asked to relinquish their party membership cards were now buying new ones, also those people to whom Natasha had once given cards that she had purloined. The party secretary asked her to record the names as he signed the cards and collected the fees. For five days, the crowds never abated, perhaps because those who held legitimate cards decided, for caution's sake, to renew their membership. A delighted Comrade von Fresser charged everyone the same, as a good Communist should.

At the end of the week, Mary, the priest's daughter, came to the Lipnoskii house to see Natasha. She modestly requested a new card for herself and her son. The next day, Natasha, as she had in the past, removed a card from the stack in Comrade Basil's office, forged his signature, and gave it to Mary.

"Like a blessed saint," said Mary, "you are deserving of glorification by Christ our Savior. Once again, you have provided me with a passport for life, even if it's only a life of warm straw that smells like cold sorrow."

THE LETTER

Dimitri Lipnoskii's letter, dated "The Kremlin, Sunday, August 27, 1933," completely upended Razan's and Anna's world.

Dearest Mother and Honorable Stepfather, Razan Shtube,

Our Beloved Leader, Comrade Stalin, has need of a barber. As you know from the history of our Great Motherland, barbering holds an exalted position among our people, dating from Peter the Great cutting the beards of his officers and passing a law requiring all noblemen to live beardless. A mustache, such as the wonderful one that our Koba is known for round the world, is not only allowed but also encouraged. I now have such a mustache myself, though mine does not compare with Koba's incomparable thickness nor does it have curled ends.

As Kremlin barber, you will be entitled to live in a government house, with other Soviet dignitaries, as well as musicians, artists, and poets, on an embankment of the Moscow River. You will enjoy all the benefits of the elite, for example, a private car, a cook, fine food and wines, travel inside the country, vacations, and of course a handsome stipend. Yefim Boujinski, the previous barber, often remarked that his was the most exacting appointment in the country. Now that he is gone, I am happy to tell you that through close Kremlin contacts, I have made known that Razan Shtube is the country's finest barber, and that his mastery of the Turkish style cannot be found outside of Constantinople, not even in Tirana. I suspect that by alluding to King Zog, whose immaculate appearance Koba often praises, I sealed the deal, as they say.

In short, Koba wants my dear stepfather, Razan, to come to Moscow, at the Supreme Leader's expense, to give him a trial haircut. On the basis of that trial will hang Razan's fate, and perhaps that of the rest of the Lipnoskii family. Our Supreme Leader said that he particularly looked forward to comparing my stepfather's Turkish technique with that of the Caucasian-Uzbeki style. It goes without saying that a burned ear could cost us all dearly. But I do not dwell on that possibility since I know that my stepfather is without peers.

As soon as you make your travel arrangements, let me know. I long to hug my mother again and will arrange to meet you at the train station in a black Packard diplomat's car. Only the best for Koba's barber!

Your devoted son,
Dimitri

No sooner had Razan shown Anna the letter than she ran through the back garden and across the square to the party secretary's house to show it to him and his wife.

"Stalin's barber?" said an incredulous Basil, and immediately telegraphed his son to return home from school. When Alexei arrived, he could not contain his joy at seeing his parents' changed attitude toward Natasha, in no small part because of her extraordinary cooking and clerical skills. But it was his father who amazed him most. What could have caused him to change his mind about Mrs. Lipnoskaya and the barber? Surely, Natasha had not become his mistress. She was far too canny to be snared by the old goat. Alexei's confusion was dispelled when his father directed him and Natasha to be seated in the living room, summoned Anna and Razan, and opened a bottle of ten-year-old wine, which he distributed liberally to his guests.

"Did you hear, Alexei?" thundered his father, with undisguised self-interest. "Stalin himself has asked our own beloved Razan Shtube to be tested for the role of Kremlin barber. Have I not told you a hundred times, more, a thousand times, that you and Natasha should think seriously of tying the knot? What greater joy for your mother and me than to see our two families united. Have I not always praised the virtues of Anna Lipnoskaya and the great Albanian traditions of her stepfather? What are you waiting for?"

As the full meaning of the letter, with its awful nuances, dawned on Razan, he said, "Don't you think we should wait until after the test? Who knows, anything could happen."

"Precisely!" cried the party secretary. "We could all be living in the government apartment house, rubbing shoulders with the Molotovs and Mikoyans."

The civil wedding took place in the local school shortly after Alexei's institute granted him a leave of absence. Gregori Lipnoskii served as ring bearer, and Pavel stood holy witness to Natasha's chastity. Anna and Razan shared the cost of the celebration, an elaborate party held at the von Fressers' house and open to the entire village. Dovgan vodka, made from grain grown in the black-soil region, triple distilled, and charcoal filtered was shipped directly from the distillery in Buturlinovsky. Nobody kept track of the refills or pirogies the hundreds of guests consumed. The couple honeymooned for two weeks in Sochi—during their stay the Krasnodar region had enjoyed fine weather—and, upon their return, Alexei was beaming from ear to ear knowing that he, and not his father, had been the first to taste Natasha's nectar. A few days later, the newlyweds left for Leningrad.

The next letter from Dimitri was brief; he wanted to know the reasons for the family's delay. He included a photograph of Stalin, neatly barbered. Anna's bags stood in a corner, packed. She was ready to leave at any time, but Razan had found Dimitri's letter disquieting. Even Anna's assurance that the words did not mean what Razan ascribed to them could not lessen his fears. Again and again he read over the letter, considering the possible interpretations.

"Dearest Mother and Honorable Stepfather." He had never heard Dimitri call his mother "dearest." Dimitri was, in fact, quite parsimonious with his endearments. And what had Razan done to be called "honorable"? Was Dimitri keen to have Razan lose his life or to improve the family's social rank? "Our Beloved Leader, Stalin, has need of a barber." The Hungarian Karl Pauker, head of state security, barbered Stalin before his responsibilities became too numerous and his travels too extensive, leading to the appointment of Yefim Boujinski, who came from Tashkent. Yefim had been trained in the Muslim manner. Was he dismissed because of his technique or for some treachery? It would be useful to know. "Barbering holds an exalted position among our people, dating from Peter the Great cutting the beards of his officers and passing a law requiring all noblemen to live beardless." Razan could read between the lines. Peter had wanted to westernize the country; the Boyars had resisted. The cutting of beards symbolized not only modernization but also the suppression of a class. That Peter was willing to execute the task himself . . . Razan paused in his reflections and trembled at the thought of his having entertained the word "execute."

"A mustache, such as the wonderful one that our Koba is known for round the world . . ." If the man's mustache had become so famous, then he must adore it. One wrong snip—and what? Perhaps Razan would be snipped. "Thickness." Would Koba tell him to thin or lengthen the mustache or what lotion to use; or would he have to guess? Some of the party members had mustaches that blended in with their beards and extended to their ears. "Curled ends." One could curl either the end or the entire mustache. From the numerous pictures of Stalin in the town, he could tell that the Vozhd preferred a bottom twist, which required a certain tonsorial dexterity.

"As Kremlin barber, you will be entitled to live in a government house with other Soviet dignitaries, as well as musicians, artists, and poets, on an embankment of the Moscow River. You will enjoy all the benefits of the elite, for example, a private car, a cook, fine food and wines, travel inside the country, vacations, and of course a handsome stipend." Razan knew the rumor: the closer one came to Stalin, the greater the danger. To work in the Kremlin, that snake pit of intrigue, he would have to note constantly who was in favor and who was out; he would always be watched by secret policemen; and he would never know whether his apartment was bugged. The benefits of obscurity—namely, freedom and the absence of fear—suddenly seemed immensely appealing.

"Yefim Boujinski, the previous barber, often remarked that his was the most exacting appointment in the country. Now that he is gone . . ." Razan pondered the word "exacting." Who drew up these stipulations or requirements that were not easily satisfied, Yefim or Stalin? Razan could undermine his skill by putting too much pressure on himself. Equally, one could falter if the recipient of his art demanded perfection. Razan wished that Dimitri had been more specific about Yefim's fate. "Gone" could mean that he had left by choice, or by expulsion, or by a bullet. Razan wanted more details.

"I suspect that by alluding to King Zog, whose immaculate appearance Koba often praises, I sealed the deal. . . ." For all his public pronouncements that he was a simple man of the people, Stalin, as Razan surmised from the many fawning newspaper articles, was the equivalent of a Red Tsar. To balance the proletarian and the princely would be no easy task. Besides the barbering, Razan would have to weigh his every word.

"A trial haircut. On the basis of that trial will hang Razan's fate, and perhaps that of the rest of the Lipnoskii family. In a personal note to me, our Supreme Leader said that he particularly looked forward to comparing my stepfather's Turkish technique with that of the Caucasian-Uzbeki style. It goes without saying that a burned ear could cost us all dearly. But I do not dwell on that possibility since I know that my stepfather is without peers." This paragraph was easily the most frightening. Stalin loved to put people on trial and see them squirm. If Razan failed, he would, like others, be exiled to the east or shot. What would happen to Anna and her children; and where had the Boujinski family disappeared to? Razan set the letter aside. Before accepting the offer, he would try to contact either Yefim or members of his family to determine whether he and Anna should move to Moscow or stay in Brovensk.

Anna was stunned. "A disgraced barber! Such a person you don't ask for advice. He was fired by Stalin. Worse, he's an Uzbek. Have you ever met one you could trust?" she asked fiercely. "Uzbekistan! It houses thieves and zealots. You must be ill and running a fever."

She had dealt with numerous Uzbek traders who traveled the old trails of the silk route. They could strike sharp bargains. One of them had even sold her a teapot that he claimed came from the Ming dynasty. It was antique, all right, just as the man claimed. Within a week, the vessel leaked and the porcelain glaze rubbed off, revealing a cheap pot underneath. No, in Anna's estimation, an Uzbek trader was no more trustworthy than a Gypsy.

But Razan had met a man in Tirana who had studied at the synagogue in Bukhara, the one with stuffed pillows made of silk and raised platforms on which the congregation rested. Did the Uzbeks resent the orient incense that infused the air or the golden lamps and shafts of sunlight that lit the shul? Not at all. After services, Jews and Muslims met at the bottom of the road and sat on a low wall dipping their fingers in the pond. Here they exchanged delicacies and stories, each familiar with the other's language.

Surely, Yefim was no different from the Bukharans, Razan reasoned. Besides, Stalin would never have hired a religious fanatic nor brought from Tashkent anyone but a brilliant barber. People weren't plucked out of obscurity for their prejudices. Perhaps then what the Bolsheviks said was true: that Stalin rewarded achievements and gave humble workers positions of prestige.

Dimitri's response to Razan's inquiries left him no less satisfied than before. Yefim Boujinski had moved from a government-issued apartment to a narrow street not far from the Arbat. He and his wife lived over a barbershop, though she never appeared. Razan pondered the meaning of her absence. Anna said, "Religion."

"That must be it! Anna, you have a genius for finding meaning where most would see nothing."

"You are satisfied, then, and we can take the train to Moscow?"

"No, I will first get Boujinski's address and write to him myself about the position. If I am not satisfied with his answer, we will stay in Brovensk. So that no harm comes to Dimitri, I will plead illness and write a letter to *Pravda* praising Stalin's generosity for his willingness to give a simple barber the opportunity to work for the Supreme Leader. Agreed?" He tried to hug her, but she resisted.

"You're wasting your time. The man will never respond. If he's out of favor, his mail is undoubtedly read."

"Then I will go alone to speak privately with Comrade Boujinski. If he tells me it's safe, I'll summon you."

"Alone!" she scoffed. "The Muscovites will immediately stamp you as a foreigner. Your accent will attract the secret police." She took his hand. "I insist on accompanying you—for your own good."

How could Razan argue with his faithful Anna when she had only his well-being in mind? So he hired a cart to take their valises and a few prized pieces of furniture to the station. The train remained in Brovensk fifteen minutes instead of five, to allow Anna time to supervise the storage of her belongings in the baggage car.

"Are you off for Australia?" asked the porter.

"Moscow," Razan answered proudly.

"I can tell you that no apartment in Moscow is large enough to hold all your things. My uncle lives there. I visited him once. Except for Stalin and his cronies, everyone lives in a coffin."

To exhibit economy, the Shtubes booked seats in the hard coach, where travelers sat on wooden benches. Razan garrulously struck up a conversation with other passengers, to the chagrin of Anna, who kept whispering that the "walls have ears." They told him that people often had to wait months for train tickets. So how had they received theirs without any fuss? Anna looked away when Razan asked her, a gesture that provided the answer. Would Dimitri always be in the background playing the role of puppet master, and Razan serving as the toy of a Soviet secret policeman? Influential people could open locked doors, but they could also spring a trapdoor. With Dimitri in control, Razan felt that the play about to unfold had as its author not himself, but his stepson, a conviction reinforced by a black Packard waiting to collect him and Anna at the train station.

"You do understand," said Dimitri, as the chauffeur pointed the car toward the house on the embankment, "that if Stalin selects another barber, you will both have to return to Brovensk."

"Immediately?" asked Anna, annoyed at the prospect.

"The Vozhd has kindly agreed to your staying for a fortnight if things don't work out, a kind of two-week vacation."

The enormous size of the gray government apartment building, built just two years earlier on the site of an old distillery, in Bersenevka neighborhood, the island across from the Kremlin, moved Razan to ask: How many families live here? "Five hundred and five apartments," replied Dimitri, "though some of them are used for offices. Twenty-five entrances, all guarded." They exited the car and thanked the driver. Razan quickly saw from the directory that one could live within its precincts and never want for anything. He counted a post office, a telegraph office, a bank, a legitimate stage, a movie theatre, a laundry, a beauty salon, a school, a medical center, restaurants, and retail stores stocked to overflowing. This building, which occupied an entire city block, belied the contention that the country was suffering from shortages. The presence of a swimming pool and gymnasium and masseurs reminded him of his father's comment that the rich live differently from the poor. He even discovered among the wealth of wares a barbershop, but it resembled no haircutting establishment that he'd ever seen. All the equipment was silver plated, including the molding on the toadstool pedestal chairs. As he soon learned, when a resident of especially high rank wished a haircut, a red light flashed. Within minutes a bodyguard appeared, followed by the dignitary, who thought nothing of displacing some lesser personage already seated.

Dimitri fished a key from his pocket and gave it to Razan. The Shtubes had been temporarily issued apartment number 349, normally occupied by A. R. Rothstein, currently on assignment in Berlin for the year.

"It's now yours," said Dimitri proudly. "Don't gamble it away."

As the three family members exited the lift, Razan hung back and slid a few rubles into the hand of the gray-uniformed operator, who appreciatively tipped his peaked cap and whispered through tobacco breath, "The famous Comrade Rykov lives just down the hall from your apartment. He has a problem with the vodka and has to watch what he says. His daughter looks after him. Her name is Natalya."

The Shtubes' apartment looked out on a chocolate factory that demonically swam in smoke, and on the statue of Peter the Great, who had fared less well in the acrid air than in his Swedish wars. The top floor of the building, reserved for Stalin's favorites, faced the river. All four wings of the apartment building had elevators that stopped at every floor. Some were quieter than others, but all of them in time became heralds of death.

A vase with cut flowers, from Dimitri, brightened the apartment, with its parquet floors, hand-painted ceilings of classical scenes, and framed picture of Stalin. He used the telephone, already connected, to order a magnum of champagne and three glasses. As the Shtubes' belongings were unloaded, Dimitri removed his jacket and helped his parents unpack. By evening, arrayed around a coffee table, relaxing in parlor chairs and drinking champagne, they decided which furniture and clothing would have to be stored in the basement bins.

"This man Boujinski . . ." hazarded Razan.

"I have brought along a map of the city and circled the street that he lives on." Dimitri placed the map on the table and pointed. "This other circle shows the location of your building."

Eventually, as the group drained the bottle and their feet grew "slippy," their tongues incautiously loosened.

"When you meet this Boujinski fellow," said Dimitri, "remember he's Uzbeki, one of those damn nationalities that continue to resist Soviet law. They're Muslims and live according to their own medieval rules. We have sent numerous cultural commissions to Tashkent to reason with them, but they insist on beards and veils and head-to-foot black clothes. I spent a week in Tashkent myself, with the peacocks screeching from rooftops. It's a place untouched by time."

"How long did Comrade Boujinski serve Stalin?"

"Too long. The Boss was skeptical from the first, but since V. K. Iasevich recommended him—V. K.'s in charge of Uzbekistan and headquartered in Tashkent—Koba let him stay as long as he did."

"What was the problem?" asked Razan.

"Koba hated his Muslim dress and the fact that his wife was veiled. If you can believe it, for Stalin's birthday party, she and Boujinski stayed home. December 21 is like a national holiday. The shame!"

As Dimitri shook the last drops of champagne into his glass, Razan asked, "But was he a good barber?"

"How would I know? I've heard that Stalin allows only three people to be present: the barber and two bodyguards."

The telephone rang, and Dimitri answered it. Pause. "Yes, yes, I quite understand. My apologies. I'll see to it at once." Pause. "Yes, comrade, you'll hear."

From Dimitri's expression, Razan surmised that his "son" was trying to formulate an idea or some words that would carefully convey his concerns. Anna, reading the pain in his face, sat on the arm of his chair and stroked his full head of black hair.

"I have some slivovitz in my bag," said Razan. "Will that help?"

"Idiot!" Dimitri exclaimed.

No one spoke. Razan wondered whether the epithet was intended for him or was a self-criticism.

"Now, now, Dima, you are no longer a little boy throwing tantrums," Anna purred as she wiped his sweating forehead.

Dimitri rudely removed her hand and whispered, "Not another word!"

Anna patted his hand, a signal that she understood, and went to Razan to mumble in his ear.

Dimitri, visibly embarrassed, stood unsteadily and straightened the crease in his pants. Slipping into his coat, he declared loudly, "I spoke in error.

Boujinski requested a transfer. And ignore what I said about the Supreme Leader's escort. No one but Stalin knows how many people are in attendance when he has a haircut."

With a gruff goodbye, Dimitri slammed the door, indicating clearly to all that he had concluded his visit to the Shtubes on their first day in Moscow. He never made another.

Razan and Anna avoided, for good reason, expressions of outrage. They now knew the apartment was bugged.

"Perhaps it's in the wall," Anna whispered.

Razan replied sotto voce. "Without removing the plaster, how can we know . . . unless it's in a light switch."

Although the only tools that Razan had at hand were related to barbering, he opened a scissor and used one blade as a screwdriver, quietly removing all the light-switch plates on the walls. Nothing. Anna pointed to the ceiling light fixtures. As Razan gently unscrewed the polished light globe for each one and delicately removed the ceiling plate, Anna banged pans together. In every case, an unfamiliar object was affixed to the wires. Anna grabbed Razan's arm and scribbled on a piece of paper, "Let them think we don't know."

Later, when he asked what led her to suspect the overhead lights, she replied that the globes had no dead insects.

Ever after, they conducted all sensitive discussions on the street, like thousands of other Muscovites.

"What if they planted one in our bedroom?" asked Razan, as they leaned on the embankment wall and peered at the river.

"I have a naughty idea," said a Anna.

Razan pretended not to hear. "We'll have to get used to writing notes," he observed, "and flushing them down the toilet."

"Did you see the warning in the hall: 'Do not put books or paper or sanitary napkins in the toilet, only government-ply tissues.'"

Across the river stood the Kremlin. Razan silently hoped that Stalin would disapprove of his tonsorial skills, and send him and Anna back to Brovensk. Yet he dared not risk injuring the Vozhd, lest he and Anna find themselves living in the cold country. He could not share his feelings with Anna, who viewed the city as an unrivaled opportunity to advance the fortunes of her family. But he knew, with a growing revulsion, that any government that eavesdrops on its citizens has forfeited the right to hold office.

As they peered at the river, Anna leaned over and whispered to her husband. His face went from pink to red, but then Anna had always been more adventurous about sex. Back in their apartment, they stood under the bedroom fixture and loudly moaned, as if transported—and sustained—by the rapture of a cascading climax. Eventually they bought a Victrola and played Beethoven symphonies at full volume to drown out their muffled words. On those occasions when an important subject had suddenly surfaced and they lacked the time to prepare the Victrola or repair to the street, they resorted to hand signals. If, for example, they wanted to show their displeasure with a person or the system, they would merely turn their thumbs down or scribble a note. In time, they agreed on a number of gestures that became their private semaphores for expressing forbidden feelings and ideas.

One day on the street, enterprising Anna remarked with a laugh, "In Moscow one could get rich teaching sign language."

"Now I understand," said Razan, "why the building's so quiet and the parks are so full, even in bad weather."

Anna found it easier to adapt. Of the two, she was the more politically cunning. "Razan, you must admit," said Anna, trying to pacify her troubled husband, "that publicly idolizing Stalin makes life easy. I'll just hang his portrait on a living-room wall."

Within a few days, the Shtubes had met their neighbors: on one side, a party official from the department of heavy industry, on the other, a member of the writers' union. Accustomed as they were to illiterate peasants, they found it extraordinary to mingle with people who spoke and dressed well, held university and institute degrees, read books, and attended plays and concerts, though Razan did find the unfailing praise of the Great Leader disquieting.

Given the constant turnover of tenants, the Shtubes quickly realized that Stalin's personal likes and dislikes were subject to sudden changes. At one time, the barber Yefim Boujinski had lived in the house on the embankment. Anna learned this fact by winning over the building superintendent and having Razan treat him to a Turkish Delight. It was he who told Razan, "Physician heal thyself."

It took a second for Razan to digest the comment. During the last month, he had neither shaved nor cut his hair, having been occupied with packing and traveling and settling into new quarters. The "super" arranged with the official embankment barber for Razan to enter his shop after hours. In return, Razan barbered both men. The super especially looked forward to unlocking the door to the barbershop, settling into one of the three chairs, leaning back, and closing his eyes, while Razan performed his magic. As the ceremony progressed, the appreciative super related in a barely audible voice the history of current and former tenants.

"What do you know about Citizen Rykov?" Razan asked.

"Ah, there's a story," said the super. And he proceeded to tell Razan about Alexei Rykov, his wife, and wonderful daughter.

Natalya, Razan learned, adored her parents, especially her father, born to peasants and a former prisoner in a Tsarist Siberian camp. He had split with the Mensheviks, and his Bolshevik credentials were sterling—a member of the committee that planned the October Revolution, a member of the Revolutionary Military Council during the Russian Civil War, premier from 1924 to 1929 (succeeding to the post on Lenin's death), and a supporter of Stalin and Bukharin against Leon Trotsky. But he fell afoul of Stalin for supporting the New Economic Policy (NEP), which was originally proposed by Trotsky and rejected, and then proposed by Lenin and adopted.

The policy, which eased restrictions on farmers, allowing them to own their farms, though not the land they tilled, was a partial restoration of the market economy, which Stalin vacillated over and finally condemned. Lenin had argued that NEP was temporarily necessary, given that the Soviet Union was principally an agricultural country, and that it would take years to develop an industrial-based economy and self-sufficiency. Under NEP, the economy prospered, farmers earned a decent wage, and people escaped the killing hunger of the subsequent years. It galled Stalin to be proved wrong.

The rightness of Rykov about NEP and his "rightist" moderate socialist views led Stalin to remove him in 1930, at which time Rykov moved from the Kremlin to the embankment, where he had lived ever since in bitterness, occasionally taking coffee with comrades who had originally made the great October Revolution. But eventually, as the show trials reduced the ranks of the old Bolsheviks, who were made to confess their treachery and admit to being wreckers, Rykov could foresee his own destiny and became ever more reclusive, staring through the window at the city he no longer trusted.

Based on this discussion, Razan decided not to wait any longer to seek out his predecessor. After all, at any moment he might be exiled to Tashkent or some less attractive place in Uzbekistan. The next day, Razan took a trolley to the Arbat, the once fashionable Moscow street and neighborhood now grown seedy. Some of the homes and shops still retained a sense of the wealth that had formerly made them the envy of Paris. He walked past the old mansions with their columns, plaster moldings, bright green roofs, and white-stuccoed facades. An image came to mind of Tirana's elegant confectioners, furriers, shoemakers, clothiers, jewelers, and horse-drawn carriages. Through the windows of run-down restaurants, Razan could see ugly crockery and frayed linen tablecloths. Natasha had said that a friend of hers lived on an adjoining street. So, too, did the Boujinksi family.

In the semi-basement of a decaying apartment building stood a small barbershop. Dimitri had circled the spot. It was no more than a low brightly lit room with faded wallpaper and a yellow-stained ceiling bulging in places, potted plants in the front window, and on one wall a cracked mirror. Razan immediately recognized the familiar smell of eau de cologne and powder. An elderly man was just vacating the lone barber's chair. Razan waited in the doorway. From upstairs came the sound of women's voices and a child laughing. The barber wore a white coat, and his expression resembled that of all Moscow barbers, grimly obliging. He exhibited a neatly trimmed mustache and delicate hands. His sad, clean-shaven face expressed care, both kinds, sorrow and sensitivity. Dressed in western clothes, he wore them tight to his thin body and, like the Persians, was tieless. Perhaps Stalin had resented Yefim's height, well above six feet, while the Supreme Leader stood only five feet six inches. Dimitri had mentioned Yefim and his wife absenting themselves from Stalin's birthday party. Surely, that didn't cause his dismissal. Perhaps the man regularly excused himself to pray. No, prayer would have been disallowed. The reason had to lie elsewhere.

Once Razan sat down in the barber's chair and in the dim, cracked mirror studied his own face with its broken nose, he worried how to begin the discussion.

"A clean shave and a close haircut. Please."

"How high do you want the sideburns?"

As the barber stropped the razor on a thick leather band, Razan smiled to himself remembering the thousands of times that with the same motion he had put a fine edge on his blade.

"Permit me, comrade," Razan said softly, "are you not Yefim Boujinski, the eminent barber who once served the Supreme Leader?"

Yefim stepped back, razor in hand, and eyed the man in the chair. "And you are?" he asked suspiciously.

"Razan Shtube, the barber from Brovensk, one of those competing to replace you." He turned to face the barber. "I need to learn what I can about Stalin. I also need a haircut and shave."

Yefim immediately concluded that Razan was a secret agent sent to draw him into a compromising conversation to learn if Boujinski was disclosing Kremlin secrets.

"How," Yefim asked, "do I know that what you say is true?"

"How many Russian barbers know how to cut and singe in the Turkish manner? Certainly not secret agents." Bounding out of the chair, Razan changed places with Yefim, reached for the alcohol, and flambéed Comrade Boujinski's ears. "Are you satisfied now?"

"You make a good case," said Yefim, pumping Razan's hand. "You are an artist. The Vozhd will appreciate your skills, and even your accent, since he has one himself." Yefim lowered his voice. "But you must be careful. Wait while I pull down the shade and lock the door. I'll hang up the 'Closed' sign."

A moment later, hot lather warmed Razan's cheeks, as Comrade Boujinski proudly exhibited his Turkish skills. "Who better than a barber knows the local gossip?" he proudly whispered. "We are at once friends, experts, counselors, and confidants. For us the town holds no secrets. We know about aging bodies, the cooling of the blood, scalps that are losing their former glories, the slackening of the muscles, the delicate creaking of frail bones, toothless gums, bad breath, the crow's-feet gathering on smooth temples. And we listen with attention to everything the bloodless lips of our customers have to confess. Am I not right?" asked Yefim, addressing the man in the mirror. "Some would say that the barber is the official city traitor, who snips his scissors and whispers the secrets of the living and the dead."

Yefim then decisively swooped down on Razan's beard, periodically wiping the blade on the stained sheet that covered him. The shave completed, he used prongs to remove a hot towel from a small steamer and wrapped it around Razan's face. Snipping the air with his scissors, he took a clump of hair between two fingers, and began shaping Razan's hair.

"Note," said Yefim, "that Stalin's mustache and pipe are a measure of his moods. When he strokes his mustache, with his hand or the stem of his pipe, he's content. When he thrusts his pipe forward like this"—he extended his arm—"blood is in the air. He will shout and wave his arms when he's angry or silently pace with an unlit pipe. When he puts down the pipe, watch out! He grows pale, his eyes yellow and bitter, his expression spiteful. Then comes the explosion and the terrible consequences." Yefim paused. "He also has a gentle side." The Uzbek put his mouth next to Razan's ear. "But here's the rub. The man I barber may or may not be Stalin. I have no way of knowing. According to the secret police, who have their own reasons for leaking such information, Stalin has a double. In fact, they say he has several. Whenever he travels he always has three cars or trains or planes leaving at the same time. They say two limousines carry decoys, and one carries Stalin. With three choices who can identify the real Supreme Leader?"

"But the Supreme Leader's voice and his doubles . . . how can they sound alike?"

"Just as the men are indistinguishable from a distance, so too are their voices. The secret police have achieved that effect with their doctored radio broadcasts and speech therapists. Besides, Russian in the mouth of a Georgian comes out as neither one tongue nor the other. From the gargle of vowels, you can't tell the difference. Speech won't help you. I've listened carefully every time the Vozhd has given radio broadcasts or public addresses. One moment I think, yes, that's the man I regularly shave. The next, I say, no, his *r*'s are wrong and his guttural *ch*'s lack a phlegmy effect. In the end, I doubt my own ears. One can't ever be sure."

Always the pragmatist, Razan tried to think of what other tests he might apply. "When you pass these men in the hall, you must know the man you barber and the man you don't."

Yefim smiled indulgently. "Who said they pass in the hall? I've never seen it. The main barbershop is on another floor. That's where his aides come for haircuts. Neither the Supreme Leader nor a decoy has ever entered the shop while I was at work." He paused, as if trying to find a way to explain the conundrum. "You see, the problem is that even if these men stood side by side, you still wouldn't know which was the genuine article. Only a few trusted aides do. And making the situation even more unclear is that Stalin has mastered numerous moods and faces and attitudes. He is a chameleon. How else could he have remained in power this long? My guess is that the real Stalin delights in pretending he's one of the doubles, and that the decoys enjoy imitating Stalin."

"But you must have some inkling who is the Vozhd and who isn't?"

"His closest associates say—and you can decide the truth for yourself—that the Boss is paranoiac about others usurping his power. He might therefore have his own trusted barber, or use a decoy, or sit in my chair or yours just to learn our thoughts. In fact, he loves to lay snares for those he thinks are un-faithful. 'To choose one's victims, to prepare one's plans minutely, to slake an implacable vengeance, and then to go to bed,' Stalin has crowed, 'there is nothing sweeter in the world.' I've often thought: What if the man I am grooming is a decoy for would-be assassins, and the real Stalin has his own loyal Georgian hairdresser who comes to his rooms or a Kremlin hideaway to barber him? Stalin is not the sort of man to let an Uzbek or a Jew put a razor to his throat. I think that just as he has doubles in two cars, while he is seated in another, he has at least two barbers. If I'm right, then the person I used to see a few times a week is a double who has been schooled with great care, even using a favorite phrase of the Vozhd, 'typically not right.' But to be safe, call him Stalin. Better to err on the side of caution."

The reference to Jews gave Razan pause. He knew the old canard that Jew-ish barbers lasciviously pandered to hair and to flesh. But any good barber soothingly manipulated the scalp, sensuously ran his fingers through the hair, and gently touched the person's face. To barber with care was as intimate as foreplay. How could Yefim not know the man in the chair? It would be like not knowing the woman in bed with you. Surely, Yefim had studied the real or counterfeit man to discover details of his life. If the man in the chair could not, for example, authoritatively discourse about Georgia or his Siberian exile, then Yefim would know the man for a double.

But a moment's thought led Razan to conclude that the secret police must be expert in preparing impersonators. They could have surgeons remake a face, and have tutors school the decoys in all the public details of Stalin's life and habits of speech. The police might even allow the men to be given information that presumably only Stalin would know, with the understanding that discovery meant death. Yes, the secret police specialized in cunning. He had heard that they were even conducting experiments on brain waves, hoping to ascertain a person's thoughts. He shuddered to think of a world in which even a person's mental privacy could be invaded.

"How can you barber a man reputed to be the Vozhd," asked Razan, "when you have no idea whether he really is that person? One slip of the razor or tongue . . ."

Yefim advised Razan on the importance of owning many faces in a country that regularly changed its political officials and manifestoes. To survive, a person had to be rubber faced and loose jointed, prepared to smile or cry, kneel or do backflips. Those who convinced themselves that they could maintain their integrity by preserving a private face, no matter how slavishly they behaved in public, usually perished. A double life was not enough; only those who could juggle eight lives, nine, a dozen, would be standing at the end. The Vozhd had learned early how to constantly reinvent himself and expected the same of others, even at the cost of friends and family. Hadn't he counseled his people to renounce their families if it served the working classes? Hadn't the Bolsheviks made a cult of the "selfless revolutionary," whose sole morality was that, in the service of the party and its cause, the ends justify the means? In the paradise to come, owing to the revolutionary sacrifices of the socialists, an ideal human being—a "collective personality" living only for the common good—would emerge. In fact, many socialists regarded the fundamental goal of the revolution as the creation of a new man and a new woman. In support of this view, they approvingly cited the example of Liuba Radchenko, who had abandoned her husband and two young daughters because she felt that it was the duty of a true revolutionary not to be tied down by family. Gorky had perhaps said it best: A new politics demands a new soul. Betrayal was thus countenanced, nay, encouraged, so long as the party prospered.

That Stalin was a different person for every interview, every audience, made perfect sense. As circumstances changed, so too did the Vozhd; even his face metamorphosed to correspond with his needs. His acting skills thus made it impossible for anyone to anticipate his behavior or to know him well. Although his lackeys and flatterers trimmed their words to suit the occasion, they were, given that Stalin could change in an instant, frequently caught off guard—to their peril. The sycophants (Mandelstam called them hyenas in syrup) had so often felt compelled to alter their personalities that they no longer knew who they were. Over time, they became all the different masks that they wore. Internalizing their different "selves," perhaps hating one self and loving another, created schizophrenia not only in the Politburo but also in the country. People sacrificed their essential core, if they ever had one, to please the Supreme Leader and the country. Certainties dissolved, killing off trust, loyalty, and love. As a result, one could never know who the man standing next to him really was: the "real" person, a double, or an actor.

"You have no way of knowing," said Yefim. "And this is true, as I've indicated, for the man you may shave. I can see you are doubtful. I readily admit that what I am saying is speculative, but if true, immensely important. Stalin's fear of assassination is so great that he regularly kills off the people around him. For us, you and me, to even entertain the idea that he has his own private barber, and that we are merely engaged in a charade, would put us high on the executioner's list. Think about it." Razan tightened his sphincter muscle as he felt his bowel loosen. He looked around, wishing for a toilet. "Since the man in the chair may in fact be the Vozhd, it is quite possible that one day you will be approached by persons unknown and offered a great bribe to disclose what you know about Stalin's daily schedule, or forthcoming plans, or current health. You might even be offered a rajah's ransom to slit his throat. Yes, I know, you are thinking such an act would be suicidal and gain you nothing. Ah, but you're wrong. Your family would be spirited out of the country to a safe one, where they could live handsomely off the money."

Although nausea now compounded Razan's fear, he forced himself to respond. "Are you saying that if the man who openly enjoys Turkish haircuts and shaves is a double, then the real Stalin can remain beyond the reach of those who would use his barber to harm him?"

"Exactly."

"Not knowing whom you are lathering, aren't you racked by curiosity?"

Yefim smiled sympathetically. Clearly, Razan was an innocent. To bring wisdom to this benighted creature, Yefim explained. "Nobody knows the Vozhd. For security reasons, he won't allow it. Except perhaps for his daughter, he lets no one get close to him. And yet paradoxically he is everywhere, with us at all times. Believers say they have seen his face in rivers and lakes and the sea."

"Am I to understand that this ghostly presence is known to only a few, all of whom are in danger?"

"Yes. The old Bolsheviks who knew the real Koba have long since been murdered. In the absence of fact, the official line in this country trumpets that Stalin is the Loving Father, the Savior of Mother Russia, and the Protector of Children." He patted Razan's arm. "Wait! You, too, will quickly learn to speak of him in this way."

Having seen pictures of Stalin, Razan knew his mustache and big nose but not much more. Yefim added what he could, based entirely on the man, Vozhd or not, whom he regularly barbered.

"He is short and has bad teeth, foul breath, a pockmarked face, and yellow skin. His left hand is crippled, and he walks with a limp. He loves moving pictures, reading history, cultivating roses and lemon trees, and drinking tea with Armenian brandy. Usual attire? Military tunics and breeches tucked into crimson-tooled, light morocco boots." Perhaps thinking of the oft-repeated saying that the walls have ears, Yefim ceased talking and concentrated on his barbering. Once he had finished with the scissors, he used his clippers to remove the tiny hairs at the base of Razan's neck, artfully flambéed his customer's ears, and applied an aromatic lotion and some talcum powder. Boujinksi then removed the sheet, shook the hairs onto the floor, and invited Razan to his lodgings. Yefim pressed a wall button to warn the women above. As Razan reached for his purse, the Uzbek barber stopped his hand and shook his head no.

At the top of the stairs, Razan saw a brass nameplate, Boujinski, and down the hall a communal bathroom. The front door opened into a cramped room divided by a curtain, behind which women were giggling. Yefim said that the voices came from his daughter and her mother.

"Might I have the pleasure of meeting them?"

"You must understand. She treats her side of the curtain like an *ichkari*, the women's quarters of a Muslim house. I tell her that she and the child need sunshine and fresh air, but she ignores me."

Without mentioning Dimitri, Razan observed sympathetically, "Your religion must have presented an obstacle to your work in the Kremlin."

"More than an obstacle, it led, I feel certain, to the loss of my position. Why else would Stalin's people have lectured me about the evils of the *chadra*? They said the head scarf was a mark of centuries of despotism and slavery, even though millions of Russian women wear babushkas. The Bolsheviks regard all religions as superstitions. When I tried to explain that Uzbek women wear the veil because it's what makes them Uzbek, they simply repeated that our women and their veils serve to resist socialist freedoms."

"I thought that the Vozhd supported the independence of national groups, like the Uzbeks."

"He did once, but then changed his mind. By putting all the nationalities under the Soviet, he took control of the country." People who constantly change their minds, thought Razan, can't be trusted. The job was quickly losing its appeal. "You do know that Stalin attended the Tiflis Theological Seminary—and was expelled?"

"Maybe that's why he hates religion," Razan replied.

"The official explanation is that the church fathers dismissed him because of his radical activities; but I have also heard it whispered that he impregnated a young girl and then went to work for the Tsar's secret police, the Okhrana."

"Stalin? A secret agent for the Romanovs?"

"That's what many old Siberia survivors say. They point to the fact that he always escaped internment easily. But the only people who know for sure are the archivists, and they live precarious lives."

Duly impressed by the range of Yefim's reflections and command of the language, Razan asked him if had been formally educated.

"In Tashkent and Odessa, I studied philosophy and economics. I trained to be a teacher, and worked in a school in Bukhara for two years, but I was sacked for setting what the head of the school called 'excessively high academic standards.' Her idea of excessive was my insistence that the students know grammar. She called me an 'elitist,' and said such people did not belong in the Soviet school system. Fortunately, my father, a barber, had taught me the trade."

"That's how I learned as well."

"We were fortunate to be taught the Turkish style. Not many Russian barbers know the secrets. Pauker didn't, even though he was hairdresser at the Budapest Opera and worked as a barber in the Austro-Hungarian Army. A bit of a dandy Pauker was. He reputedly procured girls for Stalin. I spoke to him once. He told me he used talcum powder to fill Stalin's pockmarks. I gathered that every time Stalin bared his throat to the razor, Pauker shook with terror."

Not until this moment had Razan considered how many people over the years had entrusted their lives to his own hand. He had served all classes, from royalty to runagates. If he had slit the justice minister's throat, he might have changed the course of Albanian history. The very thought caused him to shiver. Actually, Razan associated the sight of blood with tonsorial failure, and could remember no more than a dozen times that he had nicked a man's face, though never badly.

"Let me ask you a professional question. If the man you barber has deeply cratered skin, I assume you use a scissor to snip the hairs in the craters and a blade on the few smooth parts of his face."

Yefim nodded. "It's a slow process, and since it always occurs late in the evening, I'm not always properly rested."

This admission surprised Razan. "Evening? Strange. How late?"

"Two or three in the morning. He goes to bed at four or five and sleeps till noon. I usually barber him after midnight. If you replace me, you'll discover your client has numerous quirks, like never sleeping in his bed but rather on the office divan."

The trouble with quirks, Razan mused, is that unless they always expressed themselves in the same way, you could never anticipate a person's behavior. If the health of a civilization rested on the predictability of human behavior, then caprice was a danger to all. He therefore decided to learn the man's idiosyncrasies.

"Here's what he doesn't like: doors left open or slammed, people standing close to him, tall people, imaginative people—he assumes he authored every good idea—repetitiveness, as in explanations, his own or others, men who can't hold their liquor or can't stay awake late at night. He's like quicksilver."

"Have you no way to predict his good days or bad?"

"In advance, no. But his love of movies remains constant. His favorites are American westerns, Charlie Chaplin, and Tarzan."

From behind the curtain came laughter. Razan felt certain that he detected three voices; he also felt certain that to inquire would have been forward. Yefim acted as if he had heard nothing. Razan vaguely remembered Dimitri saying that the wife had a sister. Perhaps the two women were entertaining the young girl.

Hearing voices brought to mind eavesdropping. What if Yefim's apartment was bugged, or his shop? Why hadn't he thought of this before? Given Yefim's disclosures, Razan and the family could be in danger. Razan began to pace, looking for suspicious bulges in the wallpaper and eyeing the light fixtures.

"Now you remind me of the secret police. All you need is a black coat. What is it?"

Razan gestured for a pencil and paper. Writing quickly, he handed Yefim a note: "My apartment came equipped with a listening device. What about yours? And your shop?"

Unperturbed, Yefim pointed to the walls and the light sockets. "I've looked and could see nothing. We rarely speak about politics and mostly in Uzbek." He paused. "But it is true that translators are easy to find. If we've somehow been bugged, that might explain my dismissal and other things." Yefim shook his head skeptically.

"Let's look again," Razan whispered.

But all the light sockets were clean, and the walls seemed perfectly normal. "Perhaps," Razan added, "your embankment apartment was also safe, and the source was an informer."

Yefim studied his guest. His gaze bespoke pain or bad tidings. But for whom?

"Maja!" called Yefim. "Meena! Come here!"

After several moments, the curtain slowly parted and two women, each dressed in a *paranji*, which some call a burqa, shyly entered. Covered in black from head to foot, the women looked out through eye slits. Trailing behind was a child, no more than nine or ten years old, free of the paranji but wearing a head scarf.

"Let me introduce Razan Shtube, a fellow barber."

The women murmured their greetings and stood waiting to receive Yefim's direction. He told them to sit on the couch and called Yelena, the child, to him. Embracing her and kissing her head, he looked up and said without the least suggestion of concern:

"Which of you has been speaking to the secret police?"

Neither woman responded.

Yefim turned to Razan and calmly explained, "Maja's my first wife, Meena my second."

Without thinking, Razan blurted, "Then they're not sisters!" Immediately, Razan reproached himself for his rashness. His information could have come from only one source. He had unthinkingly admitted that he had been briefed by the secret police. How could he extricate himself now? He knew from Dimitri how the system infected people with two kinds of phobias: one, that everybody they met was an informer, and two, that they might be taken for one. Razan could just imagine Yefim's state of mind.

The Uzbek, in fact, was already ruing his frankness. Not to have treated Razan as a possible informer was a serious mistake. He had worked in the Kremlin long enough to know that questions were to be answered obliquely. When Razan was asking about Stalin, he had induced Yefim to drop his guard. Yefim knew that the first rule of self-preservation was to treat everyone, without exception, as an informer, even your wife. Sadly, if a spouse (for example, the husband) turned informer, the other person (the wife), unless an utter fool, was virtually condemned to silence; and since silence can be construed as conspiracy, the innocent party (the wife) became complicit in the same crime. Both were then trapped, because nothing binds people tighter than crime. The more people implicated and compromised, the greater the number of informants, traitors, and spies. As well, the ranks were swelled by the self-interested, who supported the regime to get ahead or to protect their own hides.

Even if Razan was a naif, the government would expect Yefim to denounce him; otherwise he would be putting himself and his family in jeopardy. The formula was lethally simple. If "A" failed to denounce "B," "C" could denounce both of them, a chain theoretically extendable until it tainted all the country's 170 million citizens. Another sinister possibility was that if Razan were a government agent, he could threaten to denounce Yefim as a traitor unless Yefim agreed to work for the secret police. If Yefim refused, Razan could threaten to blacken his name by spreading rumors that the Uzbek was, in fact, a secret agent. And then Yefim's friends would never trust him again.

Not having worked in the Kremlin, Razan was not as sensitive as Yefim to all the implications of treachery, and felt powerless to clear his name. How does one prove a negative? If Razan said he was not a spy, Yefim could reply that he never entertained such a thought. Why even bring it up?

It all seemed perfectly Soviet to Yefim. Razan had led him to make incriminating statements in the barbershop because it was bugged. He therefore asked Razan to join him downstairs to look for the device. A microphone would confirm his suspicions and allow him, for the taped record, to disavow all that he'd said and contend it was a trick to trap the new barber. Inch by inch the two men removed the wallpaper. When the electrical sockets proved safe, Yefim visibly relaxed, put his hands on his hips, and studied the room. Aha, the mirror behind the barber's chair! It had always been cracked. But the fissure seemed wider now than before. With a pair of scissors, he carefully pried loose a section of glass along the crack. Termites!

Yefim's relief was life restoring. While so many others were traitors, apparently Razan was not. Had a microphone been discovered, Razan could have insisted that Yefim, in light of what he had said, fully confess to being a traitor, even if his confession was false. Thousands before Yefim had been similarly trapped and had then fabricated information in the hope of staying alive.

In the apartment, except for the child, who was playing with an abacus on the rug, the women, like black idols, remained just as before, robed and silent. What a splendid disguise, Razan thought; a woman could gnash her teeth or grimace or grin and nobody could see. The burqa also made it impossible to know whether the person inside was a man or a woman. How many men, Razan salaciously wondered, had made their way into harems clothed in a burqa? Surely some Arab storyteller must have used that device for a titillating tale. Suddenly, from behind one of the burqas—Razan had no idea which—came a voice.

Yefim responded, "You ask, Meena, why I think a wife of mine works for the secret police? So often when I was shaving the man who calls himself the Supreme Leader, he would say something like, 'My guess is that you support

Caucasian independence' or 'Yagoda probably terrifies you.' How did he know my thoughts? One day, he said, 'The Five-Year Plan is proving costly in human terms,' which were my exact words spoken only to you and Maja."

Neither woman replied. Yefim reached for his Qur'an. "I want you both to swear on the holy book that you are innocent. The Prophet says that he who lies earns hell. Come now and swear."

They rose from the couch and crossed the room. Had Yefim not said, "Maja, you first," Razan would have had no way of knowing one woman from the other. On the floor, the child watched the unfolding drama, transfixed. So, too, Razan. At the last second, Maja stepped aside to allow Meena to put her hand on the book and proclaim her innocence. Maja then reached for the book, but stopped. Looking at Yefim, she cried, "Must you always torment me?"

"Why?" Yefim asked. "Tell me why, Maja."

Razan found the moment painful, as Maja broke down in tears.

"I begged you not to take a second wife, but you did anyway."

Yefim replied without rancor, "You and Meena are friends."

"Yes," she sobbed. "We agreed to say we were sisters so we could all live together."

"Have we not lived congenially?" Yefim asked.

"We have."

"Why then . . . ?"

She said nothing and turned away.

"You can speak. Razan is a friend. I give you permission."

Slowly but deliberately, she traced the outline of her grievance. "I know the Qur'an. You are entitled to take up to four wives. But I also know how I feel. Every time you wish to be alone with Meena, I have to leave the room and the apartment. I take the child and enter the street. Such is my situation. The same is true for Meena. She and Yelena leave when you and I choose to be intimate. What she feels, I can't say, but I feel shamed. Always I am asking myself, 'What's wrong with me? Why am I not enough for him? Where do I lack?'" She wiped her eyes. "That is why I agreed to inform."

"Even though you despise the Soviets?"

"I hate much about them, but not their attitude toward multiple marriages. They say many wives obstruct the advancement of all people. I agree whole-heartedly. Look around at the Muslim nations. Do women enjoy a higher status in those countries or in the Soviet Union? I think you know the answer."

From her eloquence and candor, Razan concluded that Maja had at some time in her childhood received an education, which made her unusual among Muslim women. Probably at home, he thought, and wondered what her father did. Perhaps the government had sought her out precisely because of her education. Women who had been schooled were less likely to countenance multiple marriages.

"Whom did you report to?" Yefim asked, still perfectly calm.

"I can't say."

"Informers meet their *controls*—isn't that what they call them?—in the control's apartment or in a private apartment belonging to an innocent person."

Maja refused to take the bait.

"How do I know," asked Yefim, "that you are sincere and not yourself a plant, trying at this very moment to use me?"

"You don't, but who introduced the subject, not I?"

"At some point I would have guessed."

"Perhaps."

That Razan was privy to this conversation obliged him by Soviet law to inform the authorities about what he had heard; otherwise he himself could be prosecuted for "lack of vigilance," along with everyone else who had heard it, to wit, Meena and Yelena. Yes, even the child was expected to denounce the accused, in this case, Yefim. The inhumanity of Soviet law had previously been no more than a vexation, but now he felt crushed by it. Why should he, an innocent party, be liable for keeping his own counsel? As the implications slowly spread through his arteries, he understood, for the first time, that a person's private thoughts or the verbal rambling of others were the property of the state. Not to disclose what one was thinking or hearing was like insisting on the right of private property, a Bolshevik sin. Even intellectual properties belonged to the state. A writer lived next door to him in the government house. Was he forbidden to copyright his work? And what of composers? Or, in the case of inventors, patents? The attack on imagination could not have been clearer; the state had declared war on originality.

Razan, feeling sick, asked to be excused, but Yefim, well aware of Razan's obligation to report the scene that had just taken place, followed him down the stairs to the street.

"What will you say?" asked Yefim. "They'll know that we talked."

"Of course we talked—about barbering! I can't afford to say otherwise. The test, my stepson, my wife . . . all are at risk."

"Maja was there."

Both men watched a horse-drawn dray come clop, clop, clopping down the street. On the driver's board sat an old man and a child. He was showing her how to hold the reins and drive the horse. A black Volga, the official car of mid-level Soviet officials and businessmen, was honking for the drayman to let him pass.

"Your daughter," said Razan nervously, "who is her mother?"

"Maja."

"She's a lovely child. Most women would wish to have her large dark eyes and perfect complexion. How old is she?"

"Yelena is ten, and the sweetness of our lives."

As the car drew even with the two barbers, Yefim turned his back to the street. Razan instinctively understood, and did likewise. Stay out of sight. The nail that sticks up gets hammered.

After the Volga disappeared, Yefim remarked, "I can't even imagine what it's like to own a car. They say that in America, working people own Fords, but I don't believe it. In America there's a depression. In fact, they're sending experts to see how the Soviet system works, perhaps to adopt it. Fools!" Turning to Razan, Yefim added, "You do know that if you reported me you would put yourself in good standing with the secret police."

"Yefim, I owe you a favor. You shared your experience and knowledge. For your own safety—and mine—I beg you: take your family and leave for Tashkent. I might even be able to help you with train tickets."

Yefim smiled warmly. "So you are a secret agent after all!"

Razan took the Uzbek's hand and mumbled, "No."

For a moment, Yefim studied the street and shops, as if silently saying goodbye. "I'll arrange to leave at once. A thousand thanks." He put his hands on Razan's shoulders. "Let me hug you." As he did so, he whispered, "I have slipped into your pocket a picture. It is the man I barber. Don't ask how I got it." Releasing Razan, he opened the door to his building and stopped. "Tell me one thing: Why did you think they were sisters?"

"It's my biblical upbringing," replied Razan, feeling his ears. Yefim had given him a true Turkish Delight.

"But in the Old Testament," said Yefim, "the patriarchs often have more than one."

To protect Dimitri, Razan had lied about the source of his information. But it wasn't his deceit that disturbed him; it was that lying had come so easily and seemed so natural. A quotation came to him: "Beware the temptation to ignore what is true." Would the future, he wondered, mimic the past or would new generations live in a world where falsehood was less useful than truth?

IOSIF VISSARIONOVICH DZHUGASHVILI

The day that Razan Shtube met the man who called himself Stalin, a fierce frost coated the city. Icicles hung from the Kremlin. Razan wore his new overcoat, the one Petrovich had made to order with a fur collar of marten, a hood lined with velvet, and a thick padding of calico wool sewn with fine double seams of heavy silk thread. Razan had never owned such a fine garment; not even his childhood bear suit could compare. Petrovich's creation was like a protective womb that helped him endure the cold of subzero Russian winters.

Dimitri had intended to collect Razan and drive him to his interview, but an emergency arose, and a courier brought Razan an official pass. Instead of taking a cab, Razan decided to walk across the bridge to the Kremlin. The bitter wind would concentrate his mind. Passing under the vaulted archway of the white Kustafya Tower, the barbican of the Troitsky Gate, he came to a guardhouse, flanked on either side by soldiers. Through a grille, Razan poked his pass at a stony official.

"This warrant was issued by one Dimitri Lipnoskii of the secret police. I have to check on his authority to issue passes."

Razan stamped his feet on the icy pavement to keep them warm. As the soldier held the phone, waiting for clearance, he misconstrued Razan's behavior.

"Impatience, Citizen Shtube, will get you nowhere." He then thanked the person on the phone and said to Razan, "I was instructed to ask, what is the purpose of your appointment?"

"I'm here to interview for the position of Stalin's barber."

"Are you in possession of any weapons?"

"Just my scissors, shaving equipment, and combs."

Handing Razan a basket, the soldier directed him to empty his briefcase, which included the teakwood box and razor that the barber's father had given him in Albania. It took a minute before the guard returned the contents, with a permit noting that the barber was carrying a razor.

The two soldiers, who had been flanking the guardhouse and standing rigidly in the cold, led Razan to the armory and the desk of a man in a black suit, who introduced himself as a security agent. With the guards looking on, he closely studied Razan's pass, opened his briefcase, examined the contents of the teakwood box, and conducted a body search of the barber. Then he reached for the phone on his desk, said something about "clearance," and told Razan to wait, adding:

"Comrade Poskrebyshev, Stalin's secretary, will be down shortly to collect you."

Dimitri had told his father-in-law that Alexander Nikolaevich Poskrebyshev, in his capacity as *chef de cabinet*, screened all of Stalin's appointments and many of his official documents. Absolutely devoted to Stalin, he actually lived in the Kremlin, near Koba, to serve him when needed. A few minutes later, Poskrebyshev brusquely introduced himself and snarled contemptuously from a pockmarked face, a physical disfigurement that he shared with the Boss.

"You are Razan Shtube, from Brovensk," he said looking at a paper. "An Albanian, you lived briefly in Birobidzhan. No doubt a Jew who wants to pass for a Russian." Before Razan could reply, the pox-scarred man said, "Married to Anna Lipnoskaya, whose son Dimitri works for national security."

Poskrebyshev's familiarity with Razan's history persuaded the barber that the more Stalin's gatekeeper knew about him, the better. He'd then know that Razan presented no danger.

"Are your nails clean?" Before Razan could respond, Poskrebyshev snatched his hands. "I've seen worse."

On the advice of Dimitri, the barber had carefully pruned his nails, cut his cuticles, and, of course, scrubbed his hands. Why, Razan wondered, would anyone employ this loathsome aide?

"You types are all the same," said Poskrebyshev. "You come here expecting the Beloved Leader to give you easy work. Under socialism, labor is a full-time job, not a one-hour haircut and shave. Follow me. Count yourself lucky to be in the Kremlin and meeting our Beloved Koba. But I must advise you that the Great Builder of the Soviet Union has already turned away three barbers, not counting the traitor from Tashkent. So don't whine to me that you weren't warned."

The phrase "the traitor from Tashkent" nearly persuaded Razan to turn on his heels and make straight for the door.

"Will Dimitri Lipnoskii be joining us?"

"His special assignment will take a few days to complete. Our Courageous Stalin normally disdains doing favors for friends, but he has made an exception for Dimitri, who recommended your skills. I'm sure your son will regret it."

Yefim had damned Poskrebyshev with just a whisper. "That toad would kill his own family for Stalin." Comrade Ugly, as he was called by his detractors, snapped his fingers for the barber to follow, as if summoning a dog.

To awe the few simple citizens who made it past the Kremlin gates, and to make them think that the Great Kremlin Palace was the people's house, Stalin had Poskrebyshev guide visitors through the magnificent rooms to gape at Russia's rich past. Today, however, he seemed out of sorts and ill disposed to lead Razan on a Kremlin tour.

At the front door of the palace, he said peremptorily to a uniformed attendant in a black jacket with golden epaulets, "Artur, show this *cit* the Catherine Room. The Congress Hall is being used. I have work to do." Poskrebyshev then disappeared.

The eighteenth-century Catherine Room, which was furnished with chairs and divans bearing the monograms of Catherine the Great and had walls covered with green silk wallpaper and portraits of royalty framed in gold, left Razan breathless. He slipped his guide several rubles and asked the man to permit him a peek into the other palatial rooms. Artur took him directly to the Georgievski Hall, adorned with hollow zinc columns, ornate crystal chandeliers, and an intricately patterned parquet floor built with twenty different kinds of wood. "When the room is lit," said Artur, "the light luminously reflects off the floor." Mirrored doors led from the Georgievski Hall to the octagonally shaped Vladimirski Hall, in which a glittering three-tiered crystal chandelier hung from a dome. After the Vladimirski Hall, they went to the Palace of Facets, where the walls blazed with every color of the palette, then to the Tsarina's Golden Chamber, and, through the gilded doorways of the Holy Vestibule, into the Terem Palace. The last two stops on the tour were the Palace of Congresses, which looked like an enormous wooden schoolroom, and Stalin's glittering scarlet and gold reception room, used for entertaining foreign dignitaries. From the large conference chamber, formed out of the joining of the Alexandrovski and Andreyevski halls, Razan could hear voices, clinking glasses, laughter, and a balalaika. Artur said that a meeting of Soviet delegates was in session, prompting Razan to look through the slightly open door on a scene that remained with him for the rest of his life. On an easel stood a large portrait of Stalin. Party members were celebrating the successes of their different provinces. People of all hues and races and dialects and languages were singing the praises of Soviet life and drinking the health and wisdom of the Supreme Leader. Many of the faces would surface again, both in Poskreby-shev's office and in newspaper photographs that recorded the achievements of these "Soviet heroes" and, subsequently, their unlamented deaths.

A commissar from Georgia—how could one mistake the accent?—was speaking. "Knowing how much the people love him, I sometimes think I love him because he's so much loved. If my reasoning sounds circular, think of it this way. Don't we love what we have helped create owing to our love?"

Razan stood transfixed as these men vied with one another to show how much they adored Stalin.

"Iosif has my unqualified and boundless love. So I know how great is the love bestowed on him, and how he in turn lavishes it on the people."

Others chorically added their praises.

"The people bask in his love."

"It warms them."

"Inspires them."

"Enlightens."

"Makes us all better Soviets."

"Enables us to harness rivers and build canals."

"Emboldens us to defeat our enemies."

"Gives us the strength to build a Utopian life."

"Leads us along the path to paradise."

"Opens the doors . . ."

"All drink to Comrade Stalin!"

The throaty huzzahs and upheld glasses sent a shiver down Razan's back. Their blind loyalty to Stalin suddenly made clear the meaning of a Utopia. To have such a state would require everyone to agree on what constituted the good; the members of the society would have to share the same values. Choice would be disruptive, contentious, tantamount to chaos. Therefore, those who refused to conform to the rules would be pariahs, living outside the commu-nity; only believers could be insiders. What, then, was to become of dissenters: exile, execution? Stalin believed that forced conformity to the rules rooted out "parasites," namely, those who enjoyed the benefits of socialism but were un-willing to invest the necessary zeal in the enterprise. But if freedom issued from choice, and if Utopia meant no choice, then . . .

By the time Razan and his guide reached the Senate Building and Poskre-byshev's office, Citizen Shtube was weighing the advantages and tallying the arithmetic of barbering Bolsheviks. The position of Kremlin barber was a plum, but familiarity inevitably bred contempt. Look at Yefim. Razan swore he'd never be a lackey. Apparatchiks abounded. He valued his own identity, his own sense of self. To wear other masks would mean no longer being a Jewish barber seeking a better life and married to an enterprising, faithful woman. Masks could lead anywhere, and anywhere was a state of imbalance.

Although he feared displeasing Stalin, he could not compromise the principles he held dearest, justice and fairness. Democracy, he knew, had much to recommend it, but also much to rue. The tyranny of the majority, namely, a poorly informed citizenry that elected the leaders of the country, had no special appeal. Stalin was right on that point, but what of the excesses ascribed to the Vozhd? Surely, Stalin had not overseen the starvation of millions of Ukrainians? Word would have seeped out and Stalin's critics would have howled loud enough to reach every Russian ear. And those who were sent to camps and suffered capital punishment . . . were they all innocent? If people were being jailed or executed for nothing . . . how could that be?

He would mind his own business and avoid politics. Perhaps then he could become renowned as Stalin's barber. Important people would notice him. Favors would come his way. He need not fawn like those men toasting the Supreme Leader's health. He would keep his own counsel, and his independence. As dangerous as Stalin's critics said it was to come within his orbit—life expectancy for his functionaries was short—he knew that the Soviet Union was a juggling act, and that he had the skills to stay alive.

Artur led him to Comrade Ugly's office, adjoining Stalin's, and pointed to an armchair under the Vozhd's picture. Those fortunate enough to pass beyond this room discovered, as Razan eventually would, a tiny nook, no larger than a closet, where Stalin's personal bodyguards stood watch. Beyond this nook was the inner sanctum, known to Stalin's aides as the "little corner." Positioned at the angled juncture of two wings of the Senate Building, Stalin's rectangular office resembled a long coffin. Though airy, the room was dark; heavy drapes covered the windows, preventing some distant sniper from taking a bead on Koba. Red and green carpets ran down the center of the polished floor. Along the walls, with their shoulder-high paneling, stood a row of ornate ceramic Russian stoves that Stalin often leaned against to relieve his many arthritic pains. To the left stood a long table, with a green baize cloth, surrounded by straight-backed chairs upholstered in white. Here sat the Court of the Red Tsar, conducting affairs of state; and above and behind them, on the wall, looking down on the proceedings from framed portraits, peered the two greatest Bolshevik heroes: Karl Marx and Vladimir Ilyich Lenin. To the right rested an enormous desk, one suited to a man who measured five feet, six inches tall, and wore elevated shoes.

Piled high with official documents labeled in folders, his desk held numerous colored telephones, including a "safe" one. A pool of sharpened pencils suggested the exactness of the man. His fountain pen, which he used to sign death decrees, lay ominously at hand. A door behind the desk led into two other rooms: a lavatory and the signal room, which housed a sofa and parlor chairs, telegraph equipment that connected Stalin to every reach of the country, and a globe that the Supreme Leader frequently pored over when he discussed issues of political importance with statesmen.

The Supreme Leader's living quarters were situated on the first floor, virtually right under his office. He had moved here from his former rooms in the Poteshny Palace and the Zubalovo mansion because he associated them with Nadya, the wife who had shot herself. Some attributed her suicide to mental instability, some to doctrinal differences between husband and wife, and some to jealousy. Even with his bad teeth and halitosis, Koba was attractive to numberless women. His flirting may have been clumsy and his advances rude, but he engaged in numerous affairs during his marriage. Wishing to put behind him his wife's death—in the Bolshevik paradise, wives did not kill themselves, and certainly not those who enjoyed the privileges of high places—he had moved into the Senate Building, displacing a friend and then converting a high-ceilinged first-floor drafty corridor into an apartment for him and his motherless children.

In the antiseptic colorless anteroom of Poskrebyshev's immaculately clean and austere domain, a guard insisted that Razan hang up his overcoat. The barber hesitated, inviting sharp words from the chef de cabinet. To ensure safety, control was paramount. The fewer items allowed in the room, the less chance one might prove lethal. Here sat Poskrebyshev, who had snubbed him earlier. Authorized to use a rubber stamp bearing Stalin's signature, he wielded from his desk the power to decide who would see the Supreme Leader. This arrogant man was Stalin's indispensable, servile aide, privy to the names of those sent to camps or to their death. On his desk stood a signed picture of the Boss.

"Who knows what one may have spirited away in a pocket, even though that person was searched?" Poskrebyshev peevishly said.

The barber, to Poskrebyshev's annoyance, wanted reassurance that when Stalin summoned him, the overcoat would be safe.

"You're behaving like a child, a regular Akaky."

Two hours later, he was still waiting—and fuming at being called an Akaky, a child's word for excrement. His handsome coat hung from a corner rack. He had hoped to wear it on being introduced to the great man. But Stalin was out of his office. Having risen late, the man distantly familiar to all, owing to his cratered face and large mustache, had sped from his dacha at Kuntsevo in a convoy of Packards and stopped at the Hotel Metropol for a lunch of blintzes with the head of the writers' union. Had Razan been present, he would have heard the Very Important Person vociferate that most modern literature smacked of elitism and neglected the common man.

"Readers want to learn about life in the factory, on the docks, in the fields, not about the love affairs of rich people and other criminals," the Very Important Person raged. "As for the dissonant music and the unconventional books, they have to go. When I leave a concert, I want to be able to hum the music. When I read a book, I want to understand the story. Symbolism is a decadent western idea."

Throwing his linen napkin on the table, the Very Important Person stood and silently glared at the sweating face of the man whom he had appointed as head of the writers' union, and then he stormed out of the restaurant, leaving his guest to pay the bill and perhaps the piper. The Very Important Person took badly to his driver reminding him that the Kremlin's new barber was at this moment waiting to be tested as a replacement for that traitorous Uzbek; if found wanting, he would be packed off for the provinces from whence he had come. The Very Important Person was annoyed at himself for having allowed Dimitri, a lowly secret policeman, to beg that the Vozhd consider Dimitri's stepfather for the position of Kremlin barber. Utterly preposterous! The old fortress was already rife with nepotism. Every time he turned around, he tripped over someone's nephew or cousin or uncle. But of all his complaints, he found wives the worst. Once their husbands were given apartments in the house on the embankment or in the Kremlin, they assumed the airs of royalty and dressed richly. To restore proletariat values, he would have to start deporting wives as well as husbands. The Bolsheviks had sworn allegiance to the common people, not to the costumers and hairdressers and shoemakers of Arbat Street. He reached the Kremlin more than two hours late.

Comrade Poskrebyshev glanced at the clock and snidely suggested that Razan would be better served if he returned another day. But the barber, who knew the lengths to which Dimitri had gone to arrange this interview, and who knew the hopes of his family, decided to wait, to the annoyance of the chef de cabinet.

"I have waited this long," said Razan, studying his nails. "I can wait a little longer. Waiting is good for the appetite."

The proverb was lost on Poskrebyshev, who seethed at the thought that this nobody from nowhere had the gall to countermand the Vozhd's right-hand man. Citizen barber would soon learn how much power Stalin's aide commanded. Poskrebyshev sniffed at the thought of the man's naiveté—and recklessness. Razan, whether he knew it or not, was playing Russian roulette.

At the sound of a buzzer, two armed guards opened the door to Stalin's office and positioned Razan at the threshold. But the barber saw before him only an unoccupied, narrow, dimly lit room. Looking back to see that his coat was safe, he stuttered into the black vacancy, "I have come, Supreme Leader, to give you a Turkish shave."

A voice sounded from a dark recess. "How dare you address me in this manner? Do you know whom you're talking to? Do you realize who is standing before you?"

"I had an appointment. My stepson Dimitri . . . he received your approval for me to interview . . . have you forgotten?"

"What? What did you say?" growled the voice. "What kind of language do you use with me, and in what kind of accent?" The voice rose to a frightening level. "What impudence, country barber!"

Razan felt faint and staggered backward. He might well have fallen but for the support of the two armed guards.

"I see no one," sputtered Razan. "Where is he?"

One of the guards replied, "The Supreme Leader is everywhere."

The guards settled him into an armchair next to Poskrebyshev's desk. Had Razan left quickly—an impossibility on his unsteady legs—he would have missed his opportunity, because ten minutes later a Very Important Person entered and warmly greeted Razan, inviting him into his office. Given Razan's nervous state, the two soldiers virtually had to carry him over the threshold and lead him to the settee, where the terrified barber quaked and waited. While one of the guards turned up the lights, the Very Important Person seated himself in a chair with a headrest. A guard filled a basin of water; another covered him with a barber's apron.

Watching the dispatch of the soldiers had a calming effect on Razan, who had quit shaking, his fear displaced by the euphoria a pardon bestows. He reasoned that Stalin had not been himself. As Dimitri explained, the world was in a chaotic state, with Germany threatening to annex western Poland and the Baltic states, Belorussia in ferment, and Ukraine torn between independence and union with Russia. Stalin clearly had more on his mind than welcoming his new barber. The very grandeur and history of the Kremlin stood as a reminder to every Tsar and Tsarina, royal or red, that on their backs rested the fate of an empire that embraced hundreds of nationalities and languages. The crushing responsibility that attended the Kremlin leader would cause any sane person to behave unpredictably.

Rocking on the settee like a davener, Razan clasped his hands and silently prayed that his test would go well, and that he would not have to return to

Anna empty-handed. He could hear her now. "Tell me everything, just as it happened." And he would try to recall each detail, as she listened intently, prepared to tell him where he had erred. She was a wise woman, and Razan held her words dear.

One of the guards helped Razan from the settee to a position at the Boss's side. With as much presence as he could muster, Razan lathered the Vozhd with the Kremlin's shaving cream.

"I prefer to be barbered from the side," Stalin said politely, "because I am uneasy when people move around behind my back."

Razan laid out his barbering tools: razor, combs, lotions, and alcohol. Shakily stropping his razor, he wiped the blade on Koba's apron, breathed deeply, and, watched by the two guards, slowly began to shave the Supreme Leader, starting from just below his right ear.

"Don't touch the mustache," said Koba. "The last person to interview trimmed it too close."

Suddenly, Razan lost his nerve. A riot of fears ran through his head, all bearing on what might have happened to the barber who had poorly cut the Very Important Person's mustache. What if Razan nicked him? He might never leave the Kremlin alive. On the verge of retreating, Razan stifled the impulse when the Boss sat up suddenly in the chair and told a joke.

"My driver told me this one. Stalin calls in Pauker and says, 'Listen, Karl, you tell jokes about me. It's impertinent. I am, after all, the Great Leader, Teacher, and Friend of the People.' And Pauker says, 'No, I haven't told that joke yet!'"

The Boss's robust laughter happily surprised Razan, who had been cautioned that anyone telling jokes at Koba's expense could be exiled or worse. Dimitri had warned that exile could await the person who merely heard a Stalin joke and didn't report the speaker. But the Vozhd was laughing at his own expense. Was the Boss testing him, daring him to be amused? The barber took cover in silence.

"Come now, Citizen barber, surely you must have found my joke amusing?" He turned to his impassive guards and said, "I give you permission to laugh," and they dutifully guffawed. "You, too, Citizen barber, you have my permission."

His nerves as taut as tendons, Razan eased his tension with one explosive belly laugh.

"Easy, Citizen barber. I didn't think the joke was *that* funny."

"I was laughing at the artful way that you told it," lied Razan.

Contented, the man leaned back and let the now perfectly relaxed barber shave his drooping jowls and heavy chin. Razan reminded himself that he might never have another chance to shave the Very Important Person, so he made it a point to note his features: the low forehead, the heavy eyelids, the raisin brown skin, the deep pockmarks, the decayed teeth, the protuberant stomach, and the fact that he rarely removed his hands from his pockets; and if he did, he almost always used his right hand to adjust his attire or stroke his mustache. His left hand he kept out of sight, tucked up to the wrist in his pocket or belt.

With infinite care, Razan shaved the Very Important Person, removed the remaining soap, and skillfully applied talcum powder to the craters. Now came the most delicate part of all, singeing the ear hairs without burning the auricle. He handed a guard a stick match.

"Please strike it and wait a second."

Deftly sprinkling alcohol on one ear, Razan took the match and ignited the alcohol. The guards stood poised to pounce. With a towel, at precisely the right moment, he extinguished the flame. He followed the same procedure on the other ear and then twisted one end of the towel into a corkscrew to wipe away any remains from inside the ears, which he now dabbed with a cinnamon lotion. Putting away his barbering tools, he waited. Nobody spoke. At least twenty seconds expired as the Boss raised a hand mirror and studied his pockmarked face and torched ears.

"This man is an artist!"

"I'm hired?" Razan gulped.

"Not yet," said the Very Important Person in the chair. "I will want to consult with the members of my inner circle whom you will barber tomorrow. Let us then meet in two days. Will that suit you?"

Barely able to reply from the exhilaration of having survived, Razan nodded yes, took his briefcase, and left in the company of the two guards, one of whom helped him on with his coat. In the street, the guard hailed a cab and paid for the barber to be returned to the house on the embankment.

When Razan next returned to the Troitsky Gate, his guide was a young functionary who led him not on a tour of the Kremlin but into a guardhouse to be searched and then to Poskrebyshev's office, where the aide greeted him bluntly:

"Same overcoat but a different scarf and gloves."

Razan marveled at the man's memory, reputed to be like a card file—and unfailing. Razan sat hunched over in his overcoat, hoping that he'd have the chance to appear in it before the Vozhd. No one had yet ordered him to hang it on the coatrack. The buzzer rang and the same two guards, his official bookends, started to parade him into Stalin's office.

"The overcoat!" said Poskrebyshev.

Razan stalled. As he had hoped, the buzzer rang again. Stalin had a reputation for expecting the people he summoned to materialize immediately. His chef de cabinet barked: "The hell with that vile coat, take him in as he is!"

Like the first time, the guards held him fast at the threshold. Stalin came forward and shook his hand. The Boss appeared taller. Razan guessed that he was wearing higher elevated shoes. For some reason, this pleased him, perhaps because a show of vanity on Stalin's part justified Razan's wanting the Vozhd to see his new coat.

"That's quite an overcoat you have," said Stalin, earning Razan's immediate gratitude. But for some reason, Razan was not asked to remove it. "Although humility adorns a Bolshevik, I do not begrudge a man a fine piece of cloth—and a warm one."

So appreciative of Stalin's admiration was Razan that he found himself slightly bending a knee and bowing before the Supreme Leader. Years later, at the thought of this moment, he would swear to himself that it had all happened involuntarily and in the presence of a ghost.

Razan reached into his briefcase for the teakwood box that held the implements of his trade. "It's been two days. Permit me to shave you again in the Turkish manner."

Stalin replied, "Not now. But you'll be glad to hear that I spoke to my people. They heartily approve. You shall become the official barber to our Kremlin vanguard. Poskrebyshev will make all the formal and financial arrangements." Stalin then patted Razan on the back and disappeared into the adjoining room.

That Razan Shtube was not Poskrebyshev's favorite became amply clear when the aide grumbled, "Here are your working papers. Sign here, assuming that you can read and write."

With a flourish, Razan signed his name, reading the key clause loudly, "Will serve at Comrade Stalin's pleasure." Razan brushed an imaginary speck off his coat and said, "I trust that the Vozhd and I can conduct our future business without the interference of *others*."

"There is hardly a single matter," Poskrebyshev crowed, "that Comrade Stalin does not consult me about. In fact, some people say disparagingly that I am his shield bearer, but I regard that statement as a badge of honor."

A young functionary summoned to escort Razan from the Kremlin asked in a whisper, "Is it true that you are the new barber to the Red Leader's Court? That's the rumor racing through the building."

"Court?" repeated Razan. "I thought Bolsheviks promote humility. That's what Stalin said."

The functionary corrected himself. "A slip of the tongue."

At the Troitsky Gate, Razan asked, "Doesn't a court mean dachas and Packards and lodging in a government house and fine foods and . . ."

"My mistake. It is always best to keep one's thoughts unspoken."

Each day, Razan observed the same schedule. He shaved the staff during working hours and Stalin by night. That first evening, Koba had greeted him warmly:

"You have a gentle touch, citizen, or should I say comrade? No, we have not yet arrived at that point. So tell me, how do you keep your hand from shaking when you shave the Vozhd?"

The barber could have taken the opportunity to sing his own tonsorial praises, but from the constant deference paid the Supreme Leader, the genuflecting of the courtiers—"courters" would have been more accurate—he suspected that the air around Stalin could oxygenate only paeans for the Red Pope. Razan's mind wandered. Red. Antonio Vivaldi's hair color led to his nickname, the "red priest." One could be caught "red-handed," a phrase that suited a felon. As a child, Stalin's hair was reportedly red.

"Fear," he finally said, "fear of offending you and what might then ensue."

"That, Razan, describes precisely the state of mind I want to instill in my people." He coughed. "So you see, we think alike."

"I find," said the barber, recalling his parents, "that a gentle hand that lightly leads may be equally effective."

"I have a son," Stalin scoffed, "a wayward boy who resents any lessons and revels in rebellion. Would you advise I whip the whelp?" Before Razan could reply, Stalin added, "Alliterations amuse me."

"My mother raised me. My father worked early to late in the barbershop." He pointed to a bookcase. "She read to me and always repeated the words that resonated most with her."

Stalin kindly placed the palm of his right hand on Razan's cheek. "You're a lucky man, citizen, my mother . . . never mind. Such stories are off-limits. Just be glad of your good fortune. Pain and death are every man's moiety. Tenderness is the exception."

On Dimitri's return, he took Anna and Razan to dinner at the Stray Dog restaurant. They sat next to the front window. Among the clatter of dishes, the forced gaiety, and insincere laughter, their quiet conversation was unlikely to be overheard. The windows, frosted outside and fogged inside, made it impossible for them to be observed from the street. Dimitri, who had been absent from Moscow for over two weeks, looked ill.

"It's nothing physical," he said, in response to his mother's questioning, "nothing that medicine can cure."

His response led her to rush into questions that she might normally have waited to ask. "How is Gregori? You saw him at the theological institute. And how are Natasha and Alexei? Natasha wrote and said you spent a few hours with them in Leningrad. We want to hear all about it. Gregori hardly ever writes. Is Alexei passing all his medical courses?"

The combination of heated bodies and steaming dishes humidified the restaurant. Dimitri looked around and then used his napkin to wipe away the sweat that ran from his forehead to his chin. Razan had the impression that if Anna had not been so anxious about her children, Dimitri would have bolted. He had always been close to his mother, much more so than were the other two boys. Although as a child he had kept to himself, Anna had made it a point before bedtime to take him aside and ask what troubled him most? Her gentleness never failed to elicit a response and to dispel his fears.

"I'm worried about *both* Gregori and Alexei."

"Gregori? A theology student who belongs to the Soviet-approved Renovationist Church! What trouble could he have made for himself?"

"It's complicated," said Dimitri. "I spoke to Comrade Chicherin, the previous foreign minister in charge of relations with Rome. Gregori's distrusted. To clear his name, I advised him—and he agreed—to meet with those Roman Catholic agents who are working to recruit the Russian Orthodox and undermine our government."

The waitress brought each of them borscht, with a large, steaming beet. While the men spooned the soup, Anna left hers untouched. Leaning across the table, she whispered:

"If he's working for the Soviets, what's the problem?"

"If, if, if. With Gregori, you never know. He's so changeable."

Theological discussions, in Razan's estimation, took place in a gossamer realm and were of no interest, except for their consequences. But with Gregori being the principal lawbreaker, he found himself listening.

"Rome wants to undermine the Soviets by restoring the Patriarchal Church," said Dimitri, rearranging the salt and pepper shakers.

"But Gregori is anti-Rome and prefers the Renovationists."

"The government says that Gregori is playing a double game."

"Did you warn him to be on his guard?"

"The promise that the Renovationists will be allowed to worship freely may have blinded him to the danger of Roman proselytizing."

"But you said you asked him to spy for the Soviets against Rome."

He shrugged. "Actually it was Chicherin's idea."

Anna silently brooded. Her soup and beet had quit steaming. She pushed the bowl toward Dimitri, knowing his hearty appetite.

"All his mail is being read. And I can't see him again."

Anna asked anxiously, "What do you suggest?"

Covering his mouth with his hand, he said, "If the Soviet secret police send him to Rome as an agent . . . he should stay in the west."

"We could all be arrested."

"Not if he disappears without a trace."

They said nothing further until the boiled beef and cabbage arrived. A few bites of the main course restored their speech.

"When it rains it floods," said Anna. "Tell me about Alexei. Natasha's letters sound anxious."

"First, dear mother, let me assure you that Natasha is in perfect health and is planning to have her eyes operated on."

"An operation!"

Razan patted Anna's hand. "The surgeons in Leningrad are reputed to be the best." What he didn't say, and certainly not in front of Dimitri, was that a great number of them were Jewish, some of whom had trained in Vienna.

"Then what?" asked Anna.

"She's been promised a position in a publishing house."

"I can guess the reason, and it's not because of her editorial experience. Beauty," she mumbled, "can be a curse. And Alexei?"

Dimitri pointed to his mouth. He had a mouthful.

Anna continued. "Basil von Fresser wrote us shortly after we arrived to ask if Razan had been appointed Stalin's barber and, if so, could Razan get him and his wife party work and a flat in Moscow."

Dimitri put down his knife and fork. "When was the last time you heard from him?"

"Just that one letter."

Dimitri scraped some frost from the window and peered out.

"I can tell," said Anna, "you know something."

"They've both been exiled, along with other Germans, to some camp in the taiga."

"Will the Albanians be next?" Razan asked into the vacant air.

For his stepfather's sake, Dimitri said, "At least for now the Jews are protected, so you needn't worry."

"I wonder how long that will last," replied Razan.

"Let's not suppose," Anna said. "We have to respond to what's in front of us. Why is Alexei under suspicion? You haven't said."

"At the medical school, he and Natasha have a room. Students often meet there to read poetry and talk about literature. Someone recited an anti-Stalin poem, and an informer told the secret police. Although Alexei and the wrongdoer will be allowed to complete their courses, they will be sent to Voronezh. No wives allowed."

In an attempt to lighten the mood, Razan said risibly, "Some of our best poets have been exiled to Voronezh. At least the city isn't lacking in culture."

Anna gave her husband a cutting look and said plaintively, "He's married to my daughter, not yours!"

"The source of my humor," Razan replied, "is not joy but sorrow."

Anna was already thinking ahead. If Dimitri could not quash the order for Alexei's banishment, perhaps Razan could appeal to the Supreme Leader. And if neither her son nor her husband could effect a remedy, perhaps some official could be prevailed upon to assign Alexei to a military camp, where the rations would be plentiful. The only thing that could be said for Voronezh was that one could reach it easily by rail from Moscow and that it wasn't Siberia.

"Military camps always need doctors," she said.

"And Natasha?" Dimitri asked.

"She can live with us in Moscow, in our apartment. We have enough room." Razan said nothing.

At the end of the meal, Dimitri pushed back his chair from the table and sighed, "Sadness everywhere."

Anna, painfully disturbed about Alexei, reproved her son. "And who ever said we were entitled to happiness?"

"Alexei!" Dimitri said carelessly. "He got off easy."

In no mood to be consoled, Anna shot back, "Don't be an idiot!"

Dimitri parried, "You have no idea what some people suffer."

"Death! Is there anything worse?" Anna paused. "I take that back. Torture and illness are worse."

"On my last assignment, I saw things that no one should see."

He broke off sharply. A rouged young woman, hidden beneath layered lipstick and thick mascara, sat down in the company of a uniformed officer, much her senior. All the signs pointed to a tryst, which meant that they would be sensitive to other voices around them.

Tapping her chest, Anna knowingly said, "I need fresh air. It's too close in here. Let's take a walk down the street."

Razan smiled at her perspicacity. Had she been overheard, no one could accuse her of retreating outdoors to hear or say the forbidden. "Yes," said Razan, "the heat and steam in here are suffocating."

Dimitri smiled knowingly. He had no wish to speak in a public place, a restaurant, about something that could cost him his life. "Yes, let's take a walk."

They paid the bill and left. For several blocks, they leaned into the frigid blasts, particularly at the wind-funneled cross streets. Fortunately, Razan was wearing his wonderful Petrovich creation, and Dimitri a military greatcoat that covered him from nose to ankle. Anna wore a stylish wrap, but not even the several sweaters underneath could keep out the cold. Razan told himself that with his first paycheck he would take her to the Arbat to select a fur coat.

The three of them eased into a doorway, with the two men sheltering Anna, their backs to the street. Dimitri began to speak and then paused. He waited until one couple and then another passed on the sidewalk.

"I was in uniform escorting four Uzbeks to the train station, a man, a child, and two women wearing burqas. The man's right hand was broken." Dimitri flexed the fingers on his right hand. "I was instructed to tell them that they were being sent back to Uzbekistan for security reasons. We boarded a special train. All the coaches had wooden seats. No one spoke. I noticed other nationals in the car—Asians, Mongolians, Turkamen—but they never looked at us. Fear! At Voronezh, I took one woman off the train. She must have been in her twenties. Two soldiers were waiting to take her away. An hour out of Voronezh, we stopped at some work camp, actually a lumber town, where I steered the man off the train by the arm, and three soldiers handcuffed him and drove off in a staff car. We arrived at the next station in a snowstorm. Drifts had blocked the tracks; the train had to wait to continue. I took the child and rushed her into the small station to keep warm next to the charcoal brazier. When the officials from the orphanage finally arrived—they had been delayed by the storm—the little girl looked at me with such big black eyes that my heart nearly stopped. The train made a loop, as scheduled, and we returned to Moscow. Mind you, this particular rail journey has been in service for only a year. It's designed for transporting prisoners. At the Moscow Station, I handed the second woman—young, in her twenties—a one-way rail pass for Tashkent, and told her that she was lucky to be free, even if she did have to report to the local police once a month."

Dimitri stopped, his voice arrested by emotion. Although Razan fought to hold back his tears, he finally conceded and unashamedly cried. Anna guessed the reason, but kept her own counsel.

Through his sobs, Razan asked, "Who was he?"

In a croaking voice, Dimitri replied, "I forget his last name." He shook his head. "Can't remember." But clearly, Razan did.

"And the women?"

"The one exiled to Voronezh . . . Maja. The other, I believe, introduced herself as Meena."

Razan blew his nose into his handkerchief and wiped his eyes and face with the arm of his overcoat. "Let me tell you, Dimitri, the name of the child. Yelena."

"Yes, that was it. But how do you know?"

As briefly as he could, he told Dimitri about his two hours with the Boujinski family. The wind had increased and with it the cold, Arctic cold that turned spit to ice in the air.

"I could have done nothing," said Dimitri, "even if I had tried."

"No, but I can. Give me the name of the orphanage and the town."

That night, as Razan and Anna lay in bed, they slipped under the goosedown comforter to talk.

"I want to adopt Yelena," said the barber. "She's a beautiful child. Gentle, clever, and affectionate. It's a feather in the cap of all Bolsheviks who adopt, and I certainly wouldn't be hurting myself with Stalin and his favorites. Most of them have adopted children. My only concern is room. What if Natasha comes to live with us?"

"We'll somehow manage."

At moments like this one, when Anna's generous nature eclipsed her practicality, Razan felt rewarded for marrying her. He knew that together they could survive; alone they would perish.

The next day, he left a note at the Troitsky Gate for Alexander Nikolaevich Poskrebyshev stating that he would have to absent himself to travel out of town to adopt a child, like a good Communist, and would return in a week.

Without Dimitri's help, the barber would have had to wait a month to secure a train ticket to M____. People often slept on the train platform in the hope of finding an empty seat. Although he had to sit in hard coach, he rejoiced at the thought of having a child and the gleeful play that would consume their lives in the coming years.

Before leaving the house on the embankment, he took stock. He had packed his satchel with a change of clothes, brushed his overcoat, checked his galoshes for leaks, and put his work papers, the ones with the government imprimatur and official signatures indicating his position as barber to the Kremlin, in his elongated leather wallet, which he kept chained to his belt.

At the station in M____, he hired a driver with a sleigh and horse to take him to the orphanage. The driver, a bewhiskered fellow smelling of rum, threw a heavy rug over Razan's legs, snapped his reins, and hurtled into the night.

The sleigh's runners raced along the icy ruts as the horse galloped down the middle of the road.

"I usually charge more," said the Dickensian-looking man, his head and feet wrapped in rags, and his body bound in the salvaged parts of discarded jackets and coats that had been stitched together to make one garment. The remnants, all different colors, had come from pigskin, chamois, ox hide, suede, kid, and fleece. "If the local Soviet thinks I'm overcharging, I'll lose my license." He muttered an expletive. "Fares should depend on the weather and not some list posted in an office. Don't you agree?"

In fact, Razan did, but living in a country that looked upon every citizen as a possible traitor made it impossible for the barber to say he agreed. Once again, Razan found himself caught in the tentacles of Soviet logic. If the driver was trying to trap him, Razan would be a fool to respond; and if the man's suggestion that the country was less than perfect went unreported, Razan could suffer. Leaning back to let the cold flakes fleck his face, Razan mutely agreed with Stalin's critics. Only the Soviet faithful failed to see that life had been reduced to two choices: one could either lie to himself and others, or inform. The threat of Fascism had driven Razan from Albania; now the need to speak in euphemisms or resort to silence was robbing Russia of all individuality.

Razan took refuge in a harmless question. "What's the orphanage like, large or small?"

The driver spat into the snow. "Neither, just soulless." This fellow, Razan concluded, was either fearless or a brilliant front man for the local Soviet. "The children of those who are shot, exiled, or blacklisted are brought to places like this one, where military officers and government functionaries come to adopt them."

"What if the children are older?"

"Makes no difference. They take the name of their new parents."

"I meant that older children are inclined to resent a new regime. They remember their parents and the old ways of behaving."

"A general once said to a kid he'd just adopted, as he was climbing into this very sleigh, 'A good whipping will change *your* mind.' I suppose that's how they do it."

Razan suddenly felt chilled to the bone.

The two-story building, putrid yellow with barred windows, featured a circular drive that took the sleigh to the front door. Off to one side of the orphanage, Razan could see a few official cars. The observant driver, noting his gaze, said, "Some of 'em belong to the orphanage, but the others, I'd guess, belong to the customers."

Customers! thought Razan. What can that word possibly mean when applied to children being readied for adoption? Are they fattened? Schooled in manners? Indoctrinated with Marxist principles? Presumably, the children had few alternatives. They could make themselves look presentable and leave the yellow jail, or misbehave and remain, incurring, no doubt, the displeasure of their keepers.

The more he analyzed the plight of the children, the angrier he grew, until he reminded himself of the rider in the woods whose horse suddenly took lame. Setting out on foot, the man kept telling himself that whomever he met would charge him a fortune for help. The longer he walked, the greater his ire. When he finally arrived at a farm and was greeted by the farmer, the rider said, "You can keep your goddamn help. I would rather walk than pay your fee," and stormed out.

At the front door, a matronly woman in a faded green uniform greeted Razan. She wore her gray hair in a tight bun in back and used no cosmetics. High-cheeked and blue-eyed and large busted, she looked Ukrainian, and spoke in an accented Russian.

"As you can see," said Razan, with the joke still in mind, "I come bearing no outrage or prejudices."

The buxom attendant rang for the director, who came on a run. She whispered, "We have a madman on our hands. While you talk to him, I'll call the police."

Comrade Vadim Maximovich Dibratov, the image of an albino ferret, with white hair, a lanky body, a narrow face, and kinetic energy, asked Razan into his office, where he intended to detain him long enough for the local militia to arrive and remove him. But the conversation took an unpredictable turn when the director mentioned that his father had come from Tirana.

Razan asked the name of the street and, upon hearing it, slapped his forehead and mendaciously said, "The very area where my family lived! Your favorite pastime?" Again, he slapped his forehead. "Chess! My father loved the game; me too."

After an exchange of facts and memories, Razan insisted that the two fathers had probably traveled in the same circles, and shared the same views. The director grabbed his desk phone and dialed, excitedly ordering the person at the other end "to cancel the call. Yes, that one. Immediately!"

"Would it be wrong to assume that you were talking about me?"

"It's nothing! Trust me, nothing," the director sputtered in confusion. "Lyubov, the head of admissions, you know, the lady you met when you first came in, she thought, well, you know, these Ukrainians, all emotions." He raised his hands in defeat. "She mistook you for someone else." Dibratov offered Razan a cigarette. Razan declined. "Wise, very wise. An awful habit, but I'm addicted. So tell me, what brings you here, all the way from Moscow."

Razan explained that he wanted to adopt a child, but not just any child; he wanted to adopt Yelena Boujinskia. "Dimitri Lipnoskii of the secret service brought her here recently. She's from Tashkent. Brown skinned. Curly hair and large dark eyes. Perfect teeth. A pretty child, ten years old. Her parents . . . you understand."

"She's been given a bed in the east wing. I agree: a lovely little girl. But I fear there's a problem. Let me check." Dibratov opened a wooden filing cabinet and thumbed through the alphabetically arranged folders until he found the one that he wanted. He studied it briefly and sighed. "Just as I thought. Colonel Ilia Krichevski has already signed the papers. I knew that he and his wife liked the child, but I didn't realize that Lyubov had already processed the transfer. Sometimes Lyubov is too accommodating, especially when one of the adoptive parents is a high-ranking officer."

"I gather Yelena is still on the premises," said Razan, removing his working papers from his wallet and spreading them out on the desk.

Breathless at the sight of the Kremlin stamp, Dibratov nattered on more confused than before. "Perhaps, if I'm lucky, something, I'm not sure what, can be done. She's with us, that is, here at the orphanage, for at least a week more, yes, at least a week. Maybe more. We are waiting on Tashkent, our counterparts there, to send us copies of her medical records. Vaccinations, you know, are particularly important. We couldn't possibly, not at all, let our children, I'm sure you agree, leave here without a clean bill of health. What if—I shouldn't even think it—the child, to cite just one example, died in the Krichevski house, heaven forbid, of some exotic disease? Moscow would, I have no doubts, hear about it. The party secretary for our oblast would undoubtedly insist on an investigation, and, as you know, our Blessed Leader loves little children, even 'strange orphans,' whose parents have been exiled."

"Can you give me the colonel's address?"

"Kursk. I'll write it all down." He reached for a pen. "But I beg you, please, for the sake of our fathers' memories, do not compromise me. The colonel's wife, Polonia, nearly swooned over the child. I could show you other youngsters, all in perfect health."

Again, Razan experienced that unpleasant sense of being treated as a customer expected to look over the goods. Dibratov made the orphanage sound like a horse market, where buyers could evaluate flesh on the hoof.

"They are children," mumbled Razan, "not animals."

"Pardon me, I couldn't hear you."

"I said that children love animals. Have you no pets here?"

"Hygiene comes first. I think you'd agree that the health of the children is more important than a dog or a cat."

For Razan's tenth birthday, his parents had presented him with a shaggy Scottish terrier that had become as much a part of him as any of his appendages. The dog would accompany him as he made his way to class and return to meet him for his journey home. In Razan's last year of school, his dog was trampled by a horse-drawn coach, which had careened down the street and jumped the curb, bearing some minor members of the royal family late for an appointment. A few days later, he received an apologetic note with a bank draft worth one pair of shoes, no small sum, but not a substitute for his faithful terrier. In fact, he bought a pair of shoes that he hardly wore. The sight of them painfully reminded him of the first meaningful death in his life.

Before leaving the orphanage, Razan asked to see Yelena. She came down the stairs mechanically, dressed in a dirty yellow jumper, her shining eyes now dull. When she saw Razan, a familiar face, she walked and then ran across the uneven linoleum floor. She wanted to see her parents. Could he take her? They spoke in whispers.

"Not now. I have to make arrangements for you first."

"You mean that family who wants to adopt me, don't you?"

"My wife and I would like you to live with us."

"What about my mother and father?"

"We will care for you until they return."

Yelena, who had buried her face in his chest and had been speaking from this protected position, now looked him in the eye. "They may never come back. Isn't that true? All the kids say so."

Unable to answer "yes," he nodded in agreement.

She reached up and touched his cheek, which he lowered to her lips, expecting her to kiss him goodbye. Instead, she murmured in his ear, "I'm scared to remain here . . . waiting . . . not knowing where my parents are. Promise me you'll come back."

He sank to one knee, hugged her, and promised.

The train to Kursk had no vacant seats, none in fact for several weeks, but the stationmaster, a true humanitarian, ordered that the cattle car be opened so that anyone willing to transit amidst the animals, smells, and straw could ride for free. Several people peered into the car, sniffed, and declined the offer. Razan, who had known worse conditions on his trip from Albania to Birobidzhan, took his satchel and boarded. Once the train had left the city precincts, he opened the doors. Using the wooden pitchfork lying in the cattle car, he shoveled out the offal, made a bed of straw, and fell asleep.

"Kursky Station!"

The announcement awakened him. Among excited voices, the doors of the cattle car slid back, and he exited, smelling of black pied cows. The first thing he did was ask a station worker the location of the city baths. With his satchel in hand, he paid the attendant for a towel and a sliver of soap. Lying in the steaming bath reminded him of the writer who had said that heaven was a hot roll every morning. Almost right, he mused, but first a hot bath.

Having dressed in his clean change of clothes, he now wondered about his exquisite overcoat. He couldn't step outside into the cold without it; and he certainly couldn't show up at the Krichevski house reeking of cattle. But where could he find a cleaner? And while it was being cleaned, he would have to remain at the baths. Could he trust someone not to make off with Petrovich's incomparable creation? He felt like a character out of Gogol, and had no intention of ending up the same way, trying to locate his coat.

The sallow attendant, who looked as if the steam baths had drained all the blood from his body, his face and hands exhibiting only a tracery of thin blue veins, offered to help. His cousin, a baker, worked next door to a tailor who also cleaned clothes. For a second time, Razan unfolded his official work papers.

"I can't read," said the attendant.

"Do you see this seal?"

"Yes."

"I work for Stalin in the Kremlin. That's what the seal means."

The attendant ran one hand through his thinning hair. His mouth opened, as if he intended to speak, but said nothing. When the man reached for a towel, Razan anticipated a flood of tears. Instead, the man bit the towel, like a person in the throes of a seizure. At last, after slowly lowering himself on his haunches, the man said:

"I have no cousin."

"Call the local police."

"You wouldn't . . ."

"Tell them that Stalin's barber needs a ride to the home of Colonel Krichevski." This would not be the only time Razan used his exalted position to advance his cause. In fact, he went a step further. "And have the police call the home of Colonel Krichevski to tell him and his wife that Stalin's barber would like to see them."

A car came almost immediately. Razan flashed his papers and followed a uniformed soldier outside, holding his coat at arm's length. He would have stored it in his satchel had it not been so bulky. Perhaps the intense cold would lessen the smell.

"Your coat, comrade, put on your coat," said the soldier. "The temperature is forty degrees below freezing."

"I'm sure the car is heated."

"As you wish."

The soldier opened the backdoor for Razan, and then sat in front with the driver. Even though he put the coat at the other end of the seat, Razan could smell the pungent odor that suffused the material.

"We must be approaching some cows," said the driver.

"Strange," said the other, "I don't see any."

Both soldiers began sniffing. Razan tried to pretend that nothing was wrong and hoped that his official position would dissuade the soldiers from identifying the source of the smell. Although his two escorts occasionally glanced at each other with a knowing look, neither man spoke. When they dropped him off at the colonel's house, instead of accompanying him to the front door, the driver said:

"If I were you, I'd leave the coat in his garden."

Standing in the bitter cold without any means to keep warm, other than taking refuge in the foul-smelling coat, Razan rang the bell and pressed into the narrow doorway, holding his coat apart from his body. When the door suddenly opened, he nearly fell into the vestibule.

"Are you the barber?" said a young man in a starched tunic and trousers tucked into high leather boots, in the manner of the Vozhd.

"Yes." Handing the man his coat, he said, "I've had an unfortunate accident. Please deposit this coat in the garden."

Holding it with his thumb and forefinger, the young man carried it out the backdoor, as if it were an offending pet that had soiled the rug. When he returned, the fragrances issuing from the greenhouse, an effect that the colonel prized, had been eclipsed by the hint of a stockyard. To make matters worse, Polonia Krichevskia managed a perfume factory and had the nose of an aromatic chemist. When the colonel, with his walrus mustache and florid face, invited Razan into the sitting room to meet his wife, Polonia looked past him, trying to detect the source of some bovine ordure. She and her husband exchanged baffled looks, sat on the French settee, and invited "Comrade Shtube" to explain why he had come to their house.

The sitting room, decorated in rococo, belied all the Soviet talk about humility and the common man. Every piece of furniture, every table lamp, every figurine and hand-painted plate exhibited delicately executed ornamentation imitating foliage, shell work, and scrolls. In addition to the French frills, two objects captured the eye: a large white ceramic stove, equipped in the Austrian manner to sleep a person on top, and a samovar resting on an elegant sideboard. Razan could see the whole room reflected in the silver gloaming of the stately samovar, with its old Slavonic inscriptions, a runic reminder of glories past, a fading memory of the old order.

"Tea?" asked Polonia.

"I really can't stay long."

The colonel and his wife waited stiffly for Razan to explain the reason for his presence. When he had finished, Ilia and Polonia spoke with one voice in opposition.

The colonel, barely keeping his temper under control, asked, "Why should your claim to the child eclipse ours?"

"I knew her grandparents," said the barber disingenuously. "I met the child when she was staying with them."

"You have a great heart, worthy of a Soviet," said Colonel Krichevski, with just the slightest hint of sarcasm, "but we've made up our minds. Besides, children are taken from their parents and friends every day—for the good of the motherland."

"Patriotism, like any feeling, is hard to argue with."

"Comrade Shtube, you have no idea the impression the child made on us. Her delicate gestures . . . her balletic movements," said Polonia, who herself strode across the carpet with feet pointed outward like a trained ballerina and moved her hands and wrists as if they floated in air.

The colonel, as everyone in the military knew, had fought for the Tsar against the Germans. He had been a White Army officer, a fact that Razan now elicited. Most, if not all, of these officers were repugnant to Stalin, who had famously said:

"Prick the skin of every Red officer who once fought for the Tsar, and he'll bleed White!"

As much as Razan disliked blackmail, he felt compelled to keep his word to Yelena. "As Stalin's barber . . ."

"You must tell us about it," the colonel said sincerely. "You must be privy to a great many . . ." He laughed. "State secrets."

For effect, Razan looked around as if checking his surroundings for eaves-droppers. "He has his assistant, Poskrebyshev, look at all the adoption lists, even though they run into the thousands. Anyone who once fought for the Whites, or is suspected of harboring sympathies for their cause, is struck from the list. But I'm sure, Colonel, that you and your lovely wife can make a special case for your adopting Yelena Boujinskia. If I could, I would help, but given my own feelings, I'm hardly the one to advance your case."

"You are absolutely right, Comrade Shtube, about our Supreme Leader, but what you don't know is that in Georgia, I once saved his life. An assassin fired at close range. In fact," said the colonel, pulling up a trouser leg, "I . . ."

He never completed his thought, because Polonia interrupted. With a hitch in her voice, she said, "Ilia nearly died defending the Vozhd. He took a bullet intended for Stalin."

Razan had played his best card and had lost. An awkward silence ensued. Spying the library in the adjoining room and playing for time, he asked if Ilia and Polonia had any objection to his looking at their collection, which was handsomely displayed in Moroccan bindings. They welcomed his interest.

"Polonia, besides being a dancer and chemist," said the colonel, "is a translator. So we have a great many volumes in English and French, her two other languages."

Razan saw a collection of O. Henry short stories and smiled; his mother had read them in English and repeated them in Albanian. Perhaps, just perhaps, he wondered . . .

Returning to the sitting room, he said, "If you don't mind, I think that I would like a cup of tea, after all."

Polonia glided across to the samovar and returned with a cup bearing an incised design. As Razan sipped his tea, he deliberately sighed and casually remarked:

"Yelena, such a delightful child. I envy you . . . except for those few times . . . but then I'm sure Comrade Vadim Maximovich Dibratov has already told you about her occasional—what should I call them?—oddities or rather bouts of misbehavior. But then what can you expect? She is the child of enemies of the people."

The colonel put down his cigar and repeated, "Oddities? Bouts?" He leaned toward Razan. "What can you possibly mean, comrade?"

"I spoke out of turn. Forget that I said anything. After all, am I not here because of her effect on me? Your feelings are mine. We both love her. She is a most charming little rascal, particularly around matchsticks."

"What did you say?" asked the colonel.

"She nearly burned down the Boujinski apartment on several occasions, and she somehow managed to set fire to her mother's best dress. But all children have a touch of pyromania in them. Right?"

"When we interviewed her," said Polonia, "she was a model of good manners. And there's nothing in her file . . ."

"So she didn't howl like a calliope during the interview? Good. Perhaps she's over it. I can't tell you how many nights she kept her parents awake."

Polonia and Ilia exchanged worried glances.

"I do like my sleep," said the colonel.

"As a precaution, you'd be well advised to soundproof your room or house the child in another wing."

"Surely that sweet little girl . . ." Polonia broke off. "Many of these children have suffered terribly. Perhaps . . ."

"I'm sure by now she's overcome her habit of kicking and biting."

Training his experienced battlefield eyes on Razan with the hope of detecting a flaw in the enemy, a now troubled colonel asked, "Then tell me, comrade, why would you want to adopt an unruly child who is, according to you, the embodiment of her parents' sins?"

"Friendship knows no defects and needs no reason. Yelena's grandparents and I—same apartment building. That's the all of it."

Razan said nothing further, letting his comments sink in. If the colonel and his wife insisted, he would have to withdraw.

The colonel took his wife by the elbow and they walked into the library. For several minutes, they whispered. When they returned to the settee, Polonia's eyes were moist. The colonel cleared his throat:

"Comrade Shtube, she's yours. We'll just have to try elsewhere."

TO MOSCOW, TO MOSCOW, TO MOSCOW!

As two policemen led Alexei through the Leningrad train station, Natasha caught up with her husband on the platform and, ignoring his guards, tearfully embraced him. She swore to write every day, a promise she kept, and to visit him often in Voronezh, which proved impossible. Dimitri had tried to arrange for Alexei to serve his five years treating soldiers at a military camp. But the harder he tried, the testier the head of the secret service became, until Dimitri feared that the length of Alexei's sentence would be doubled.

The Leningrad publisher Kazimir Ouspensky, who wanted to employ Natasha, had, by a stroke of good luck, been promoted to an official position in the Moscow archives, where he oversaw the cataloguing of thousands of secret documents. Within a month of his arrival, he approached his superior, Efim Smilga, a Very Important Person, to ask if Natasha von Fresser could receive a special dispensation to allow her to work for him in the Archive of Denunciations.

Adjusting his metal-framed spectacles, Kazimir initiated the discussion with a series of falsehoods. "So desirous is she of working in the archives that she went to the trouble of having her eyes operated on to correct an impairment. And although married to an enemy of the people, she deplores his behavior and has indicated a willingness to divorce the traitor. She has, should you wish to note it, privately denounced him to me."

"Have you told the authorities?"

"Better! The man has already been deported to Voronezh without any means of support. His medical training will be worthless. What self-respecting Soviet citizens would let an exile treat them?"

Whether because of Natasha's own pleadings or of Kazimir's blatant lies, she received permission to work under Comrade Ouspensky, a condition that he greatly desired, given her rapturous looks and fetching figure.

Razan and Yelena quickly adapted to their new relationship, in part because both of them felt outsiders in Soviet society. Most late afternoons they spent playing chess. When not at the board, the child liked to sit at Anna's feet while her stepmother brushed and combed her hair, or braided it Ukrainian fashion in elaborate and swirling designs. Razan accompanied Yelena, in her starched uniform, to class each morning and along the way told her stories about his youth in Albania. She sometimes related what she remembered about Tashkent. At the front door, Yelena always turned and waved before disappearing from sight. Razan felt closest to her at these moments of silent parting.

He would then cross from the island to the Kremlin and show his pass with its official stamp and photograph, enter the Troitsky Gate, and continue to the small barbershop used by Soviet officials, a space distant from Stalin's quarters, and one that Poskrebyshev had ordered newly equipped for Razan. Although not as comfortable as his father's barbershop in Tirana, it had all the necessary fittings and tools: a proper chair that could be raised and lowered and the headrest adjusted, a deep sink with porcelain faucets, a small rubber hose that could be attached to the sink nozzle for the purpose of washing and rinsing hair, a steamer for towels, a wall mirror and looking glasses, and imported Swedish scissors, clippers, tweezers, combs, clips, and razors. Everything was silver coated and gleaming but not as comfortable to the hand as his own set of barbering tools, which he reserved for the man who answered to the name "Stalin."

Given that Koba usually didn't sit for a shave until two or three in the morning, Razan designed his day in two shifts. He slept from 4:00 a.m. until he walked Yelena to the nearby Moscow Experimental School (MOPSh), and then returned to bed. Such a schedule meant that when not on call, his evenings were free to take his family to operas, stage plays, ballets, and, of course, the wonderful circus. Anna's favorite entertainment was movies, and she had a special fondness for musicals, mysteries, and comedies. Natasha's imagination took flight the moment the curtain rose on a play or a romantic ballet. Yelena would attend these diversions when her homework allowed. It was not until she saw the art exhibition at the Kremlin that Yelena discovered her vital element: drawing.

The winter, as always, made excessive demands on one's energy. Just to walk through the snowdrifts and keep warm exhausted those not properly dressed. With his Kremlin salary, Razan insisted that his family buy the best and most durable clothing, which could be found in the basement government shop, the one accessible only to the party faithful. Here the goods were functional and stylish because most were imported from France and Italy and the United States. Here, and not on the Arbat, he bought Anna her fur coat. When Razan and his family walked down the street, no one could have failed to notice that they dressed like the favored Soviet class, the bureaucracy.

On the street, cabs appeared out of nowhere while other people huddled in the cold, waiting. Tables in restaurants materialized while other customers were asked to wait or turned away. Seats for plays or ballets always turned up, although the sign in front of the theatre said SRO. Even train tickets, so difficult to acquire, became available, allowing Anna to visit her sons in Leningrad and Brovensk. Had Razan requested a car, the Kremlin staff would have provided one to travel the short distance from his apartment to work. Invited to a few weekend parties at the dachas of Molotov and Yagoda and Malenkov, though not Stalin's, a car always took Razan and his party to the front door. Paradise, an abstraction for some, was a perk of the privileged. Alas, even in a classless society, some drink champagne and some only cheap vodka.

Natasha had moved in with her mother and stepfather, occupying the living room with Yelena, whom she treated as a younger sister, often and proudly reading to her now that her vision had been surgically repaired. After several months, they became confidants, which confirmed Razan and Anna's decision to adopt Yelena. The child idolized the lovely Natasha and would often come directly from school to the archives, where she sat in the waiting room among dozens of people, all hoping to uncover some document that would exonerate them or their loved ones or prove to the contrary some damning assertion. On entering the building, she was, like the others, always searched. A guard would shake out her notebook and primers looking for contraband. But when Natasha appeared, slipping her a spool of film to pocket, they would leave undetected. It was the introduction of forbidden objects that concerned the guards, not the removal of ones that citizens studied under the watchful eye of an attendant.

On the days that Natasha asked Yelena not to meet her, the blond beauty usually left the building in the company of Comrade Ouspensky, who took her to the Metropol Hotel for a drink and then to one of the few fashionable Moscow restaurants for dinner, always to be followed by dancing. The same barbershop that Dimitri patronized, Paul's, styled Natasha's loops and curls and waves. In fact, Paul himself cut her hair. The first time she sat in his chair, the one that was closest to the door and that rested on a platform six inches higher than the other two, he stepped back and studied her face as if planning to paint it.

"A woman's hair," he said, "is the elegant frame for her face. It should not clash with her coloring and certainly not with her bone structure. Your face reminds me of Bernini's marbles, the same whiteness, the same passion, the same angularity to the neck."

She made it a point, though she could barely afford it, to have her hair styled weekly. What made the cost possible was the fortuitous arrival one afternoon of Dimitri, who had come to collect Comrade Yuri Suzdal. Her brother, who had eyes only for Yuri, failed to notice her until he and his companion had reached the front door. Dimitri knew at once that she would discover their relationship, if Paul hadn't already disclosed it. Insisting on paying half the cost of her hairdressing visits, Dimitri made no demands in return, but Natasha was now worldly enough to know the meaning of a quid pro quo. Didn't she, in fact, have one with Kazimir? She let him kiss her and fondle her in return for nights on the town and costly presents. Although he had often tried in the privacy of his own apartment to seduce her, she had unfailingly slapped his hand; but she knew that one day, when the conditions were propitious . . .

A positive response to the right person would guarantee her more than cocktails and dinners and fluffy dresses and cosmetics and fashionable shoes. She would ride in a chauffeur-driven black car, be collected from the embankment each morning, and driven on weekends to dacha parties. She would receive regular promotions and pay raises. And perhaps most enticing of all, she would have access to the holy of holies, the vault with top-secret documents.

Diminutive and dapper, dedicated and devious, Kazimir Ouspensky had first married for money and then for position. His first wife came from a farm family that owned hundreds of acres, until the government appropriated the land. Wife number two came from a Bolshevik family with connections to Bukharin, who eventually fell out of favor. Kazimir's brood, four children, could be found in Leningrad, but he had not spoken nor seen them for years. His second marriage had made possible the small but prominent government publishing house he ran for the principal purpose of printing the theoretical musings of party officials. To his credit, Kazimir would occasionally publish writers not on the government list. His favorite poet, Marina Tsvetaeva, best known for her lines,

> And soon we all shall sleep beneath the soil,
> Who would not let each other sleep above it,

was always in need of money, small sums of which he arranged for her to receive secretly. Although chastised for publishing poets out of favor with the government, he found more pleasure in the works of the pariahs than the doggerel of hacks celebrating a new tractor or dam or canal.

His not unhandsome features, pale blue eyes, clear skin, small mouth, blond hair, gentle hands, had over the years attracted a number of women, but none of them as bewitching as Natasha, who held him spellbound, even to the point of danger. When he had transferred to Moscow to become the archivist of denunciations—an entire wing of his ministry screened the thousands of denunciatory letters that arrived every week—he had distinguished himself by exhibiting an unerring sense of knowing which letters to credit and which to ignore.

"Dear Comrade Stalin" was a typical salutation. "I live in an apartment building with Galina Sobol. Whenever your name is mentioned, she makes the sign of the *figa*, like an illiterate Italian peasant, to keep the evil eye away. She should be reeducated in a camp, and I should be given her apartment, much roomier than my own with a view of the garden." A letter of this kind would seem to beg for the reject pile, but Kazimir was struck by the candor, the name Sobol, and the word "figa." After an undercover investigation, Kazimir discovered that the writer, a man, belonged to an anti-Semitic group, which the police subsequently broke up, and was himself an Italian Fascist agent with family in Rome.

"Dear Koba" immediately suggested to Kazimir that the writer was a love-sick woman who wanted to insinuate herself into the presence of Stalin. "I have uncovered a nest of spies in the alley across from me. If you will send me a train ticket to Moscow, I will bring you their names and show you my proof."

"Dear Defender of the Motherland" normally meant that the letter writer was going to engage in self-denunciation. "When asked by the authorities, I originally said that my father worked in a metal shop. But now I see how my lies have poisoned my life and cost me my health. The truth is that my father was a policeman for the Tsar. I hate myself for having lied and wish you to tell me how I can make amends."

Kazimir usually arranged for the self-denouncers to be brought in for questioning. In most instances, they proved frightened and no threat to the state, though some of them had to relinquish their current positions to make way for patriots. The ex-children of priests, for example, could not be allowed to obstruct a true Soviet.

Eventually Kazimir's good work caught the attention of Stalin's favorite secret policeman, Genrikh Yagoda, deputy chairman of the GPU. A ferret-faced jeweler's son from Nizhny Novgorod, he sported a brush mustache, loved orchids, watched German pornography, and cultivated literary friendships. He was principally responsible for the purges in the countryside, having persuaded Stalin to root out the kulaks as plotters against the party and Supreme Leader. Yagoda asked to see Kazimir, whom he found immensely clever, and offered him any archival job he desired. Comrade Ouspensky requested the sensitive position of cataloguing Koba's secret files.

"Ah, the crown jewels," said Yagoda.

"And if I might be so bold . . ." Yagoda shook his head yes. "My assistant, Natasha von Fresser, should replace me as head of the Archives of Denunciation."

Stroking his pointed chin, Yagoda said, "Let me guess. She is very beautiful."

"And a gifted archivist. I trained her myself, if you'll excuse my lack of modesty."

"Excused. I'll see to it that she is given the job, the title, and the increase in pay."

When Kazimir left Yagoda's office, he was convinced that Natasha would appreciatively give herself up to him, perhaps that same night. But Natasha was so excited by the news that she felt in no mood for romance. She wanted to dine and dance, and get blissfully drunk.

Thanks to Ouspensky's connections, Natasha met men in government of all types and ranks. Her desk in the archives, like honey to bees, drew swarms of admirers, both married and single. Within weeks, she found herself escorted to dacha dinners, excursions, theatricals, readings, concerts, and men's apartments. Although Ouspensky was her original sponsor, she soon found little need for him. The poor man wondered if others were enjoying what he had failed to receive.

Shortly after her installation as the archivist of denunciations, Natasha had begun spiriting documents from the office and passing them to Yelena. Had she been caught, exile or death would have ensued; and yet she harbored no fears. She engaged in this illegal practice for two reasons: one, she was light-fingered by nature; two, she thought that in the future she might be able to make good use of some of these odious letters.

Yagoda saw Natasha for the first time during one of his periodic archival visits in search of damning evidence to condemn some poor soul. He stopped at her desk and, struck by her Scandinavian mien, could hardly unscramble his jumbled syntax. When he learned that she was Kazimir's protégé, the woman Kazimir had recommended as his replacement, he insisted that Comrade Ouspensky bring her to his dacha. Given that Yagoda was Kazimir's superior, Ouspensky feared that the chief would have his way with Natasha.

"As you know," said Yagoda, "I love to host parties. Bring her to the next one, Kazimir. She'll brighten up the company."

Kazimir knew about Yagoda's lecheries, but he could hardly say no to the head of the secret police, to the man upon whom he depended for his job and his life. Several weeks passed before Kazimir and Natasha motored out to the dacha, because Yagoda had been called to the Caucasus to quell a minor revolt over the nationalization of privately owned shops.

In the meantime, for the enjoyment of Soviet bureaucrats, several of Claude Monet's paintings from Leningrad's Hermitage Museum were on exhibit in the Kremlin Palace. Some well-placed calls enabled Natasha to bring Yelena to see the masterpieces. The child's eyes fixed on four particular canvases, *Waterloo Bridge, the Effect of Fog; Haystack at Giverny; The Grand Quai at Havre*; and *Jeanne-Marguerite Lecadre in the Garden*. After leaving the exhibit, Yelena requested postcards of these paintings and a drawing pad. While Natasha made the purchase, the child pored over a book of photos entitled *Iosif Stalin: His Life and Times*. As soon as they reached government house, Yelena spread the pad on the floor and began to copy the postcards. To her family's amazement, her reproductions, although only in black and white, looked professional.

"We will have to get her art lessons," said Razan.

Anna agreed, and Natasha allowed that through her contacts she could probably arrange for Yelena to attend the official art institute for nothing. When Yelena told Sasha Visotsky, her best friend in the embankment house, he seemed strangely unenthusiastic. At first she attributed the reason to her spending less time with him crawling through the heating ducts that circled the building and eavesdropping through the vents, an activity they held sacredly secret between them, for had their parents known, the two children would have been severely reprimanded and perhaps even forbidden to see one another.

Almost immediately, she was admitted to the institute and sat through her first class, an evening session that allowed talented children to attend school during the day and art classes at night.

"Pretty dry, wasn't it?" said Sasha the next afternoon, a Saturday, as they were putting on their ice skates in Gorky Park.

Yelena looked at him stoically until he admitted the source of his comment. Without looking up from his skates, which he was lacing a second time so that he wouldn't have to face Yelena, he said, "Benjamin Levitin, a painter friend of my parents, said that the institute discourages imagination. Is it true that the students copy only classical models?" She said yes. "You're better than that."

A flattered Yelena smiled and replied. "I agree!"

"Why don't you get *him* to give you lessons? I know he has students. My parents said that because he does abstract paintings, he can't show them in galleries."

"I don't want to draw lines and circles. I want to draw gardens and fields and people."

"You can draw me!" he said, standing up on his skates and holding out his arms as if readying himself to take flight across the ice.

"Hold that pose a second longer so I can remember it. You think I can't draw you, well, you'll see."

Yelena put her small hand in his and they skated off together.

Yagoda's dacha, one among several Soviet retreats in the area, nestled in a beech forest. Armed guards circled the property and parked cars stood in strategic spots near the house. When Kazimir and Natasha arrived, a secret agent inspected the chauffeur's papers and waved the black Packard past the gate. The cedar paneling of the house exuded a pleasant aroma, and the paintings on the wall indicated that Yagoda did not share the official dislike of abstract art. Among his collection was a small cubist work by Picasso.

Natasha recognized Molotov and Malenkov, and repeated their singsong names to herself, "Molotov-Malenkov, Malenkov-Molotov." She also recognized Yagoda's aide, Nikolai Ivanovich Ezhov, the man soon to become known as the bloody dwarf. Short and slight, Ezhov had dark wavy hair and a youthful face. Natasha thought him handsome, a judgment shared by many women, and calculated his age at no more than twenty. Kazimir seemed to know everyone in attendance and introduced her to the famous and infamous, as well as a few writers and artists whom she had never heard of; but then she had only herself to blame for this lapse. She admittedly read little and had found art rather boring until Yelena's talent had surfaced. Scanning Yagoda's bookcase led her to make a promise: she would in the future read Pushkin and Gogol and Dostoevski and Turgenev. As she listened to the wives of the dignitaries mention authors and composers, she realized that her beauty could take her only so far. Her husband, who often alluded to her infatuation with things rather than ideas, had one day observed: "After men have spent themselves, they want the richness of wit."

At first, she had thought that he was referring to humor, but eventually, she realized that wit cast a larger net. It referred to high culture and learning, both of which she lacked. Her failings had become painfully clear to her in her daily letters to Alexei. After the first week, she had nothing of interest to say; and whatever she said, she always framed in the same mundane manner. Catching up with these other women would take some time. For the moment, she would have to exploit her exciting appearance and her feminine wiles to attract the attention of men like Molotov-Malenkov and, not least, Yagoda, who rested his hand on her arm and offered to show her the house and his bust of Stalin.

"But cook is ringing the dinner bell," said Natasha, "and I can smell the goose."

"Afterward, then, when my guests have driven off or are dozing in a corner, we can be alone. I want to show you my private collection of German films." She smiled at Kazimir across the room and started toward him, intending to accompany him for dinner. "No, my dear," said Yagoda, "you must sit next to me."

"But your wife . . ."

"She understands completely. She is not bourgeois."

Kazimir, seated at the end of the table, kept eyeing Natasha, while harboring murderous thoughts about Genrikh Yagoda, the Jew! Bad enough that Kazimir had to report to a Yid, but the man had appointed innumerable Jews to the secret police. No wonder the GPU had a bad name. "Keep your temper under control, Kazimir," he thought to himself. "A day will come . . ."

By the end of the evening, as Yagoda had predicted, most of the guests had been driven home or were horizontal from drink. Kazimir simulated drunkenness, though perfectly sober. He waited a few minutes and then tried the door of the room into which Yagoda and Natasha had disappeared. Finding it locked, he gently knocked, but no one responded. His worst fears had a basis in fact. Yagoda and Natasha sat nestled on a couch watching a blue film. Her left hand, like that of the woman on the screen, was masturbating Yagoda. To bring her to this infamy he had promised to give her an apartment, where she could live on her own. His intention, of course, was to use it for trysts and for secret meetings with informants. She would make a perfect front for such rendezvous because no one would suspect that a love nest was also a place of political intrigue.

When Natasha and Yagoda finally emerged, her lipstick was smeared and her dress disarrayed. Still feigning inebriation, Kazimir staggered from his chair, smiled at Yagoda, directed Natasha to take her coat, and pushed her out the front door to his waiting car. The chauffeur, wrapped in a car blanket, lay snoring on the front seat until Kazimir rapped on the window. Snapping to attention, he opened the back door for his boss and Natasha, and roared into the bleak moonless night. They sat apart in the car, saying little. Kazimir chose to express his displeasure by ignoring her and told his chauffeur to see her to the door of government house. If she thought that without his help she could decipher the myriad letters that crossed her desk, she would learn soon enough Kazimir's full value.

Anna and Razan helped her move to her new apartment, situated in a cement block that, like most tasteless Soviet architecture, looked like a prison. From her window, she could see the Lubyanka Prison, with its long line of women and children waiting to bring parcels to incarcerated dear ones. Where do the men go, she wondered, because she never saw a woman leave the Lubyanka with a man. Her faith in the government was wavering, particularly since she now worked for the Archive of Denunciations and knew for herself that people daily accused others of crimes. When Razan, increasingly skeptical, mumbled about the numbers sent to camps for five, ten, and twenty years, Natasha repeated the official line that "they must have done something wrong, because the government doesn't act without cause."

"No doubt," said Razan, "but it's the nature of that cause that troubles me. A poem, a painting, a joke, a symphony, a play . . . any of these things, I've learned, can land you in jail. When I shave the bureaucrats, they all want to see a person suppressed. And for what? Smoking a foreign cigarette, hoarding a turnip, praising life in the west, failing to own the Vozhd's picture . . ."

This conversation, like so many others, took place on the street, because Razan feared that Natasha's new flat would be bugged. In that event, the eavesdropper would have learned that both Yagoda and Kazimir had enjoyed Natasha's physical charms. But Yagoda shortly stopped visiting, and one of his men stood sentinel in the apartment as a contact for informers. During most of those investigative sessions, Natasha excused herself and left the apartment, often passing the informant ascending the stairs to her second-floor safe house. On two occasions, when illness kept her at home, she left her bedroom door slightly ajar to hear the conversation.

The first time, a secondary-school teacher was denouncing a student—his own!—who had asked the teacher how Trotsky's view of the state was any different from Bukharin's, and why Stalin had changed his view about private ownership of farms?

"I regard all these questions as provocative," said the teacher. "Clearly, someone has suggested he ask them."

"Without a doubt, the student is a provocateur," Yagoda's man answered. "Give me his name and address. We will bring him in immediately and get to the bottom of this conspiracy."

"Conspiracy?" said the teacher, his voice registering alarm. "I didn't intend . . ."

"These people never work alone. Scratch the surface and you inevitably uncover a nest of termites devouring the foundations of the Soviet state."

The second time, a glazier came to the apartment to denounce his local barber. For obvious reasons, Natasha took careful note. Her stepfather, thank goodness, worked in the Kremlin and not in the general precincts. The man identified his neighborhood—one well known for its bakery and barbershop—

and said that Rebkov, the barber, kept suspicious company, underpaid him for a new mirror, and had a penchant for telling anti-Stalin jokes.

"Here's one he told in front of several customers waiting for haircuts—and they all laughed! At the May Day Parade, a very old man was carrying a placard that read: 'Thank you, Comrade Stalin, for my happy childhood.' A policeman approached the old man. 'What is this? Are you deriding our party? Everybody can see that when you were a child, Comrade Stalin wasn't yet born.' The old man replied, 'That's precisely why I'm grateful!'"

She gathered from the silence that the interrogator was transcribing the joke. And where would his report be stored? In the building where she worked. As in Brovensk, she could alter records or destroy them, if she chose.

"Just last week," said the informant, "I was polishing the new mirror when Rebkov told this story: 'A dozen workers from the Urals were visiting Stalin in his office. After they left, Stalin was missing his pipe. He told Poskrebyshev to see that all the workers were questioned. A few minutes later, Stalin found the pipe in his desk and told Poskrebyshev to release all the workers. 'But Comrade Stalin,' said Poskrebyshev, 'they've all confessed.'"

Natasha assumed that the other denunciations were not unlike the letters she opened each day, hardly a one of them written by a disinterested patriot. Most of the authors wanted to be rewarded with the denounced person's apartment or overcoat or pension or some other prize, such as access to the person's spouse or lover. She found it all so sordid that she began to worry about her own behavior and how she had betrayed her husband. Yagoda had said that after the first betrayal there is no other. She understood his meaning. A person can't lose his innocence more than once, but repeated offenses did not justify or assuage the first betrayal. His comment gnawed at her. Alexei wrote to her every day, and she replied swearing her undying love and faithfulness. What she wanted to include in the letter, but could not, would be the qualifying phrase: from this day forth.

Yelena became Natasha's innocence, her golden chalice held above the unsavory throngs. The child's art lessons, now in the hands of Benjamin Levitin, had tapped a well of imaginative talent. From drawing city and country scenes, Yelena had progressed to sketching people. Her unerring eye and playful personality led her on more than one occasion to draw an occupant of the government house. Natasha thought she knew most of the embankment bureaucrats, but she found among Yelena's portfolio a few strange faces. Taking some of the sketches to the archives, she kvelled as her fellow workers said that the child would be a master portraitist. Kazimir took vicarious pride in the artwork and insisted on showing some of the pictures to Yagoda, who fancied himself an art connoisseur, but Yagoda's response startled both Kazimir and Natasha.

"Where were the sketches done? These two men, for example, their heads nearly touching, as if conspiring?"

Natasha said that she had never seen the figures in the picture and would have to ask Yelena. The child claimed that she had observed the scene, which she had then drawn from memory.

"She has been spying on our people!" cried Yagoda.

"Spying?" said Kazimir shocked.

"On our people?" said Natasha incredulously. "What in the world do you mean?"

Yagoda, clearly uncomfortable, explained that one of the two men was a secret agent who used an embankment flat to meet his informers.

"There's only one way she could have seen these men and that's if she had been spying on them."

Natasha said, "She has no key to any apartment but my parents."

"We shall find her hiding place," hissed Yagoda, "even if we have to tear down the walls."

The next morning, the secret police were swarming over the house on the embankment and discovered to their unease that a child or small person could squeeze through the heating ducts. When Yagoda received this report, he ordered that all the ducts be installed with metal grilles, and he summoned Natasha and Yelena to his office.

Although he assumed his most menacing scowl, the child utterly disarmed Genrikh with her frank admission, which in no way contradicted her original explanation, that she and a friend were playing tag in the ducts and she peered through a heating vent and mentally registered the scene: two men huddled in whispered conversation.

"I want the picture destroyed!" he shouted, forgetting that he had removed it from the archives himself. When reminded of this fact, he made a show of tearing it into little pieces.

On the street outside of Yagoda's headquarters, Yelena cheerfully said, "I drew the first one from memory, and I can draw a second the same way."

Although Natasha tried to suppress her merriment, she chuckled at the idea that authority could efface an idea or an image. Alexei had told her often enough about the power of both; for the first time, she had witnessed the truth of his words.

A disconcerted Kazimir indicated that he would like a private word with Natasha, but although he had mentally composed an elaborate justification for Natasha distancing herself from the child, the subzero weather demanded brevity. "Yelena will compromise you. See her as little as possible."

"*Etta govnaw!*" exclaimed Natasha and hailed a taxi.

Once inventive Anna heard about the incident, she came up with a plan, one so simple and so ingratiating that it just might possibly work. Now that Mrs. Yarmilova's apartment was known to have housed a secret operation, the GPU would undoubtedly feel the need to establish another.

"If one person knows a secret," Yagoda had often said, "it is safe. But if two know, then eleven know."

Mrs. Yarmilova, a widow with white hair, rheumy eyes, and a wrinkled face, had been given her apartment because of her husband's heroism during the Civil War. With the exposure of her apartment as a nest for political intrigue, the government withdrew its agent, and, as well, the small allowance Yagoda's department had paid for its use. Anna, taking advantage of Mrs. Yarmilova's straitened conditions, proposed to the old woman that she turn her flat into a gallery exhibiting Yelena's artwork: oils, watercolors, pencil and charcoal drawings, and crayon sketches. Of late, she had taken to painting canvases of Stalin and his mustache from Yefim's secret photograph. Its originality had captivated her the moment she spied it in Razan's drawer. The embankment residents would probably pay handsomely for such a rare aspect. They'd regard it as a relic or an icon.

"I know an icon, but this thing you call a relic," said Mrs. Yarmilova, waving an arm in circles, "explain it to me."

"It's an object that brings good luck to the owner, like a splinter of the true cross, or a toe bone from a saint, or a strand of hair from a martyr." Anna touched her arm. "In your youth, do you remember attending church and seeing vials of saints' blood?"

"I don't believe in magical charms. Maybe then, but not now."

"You don't have to believe, nor does the buyer. Think of it this way. When your daughter comes to visit, you wear the sweater she gave you." Anna fingered her own woolie. "Why? To show your love."

"So we'll be selling lucky sweaters, is that it?"

The poor woman had sadly lost most of her wits when word came from Kiev that her husband, fighting for the Reds, had died at the hands of the marauding White Army.

"No, Yelena's pictures. We can even put up a banner saying: 'In devotion to Iosif Vissarionovich.' Maybe we'll have a Victrola playing the *Internationale*. No candles or incense, nothing to suggest religion. Maybe the hammer and sickle displayed on the wall."

"You would sell pictures of our Beloved Supreme Leader for a profit? It's unpatriotic and probably against the law."

"I was thinking only of you, Vera Yarmilova, and the modest stipend the secret police will no longer pay." She took an apple from the sideboard. "Food stuffs like this are expensive, maybe not so much for you, but for your daughter and her beautiful little boy and girl." She sighed. "We should all be so lucky as to have such well-behaved and talented grandchildren. What are their names again?"

"Lev and Karolina."

"Yes, of course. I've seen them in the hall when they come to visit you. Such children! It's a shame they don't have sweaters without holes in the elbows and sheepskin coats to protect them from the awful flu and pneumonia we've been seeing of late."

Mrs. Yarmilova's senses were not so diminished that she didn't want to provide winter wear for her family. Lev and Karolina would be the envy of every schoolmate, not to mention her daughter's neighbors. All the gifts she could lavish on her daughter would make up for the times that she had scolded her for marrying a drunken lout. She paused, struck by a terrible thought. What if that sot drank up the allowance she gave to her daughter? Anna put her mind to rest. "Never give cash presents." She hugged her purse to her chest. "Buy the sweaters downstairs in the government store, and anything else that you want: wooden plates, nested toys, shawls, coats. In the foreign-goods store, if you have the money, you can purchase items from France and Sweden and Norway, even Germany and America. With the kopeks we bring in, you will be Sneshkus's best customer. Wouldn't you like a new handbag, from Italy, made with soft leather?"

To Anna's delight, Vera agreed, but selling Razan on the idea proved far more difficult. They talked in the street.

"Your idea is insane. You'll endanger the family. And for what: kopeks and rubles? We'll all be sent to Siberia."

"I have no fear. Growing up in Brovensk, I spent my youth watching the Tsar and Lenin. These peacocks will forgive any sin, any transgression, so long as you fawn over them. Honey-coated lies about their accomplishments make them roll over and purr. The Vozhd is no different. You of all people ought to know *that*."

"Which Vozhd, the humble Bolshevik or the vengeful autocrat?"

"Yes, I know, the man is subject to moods that you say radically alter his behavior. But the Stalin who was thrown out of the seminary because he wouldn't kiss the feet of the clergy has always wanted others to lick his boots. Should he hear of my scheme—I admit, it's a nepman's scheme to make money—he'll throw a tantrum and then go back into his corner, refill his pipe with cigarette tobacco, and lie on his divan, immensely pleased that the people love him so much that they treat him like God."

"The corner, the pipe he fills with Herzegovina Flor tobacco, the divan . . . you heard all those things from me. Don't ever repeat them. They are treated as state secrets. If Poskrebyshev knew . . ."

"At Molotov's dacha, when I met this Poskrebyshev, I knew at once that he wore the clothes of human loathing. Remember how he bragged that no person, no fact, could insult him? He's proud of his slavishness. If you think that I would ever say a word that would put you in that man's power . . . I would hang myself first."

Razan embraced his wife and suggested that they escape the cold street and have a cup of tea and a roll in the nearby restaurant.

"Not until we settle this matter," said Anna, unyielding.

Razan had come up against her intransigence before and always lost. But this time, he felt that she was peering into the abyss. "What you are proposing is that we open a gallery for profit and trade on Stalin's person. How do you know that people will pay for Yelena's pictures?"

"Stalin's mustache is his most famous feature. Think about how men used to travel leagues to see the arm of some dead martyr in a silver sleeve. Human nature hasn't changed in all these years. Men would sooner pay to have a picture of Stalin's mustache than buy a starving child a crust of bread. I know these people. Come!"

Over tea at a small neighborhood café, Razan spooned honey into his cup and plaintively said, "Anna, our lives before . . . we never wanted for essentials. Have I ever denied you anything?"

She stirred some sugar into her tea. An attractive woman, with a small enticing mouth—her slightly protruding lower lip was especially seductive—she was also a clever one. When her peasant's cunning came into play, her eyes would narrow and her generous bosom rise mysteriously, revealing its bounty and seeming to say, "If you hope to see more of me, you'll do as I wish." Had someone told her that squeezing kopeks makes them multiply, she would have purchased a pair of pliers. She loved Razan's inherent gentleness and took pride in his skills, but she wondered about his indifference to money. In Brovensk, the peasants had a saying: "Only Jews can shit shekels." Had she married the exception?

"God takes care of those who take care of themselves. For the future and my family's security, I put my trust in money—and you. After my husband died, a number of men expressed their interest in me, one or two of them, in fact, quite handsome. But none of them showed me any real kindness. They treated me as a cash cow. You were different, are different, and I love you for your gentleness. I know you have no passion for money, but I do. You have told me about your comfortable house in Albania. But I have tasted the dry bones and thirst of poverty. My family was so poor that to keep the hunger at bay I chewed on my own clothing, just to have something in my mouth. Now I see a chance for us to become rich. Like the church, we will be exploiting people's fears. If they don't show their love of God or, in this case, Stalin, are they not then running the risk of being cast into hell or into a hellish camp? The bureaucrats will come, and they will buy; and they will want everyone to know that they have purchased a share in Bolshevik heaven." She reached across the table and took Razan's hand. "Trust me. When the time is right, we shall cash in our kopeks and leave . . . maybe even cross the border into Finland."

Initially, the embankment residents came to Vera Yarmilova's gallery out of curiosity. Her next-door neighbor, Alexei Rykov, was the first to hazard a look. His black curly hair had, since his fall from favor, turned gray, and his mustache and Van Dyke beard needed trimming. His nose, pinched at the bridge, always made Anna think of a man who had been cut in half. With his sad, piercing eyes, he studied colleagues whom he despised for their bloodlust. He had stood for social democracy and a humane application of Communism. But his so-called rightist views had cost him the chairmanship of the party and led to his abased position as minister of post and telegraph. Slowly, the erstwhile leader lost everything, including his life. Demoted to a nonvoting membership in the party's Central Committee and expelled from the Communist Party, he retired with palsied hands and yellowed skin to await his fate at the house on the embankment.

The lower half of his face reflected his internal pain: his quivering lips, his disordered speech, his untrimmed facial hair. Sadly, his slow descent could be charted in his physiognomy and in the progressive deterioration of his wife, who was now bedridden from a stroke. Taking solace in drink, he had become a pathetic alcoholic, dependent on his daughter for his needs.

When he saw Yelena's work, he raised a shaky arm, clenched his fist, and mumbled, "May the devil take him." Moving his head from side to side, he added, "It could have all been so different." He then did something startling and dangerous. With others in the room, he shouted, "You are a cutthroat Georgian, an uncouth barbarian, and nothing will change you but death, which can't come soon enough."

Most of the visitors promptly left. The two who remained tepidly asked, "How do we know it's really the Vozhd?" And "Does Comrade Stalin know, and if he doesn't, couldn't we be punished?" Anna assured them that the drawings of the famous mustache were based on their own Beloved Leader, and that she would never run the risk of counterfeits. "If you are worried about inviting Stalin's ire," she said, "I ask you: have you ever known Koba to resent the love of his people? Ridiculous! I've never heard anything more absurd."

To capitalize doubly on the project, Anna had Yelena set up an easel and draw those tenants who would pay a ruble to sit for their portrait. Before long, the walls of Vera's apartment were hung with Yelena's drawings, which in fact lured quite a few buyers. As Anna had predicted, votary lights began to appear in the apartments of people who had purchased a picture of Stalin's mustache. Anna hoped that one day Stalin would actually sit for a painting, and that Razan could be included in the background. The papers had run stories on Stalin's doctors and dentist. Why not a picture of the Vozhd and his barber? Given the Boss's international reputation, Anna knew that if Razan appeared with him, her husband could command a great deal of money for interviews with foreign correspondents, biographers, and historians. Making a bullet out of shit might be impossible, but making money from celebrity was not.

Yelena produced the greatest bonanza of all when she painted on a neutral background a huge Stalin mustache—and nothing else—that covered virtually the entire canvas. Of all her artwork, this painting proved the most popular, so much so that numerous residents bid to buy it. Anna eventually auctioned it off to the highest bidder, but not before she had a local photographer duplicate it hundreds of times. Razan even presented a copy to Stalin, who asked if he could have Yelena paint another, for which he would sit. Anna's dream had come true!

Shortly after Stalin's request, Anna received a note in the mail from Serjee, the Kremlin's official photographer requesting "an audience." From the formal wording, she couldn't decide whether the man wanted to talk or snap her picture. To be on the safe side, she responded, "You asked for an audience. Certainly. Just tell me when," and signed her name. A few days later, a second note arrived: "Would Tuesday next suit you?" These high government officials, she concluded, wrote and spoke a language unlike her own. When the man knocked on the door, she saw standing before her a short heavy-shouldered Tatar. A model of politeness, he asked if they could "retire to her sitting room for a tête-à-tête," whatever that meant.

He introduced himself only as Serjee, the single name that appeared on his letters. His Russian was perfect. Did he have a last name or a patronymic? He explained that in the 1920s, the government banned all but first names for Mongolians.

"My family came from Ulan Bator. During the Civil War, we lived in China. My father was a chemist. I went to school in Peking, where I learned how to use a camera. Comrade Stalin, who is a great and generous man, made me a Kremlin photographer."

Anna poured him tea. She explained that her husband was napping, and that her young daughter would soon be returning from school. "Your note never said what you wished to see me about. Does it touch upon Stalin? Is there a problem?"

"Problem? No, I wouldn't call it that. You had someone paint Koba's mustache. A photograph was then taken of the painting. If you will excuse me for saying so, the lighting in the picture is poor and, as a result, Stalin's mustache lacks luster. Neither the picture nor the painting quite do it justice. I would like to buy the canvas and, as well, remove all the photographs from circulation. Your daughter can then paint a new one, and I can photograph it."

"The painting was sold to a diplomat who lives in this building. I'm not sure he'll sell it."

"I have been . . . that is, I am prepared to pay twice the amount or more, if necessary."

Anna noted the revision in language from "I have been" to "I am." She wanted to ask if Stalin had directed him to buy the painting, and would he really commission a new painting?

Sensing her reluctance, he said, "Mrs. Shtube, let me assure you that no harm will come to you or the painter. I merely want to photograph a new canvas properly, with the right lighting and lens."

To suggest harm was to admit its possibility. The absence of evidence, she knew, was not evidence of absence. You learned that fact at a young age living in a Soviet society.

"And the original painting: Will that also be safe?"

"Absolutely! You have my word."

"Excuse my provincial habits. I am a cautious person. So tell me, is it you or the Vozhd who's dissatisfied?"

Serjee began to perspire. His hands trembled, and he began to tug at his buttons and pull on his chin, all the time looking at her pitifully.

Although Anna had a nose for trouble, in this instance she couldn't frame the source or nature of it. Perhaps the problem wasn't Stalin or Serjee, but rather the object itself. Serjee wished to remove both the canvas and the photographs. Perhaps, though, the problem was the very idea of the mustache.

Since Serjee offered no further explanations, she led him through the building and introduced him to the owner of the canvas, Dr. Efraim Slonim. She would have liked to remain to hear what was said, but Serjee made it clear that he wanted her to leave.

"Thank you, Mrs. Shtube," he said. "I will now conduct my business with Dr. Slonim."

He slightly bowed and turned up his right palm, as if to point the way out. Anna turned to Dr. Slonim, who was so bewildered by Serjee's invasion that whatever thoughts he might have wished to express remained stillborn. Out in the hall, Anna wondered and worried. Perhaps Razan had been right: Her financial finagling would earn them all a five-year stay in the cold country. She wished at that moment Yelena could crawl through the heating vent and listen to what this Tatar was saying. Tatars! She had never trusted them.

Anna rose early the next morning to catch Dr. Slonim on his way to the Kremlin, where he removed gall bladders and benign tumors, and the occasional appendix, leaving the more serious surgery to Dr. Ginzburg. Like Stalin's dentist, these men were all Jews, even though the Vozhd railed against "Zionists." Anna wondered.

"Dr. Slonim, excuse me, I know you have appointments to keep. But that man last night, Serjee, I never had a chance to explain. He was a complete stranger to me. To this minute," she falsely said, "I don't have the slightest idea what he wanted, do you?"

"He wanted to buy your daughter's portrait of Koba's mustache. He offered me three times what I paid."

"Did you sell it?"

"His offer made me suspicious. I thought: Maybe this painting is the work of a budding genius. Although I sometimes buy paintings, I am no connoisseur. The art dealer Henrik Hilgy is. I want to ask him. Then I'll decide." He shook his head in wonderment. "Three times what I paid!"

"Dr. Slonim, my advice to you is if your expert says the painting is the work of an amateur, don't let that stop you from asking for ten times the amount. The Tatar will pay it. Trust me."

Dr. Slonim looked at his watch. Anna could see that his car was waiting at the curb. He buttoned up his English duffel coat, reached for the door, paused, and said, "Do you know something I should know?"

She looked around and whispered, "In God's name I don't. My husband—the Supreme Leader's barber!—even he claims to know nothing. In fact, he advised me to avoid the subject. But every bone in my body tells me that the Tatar came because of Stalin's mustache."

Later that evening when Anna told Razan the story, he agreed with her view and opined that the mustache had become incendiary. Her lucrative business would have to come to an end.

"Tell all your buyers that somehow Stalin learned about their votary lights and worship of his mustache. Tell them, he said that such worship resembled a religion. He has therefore forbidden the selling of any unauthorized paintings or photographs of him."

Anna was pained to think of the money she'd lose. "And what about authorized pictures? Are we allowed to worship those?"

The barber's annoyance was palpable. "If you insist on behaving like a nepman, then have Yelena paint landscapes or city scenes, but stay away from Stalin. His face already haunts every home."

Anna reluctantly agreed.

IN VORONEZH, A CITY PETER
BUILT AND POETS BRAVED

Before the train departed for Voronezh, Alexei von Fresser was bound over by the two secret agents to a young soldier, no older than a teenager, whom Alexei cultivated, treating him to a cup of hot tea and a buttered roll that he bought from the porter in charge of the food cart. The soldier, Konstantin Gilyarovsky, came from a small village on the Volga and regularly brought exiled men from Moscow and Leningrad to one of the camps in the eastern zone. He preferred escorting women, not because their company was more pleasant but because they were less likely to be sent to Siberia. An exiled woman was usually a "hundred-and-fiver," a *stopiatnitsa*, who had to live at least a hundred kilometers away from Moscow. Voronezh qualified.

One-day journeys enabled Konstantin to sleep at home. Although Voronezh lacked the amenities of great cities, it offered free concerts and poetry readings by exiled artists. Had his commanding officer known that he attended such gatherings, he could have suffered a loss of pay—his rank was too low to be reduced—and perhaps even a few days in the guardhouse. He sat next to Alexei on the hard wooden seats, and enviously watched his prisoner reading a book. Eventually, Alexei noticed Konstantin's raptness.

"Would you like to share it?"

He held up the cover to exhibit the title.

"I can't read," said the boy.

"Then let me read to you. Have you ever heard of Pushkin?"

"Yes, yes," he replied excitedly. "I have even heard some of his poems read out loud."

"At poetry readings?" asked an incredulous Alexei.

"Please don't mention it."

As Alexei recited some poems, the train car came alive, and the babushkas shared with him and Konstantin their wicker baskets of food. When the tea man returned, pushing his trolley with its steaming samovar, Alexei treated all his benefactors.

"More poems!" said a partially paralyzed elderly woman, waving her cane in the air like a baton.

"A love lyric, if you don't mind," said a man with silver hair and matching spectacle frames.

"Do you know Pushkin's poem 'Night'?"

To the surprise of all, the conductor, just then making his way through the car, stopped and recited the short poem by heart.

"Wonderful!" exclaimed Alexei. "I have used the poem for my own purposes. It's dedicated to my wife, who stayed behind. Permit me to read my revision."

The passengers begged him to do so.

Alexei closed the book on his lap, leaned back, closed his eyes, and recited:

"My voice for you Natasha is so gentle
It's like the dark night's velvet mantle.
By my bedside rests a candle, my sad light
That flutters, lifts and falls, like a tailless kite.
But always my thoughts return to you alone,
And in the dark, your eyes shine like precious stones.
Your smile outshines the light and brings back your voice;
My dearest wife, sweetest one, you are my choice."

The conductor's sour expression presaged his judgment. "You're no Pushkin, but I understand your feelings."

In Voronezh, the soldier led Alexei, with his one valise and satchel, to the main police station, where the exile was required to register and then report weekly. Ossian Oblomov, the commissar of police, an insecure fellow who disguised his fears of inadequacy through bluster, looked at Alexei's papers and asked in a loud authoritative voice:

"Where is your medical degree? The official certificate? The stamp that says you are actually a real doctor? With all the quacks running around, we don't need another. Is that why you were sent here, to peddle poisonous potions, or was it to maim patients with the so-called mercury cure?"

Oblomov leaned back in his chair proud of his authoritative voice and his pronouncements about medical malpractice. The chief medical examiner for his district had in fact damned him as "passive," a serious Soviet crime, for not rooting out all the faux physicians under his jurisdiction. Oblomov remembered this exchange with some embarrassment because, in addition to being reproved for his laziness, he had been forced to ask the medical officer the meaning of the word "faux." Bad enough he even had to ask, but the man merely exacerbated his insecurities by exclaiming:

"You are the commissar of police and have never studied French?"

Oblomov had left school in the sixth grade and felt superior to most of his men because he could read and write, and he knew the difference between classical Russian and modern, a dual system that remained a mystery to most native speakers. Prepared to take out his frustrations on this exiled medical graduate, he had a brilliant insight. Who better than this young man to uncover the medical quacks in Voronezh oblast?

Oblomov's idea handsomely served at least two people: himself and Alexei. Shortly, Moscow would give Oblomov a medal with a red ribbon for exposing the medical mountebanks who swarmed through the area. He immediately found Alexei lodgings and work. The implications of this happy conjunction meant that the commissar of police had to trust Alexei's judgment, even when it contradicted his own, a hard pill to swallow, and that Alexei was free to travel outside Voronezh oblast, a liberty that few exiles enjoyed.

The city itself, in the southwestern black-earth region and located on the Voronezh River close to the spot where it empties into the Don, lacked Leningrad's architectural grandeur and Moscow's political influence. Founded in 1585 by Tsar Feodor I as a fortress town to protect Russians from Tatar raids, Voronezh grew into a city when Peter the Great established a large naval shipbuilding yard on the river. Like the Tsars, the Soviets favored this city for exiling poets, painters, and intellectuals for antistate activities, inadvertently creating a hotbed for artistic and dissident ideas. Although exiles often went hungry and suffered the cold—the government offered no subsistence—the pariahs managed to organize poetry readings and concerts and lectures, making police surveillance a necessary activity, to the chagrin of Oblomov and his constabulary, who generally had no interest in hearing poetry or Beethoven sonatas. Of course, there were exceptions, such as Konstantin, men and women who loved the sound of words and classical music. These secret agents kindly chose to overlook travel violations, curfews, and printed material passed among friends. A few of the police even asked the artists for their autographs, surreptitiously. Konstantin, for example, always wore civilian dress when he attended a poetry reading. He knew that the audience would comprise as many secret agents as genuine lovers of language.

Oblomov's first instinct had been to house Alexei in Lena Goracheva's boardinghouse. When his wife died from typhus, he took Lena as his mistress, and he often directed travelers to her address. But on further reflection, he decided that since the young man would be scouting the countryside, he couldn't properly take advantage of Lena's hospitality and cooking. Instead, he found him quarters in a run-down barrack on the grounds of the military training camp; and to navigate the oblast, he assigned him one of his dissolute colleagues, Yevgeny Peterov, who was given the authority to arrest any purveyor of false medical treatments.

Peterov requisitioned a horse and a low Finnish sleigh. In winter, the ancient Fiat car assigned him would not carry them any farther than the city limits. Having grown up in a farming family—his father had once owned land, though Peterov steadfastly denied it—he felt at home around horses. At the outbreak of the Civil War, a group of Red Army men had swept through his village and inducted him into their company. Wholly uninterested in politics, he never knew exactly what principles he was fighting for, but did know that the availability of drink and whores perfectly suited his tastes. His comrades called him Casanova and Romeo; they also called him brave because he seemed oblivious to his own safety, frequently charging enemy positions with only a rifle. When the Soviets accused his father of holding land and charging interest on loans to peasants, Yevgeny pleaded ignorance, saying that he and his father rarely spoke, a statement supported by neighbors who said that the father beat the boy as a child, and that in later years the boy beat the father.

Together, Alexei and Yevgeny set out, like Don Quixote and Sancho Panza, on a quest more illusory than real. Although the countryside was rife with illness and the two men slept in barns and huts and on the floors of hovels, eating what others ate, earning the trust of the peasants proved difficult. The moment the two arrived in a village, no one would identify the potion peddlers. Alexei would ask to speak to the nurse or midwife, since doctors were virtually nonexistent. Most hamlets housed neither. He would then question the villagers about their medicaments and treatments, as well as the advice they had received on how to prevent cholera, typhus, scrofulous, botulism, and polio. Frequently, Alexei would gather the locals and lecture them on the origins of illness: on the nature of germs and viruses. During these presentations, he never failed to notice how many young people supported themselves with crutches, usually the result of polio. As for Yevgeny, once he had heard the lecture, he saw no need to hear it again. So he would find a bottle of vodka or a plump peasant girl or both and disappear for the rest of the evening.

Eventually, word spread through the oblast that Alexei had been sent by the government to improve their well-being, a rumor that led people to reveal their maladies and remedies, but not the toadstool doctors on whom they relied. After all, Alexei would be leaving, and the quacks staying. What other alternative did the afflicted have? Folk medicine filled the void. Alexei therefore begged the villagers to heed his warnings: Mercury, as surely as arsenic, poisons. Radium burns and leads to a painful lingering death. Snake venom paralyzes the nervous system and fails to cure seizures. Horseradish and turmeric do not arrest cancer, nor do electric shocks. Hot baths and petroleum soaks may feel good but cannot cure or relieve tuberculosis. Ice baths or winter baptisms do not dispel killing fevers, even if the patient's temperature falls temporarily. Powdered tiger teeth or monkey testicles or rhino horns do not restore virility. Mandrake roots are a fiction, and medical science, as yet, has no remedy for female sterility. Holy relics are probably not holy, and they have never proved a balm for palsy or dropsy or ague. If found trading in such items, the dealer could find himself imprisoned for five or ten years, perhaps longer.

A favorite "cure" that had lingered in illiterate communities, and one which fraudulent healers and itinerant priests exploited, was the casting out of devils. Alexei told the people that they were not possessed, that the idea of exorcism came from the Middle Ages, that devils did not exist, and that those who foisted on the sick this superstition were saying, wrongly, that they had made themselves ill. Could a person make himself sick? Yes, from frequent drinking, excessive eating, smoking, living in unhygienic conditions, and resorting to quack remedies.

When medicine was unavailable were prayers an alternative? Alexei knew the penalty for promoting religion, but in the midst of such abysmal poverty and endemic ignorance, he felt that he could not rob the people of all hope; he therefore told them that if prayers made them feel good, and if they were convinced that they helped, then by all means pray, but not in lieu of seeking legitimate medical help.

After weeks on the rutted roads, caramelized with ice, they found, like Peter the Great, that the icy sledge paths made an ideal highway. Had they been traveling in spring, they would have cursed the ankle-deep mud brought on by the thaws. But they returned to Voronezh in the dark of February, heroes of the countryside and, except for their failure to apprehend felons, celebrities in the city. How many bastard children Peterov had fathered would not be known until fall. The last leg of their journey, the fastest, had been by train, which Alexei cursed for its stopping at every station, so great was his desire to receive Natasha's letters, even if they were banal. But outside of Voronezh, at an army garrison, several soldiers had been diagnosed with cholera. A telegraph sent to one of the train stations directed Alexei to stop at the camp.

Working next to an army doctor, Viktor Gubin Podol, he instructed the soldiers on proper hygiene and suggested to Viktor that the sewage system might be the source of the outbreak. An investigation of the clay pipes discovered numerous leaks that had affected the well water from which the garrison drew. Viktor congratulated Alexei on his good thinking and said that a celebratory drink was in order.

"I'll have my driver take us to our glorious state-run inn," said Viktor derisively. "I want to get away from this pestiferous base."

That evening a black Zim car carried the men into town, where Viktor, who had a low threshold for alcohol, quickly succumbed to drunkenness on the hundred-proof vodka. Alexei sipped his drink, fearing the effects. The half-timbered inn brought to mind Falstaffian revelers and buxom barmaids, even though the flat-chested woman who served them was glum. Their table, with innumerable names and symbols carved into the wood, the low ceiling, darkened from years of smoke, the roaring fireplace, the oak logs, and the formal barkeep, wearing a leather apron, pouring drinks and toting up Viktor's bill on a tab that he kept in a drawer, invoked England not the USSR.

"Did I ever tell you," Viktor slurred, "how I came to be posted at this god-forsaken place?" Before Alexei could answer, Viktor continued in his drooling fashion. "Because of a woman. A beautiful girl at a state clinic. I took her for a meadow walk . . ." He laughed. "I needn't tell you what I mean by *that*, and the bitch reported me. Can you imagine? There we were by the creek, birds singing, may flies thick as dust. I did what any red-blooded Russian would do. But when I unbuttoned, she refused. None of the other women ever complained. I had to put a pistol to her head."

Sprawling across the table, he passed out.

As Alexei expected, Oblomov handed him a full bag of mail. With Natasha having promised to write every day, he could hardly wait for the evening, to sit, read her letters, and picture her incomparable face. After two months of listening to Yevgeny's stories, repeated endlessly, and having to save him from irate fathers who insisted he marry their daughters, he was glad to be rid of the drunken Casanova. Had Alexei not been faithful to his wife, he could have acted on the numerous offers that women, lovely and ugly, had extended to him. One young widow, in particular, had caught his eye, and although he took a modest supper with her and a sip of homemade vodka, he refused the offer to share her bed. Thoughts of Natasha kept him pure.

Upon receiving his mail, he quickly rustled through it, identifying dozens of postings from his Leningrad friends, most now certified doctors and practicing in various cities. Pocketing the numerous letters from his wife, he soon discovered that she seemed unable to rise above the boring and bromidic. He could have cried. One of the letters he actually burned.

My dear Alexei,

Life without you is tedious. I go to work each day and come home. Razan adopted a little girl. She's ten. I like her. We sometimes do things together. Mother is mother. She's always looking for ways to you know what. Would you believe that I saw a woman in a mink coat? She was walking on Arbat Street. I guess she's the wife of some high official. I'm hoping that Razan will become a high official and buy us a car. How are you? Do you think of me? I try to keep busy so as not to think of you. Write me!

Love and kisses, N.

Since Natasha had no way of knowing when Alexei was returning to Voronezh, he took his time writing back.

Dear Natasha,

I received your many letters and read them several times. Their shortness I can ascribe only to your busy schedule. You say nothing of the child your parents adopted; you don't even mention her name. What is she like? What led Razan to select her and not some other child? You say nothing of your stepfather's work in the Kremlin. Surely he must see and hear things that would make for an interesting tale. Or is he forbidden to talk about his work and the people he meets? I was glad to hear that your mother has not lost any of her energy for you know what. She's an amazing woman.

In the town of N____, I met a woman who had been stricken with polio as a child. She walks with two sticks, and yet she manages to raise three children and care for her house. Her husband died the year before in a farm accident, but she soldiers on. She asked me if I had any medicine that could ease the pain in her stick-thin legs and could keep her own children from the crippling disease. (I even enjoyed her cooking one night.) You have no idea how many children have died or been disabled by this terrible disease. Some are reduced to pushing themselves around on boards with wheels. The peasants seem not to notice, a fact that horrifies me.

Can you imagine what it would be like to have a child stricken so badly that he can't lift his head off the pillow or move a limb? Polio epidemics are the scourge of the world. We must find a cure for this dreadful disease. Worst of all, though, is the widespread hunger. The government blames it on hoarders and looters, but I saw no evidence of either. What I did see were children with distended stomachs and lolling tongues, adults with no more skin on their bones than a rotting carcass, empty storage bins, silos, and larders, withered crops, blasted fields, and failed farm equipment. I could not help but think that this disaster was man-made. And yet we are told that the people are well fed and warmly clothed. No one decries the cholera and typhus. I begin to wonder what world the government is describing, certainly not the one I have seen.

The man I traveled with was a jovial drunk who ran after women. Had it not been for his ability to handle our horse and sled, I would have dumped him at the first tavern. Except for driving us once into a snowbank when besotted, he negotiated the frozen roads with skill. He also loved telling jokes. Here's one you might enjoy. An illiterate peasant was told to report to the local military officer for induction into the army. The man showed up and said that he was unfit for service. "Why is that?" asked the recruiter. The peasant held out his right hand. The index finger was retracted, as if paralyzed. "It's my trigger finger," said the peasant. "It's been frozen in this position for years." The recruiter shook his head. "I see. But tell me, Ivan, what was the finger like before the paralysis?" The peasant straightened his index finger and held up his hand. "Like this!" he said.

Given what I have experienced on this trip, I find Yevgeny's jokes my only relief. Write me with some details. I long to hear about your life.

Love, A.

When Alexei returned to Voronezh, his meritorious record persuaded Oblomov to house him with his mistress, Lena Goracheva, the widow of Major Gorachev, a hero in the Great War, who had left Lena a house with an attic apartment that she rented to supplement her modest pension. It was here that the commissar of police brought Alexei, leaving the barrack behind. Lena was delighted to have as a tenant a young medical student, even if he was labeled an enemy of the people. Her usual renters were government bureaucrats who bored her with their constant repetition of official phraseology that celebrated the "New Soviet Man" and "Five-Year plans" and "engineers of the human soul" and "phases" and "the dictatorship of the proletariat." She looked forward to talking about actual events and to consulting Alexei about the sciatic nerve pain at the back of her leg.

Lena and Oblomov were very proper in the presence of Alexei. As the commissar left the sitting room, he said to the young man:

"Lena's specialty is potatoes and beets. She can prepare them a hundred different ways."

Alexei replied dryly, "I can't wait."

As the door closed, Lena lifted Alexei's valise as easily as a down pillow and carried it to the attic. A muscular peasant woman with a broad Tatar face and narrow eyes, she had a man's shoulders and a braid that ran down her back like a Chinese coolie. Before Alexei could object, she had snapped opened his valise and started to store his belongings in the armoire and small chest of drawers.

"These shirts," she said, "who's been pressing them? They need a woman's touch."

She gathered them up and disappeared downstairs.

Alexei smiled thinking of how her robustness would appeal to Oblomov. He could imagine them engaged in sweaty lovemaking, though "wrestling matches" would be more accurate.

By the time she returned, Alexei had put his trousers and jackets in the armoire—his overcoat didn't fit. Having filled the two drawers in the chest, he left his sweaters in the valise and emptied his satchel of the half dozen medical books he had brought into exile. All of them treated maladies of the brain and psychiatric subjects, the very studies in which he had intended to specialize during his residency.

When Lena neatly laid the shirts on the bed for Alexei to admire, she remarked, "You'll never hear a mean word out of me. I'm not like that harridan Mrs. Minkskovia. But whoever's been mending and ironing your shirts neglected a few rips and took no time with the pressing. The missing buttons I replaced."

"You're a wonder."

"Now, some of these women who keep boarders . . . like Mrs. Minkskovia across the road . . . the things I could tell you."

Alexei added ironically, "But you won't."

"Not unless, of course, you really want to know," she said, hoping to be asked.

"Perhaps some other time."

Lena opened the chest of drawers. "Just checking to see if you put away your clothing in an orderly fashion." She held up a pair of suspenders. "Are these yours?"

"I wore them in medical school."

"In Voronezh, unless you want to stand out, which is always a mistake, I'd suggest you wear belts. My late husband had some nice ones I gave away. But I still have a few you can choose from. The last person I ever saw with suspenders was a doctor from Leningrad who stayed in this very room for two months while treating patients and holding . . . what's the word?"

"Seminars?"

"Yes, running seminars in the local hospitals. His name will come to me in a minute."

"If you don't mind, Mrs. Goracheva, I need a place to hang my overcoat. The armoire is too small."

"I'll put it in the hall closet. Hasn't this weather been bitter? The doctor who stayed here briefly, he too came in the middle of winter. Never dressed warmly enough. Rarely wore a muffler. Chulkaturin! That was his name. I knew it'd come to me."

"Not Dr. Semyon Chulkaturin?"

"That was him. Like I said, he slept in this very room."

"I studied with him! He worked with Freud."

"Never met Mr. Freud. But as for Dr. Chulkaturin . . . where else would a gentleman stay? Certainly not with Mrs. Bizmionkova—that shrew! Oh, you can be sure she tried to steal him away, with her jam tarts and honeyed words. But he knew which boardinghouse was the better one. I always mind my own business. Why, I've never even peeked at the notebook he left behind."

"A notebook here in your house?"

"On top of the armoire, like he was trying to hide it. But since I keep a house as neat as a pin, when I dusted I found it. A lined notebook, filled from front to back."

"May I see it?"

"Well, I don't know. It's not my property. I don't want any trouble. I should have turned it over to the police long ago."

"The fact that you haven't leads me to believe . . ."

"I'm not a poor woman, Dr. von Fresser, nor a rich one."

The construction of her sentence led Alexei to ask, "How much would you accept for the notebook?"

"You won't think me mercenary?"

"Not at all."

"Thirty rubles."

Alexei had been receiving regular money transfers from his mother during his medical studies in Leningrad. He and Natasha could barely live on the government stipend. When she learned of his exile, Anna had sent him a large sum, but how long could he live off the largesse of his mother-in-law and Razan? He needed to practice economy.

"Commissar Oblomov said, 'Anything you need, you just ask Lena. She'll tend to your needs.'"

"I'll settle for twenty."

"Perhaps you really should turn it over to the police."

Mrs. Goracheva was now torn. She could give it to the authorities, hold out for her price—but who would buy it?—or sell it for less. Alexei was unlikely to inform and to risk his own safety.

Trying another approach, Alexei soothingly said, "For helping medical science, I should think they'd give you a medal."

"A medal!"

"With a picture of Stalin."

Lena sighed, "Iosif Vissarionovich Dzhugashvili, I think, is the handsomest man in Russia, don't you? His portrait hangs in my room."

"No doubt about it. He cuts quite an imposing figure."

"Ten rubles and no less."

"Agreed."

"I'll get the book in the morning. It's stored in the basement."

That night Alexei dreamed of standing before the king of Sweden to receive the Nobel Prize for medicine, while Dr. Chulkaturin sat in the first row tapping his foot. "For original contributions to psychiatry . . ." said the king, a statement that elicited mocking laughter from Dr. Chulkaturin. Alexei was glad to see the morning. He had just finished dressing when voices sounded in the entry hall. Opening his door, he heard his name, but couldn't follow the discussion, except for the mention of a "Dr. Leshin," followed by the title "medical examiner." Had some high official resented his good work and come to tell him to pack his bags and live on the street?

After several minutes, Mrs. Goracheva called to him. He quickly put on a tie and jacket and descended the stairs. Lena said that two men, in the sitting room, wished to speak to him. Tucked under her arm was a notebook.

"I tried to worm their business out of them," she murmured, "but they're as stony as the secret police," a reference that so unnerved Alexei that he excused himself to stop at the lavatory.

A man resembling Lenin, with wide nostrils, searching eyes, and a Van Dyke beard, stood in front of the stove. Thin and rabbitlike in his movements, he first introduced his associate, Leonid Basmanaya, a portly well-dressed fellow whose jelly jowls shook in unison with his head movements, and then himself.

"I am Dr. Leshin, Andrei Leshin, the medical examiner for Voronezh oblast. Commissar Oblomov reported glowingly on your work in the province." He shook Alexei's hand. "I have already made some telephone calls this morning to Leningrad and discovered that your interest lies in psychiatry. Is that right?"

"Yes."

"I see no reason to waste your talents hunting quacks. We have a clinic with a mental ward reserved for the commissariat and special cases. Interested? The previous doctor was transferred."

"And you," Basmanaya chuckled, as he extended a hand to Alexei, "are now a Voronezh regular. You're a fiver. The years go quickly."

A stoic Dr. Leshin observed, "That ought to give you enough time to reorganize the ward and put in place current psychiatric theories. Of all the specialties, I think psychiatry is the most misunderstood, even though one of the most important."

"After Leningrad," said Basmanaya, "you'll find that life here lacks city refinements. The clinic, though, relieves the boredom."

"Comrade Basmanaya," said Dr. Leshin, "is in charge of the clinic. He can tell you about the wards, the pharmacy, the staff, and the patients, only a few of whom are in the mental ward."

"We have our rules," said Basmanaya. "Ward One is for physical care, surgery and the like. Ward Two for mental patients. Ward Three is the isolation ward used for special mental cases."

"You have patients whom you quarantine?"

"One. The subject insisted on writing articles critical of the state and is hostile to treatment. So we had to resort to isolation."

"You will find," said Dr. Leshin, "that we have a rather good library at the clinic."

"Journals, too?" asked Alexei.

"I hope your question means," said Dr. Leshin, "that you want to engage in research. Have you ever published a scientific paper?"

"Yes, a theoretical one."

"So have I," said Dr. Leshin, "several."

"May I ask about what?"

"Human nature. I have a theory, based of course on my many years of observations."

Alexei nodded approvingly. "In medical school we learned that theory without observation is blind."

"I am preparing a paper right now for the *Red Army Review*, in which I argue that freedom is just another name for indecision. Accomplishments are fathered by rules."

"My paper treated the use of stories to help the mentally ill. Perhaps I could treat the person in quarantine."

Dr. Leshin's laugh sounded like boots crushing glass. "The patient fancies herself a musician, not a lover of fairy tales."

"Actually," Basmanaya added, "she plays the flute rather well, but we deny her requests for sheet music. Slander has its penalties."

"Are you sure that's the best way to proceed?"

"I love music," said Basmanaya. "My wife and I both play the violin."

"If you'd let me see her . . ."

"Ward Three? Impossible!" interrupted Dr. Leshin. "Denial of desire is the best way to discipline a recalcitrant patient. When she agrees to behave, she can have music."

Alexei, well aware that a long prison sentence or exile frees a person to act and say what he will, decided to personally exploit that fact. What more can they do to me now? he thought. Extend my sentence? Freedom cannot be counted in years. Death? Isn't that also a kind of freedom, albeit a different kind?

"We know," said Alexei, "that stutterers lose their speech impediments when they sing. I believe that stories can equally clear the malaise in the minds of some mentally ill patients."

"Perhaps," replied Dr. Leshin, unmoved. "I'll keep your theory in mind. In my experience, however, some people are never able to dispel the stone in their brain. They get an idea and then marry it."

"How many patients are currently in the mental ward?"

"Four in Ward Two."

"And the previous doctor?"

"A headstrong type," said Basmanaya, "recalled at our request."

"I assume his medical charts and notes are available. I'd like to see them before meeting the patients."

Basmanaya looked torn. "You can have all but Ward Three."

"Where are those records?"

"Comrade von Fresser," said Leshin, "you will discover that life here runs smoothly when one, shall we say, keeps his own counsel."

"I see. No records."

"Not that we have anything to hide," added Basmanaya. "Quite the contrary. It's just that we try to keep the clinic safe from the stain of scandal."

"Are you suggesting . . ." said Alexei, unsure of how to continue.

Dr. Leshin stroked his pointed beard with his index finger, and with the toe of his boot traced a pattern in the Asian rug. "Comrade von Fresser, I started my medical career at the front during the Great War. From my army comrades, I learned a useful lesson: Rules free a man from the vagaries of choice. Follow the orders of your superiors, and you'll fit right in."

As soon as the door closed behind the two men, Alexei paid Lena Goracheva for the notebook and repaired to his attic room, with its sloping roof and front window that looked out on an oak tree and the street. He sat in the rocking chair and turned on the floor lamp. In the orange glow, he held Chulkaturin's notebook gently, as one might a rare manuscript. Chulkaturin, an eminent scientist whom Alexei had eagerly studied with, had an international reputation for his work in the field of schizophrenia and what Freud called "the talking cure," psychoanalysis. His colleagues often said that if any patient had unhealthy, buried sexual memories, Chulkaturin could unearth them and neutralize their harmful effects.

The notebook began with the following entry.

Thursday, December 5th, 1931. Once again Rissa was terrified at the mention of Dr. P___. Her hatred of authority runs deep, or is it merely a fear of military personnel? Although Dr. P___ seemed competent when I interviewed him in his new quarters, if I mention his name to Rissa she becomes uncommunicative.

A knock at the door interrupted his reading. Mrs. Goracheva had brought him a cup of tea.

"It's spiced with a special mushroom," she said, "which settles the mind and brings on sweet dreams. A Persian apothecary stops in Voronezh once a month. I buy it from him."

Alexei had read about mushrooms in one of his pharmacology books. Some were quite poisonous; some induced hallucinations. Indians in various countries were known to use mushrooms for their religious ceremonies and regarded them as beneficial. He thanked Lena for her thoughtfulness, sipped the drink, and resumed reading the notebook. A short time later, he heard his name being called and recognized Dr. Chulkaturin seated on the floor, in front of the armoire.

"I confess: After just a few weeks, I was in love with her."

"It's apparent," Alexei replied, "from your notes."

"She's exotically beautiful. Thick dark hair. Her movements," he moved his hips, "remind me of dancing girls in Marrakech."

"Doctors shouldn't fall in love with their patients."

"But they often do. She has an American blues singer's throaty voice, but it's her rapturous flute playing . . ."

"This information will prove useful."

"Ah, to be young again, no wrinkles, no warts. And yet . . ."

"What?"

"I worry about her obsessiveness. She always plays the same music and repeats certain measures. According to Freud, it must be something she's suppressing. I should have tried sodium pentothol."

"Hmm, that's an idea. According to your own articles, it's not unusual for patients to be confused about their identity. You suggest in your notes that her fondness for riddles indicates as much."

"And those damned flute passages that she plays hours on end."

"Perhaps she is trying to signal what she can't say."

"Whenever I ask her to stop, she always obliges."

"Someone right now is playing the Mozart Flute Concerto no. 2 in D Major. Do you not hear it in the distance, Dr. Chulkaturin?"

"I wrote her a poem.
In Samarkand, where I am bound,
I'm told that peacocks perch on every roof,
And cry their soulful sound."

Alexei held up the notebook and pointed to a passage. "You said: 'The more I learn about Rissa Binderova, the greater my feelings for her. Perhaps I should stop now before it's too late.'"

"I should have followed my own advice. What a fool!" He shook his head. "I was warned not to go near her. But once we . . ."

"A man away from home, especially in a town of exiles, craves the touch of a woman. Was that it?"

"I held her hands as we spoke, and as her fingers mingled with mine . . ." He entwined his fingers. "I was caught, like a magnet drawn to metal. Nothing else mattered."

"When you wrote, 'Such a shame, such a waste of a young Jewess in the bloom of life . . . if only I could take her with me back to Leningrad,' did you actually have a choice? Would the authorities have released her to your care?"

"Probably not, but then I never insisted."

Alexei felt an inexplicable anger. "You're asthmatic. Married. Two grown sons. You're an old man. What are you talking about?"

"I could have kept her as a mistress. I wouldn't be the first. Just consider all the men around Stalin who keep girlfriends in rich apartments. And just imagine her devotion to me for arranging her release from this jail!"

"Filthy bastards! I'll bet Stalin's aides are all married."

"Of course, but marriage grows stale."

"She's my contemporary, not yours!" Alexei said, furiously shaking the notebook. Surprised by his anger, he pondered its source.

"You don't even know her. Idealization has its dangers, Alexei, as you know from your psychiatric studies. Besides, you've recently wed. Why the sudden change from purist to playboy?"

"Natasha's in Moscow, and her letters bore me silly. Besides, I'm here, and she's there."

"Perhaps she's saying the same thing. Has she requested permission to visit you in Voronezh? But of course, it's forbidden." He smiled. "Maybe you ought to meet Rissa and make her acquaintance. It won't be easy. Ward Three. She's mad, you know."

Chulkaturin laughed teasingly and slowly disappeared, as Alexei slumped in his chair profoundly asleep.

The next morning, Alexei gave strict instructions to Lena never again to lace his tea with a mushroom. "Persian or no Persian apothecary. The mushrooms you buy have psychedelic properties that act like a drug and induce dreams."

He took his coat from the front closet, stepped into the cold, and hailed a Fiat taxi to take him first to the post office and then to the clinic.

Basmanaya greeted him warmly in the lobby under a large picture of Stalin, and started his tour of the facilities with a stop at the pharmacy. Alexei had anticipated seeing a counter and an attendant in a white coat waiting to serve the staff. Instead, he saw an old man with a scraggly beard tending a storeroom of a few shelves that held boxes marked "Cotton Balls," "Rubber Gloves," "Benzodiazepines," "Sodium Pentothol," "Ether Masks," "Sulfur," "Syringes," and similar medical names. The old man, who was introduced as Comrade Lvov, exhibited courtly manners. Alexei guessed at once that the man hailed from the old school, the landed aristocracy.

"Comrade Lvov is indispensable in the dispensary," laughed Basmanaya, amused at his own play on words. "He works long hours and will open the pharmacy in the middle of the night if we need him."

Alexei gathered from the stock in the storeroom that although the doctors in the main ward, the one that treated physical ailments, frequented the pharmacy, the clinic stood ready to use psychotic drugs when the need arose. Before he and Basmanaya continued their tour of the premises, a young doctor entered and handed Comrade Lvov a book. Alexei could see the title: *What Is to Be Done?* What he couldn't see was whether the book was the novel by Nikolai Chernyshevsky or the political tract by Lenin, who had appropriated the title for his own book. Alexei smirked. Lenin had already shown, disastrously, what was to be done, and now Stalin was having his way. What did the title augur for him?

Comrade Lvov took the book, thanked the doctor, and remarked insincerely, "Such an important book. I have always wanted to read it." He looked blankly at Alexei, who slyly winked.

Basmanaya led his charge out of the pharmacy and into Wards One and Two. The director introduced the other members of the medical staff, all of whom seemed dedicated doctors as well as patriotic Soviets, who hailed him as "comrade" and "a hero of the people" and "one of Stalin's vanguard."

Alexei smiled appreciatively. The women's section of Ward Two housed six beds, only one of them occupied. Helena Schmidt came from a wealthy German family that dated back to the building of the Voronezh shipyards. A stately gray-haired doyen of Voronezh, she had frequently hosted salons that brought together artists of every political persuasion. Her numerous lovers were all conquered by her stately Nordic face, with its unblemished pale skin, brilliant blue eyes, small mouth, and perfect teeth. Proud of her Teutonic forebears, she made no effort to hide her critical views of Lenin and other so-called Bolshevik philosophers, all of whom she regarded as muddled.

"You are marked down as 'politically insane,' not 'criminally,'" Alexei said, as he pulled up a chair. "What put you in trouble?"

"Lenin," she said, "*das Ekel*, the horrible man."

"Did you know him?"

She laughed. "Au contraire. I never wished to. But I have read his nonsense and often said he was a dreamer, a man who took irrational German thought—romanticism—and fused it with French *idéalisme*. The result was, *horribile dictu*! an unsystematic belief that everyone could be equal and free and could finally *Live*, with a capital L, whatever that means. I used to bring together people interested in high culture. During these soirees, I'd speak my mind. One of the guests told the secret police that I had spoken derogatorily about Comrade Lenin. The head of the GPU called on me to ask whether the charge was true. 'I do not cavil,' I said, 'nor do I countenance falsehood. Your odious informant spoke the truth.' The idiot told me that just because I had earned a degree in philosophy, I had no right to question orthodox Soviet thought. 'Even if I'm a democratic socialist?' I asked. 'How can you be a socialist,' he replied, 'if you do not agree with Comrade Lenin?' 'Neither do a great many others,' I answered. An otiose judge subsequently charged me with crimes against the state. The local Soviet found me guilty without allowing me to voice my objections. No doubt because of my family's affiliation with Peter the Great, they offered me two choices: a work camp or a mental ward. And here I am."

Well aware that thousands of people thought Lenin's ideas vague and airy, Alexei concluded that Helena's position in the community, as a grande dame and the daughter of a distinguished family, explained her having been brought not to the city hospital but to the commissariat clinic. He would compare her statements with Basmanaya's records to double-check her story.

As Alexei and Basmanaya strolled out of the woman's section of Ward Two, Alexei asked, "Where is Ward Three, where your other female patient is lodged?"

The director pointed to a branching hallway at the end of the ward. "Miss Rissa Binderova is confined to her own quarters down there, behind a locked door, but she has permission to play the flute and dress as she likes. She has limited freedoms."

"Exercise?"

A stoical Basmanaya said, "Twice a week. When she agrees to write in the Soviet mode, and not seditiously, she can go."

"But certainly she's no worse than Helena Schmidt, a 'political' also. What crime would justify two years of solitary confinement?"

Basmanaya, looking as if someone had squeezed his testicles, wheezed, "Her scribblings were the work of a mad person and reached a far larger audience than Helena's artist friends. To rail against paradise indicates the presence of a dangerous malady."

"Until now, Comrade Basmanaya, I had never really heard the diagnosis for dissidents so clearly expressed. The Soviet Union is paradise. Those who cannot appreciate paradise are mad and therefore need to be treated. Thank you for the exposition."

"Worse than mad! Miss Binderova comes from a prominent family, a fact that we have taken into consideration by giving her a private room and special attention."

"I would like to speak to her—to confirm your diagnosis. Besides, I have treated dissidents before, with some success."

Basmanaya's grim expression argued that Alexei would not be allowed to see this particular patient, and certainly not alone.

"What if you accompanied me when I talked to her? Call it a test case." He winked at Basmanaya. "After all, if one of your patients exiled for unsocial behavior was cured of her pathology, you would be written up in the medical annals and acclaimed."

Basmanaya, always susceptible to honors, felt the force of Dr. Leshin's orders weakening. What if this man was right? To save so many people from error might earn the clinic director a medal.

"Dr. Leshin will surely object."

"I'll assume the responsibility for the decision, and if it proves wrong, I'll shoulder the blame."

Basmanaya looked left and right. "When do you have in mind?"

"Tomorrow or the next day. In the meantime, I can speak to the men assigned to Ward Two."

"Tomorrow, then."

Basmanaya and Alexei entered the men's section of Ward Two. Here he introduced the doctor to the three men, and excused himself, but not before Alexei reminded him that he had not yet received the medical charts. The director assured him that by the end of the day, they'd be available. Alexei huddled collectively with the patients in the ward to determine how they perceived their maladies, which in turn might indicate a pattern of anti-Soviet madness.

"I am perplexed," he said, sitting on a stool, "that you three gentlemen have been singled out for the clinic and not the general hospital. Tell me about yourselves and how you got here."

The men, only too glad to share their personal histories, all started talking at once.

"Let's begin alphabetically," said Alexei diplomatically.

Benjamin Federov, a sunken-cheeked balding fellow, sat on a stool with ramrod straight posture and pronounced his consonants with the purity of a voice teacher. Claiming that his parents had owned a distillery that was confiscated by the government, he explained, "In the company of my parents I traveled to Moscow to speak to Comrade Stalin. At the gates of the Kremlin we were arrested, questioned, and told that the government knew we were hoarding money and other valuables, like jewelry. They would allow us to go free only if we turned over our treasures." He turned out his empty pockets.

"Nothing! What we didn't know, until the police questioned us, was that our family had been denounced. They said they had letters that proved we had grown wealthy on the backs of the poor. My parents, aristocrats by nature, refused to reply, and were sent to camps where they died in less than a year. The Soviets figured that if I also passed away they would never recover our hidden wealth, so they sent me here, with the understanding that I could leave when I revealed what they wanted to know." He made an obscene gesture. "They should all bite their tongues and die of the poison!"

Alexei noted that Benjamin Federov's narrative did not include a denial of secreted wealth. But then, under these circumstances, a man might say anything. Again, he would have to check Benjamin's statements against the first doctor's notes.

Arkady Gorbatov came from a family of actors celebrated for their satiric impersonations and miming of famous people. A tall man, his body, thin and sinewy, exhibited a contortionist's flexibility. When he spoke, he repeatedly used his left thumb and index finger to stroke the enormous handlebar mustache that reached to his chin.

"I learned the art from my family. We traveled through Russia and most of Europe. My father's specialty was poking fun at famous musicians, like Rachmaninoff and Paderewski, and my mother's realm was ballerinas. In the Baltics, I started satirizing Stalin, using a false mustache and, because I am tall, walking on my knees to imitate that dwarf." He fell to his knees to demonstrate. "The GPU heard, and I was put in irons and brought here from Estonia.

Since they won't let me write letters, I am lost to my parents, assuming they are even alive. Like most prisoners in this country, you get a choice: obey and perhaps be released or resist and be jailed. I too was given a choice. Koba wanted me to perform in Moscow. I was to impersonate Tsar Nicholas Alexandrovich Romanov and the Empress Alexandra Feodorovna. But how can you lampoon a couple who once governed this country and were savagely murdered? I couldn't."

"Are you a monarchist?" asked Alexei.

"No, an artiste. I respect all people. Satire, when used as it should be, is directed at people we wish to correct."

Alexei was willing to wager that Arkady's family had once performed for the Tsar. It would be easy enough to find out.

The third man, Sviatoslav Sarkaski, a nuclear physicist, looked as if his neck and chest had melted into his abdomen. He was a trinity of legs, stomach, and head. Alexei likened him to a three-act play with a final fourth act yet to be written.

"You ask," he said to Alexei, "why I am here and not in the city hospital. A good question. I told the secret police that if I was truly out of my mind they should lock me up with real madmen so that I could escape to the garden, like the writer Vsevolod Garshin, and pluck red flowers."

Alexei knew the story to which the physicist was alluding, one in which the mental patient wants to take upon himself all the suffering of the world and, by plucking the bloody blooms, dispel evil.

"Are you Christ?" asked Alexei, trying to determine whether the man suffered from delusions. "Or do you feel like a savior?"

"Sometimes, but not in the religious sense."

"Then how?"

With his hands at his back, he paced. "Nuclear physics can save the world or destroy it, which endows people like me with awesome powers, a fact that I have repeatedly tried to impress upon my colleagues, who seem not to realize how great is their moral duty to do good and not evil."

Alexei had taken courses in physics but felt out of his depth discussing the subject with a man as prominent as Dr. Sarkaski, whom both Lenin and Stalin had once honored. The scientist had presumably fallen out of favor by choosing not to work on nuclear projects he feared might accidentally incinerate the globe.

"Do you think of scientists as the new gods, the modern messiahs, who can create the world anew, so to speak?"

"Do they have the means? Perhaps. Are they gods? Absolutely not. Most of them are prisoners of their own science and, all too often, prisoners of the official ideology."

"I suppose that you, too, have been told that if you agree to do as you're asked—in your case, resume your research in nuclear physics—you'll be released. But you have refused."

"Your diagnosis is correct, Dr. von Fresser. Your predecessor insisted that my presence in the laboratory might restrain the zealots. Might or might not, I said. More likely my presence would be interpreted as a vote of confidence. That I could not allow, if you see my point."

"Then you regard my working in this clinic in a similar light?"

"Yes."

"I am putting my medical knowledge in the service of a government that you find . . ."

Turning his head to one side, he said, "Reprehensible."

"So you, too, are a 'political'?"

He shook his head yes. "When Thoreau was arrested for refusing to pay his taxes because he said they would go to support an unjust war, Emerson visited and asked him what he was doing in jail. Thoreau responded, 'What are you doing outside of jail?'"

Alexei found this exchange disquieting. He would have preferred to keep the discussion on a philosophical level, not a personal one. But Dr. Sarkaski's comments had made it appear that Alexei was just another apparatchik.

"I have been exiled for five years—for political reasons," said Alexei calmly, producing a document of his sentence. "I could have continued working in the countryside among the poor or work here. Once you have seen the ninth circle of hell, and tried to ameliorate the suffering there, you gladly accept the chance to serve people like you. Frankly, the task is lighter and I enjoy the company of well-educated people. If my impulses offend you, tell me, and I promise to maintain my distance."

"The better choice," said Sviatoslav, before taking to his bed and burying his head in the pillow, "would have been to suffer the cold of the street and to beg for your bread rather than serve these villainous creatures."

As Alexei exited the clinic, he chose to walk home in the frigid air to clear his head, which at the moment was in turmoil over Thoreau's point that conscience matters more than the law. He headed for the post office to collect his afternoon mail, hoping to find one from Natasha full of love and well wishing—and wit. The postmaster chuckled as he removed mail from a special slot marked "Exiles" and sorted through it to find Alexei's.

"That was quite a good joke about the peasant and the paralyzed finger. I laughed heartily."

Yes, all the stories were true. Any mail posted by an exile was read by the authorities and censored for speaking ill of the state. But which subjects and words constituted "ill"?

"What was omitted?" asked Alexei, hoping that the letter wasn't completely gutted.

"Comrade Lipnoskii, you know there's no famine in the countryside. Stalin has forbidden the use of that word."

"I used the word hunger, not famine."

"Same thing," said the postmaster, who shrugged and returned to his desk, opening envelopes and reading through other people's mail.

Basmanaya, as promised, gave Alexei all the files of the former doctor, except Rissa Binderova's folder. He would read the notes at his leisure after Lena's dinner, which he prayed would not include potatoes or beets. Outside his bedroom window, the shape of the tree limbs fascinated him. He could stare for hours at nature's contours and marvel at the fact that no two trees or flowers were exactly the same, just as no two patients behaved identically; and if they did, madness would truly be afoot. Relaxing in his rocking chair with the files in his lap, he thumbed through them. For some reason, the former doctor's name had been blotted out, but not his medical notes: clinical facts about temperature, height, weight, physical abnormalities, toilet habits, and, of course, obsessions, by which the Soviet medical establishment meant wrong thinking. Alexei skimmed over the numbers and figures to look at the summaries, which had been written in a graceful hand and prose.

"Helena Schmidt is a 'political.' As with all the patients in the clinic, Dr. Leshin hopes that a mental hospital, by means of Freud's talking cure, will be able to reorder a person's mind. Although Dr. Leshin has allowed me the liberty to experiment, and although in her case I have, on more than one occasion, resorted to drugs, I have had no success in trying to alter the brain chemistry. In the end, I have to admit that talking with Helena has been more effective than trying to expunge her heresies with drugs.

"Note: I had far more success with drug therapy when I was assigned to the military hospital. Was it because the Red Army men were less educated than patient Schmidt, or was it because they so enjoyed the effect of the drugs that they said what I wanted to hear? Surely this conundrum is worth a scholarly paper.

"The hours I have spent talking to Helena Schmidt have led me to observe certain patterns. One, she resents being talked down to. At times she resorts to Russian Church Slavic, laced with lexical borrowings from German, English, Polish, Latin, and French. Her archaic language is clearly intended to reinforce her previous position among the aristocracy. When I ask her to speak simply, she says that she prefers the high style. I don't believe it will be possible to persuade her to avoid philosophy and learned diction for the sake of becoming one of the people. She abhors bad grammar and sneers at syntactical confusions. Her identity is wedded to her education in philosophy, her command of languages, her preference for Hobbes and Locke over Engels and Marx. Well aware that she has been sent to the clinic instead of the city hospital because of her family's history in the community, she feels it her duty to remain steadfast and not succumb to the bribe of Bolshevism."

"Benjamin Federov is an interesting case. He loves to talk about his former walks in the woods and bird-watching. By just sitting at his clinic window, he has amassed a great deal of data that any ornithologist would envy. He can even imitate the sounds of birds and identify avians from afar. This last activity takes place when he walks in the clinic garden. He will say, 'Did you hear that? It is the sound of a cuckoo.' Or is he merely engaging in self-parody? I sometimes wonder.

"I think that if his parents had not died in a camp we might have persuaded him to reveal the location of the family wealth. He knows the government wants to find it, so he deliberately teases me and others with comments like 'Have you ever seen a ruby as large as an egg, or a diamond as big as the Ritz?' This last comment, I think, is a literary allusion, but to what I don't know nor do I have the time to find it. He also speaks of rubles wrapped in canvas, neatly stacked in bundles of a thousand each. I suspect he's goading us, but I have no doubt the family hid away a great deal of money. Perhaps one day some peasant will unearth the treasure. I certainly hope so. But would the peasant notify the authorities or keep everything for himself? If I had to wager, I would bet on the latter.

"The family distillery, which has of course been confiscated, looms large in his speech. He describes the copper kettles that shone like the sun, and neglects to say that some exploited workers were undoubtedly assigned the task of polishing them. At the end of each day, the floors were always swept and the office windows washed. His father apparently sat at a large desk—a sexual allusion?—from which he commanded the workforce. I get the impression that patient Federov is expressing a subconscious desire to make love to all the women who worked in the distillery. Perhaps, though, if I used Marx instead of Freud, I would discover that Benjamin wants to lord over his workers not his sexual prowess but his financial power."

"Arkady Gorbatov has been investigated repeatedly by the secret police, and his family background scrutinized for aristocratic leanings. But nothing criminal has been reported. My sessions with him make me think that at some time he had a girlfriend or lover who came from wealth. He once said to me, 'I have known a woman from a loftier realm.' Surely, he could not have intended the statement to refer to the Virgin Mary? I must make a point of telling the police to check his past romantic relations. Once Russians come into contact with the aristocracy, they never recover. Their natural dreaminess is reinforced, and they start to assume airs. I am virtually certain that Arkady knew a woman who had once enjoyed a high estate. Why else refuse to perform for the Vozhd? And even more telling, why does he insist that the Romanovs were murdered when no one knows for sure? Rumors abound, I admit, but he seems convinced they were butchered, and he identifies with Tsarist society. Marx and Lenin rightly said a man would rather die than betray his class. But what they neglected to say was the converts are the worse. Take a man like Arkady, put him in the presence of a rich woman or let him stay overnight in a country house, and immediately he is defending the very class that has oppressed him his whole life. Even if my approach is wrong, I can't seem to make him understand that the Romanovs were no angels.

"On numerous occasions I have told him that Nicholas and Alexandra had nothing but scorn for people like him. So what makes him insist that it would be 'sacrilegious'—his word—to lampoon the two of them. The most unexpected details reveal what a person is really thinking. Who would have guessed that by Stalin's asking him to perform that he would behave like a royalist? The Vozhd is right. Constant vigilance is required because some kind of heresy is always lurking in the shadows.

"The secret police's idea that if we allowed him to write letters he would reveal the identity of the royalist relationship, and possibly a whole underground movement, proved fruitless. He wrote to theatre managers asking if they knew the whereabouts of his parents. What I have told him is untrue: that we have been keeping tabs on his parents, and if he cooperates we will put him in touch with them. He doesn't believe me. Or does he regard the respect that he bestows on the Romanovs as more compelling than a meeting with his family? An interesting possibility that deserves further study."

Before Alexei opened the last patient's folder, he was already disposed to believe that the clinic's mental ward held no ordinary people. They were all there for political reasons, yes, and had come from well-known families, but some part of the puzzle was missing.

"Sviatoslav Sarkaski mystifies me the most. By his own account, the work he was doing in physics could benefit all of mankind, but he refuses to continue his research because he fears that his work could be used for devilish ends. I have tried to explain that such an argument could be made about most ideas: They can be used for good or bad. What lies beneath the surface is a distrust of the Soviets, though he won't admit it. I have asked him would he take external exile if it were offered to him and perhaps work for England or America? He insists that he loves his country and his language, but says that his experiments in the wrong hands could put an end to planet earth. Absurd!

"When I question how any force could destroy all living things, he merely scoffs that my training is not sufficient for me to understand. The arrogant bastard! As a matter of fact, I did very well in physics at the science institute and thought seriously of spending my life working in a lab, but my humanitarian impulses got the better of me, and I have devoted my life to securing the mental health of our people.

"He likes to pace and peer out of the window through his thick binocular glasses. He reminds me of a pale shrunken monk grasping the window grating of his cell, knowing that he is vegetating, withering, drying up, wishing he had never taken holy vows. The only thing absent is a tolling bell, to summon his friends to hear a sermon sung in his honor. Like all intellectuals, he has ideas that must either find expression or become self-destructive. Every day, he scribbles numbers on a pad and debates with himself in a mumbling manner. When he arrives at some decision—who knows what?—he shreds the paper and flushes it down the toilet. Occasionally, the secret police have surprised him and gone off with his numbers, but they report that other scientists can't decipher them. I think the man is a crypto-churchman who believes in the devil, and in his case Satan has taken the shape of formulas. I have even suggested, on the advice of the OGPU, that he resume his position in the laboratory and experiment on any idea that teases his imagination. The police reason that perhaps he'll be drawn back to nuclear physics, and we'll be able to use his discoveries. If he keeps shrinking, he'll soon dissolve into a puddle, his body worth no more than a few kopeks."

The next sentence, one that Dr. Leshin could have easily missed (it was embedded parenthetically), read mysteriously:

"A body is no more than a handful of chemicals, and yet when it provokes desire, what follows? The end of a career?"

Arriving at the clinic early, Alexei asked Sviatoslav Sarkaski if the previous doctor, whose name the patients were forbidden to utter, had ever talked about the chemicals that compose a human body and how those chemicals, arranged in a certain order, trigger emotions?

"What a strange question. Why do you ask?"

"A hunch."

"Stupid man!" he replied, and walked off, mumbling, "No better than Dr. P."

A P., yes, but first or last or patronymic? Alexei would also have to learn the man's medical background and current status. He felt certain that Rissa Binderova held the key to Dr. P., and that only she could dispel the cloud of unknowing that seemed to hang over the entire clinic.

IN THE MOST HIGH AND
PALMY STATE OF ROME

A porter admitted the former commissar for Foreign Affairs into the Leningrad Theological Institute, a drab, depressing building, ill lit and poorly heated. The aristocratic Georgiy Vasilyevich Chicherin, who spoke numerous European languages and a few Asian ones, had been asked by the current minister for Foreign Affairs, Maxim Litvinov, to handle a delicate matter. Although feeling unwell, Chicherin had come to the institute personally to inform Gregori Lipnoskii that a "catacomb priest" had denounced him as a secret adherent of the Eastern Orthodox Church.

The autumnal crispness that day in 1935 lingered in the hallway that led to Gregori's room, an austere, windowless cell with a table, a single wicker chair, a narrow bed, and two wall hangings: a photograph of Stalin, exhibiting his fatherly all-knowing look, and a bad pencil drawing of the Alexander Nevsky Monastery. Chicherin said nothing about the open Bible and the religious literature resting on the table. He also noticed a Maxim Gorky novel, *Bystander*. Without being asked, he sat on the chair. Gregori paced.

"Our informant has told us that you attended Orthodox services late at night in forest caves. We even know the secret codes and ciphers you and the catacomb priests use." As Gregori opened his mouth to speak, Chicherin held up one finger to indicate that he hadn't finished. "We have apprehended couriers you employed to convey messages and confiscated false identification cards made out in the names of deceased persons."

Gregori stood and said magisterially, "Lies! All lies! I am a Renovationist Church member faithful to the Soviet government."

The erstwhile minister leaned back, folded his arms, and seemed to take great pleasure in agreeing. "You are absolutely right! All lies. But in a court of law, you'll be convicted. If you wish to save yourself from exile, and to spare your denouncer, whom I want you to meet, you will confess to being a catacombist."

"Comrade Chicherin, your reputation for subtlety is well known. Surely, you have in mind more than my simple confession."

"Your brother Dimitri rightly described you as a clever fellow. Yes, we have an assignment for you: to work secretly for the Department of Religious Affairs to help us suppress nationalistic sentiment against the government." He opened the Bible. "In the minds of believers, as you well know, religion and nationalism become hopelessly tangled. The pope has undercover agents in the country attempting to rouse nationalistic sentiment against the government, particularly in those Slavic and Ukrainian areas that used to follow the Roman Church. As your brother has already explained, many people still, sadly, believe in the western rites and recognize the pope."

Gregori, ambivalent about the Roman Church, though not about Greek Catholicism, tried to take the measure of this well-known man. Comrade Chicherin, a distant relative of Pushkin, loved classical music and particularly Wagner. He also exhibited a fondness for Gregorian chants, like the ones he heard upon entering the putative seminary. The simplicity of the musical line reinforced his own tastes. Although illness had caused him to leave office a few years before, he took on special assignments for Litvinov in religious matters. Having negotiated successfully in the 1920s with the Vatican, he had the temperament and diplomatic skills to deal with Roman machinations. A handsome man, with a mustache and meticulously trimmed pointed beard, he had a high forehead, soft eyes, thinning hair, and a somewhat bulbous nose. His dress always included a white detachable Fremont collar, a starched shirt, a vest, and a suit. Thoroughly westernized, he had used family wealth to help the revolutionary cause in the belief that modernization in Russia would not take place until the old regime had been replaced.

Without animation, Gregori said, "You and Dimitri want me to work as an agent for Rome."

"Precisely! But first you will have to confess your crime."

"That," replied Gregori emphatically, "I cannot do. Deceit may suit the government, but not my Christian principles."

"As I said, I want you to meet your denouncer. His name is Peter Filatov. Years ago, he taught theology in a Moscow monastery. He now works on behalf of the proletariat." He paused. "Lovely Bible."

Gregori's first impulse was to say that he had no stomach for consorting with Christian denouncers, but waited to hear Chicherin's final words on the subject.

"The best way to serve the Renovationist cause," he said, closing the Bible, "is to keep it from Roman designs: bringing back the old ways and expelling the new. I would remind you what the Russian archbishop called Renovationists: 'A sewer of the Orthodox Church.'"

The Nevsky Monastery, converted in 1932 into a Museum of City Sculpture, also housed offices, institutes, a warehouse, and a small room set aside for secret police meetings. Gregori Lipnoskii and Peter Filatov arrived at virtually the same time. The room, wired to record even whispered conversations, also held a hidden camera in case the participants, wary of being bugged, wrote notes. But Peter Filatov, after their initial introduction, spoke candidly. His tall, skeletal appearance looked, quite accurately, as if it were incapable of hiding a secret. Where, among the skin and bones, would he hide it?

"My own confession was untrue in every word. They said that if I did not confess to helping the Roman Church, my family and I would disappear. After I agreed to sign, they said they wanted the names of others involved in the so-called plot. 'Others?' I asked. 'Make them up if you have to,' they yelled. So I gave them names, including yours, even though I knew you were innocent of conspiring with Rome."

"Why mine?"

"They suggested it."

"They?"

"The Office of Religious Affairs. Two men interrogated me." He buried his head in his hands. "They said that if an Orthodox priest admitted to having entered into secret relations with Rome and signed a statement, it would pass unnoticed. The danger to the nation would appear greater if the state-supported church, the Renovationists, were conspiring with the Vatican. Then no one, not even the favored, could be trusted."

Gregori had lent himself to the Renovationist movement to preserve the Russian Church and to try to discover those Orthodox priests who pretended to resist the government while actually reporting to them, a practice dating back to the Tsars. Under Nicholas II and his predecessors, priests were agents of the state, a condition they swore to in their ordination oath. Even though church law banned disclosing what passed in the confessional booth between parishioner and priest, the church often reported draft dodgers, prospective recruits for the armed forces, and any antistate information. Gregori may have shown fealty to Stalin for endorsing the Renovationist Church, but he showed a greater fealty to his Lord in matters of conscience, truth, and Orthodoxy.

"What will happen," he asked Peter, "if I refuse to sign?"

"They will shoot me and my family."

"But the regime is terrified of creating religious martyrs. Your death would undermine their efforts to sway believers."

"Aren't you forgetting one thing?" said Peter, as Gregori studied him. "I don't want to die, nor does my family."

Public confession of political or religious wrongdoing, Gregori knew, served an indispensable purpose. When individuals declared themselves guilty, the state had no need to stamp them as social pariahs and run the risk of martyring them.

"Peter, if I admit guilt, I help the state crush opposition, political and religious, and undermine our church's efforts to attract the faithful."

Peter sighed, "Yes, but abstractions are not reality."

"What we know to be real," replied Gregori, "is that when people confess to plots against the state, the organizations they belong to are often exterminated. If I sign a statement conceding that your charges are true, the only way to save my own life is to agree to spy for the Soviets."

"The Vatican would protect you as a man denounced for his true beliefs. Who will protect me, if not you?"

To save Peter's life, Gregori agreed to become a Soviet agent. While espousing Latin rites, he would try to insinuate himself into the Russicum and spy on Rome, transmitting to Moscow the names of underground priests.

Before Peter Filatov was led off to prepare himself for his next "official" assignment, he hugged Gregori and, in whispered words, begged his forgiveness. Gregori returned to the institute and waited, using the time to school himself in the writings of Catholic hagiography. It took a few months before the Department of Religious Affairs could fabricate and circulate the story of Gregori Lipnoskii, ostensible Renovationist, who deviously belonged to the Catacomb Church, while furtively promoting nationalism among Ukrainians and Slavs to promote the Roman cause.

Chicherin had told Comrade Dimitri Lipnoskii it was a "dastardly business" before sending him to Leningrad to tell his brother that the fate of the family hung in the balance. The brothers had never been close, though both ironically had found work that required absolute obedience to a higher authority. As soon as Dimitri came into Gregori's presence, he could detect Gregori's unease.

"You are not yourself, Gregori. Is it the idea of spying that troubles you or something else?"

"I had hoped to take orders and enter the priesthood."

"For our purposes, all the better."

"But I also want someday to marry. And you know the rule. A married man can become a priest, but a priest can't marry."

"A widower can do both. We will arrange your files to read that you were once married and that your wife died." He studied the room, which seemed to him as cold as his brother's religion. "You will have to learn Italian. And the Fascists . . . well, it won't be easy."

"As a priest, I can inure myself to any test. Let us forget the subject. Please tell me about our dear mother."

When Anna picked up her copy of *Pravda* downstairs, she saw on the front page, in large print, the headline: "Traitorous Priest Flees the Motherland." The first sentence of the accompanying article identified the priest as "Gregori Lipnoskii." With her heart wildly beating, she flew to the elevator, burst into her apartment, cried out for Razan, and threw herself on the couch, declaring, "Our days are numbered." He reached for the paper and studied the article. His own legs grew wobbly. As Anna's eyes closed, he sat down on the floor next to the couch, rubbing her hands and her head. When she showed no response, Razan thought she had either suffered a seizure or a heart attack. From the liquor cabinet, he took a bottle of brandy and poured some of the liquid into her mouth.

Slowly she revived. Wanly smiling, she advised that they should be prepared for a visit from the secret police, who in fact came that same afternoon. Driven away in a black Packard, they entered the grounds of Lubyanka Prison and quickly found themselves sitting in a room reeking of cigarettes. An interrogator, with nicotine stained hands and teeth, had been assigned to their case.

"You know why you're here," said the man, "so let us not pretend. What do you know about your son's escape and when did you know it?"

Razan hoped that Anna's steely nerves would eclipse his fears.

"We know nothing," said Anna. "I confess: My heart cries. Our son is as dead to us as he is to you."

"Dead," mocked the man, as he extinguished one cigarette and lit another. "Dead! He can cause us more harm than a bomb-throwing terrorist. In fact, he is a saboteur on a grand scale. With what he knows about religious conditions in our country, he can cause a schism as great as the one in 1054 that divided the church."

Neither of them had any idea of what the date 1054 meant, but they both intended to find out, since it seemed to bode a great ill.

"The Vatican is never happier than when it is stirring up the Roman Catholics in Soviet territories. Your son merely feeds that fire. He will undoubtedly be quoted in *L'Osservatore*, the Vatican newspaper, spewing slander about our beloved Mother Russia."

Had the interrogator not said "Mother Russia," he would have completely cowed Anna. But the phrase gave him away. She could see that he was overacting, and that for some reason this whole scene, which lacked any of the usual violent props that Lubyanka survivors often mentioned—clubs, whips, chains, brass knuckles—was a sham.

"If Gregori contacts us, we will tell you immediately. We are faithful citizens of the country and love our Supreme Leader. Please don't exile us to a camp. Siberia would be the death of us."

She wanted to withdraw that last statement, feeling that she too was now overacting. But the man seemed not to notice and suddenly grew sympathetic, assuring them that their lives were in no danger, just so long as they continued to cooperate with the secret police.

Days passed, and then weeks. Anna comforted Razan with her belief that they would not be questioned again. Although he had his doubts and at low moments could feel the cold of Asiatic Siberia, her words held true. Little did they know that the Soviet government had arranged the priestly ordination, the escape, the newspaper article, and the benign interrogation.

Leaving by train from the Levashovo Station, Gregori was met at the Finnish border by smugglers, in the employ of the Soviets, who spirited him to the Baltic, put him aboard a fishing boat, and three weeks later landed him at a safe haven on the Sicilian mainland. To make his defection look real, Gregori arrived without papers, made his way slowly toward Rome on back roads and hay wagons, and stopped at prearranged houses. Apprehended at one of them and taken to the capital, Gregori told the Italian secret service his rehearsed story. The Fascists quickly unearthed the *Pravda* article and called in a Vatican emissary, Monsignor Schiaffone, who interviewed Father Lipnoskii, declared him *perfetto* for service in the Catholic Church, and, at Gregori's suggestion, offered him a position tutoring prospective priests at the Russicum, an institute that schooled young men in the Russian language, the Eastern Orthodox rites, and the machinations of spying. The Russicum graduates were then smuggled into the Soviet Union to exploit the nationalistic and Roman Catholic sympathies of Poles, White Russians, Armenians, Georgians, and others. They would also report to Rome on the state of religion in

Russia. This practice, far from being new, had been in place for many years, with the loss of numerous lives. When the Soviets discovered a Russicum priest, they shot him without a trial.

Gregori's Roman contact, to whom he reported Russicum activities, was an Italian Communist, aptly code named Carlo Cospirato. A short, round-faced, pudgy fellow, who could not pass a coffee bar without stopping for a cappuccino—"heavy on the milk"—he was, by day, an automobile mechanic and, by night, a Marxist, distributing leaflets, attending party meetings, and ferrying secret information to the Russians. To make their contacts seem perfectly natural, Carlo continued Gregori's Italian lessons and put at his disposal a used Fiat, a Topolino. Once Carlo had taught Gregori to drive the little mouse-car, the latter could not only traverse the Holy City, but also see the beautiful Roman countryside, where he discovered the Benedictine abbey of Farfa and its splendid library and prestigious scriptorium dating back to the eleventh century.

One Saturday afternoon, he motored over the Sabine Hills to visit the abbey. In the village of Farfa, adjacent to the monastery, hammers and saws could be heard. Under the direction of the Fascist government, workers were repairing the old houses and restoring the porches and slab fronts on which medieval merchants had displayed their wares. Here he lodged, sans his clerical garb. On Sunday morning, he entered the huge Romanesque gate, with its magnificent floral friezes, and walked between incensed candles down the middle nave to hear Mass. He passed through the two rows of ionic columns, and under the coffered ceiling with the Orsini emblem that bathed him in bronze. Presenting himself as a Russian scholar in the employ of the Russicum, he endeared himself to the resident monks by praising the worth of their library. The abbot of Farfa, the cardinal bishop of Sabina, a suburbicarian bishop, had delegated the responsibilities of the abbey to a priest, Father Maurizio, who immediately befriended Gregori. The two men conversed, to their delight, in Latin, which both men knew well. Invited to return the next week to take a meal and celebrate Vespers, Gregori eagerly accepted in fond anticipation of the silver light of the tapers, the perfume, the songs, the service. Like so many worshippers, he loved the ceremonies that he believed gave meaning to the mysteries of life. Before long, Farfa Abbey felt like his spiritual home— the library, the friendship of the monks, the smells, the sounds, the gardens— and he often returned.

After several visits to Farfa, Gregori began to wonder if his mind and soul weren't being tempted to receive nourishment from Roman Catholicism. But he knew that the canon law that prohibited Catholic priests from marrying would ultimately keep him from embracing that faith. In fact, his wish to marry and his gentle courtesies made him a good catch for Signora and Signore Credulo. They owned the Farfa Inn, where he lodged when he stayed overnight, and were the parents of Angelina, with whom he was smitten. Although her persistent frothy cough had dissuaded her last suitor, Mario Fori, from seriously considering marriage, her smile gladdened others and her sensuous lips cried out to be kissed.

Angelina, of an age when a young girl should wed, had given Gregori numerous encouraging signs and had even strolled with him unchaperoned. In the evening, they took coffee in the piazza, walked through the village, greeting families whose ancestors dated back hundreds of years, and followed a path that led up the hillside behind the town to a beautiful vantage point. Here they would sit and remark on the picturesque scene below. Bathed in the silver moonlight, she always felt alluring and desired, and made every smiling effort to bring Gregori into her loving orbit. The rustics she had known had never exhibited the learning of this man; they had never behaved like proper suitors, but rather wanted to hurry into some adjacent hayloft. The local boys had even made sport of her gifted artwork, mugging and dropping their drawers with rude cries, such as "Why not draw my ass?" What did they know of Italy's great artists; what did they know of Giotto, Cimabue, and Rafaello, names that came as readily to Gregori's lips as breath?

Had she been asked whether she loved the Russian priest, she could have said in perfect honesty that she really had no experience with love. Admittedly, Mario had often kissed her and run his hand beneath her dress, and, although she tingled at his touch and could feel her face flush, she knew better than to say that love was a hot pang. She wanted, like heroines of old, the permanence of position. Affection would grow from her happy station in life. At least, her sagacious grandmother had said as much when she counseled her to "treasure rank and reputation more than rapture." She had no fear of different languages or customs; her only fear was that she would die for want of strength before she could marry or exhibit her paintings.

She went so far as to suggest to Gregori that, on her next trip to Rome to buy oils and canvases from the merchants in the Via della Rotonda, they meet at Gregori's room. When he explained that his hostel, across the river and adjacent to the Vatican, housed only priests, she proposed they meet at the Pantheon, but not before teasing him that he ought to find his own quarters, where he could entertain friends. What did she mean, he mused, by the word "entertain"? Rather than ask, he would just keep their appointment.

On a Friday, Venerdi, Venus's day, they spent at least an hour in the Pantheon as she explained how the tombs and the sunken panels (coffers), reduced the weight of the structure and made it possible for the walls to support the enormous dome. Angelina had just purchased a new sketchbook and insisted on capturing Gregori's likeness with the light from the open dome striking his face. The rather good sketch pleased Gregori, and he asked if he could own it.

"Only if you take me to the Café Magi to see the magician, Signore Calvo. I understand he can turn catnip to Chianti," she said between coughs, "and his admirers are innumerable. Friends of mine who have seen him can't stop raving."

The café, next door to a Fascist recruiting office, attracted all classes of people, from rowdy young men to old women, from workers to intellectuals. This night, they had to wait for a table. The stage was virtually bare, except for a blackboard behind the magician, a raised thronelike chair, a wooden box, and a baton that he used to direct the café-goers. Like a prophet, Calvo told his audience that Italy, inspired by a single idea—the collective will—could reimpose its rule on the Levant, and re-create the ancient civilization that was Rome. He said that what seemed like magic was, in fact, reality, and insisted that the magic and power of ideas engendered creation.

"First from his mind and then from his brush, Michelangelo brought forth the ceiling in the Sistine Chapel. Never underestimate the power of an idea to change the world. Roman glory can once again be ours—by translating words into action."

As they waited, Angelina and Gregori amiably chatted with the *portiere*, who eventually seated them next to the stage and handed Calvo a note. The magician almost immediately began to play to the attractive Signorina Credulo, smiling, winking, and tipping his cap. Dressed in a black silk shirt and riding boots, he used the baton magically to orchestrate her response.

"Raise your right arm."

Her arm shot up as if spring loaded.

"Mario Fori, a former boyfriend, still thinks of you fondly." Angelina coughed fiercely into her handkerchief. "But then we all have secret lives." He strutted around the stage, stopped, and said, "I know that you believe in the inspirational power of faith and myth." He swung his baton. "Swear your allegiance to the higher power that will restore Italy to the center of European civilization."

Her mouth, like a ventriloquist's dummy, opened mechanically. "I have faith. I will obey and fight for the glory of Catholic Italy."

The audience cheered.

"At this moment, you are thinking: How can I act in this manner? Surely, I can resist this man's powers of suggestion. But you cannot. Why? Because I have your number."

He then took a stubby pencil and scribbled on a piece of paper, which he put in his breast pocket. He then asked Angelina and Gregori to take the stage.

The men and women watched raptly. Stepping back, Calvo admired Angelina's long skirt. "Such beautiful flowered Japanese cloth . . . such flair." Circling Gregori, he remarked, "He looks like Lenin in London." The audience shredded the silence with their laughter.

"Signorina," said Calvo, "write a number on the blackboard." Taking the chalk from the ledge, she paused and then wrote 9610. Calvo chuckled and shook his head, as if to say: "Just as I expected." Turning to Gregori, he asked the "signore" to remove the piece of paper from the magician's pocket. "Please read what I wrote."

Staring at the paper, a shocked Gregori could barely reply. First, he looked at the blackboard and then at Angelina, as if she had colluded with the maestro. Finally, facing the audience, Gregori said, "The number is exactly the same, 9610. But how . . . ?"

Ignoring the question, Calvo added, "I can also tell our audience that you are a priest, though you're not wearing clerical garb."

Gregori wanted to ask the magician, "Which church?" but felt that his accent gave him away. Without irony, Gregori thought that Calvo was a man the Soviets could use. His ability to divine a citizen's background could save the secret police money and time.

Back at their table, Gregori kept mumbling that he had to know Calvo's secret. Angelina, with her eyes riveted on the stage, hardly heard him. Gregori prompted, "Perhaps if you ask him, he'll explain. He seems much taken with you."

"Shh," objected Angelina. "I want to hear what he's saying."

The magician was talking about the power of words. "Not just any words, but words imbued with fire." Holding up a Bible, he observed, "This single book had the power—and still does—to convert pagans, erect churches, inspire crusades, and provide the subject matter for innumerable artistic masterworks. Today, we have before us a new religion, a new faith, which can make Italy the greatest nation on earth." He held aloft a sheaf of wheat. "One *fascio* can be toppled by the wind. Thousands of sheaves can support an army."

The play on words elicited a loud cheer from the audience, who raised their arms, saluting Calvo's magic. Holding up his baton for silence, Calvo waited a second and then, with a flourish, brought it down, eliciting a thunderous cheer, "*Me ne frego! Me ne frego!*" the familiar chant of the government faithful, "I don't give a damn."

"Permit me to ask our couple to return to the stage," said Calvo. The audience clapped in agreement. "Although the young woman briefly hesitated at the blackboard, she could not escape my will or yours, which in fact are one and the same. That is why she had to remain true to her original choice." Addressing

Angelina, the magician said, "Now, signorina, you know that you are just a part of a larger idea, one that unites ancient Rome and modern, an idea that is self-evident to the *cittadini*. The number 9610 itself hardly matters . . . merely a vaudeville trick." Taking her hand, Calvo told the audience, "Chance favors the prepared mind. A magician, like a general or a leader of the people, must never fail to see the little clues found in a word, a phrase, an unusual facial expression. Even a dropped vowel or slurred consonant may tell him what he needs to know to accomplish his ends." With the baton he pointed to the *portiere*. "He," said Calvo, "is the source of my information. Having overheard our couple's conversation as they waited for a table, he jotted down several interesting facts he thought I could use in the act. One, names: Angelina and Gregori. Two, the woman is an artist." As an aside, he held his hand to his cheek and, with a stage whisper, told the crowd, "I must arrange for her to meet Margherita Sarfatti, the head of Italian culture, and one of our leading art patrons." Flourishing his baton, he encouraged the audience to agree.

They chanted, "Margherita, si; Margherita, si!"

"A third fact I learned was that Angelina was born on the ninth of June 1910: 9610. She shared that information with her gentleman friend; she also mentioned a Mario Fori. Gregori, for his part, talked about his work at the Russicum and his living quarters at the Vatican hostel. Any fool would know he is a priest. In fact, I would hazard that, given his accent, he is an Orthodox one." Holding up his baton, Calvo asked Gregori, "Am I right?"

"Yes. On every point you have, as you say, our number."

"Not quite," said Calvo. "Not until I endow you with second sight can I make that claim." Calvo reached into the wooden chest and removed a miniature bundle of sticks, with an axe bound to it, the premier symbol of the current government. "The fasces indicates the people's power over life and death," the magician declared. "It even appears on the seal of the United States Senate and on a wall of the House of Representatives, as well as on the coat of arms of France. Take it as a gift from me," said Calvo offering Gregori the miniature fasces.

"Impossible."

"Why?"

"I am devoted and loyal to a different host, a transcendent one."

"Are you referring to Angelina here?" Calvo asked ironically.

Gregori blushed. "No, but I do admit that she is a lovely young woman, and she comes from a good family, a pious one."

"Our beloved pope," said Calvo, "has blessed this symbol. He and it are as one, just as the people and the pope share one spiritual body. We are all part of the same will." Putting his face close to Gregori's, Calvo said, "You will accept this gift." The magician's eyes glowed with a jaundiced yellow tint, holding Gregori in his gaze. "Who partakes of our body will enter into the mystical union with Rome that began with the Caesars and will last until the end of time."

With this grand pronouncement, Calvo held up the fasces, as a priest might raise a crucifix in a religious procession, and, facing Gregori, slowly backed toward the stage steps. Gregori followed, seemingly mesmerized. Someone screamed. Still the two men continued their twinned dance; descending the steps, they moved down the aisle toward the back of the café, where the door stood open.

"Stop!" yelled a young man who rose to his feet, while a pretty curly headed waitress, with whom he'd been flirting, tried to force him back into his seat. "Don't!" cried the man, persevering in his resistance. "Look what is happening to Italy!"

This last statement earned him a rough expulsion from the café at the hands of the Me-ne-frego crowd of ruffians. But the tumult at the door prevented Calvo and Gregori from exiting the café, at which point Calvo thrust the fasces into Gregori's hands and led him back to the stage. Gregori, who had exhibited an ethereal lack of resistance throughout the ordeal, metamorphosed when he reached the stage. While Calvo retreated to his chair, the Orthodox-Renovationist priest and double agent held up the fasces and in a mesmeric voice that seemed to issue from his soul, shouted to the audience, "Me ne frego!"

Mayhem ensued, as the patrons stood on chairs and tables, sang the patriotic anthem "Giovinezza," waved flags that mysteriously materialized, and formed a line that marched around the café and out the door, to the dismay of the café owner, who ran after the revelers, yelling at those who had failed to pay for their drinks. In the sudden quiet of the café, the three people remained onstage. Then the owner turned off the lights, except for a single spot. An emotionally exhausted Angelina and Gregori sat at the feet of Calvo, bathed in the light cast on his throne, forming a Trinitarian tableau.

As promised, Calvo arranged for Angelina and Gregori to attend an evening salon at Margherita Sarfatti's apartment. Observing the Roman preference for early weekday hours, the invitations said that the conversazione would take place Wednesday, between eight and ten.

La Sarfatti, as she was known, had spent the afternoon at an exhibition of paintings by Achille Funi and Mario Sironi, two of her favorites. She arrived in the small piazza, where she maintained an apartment, in a black Lancia limousine that was so long that to turn the corner, it had to jump the curb. The cool spring weather had given her an excuse to wear a fur piece over her black dress. A string of pearls graced her neck, now thickening from age. In her youth, she had been quite a beauty, with her tall, full body, deep gray-green eyes, reddish-blond curly hair, and stylish dresses, invariably designed in Paris by Schiaparelli and adorned with tasteful and expensive jewelry. Her Venetian family, the Grassini, issued from Jewish roots, and although some members had, for mercantile reasons, defected to the church, she was secretly proud of being born an *ebrea* and of moving easily in Italian high society.

The Grassini wealth had made it possible for her to receive a first-rate education and meet courtiers, cardinals, and bishops. Her father and her lawyer husband, from whom she took the name "Sarfatti," had always indulged her expensive tastes. Not for La Sarfatti the drab, masculine clothing of the socialist women's brigades whom she had supported before the Great War. She likewise disapproved of Fascist fashions, except for their favoring the color black. A warm and witty lady, she was famously known as "Il Duce's other woman," in short, his mistress, one of many, though easily the most cultured.

Angelina could barely contain her excitement, skipping up to every fountain they passed and, like a schoolgirl, splashing drops of water on Gregori's untonsured head. He pretended to enjoy the sport, but, in fact, he found her behavior fatuous.

"Why all this fuss about La Sarfatti?" he asked, clearly annoyed.

"She tutored Il Duce himself! Everyone says so. They say Benito was a boorish boy until she made him over."

Gregori ironically replied, "I can just imagine how much he appreciated his tutor being a woman."

Angelina coughed. "You're right. Italian men resent accomplished women." Then she dismissed the idea with a toss of her head and again tripped down the walk toward La Sarfatti's apartment, carrying a small painting of her own, a gift for the grande dame.

Margherita's apartment occupied an entire upper floor, with marvelous city views. A *portiere* answered the door and nodded his head approvingly when Angelina flashed her invitation to partake of drinks and cultured discussion. The chairs in Sarfatti's drawing room had been arranged in a conversational circle. Gregori and Angelina peeked into her study and saw a confusion of manuscripts, proof sheets, and books. On the apartment walls hung hundreds of paintings, arranged from floor to ceiling. But pride of place was given to a stunning white-marble bust by Adolfo Wildt, titled *Margherita Sarfatti*. And indeed, she held sway in all cultural matters, from painting to pottery. Her taste, which ran to the colorful and bizarre, could be seen in the artistic movement that she now spearheaded, the Novecento, known for its insane colors and its cadaver-like heads. Some of these works hung on her walls. Her collection also included ugly pieces of sculpture, for example, the head of a boxer by Romanelli that eerily resembled the head of Il Duce. But, since she preferred painting to sculpture, the room smelled of oils and resins and not marble. And of all her paintings, those of Achille Funi predominated. The shelves of one room, in fact, bore the inscription, the "Funi Library," with numerous small cards or brass labels identifying every painting and book. Gregori felt as though he were in a suffocating museum or an airtight bell jar, not in the apartment of a person who cooked and ate and slept and used a bathroom.

When the guests finally took their seats and turned their attention to La Sarfatti at the head of the circle, she immediately introduced the subject of art, and the importance of order.

"The Cubists are mad, simply insane," she pontificated, waving her arms. "They represent analysis run amok."

A twitchy thin-faced, balding fellow, lipping a drooping unlit cigarette, tugged at the red scarf around his neck and remarked, "Artists must be free to represent the world as they view it, whether crooked or straight. Both views are defensible. Greatness resides not in the subject matter per se but in the execution."

Margherita would hear none of it. "Art should reflect the moral and cultural values of our society. It should be an expression not only of a country's values but of those it wishes to inculcate."

Angelina chose this moment to hand her small painting to La Sarfatti, whom she pressed to comment.

In that instant, Gregori became memory's silent pawn. He remembered his mother hanging a reproduction of *The Volga Boatmen*, a painting by Ilya Repin, bought from a tinker. As Gregori watched, his mother hammered a nail in the wall over the couch. While she was leaning to hang the wired frame, Pyotr entered, eyed her vulnerable position, and came up behind her. Fully clothed, he gave her a great hump that sent her sprawling on the couch. Whether he had intended the action to be affectionate or hostile, Gregori couldn't tell, but she tumbled on top of the picture causing it to rip. Anna, who had never shed a tear during all the years of Pyotr's beatings, who had never let the children view her pain and humiliation, cried over the painting. Her response left Pyotr stunned. He could understand a whipped person wailing, but someone blubbering because of a cheap reproduction? In his incomprehension, he resorted to the only behavior he knew: abuse. Although Gregori was present, Pyotr dropped his pants and tried to remove Anna's skirt to enter her from behind. Roaring, "Cry, will you? I'll give you reason to cry," he failed owing to his drunken state, which had left him limp.

Margherita removed the brown wrapping paper and stared at the painting dolefully. Angelina's heart sunk, and she began to cough. But then the mistress of the salon smiled and said, "Here is an example of a *quadro*, a painting, that returns to the purest traditions of Giotto and Masaccio, and yet she does not renounce the uniqueness of our modern times." The guests clapped, and Angelina bowed her head as if she had just received a state medal. The painting, a scene of the Farfa countryside, was passed among the guests, as Sarfatti continued, "Italian art must once again become method, order, and discipline. It must give rise to definite bodily forms that are analogous to the ancients, and yet different from them. It must be independent of foreign fads and mercantile considerations."

Gregori had only an imperfect idea of what she meant. But he recognized a similarity to what Stalin called "Socialist Realism." In fact, the Supreme Leader had said, "How can we judge the art of an age if not as the expression of its moral habits?"

"Thus," La Sarfatti continued, "an orderly society produces orderly art, while, at the same time, encouraging a respect for discipline and control." Insisting that art had to be a mutual enterprise, she exhorted her guests to insist that artists abandon their individual "arbitrary" styles and work toward a "collective synthesis of concreteness and simplicity."

Yes, indeed, Margherita and Stalin were cut from the same cloth. This discovery led Gregori to the idea that all "isms" found validation in conformity, and that the "isms" closest to one another had to exaggerate their differences to maintain their separate identities. Here at last was an explanation for why those sects closest in belief, like the Catholics, hated each other so fiercely. The endless sectarian wars in the Caucasus suddenly made sense. His musing came to an end when Margherita stood to thank her guests for attending and bowed out of the room. The front door opened and the faithful cascaded down the steps and spilled into the street.

Weekdays Gregori spent at the Russicum under the watchful eye of a priest from the Sacred Congregation for the Doctrine of the Faith; weekends he drove to Farfa to see Angelina, though he had reservations about the seriousness of her commitments, whether to art, politics, or religion. He began to regard her as a dabbler, a dilettante. Even her frivolity seemed at times artificial. When he tried to broach the subject of dedication to a cause, she dismissed him with feigned gaiety. His students behaved in the opposite manner. They were dedicated warriors in the service of the Vatican. Perched on wooden benches, they hunched over communal tables, scribbled in their notebooks, and haltingly repeated the soft and hard glottal sounds of the Russian language. Gregori taught them the principles of the Orthodox faith, with its insistence that the Holy Spirit came not from the Son but from God alone, and its rejection of any rigid hierarchy, namely, the pope, cardinals, and bishops. He explained that in many Orthodox churches, the clergy shared the responsibility of leading the congregation with the laity. In some cases, the laity even elected their clergy, a practice that the novice spies felt led to anarchy.

When his handler, Carlo Cospirato, asked him how he liked the work, he lied, "I'd rather be in the Soviet Union, helping in the struggle to create a new society."

"That's what you're doing now," replied Carlo, a true believer. "You are helping the cause by rooting out the enemies of Bolshevism."

In fact, Gregori relished conspiracies, whether in Moscow or Rome, and especially papal machinations. Every restaurant and café seemed to have its whisperers and secret agents. One day, he approvingly told the Russicum priest from the Congregation of the Faith, "You and I with Him conspire." The priest's grin suggested that he understood "Him" to stand for God. But what did Gregori intend: Christ? The staunchly anti-Communist pope, Pius XI? The Soviet government? Or was it the abstract idea of a higher cause, which had become for him a vague feeling that he associated with the armor of righteousness? Although exalted causes produced high emotions, they also implied obedience. Awash in a sea of theology, Gregori argued with himself about the virtues and defects of submission and its attendant certitude.

The Russicum students liked Gregori and, in turn, their respect brought out the natural teacher in him. As students and teacher grew closer, Gregori felt responsible for the fate of these young men. They had, through his tutorials, become his "children." If he gave Carlo their names, as planned, they would likely be caught and shot. Given that he wanted to build a better world—didn't the old medieval metaphor portray God as an architect?—he would have to play God and fashion his own future instead of following the plan of some other designer. Perhaps he would even stay in Rome and devote himself to teaching others. But teaching what? Catechistic instruction was boring. One could continue for only so long training spies to undermine the Soviet regime. To make the teaching more challenging, he introduced lessons in history. He told his students how religious ideas and institutions had evolved, and gave numerous examples to prove supernatural truths and God's miracles. Deploring the split between Greek and Roman churches, he argued that doctrinal

Orthodoxy and sectarian arguments came not from the Bible but from church councils, where political power, not scripture, was at issue.

After a day of such exhilarating exposition, he would retire to his dormitory, sip a glass of wine, nibble on *pane* and some pecorino, his favorite cheese, and try to sort out his growing unease over competing theories. In the blue-black darkness of night, he would fall to his knees before a cheap icon that he had purchased from a stand outside of the Vatican—the gold paint was already chipping—and engage in a timeless ritual, a catechism.

Question: Which is the true church? Answer: The Orthodox.

Question: Do you believe in Stalin? Answer: Yes, but . . .

Question: Do you believe in celibacy? Answer: No.

Question: Do you achieve holiness through good deeds, a theocracy, or penance? Answer: Prayer. Reply: Answer the question.

When he shared these ideas with his students, word reached the Office of the Faith, and his overseer gently suggested that he should leave political philosophy to the Catholic fathers and get on with the labor of schooling his students in Orthodox doctrines.

"We count on you," said the priest, "to instruct our people in the liturgy, to illuminate for them the role of icons and the symbolic importance of priestly garments. How else can they get close to the people and bring them to the true faith?"

One evening, after he and Angelina dined in a cellar restaurant a few steps from the Piazza dei Fiori, they walked past the statue of Giordano Bruno and made their way to Capitoline Hill. Below, people were gathering in the Piazza Venezia. "Of course!" said Angelina, as they descended the Michelangelo steps. "Mussolini is speaking tonight from his balcony."

The couple joined the swelling crowd. Although Il Duce would not appear for another thirty minutes, Gregori could hear in the voices of the faithful a religious reverence, an ecstasy. For them, Benito was a religious experience. Gregori had read about the spellbinding leader, had seen numerous photographs of him in the newspapers, and had heard him on the radio. But what he experienced now was unlike any spiritual awakening he had ever known. Yes, it was comparable to a religious conversion. The man looked strikingly like Calvo. The magician was everywhere, supplanting God with his mesmerizing powers and magical plans for a new Roman empire that would engulf the Levant and much of East Africa.

When the curtains parted and Mussolini appeared on the balcony, holding up his immense jaw to the sky as if challenging the Almighty, the street subsided into obedient silence. "Although we wish to re-create the glory that was Rome, we are not *passatisti*, those captive to the past." To punctuate each point, he punched the air with his fist. "We also want a New Italy, the Italy of tomorrow, one that throbs with massive engines of production, commerce, and travel. One in which aircraft fill the skies with the thunder of their motors, and automobiles speed along ribbons of highway, and steamships, like sharpened steel, slice across the oceans. I envision great factories with tall smokestacks reaching the clouds, and electricity sparking life into every human endeavor. I see buildings that dwarf the Coliseum and rival the Pantheon, train stations that resemble artworks, marble statues in every courtyard, and all of us sharing in the beauty that was and is to come."

He spoke of the poverty and humiliation visited upon the country after the Great War; and he said that for the nation to enter into the ranks of the richest and most powerful nations, Italy must express its national interests through any viable means. How else could they escape the current worldwide economic depression?

"We will do whatever it takes to maximize the interests of the people. If the evidence argues that the nation prospers most under monarchy, Fascists will become monarchists. If the evidence shows that monarchy is unworkable, then Fascists will become republicans. If Venezia can do what we can't, then we will all become Venetians." Urging communalism, Mussolini cried, "Only in the development of the nation-state will individuals and classes find their own fulfillment. Fascism places the nation before all else. The group counts more than the individual, the nation more than the group. Think of the fascio," he said, holding up a flag exhibiting the familiar symbol.

Tumultuous applause shook the piazza. From the overflow crowd in adjoining streets came cheers as loud as those in the Piazza Venezia. The Italians were embracing Ignatius Loyola's teaching that individuals are most free when they merge their identities with the group and give their leaders the decision-making powers. Benito claimed that he was merely an agent of the people, the vehicle through which the collective will spoke. At that instant, Gregori was uncomfortably reminded that he, too, was subject to the will of a greater force, in fact, two forces, the pull of religion and the push of the Soviets. The first was freighted with sectarianism. Should one choose the Orthodox or Roman rites? The second, with its so-called dictatorship of the proletariat, was just another form of Fascism. So why prefer Stalin to Mussolini, or Mussolini to Stalin? The answer to that question would determine Gregori's future course of action.

Several days later, Gregori found himself asking: Do I want to linger in the lifeless antiquity of either the Orthodox or the Catholic Church? He felt that

Mussolini's speech had baptized him in beauty, and that to join the Fasci di Combattimento, not as a soldier, but as a spiritual fellow traveler appealed to him. His immediate problem was to find a trustworthy person with ties to the Fascists who could secretly insinuate him into the movement. He could not speak to Carlo Cospirato or to anyone at the Russicum, and he could hardly walk into a recruiting office. Given his church connections, he would be suspected immediately, even though the Fascists and the Vatican had made common cause in the Lateran Pacts of 1929.

So he sought out Margherita Sarfatti, and she in turn arranged for him to meet Galeazzo Ciano, married to Mussolini's daughter Edda. As minister of propaganda, Ciano was involved in the black work of disinformation. A week later, Gregori was standing in an ornate room, on a Turkish rug, before an enormous table, crafted by some Renaissance artist. A handsome young man with dark hair and lively eyes, Ciano would squint when focusing on a person whom he thought worth his attention. Rumor said that he distrusted Hitler. Gregori spoke with undisguised passion. "I agree with Mussolini that we must distinguish between the act, what a person does, and what a person thinks, the ideological commitment. Not to recognize the difference between behavior and belief is to falsify reality." He thumped his chest. "From within me, I hear a ringing voice that is at odds with my priestly calling. It says never rest, go forward. Where? Not toward some distant heavenly goal, but toward myself, the ideal self that I ought to be. The voice, as I understand it, is a moral admonition: *Sii uomo*, Be Man!"

Ciano wryly observed that the priest had only the Russicum to recommend him, a Catholic organization, and, at this moment, Gregori wished to leave that assignment for one with the Fascists. Gregori said, "Surely you have contacts in the Soviet Union who can report back to you on my loyalty."

"True, but tell me: What avenues, what conduits do you have access to that will allow you to tell Christians in Russia that Mussolini will guarantee freedom of religious belief?"

"I have access to the Catacomb Church. I am a leader in the Renovationist movement. The Russicum will put me in touch with Roman Catholics in European Russia, Ukraine, and the other Slavic countries. I even have contacts among some of the Protestant churches."

Playing with a wooden letter opener in the shape of a crocodile, Ciano tapped the point, the tail, on his blotter. He seemed to be calculating the advantages and risks of using Gregori Lipnoskii to spread information sympathetic to Mussolini and useful to the Fascists. Russia was fertile ground, given its size, its discontented minorities, its forced collectivization, and its antireligious laws. Every executed priest had a family, and that family had friends, and those friends had families. The chain was virtually endless. And what Gregori had said was absolutely true. The Italian government had well-placed spies who could report back on the loyalty—or treachery—of Gregori Lipnoskii, Renovationist priest.

"You will have to be trained," said Ciano, unscrewing the letter opener to reveal a pen and scribbling some notes on a pad. "Let us toast your new life." He removed from a drawer a bottle of wine and some biscotti and declared, "You have been born again!"

Resigning from the Russicum for reasons of health, Gregori underwent special training on the grounds of an army base outside of Rome, near the airport. Schooled in the crafts of propaganda, misinformation, and disinformation, he soon felt at ease with his assignment, and his tutors found him a quick study. On Sundays, the only day of the week he could see Angelina, he took her to Orthodox services and slowly inducted her into the Russian rites for the sole purpose of marriage. He had decided that her carefree behavior actually masked a profound sadness, but of what, he knew not. By the time he found out, it was too late.

Before leaving Rome, the couple married in Rome's Greek Orthodox Church of San Teodoro Megalomartire. The Credulo family attended; and Gregori's family, thinking him lost, was of course absent. During the service, Angelina held a handkerchief to her mouth to muffle her coughs, but read from the Bible with authority, as if God had cured her cough when she stepped up to repeat Holy Writ.

To prevent the Soviets from suspecting him of treachery, the Italian secret service took a leaf from *Pravda's* notebook and ran stories in the local press declaring that Gregori Lipnoskii had been unmasked as a double agent, and that the government had ordered him expelled from Italy immediately. Spared the cruelty of having to expose his students as spies, he wished them good luck sowing discontent among Roman Catholics in Russia. A few days later, an Italian military plane landed near the German-Russian border, where a car met Gregori and Angelina and sped them back to the Soviet Union.

Litvinov, of course, wanted to know how Gregori was discovered. Basely blaming Carlo Cospirato, Gregori declared that the man worked for the Italian secret service. Days later, unbeknownst to the priest, the man who had been his friend and given him a Topolino was found dead on the outskirts of Rome. A bullet to the back of the head led the police to think that he had been a member of the Mafia because he was executed gangland style.

When Gregori explained to Angelina the service that he had agreed to render the Italian government, she seemed pleased. Though not herself a member of the Fascist Party, she greatly admired Il Duce; and never having traveled outside of Italy, she found the prospect of living in the Soviet Union exciting. But their arrival in 1937, at the start of the Great Purges, was met with suspicion. Anyone who had been residing outside the country was tainted. In addition, Stalin regarded all foreigners as unreliable, even wives, so Angelina's Italian roots put her in danger. At first, Gregori's excuses kept the police from his flat. He had been working for Litvinov; he had been betrayed; he was prepared to tell the NKVD the little he knew. Then late one night, while lying in bed, he heard the elevator. He knew the rumors about such sounds. They were the heralds of a visitation. And indeed, the inevitable knock on the door followed.

His interrogation took place at NKVD headquarters, Four Liteiny Prospekt. From adjoining rooms, he could hear the cries of prisoners presumably being tortured. But he knew from Dimitri that the NKVD scared their victims by piping into the interrogating room the taped screams of actors. His inquisitor, a bespectacled former professor of biology, introduced himself as Foma Sharok, a Muscovite. Impassive and soft spoken, he had no stomach for torture, which he assigned to the criminals in his employ. The only light in the room came from Foma's arc lamp. Gregori sat in front of his desk. Training the light in the eyes of the priest, Foma made it virtually impossible for Gregori to see him, though Gregori could hear, in the dark, Comrade Sharok shuffling papers, a favorite trick interrogators used to make their victims think that they possessed large files of incriminating evidence. Foma began, not with an accusation, but with an assembly of facts that he hoped would slowly erode Gregori's confidence.

"Mr. Lipnoskii, or should I say Father Lipnoskii, you were initially recruited by Georgiy Vasilyevich Chicherin. His gentle methods, I should point out, have been replaced by more forceful ones. If we are to root out the enemies of the people, pruning is not the way to proceed, but uprooting the whole plant."

"What am I accused of? Nobody has told me."

"You are all the same—protesting your ignorance of the crimes you've committed."

"What crimes? I worked for the secret police at the Russicum in Rome and passed along my information to one Carlo Cospirato, a garage mechanic, who taught me Italian and gave me a car to use."

"I find it incredible that while at the Russicum, you never uncovered one spy. Although your own students hadn't yet graduated, certainly you must have been privy to some in the field." He paused and said kindly, "The Roman

Church is far more clever, Gregori, than you might think. All spies use aliases, so it should come as no surprise that the Russicum had assigned these men code names."

Was Foma, Gregori worried, trying to trap him by providing him with an excuse? "Whatever I learned, I turned over to Carlo."

"You spent time at Farfa Abbey with monks who hate the Soviets."

Gregori shifted in his chair. How had Comrade Sharok found out about the abbey? "I worshipped there. The political opinions of the monks were never made known to me."

"Do you know a Father Maurizio?"

"Yes, quite well. We became rather friendly at the abbey."

"He works for us."

Having no way of knowing whether Foma was telling the truth, Gregori took the safe path to avoid a possible trap. "Our discussions were always of a theological nature. At no time that I can remember did we talk about politics. In fact, we both agreed that churches, of any denomination, ought to stick to spiritual matters."

"Ah, then you did discuss the church's role in society?"

"In society, yes, but we agreed that it had no place in politics."

Foma said nothing—to let Gregori reconsider. But the priest remained calm. Foma knew that these priests, with their spiritual pretensions, were difficult to break. They always put their trust in a higher cause. Men who spied for money were easier to deal with.

"So you are telling me that Maurizio is a liar? That the money we give him is wasted?"

"I know nothing about the Soviet government's relationship to Father Maurizio and Farfa Abbey. It all comes as a surprise to me."

More papers rustled. "What if we brought Father Maurizio here and he confronted you with the truth."

"I would be delighted to see him."

Foma had taken a wrong turn. He decided to try another approach. "Your wife is Italian, and her family fancies Mussolini."

What Foma had said was true.

"My wife, Angelina, has never voted in an election. Her passion is for painting, not politics."

"We have been eavesdropping on your conversations. Now what do you have to say?"

Gregori saw yet another trap being laid. Whatever he said could be used against him. For good reason, his brother had told him never to volunteer any information. "We have nothing to hide."

"Your wife says she misses Rome."

"True."

"Anyone who doesn't appreciate the Soviet paradise is either mad or an enemy of the people."

"As a matter of fact, Comrade Sharok, she is ill, but not mentally. She has been coughing blood. We are seeing a specialist."

Foma decided to terminate the investigation. This priest, as far as he could determine, was harmless. If information should turn up later . . . well, the case could always be reopened.

After months of spitting blood, Angelina was diagnosed with tuberculosis and sent to a sanitarium outside of Leningrad. Gregori sat at her bedside, his distress and hers made all the more acute by the fact that she was in the early stages of a pregnancy.

"Why didn't you tell me in Italy that you suspected your cough was from consumption?"

"I didn't want to believe it."

"That's why you often feigned gaiety."

"Yes, even though I knew you thought my behavior peculiar. My lungs were a constant source of worry. I felt that my life would soon end. My mother used to say we are born, and we die, and in between, we dance. Soon, I shall slip off my dancing shoes, which of late haven't fit very well. When I laughed and teased, I was dancing on my own grave. But now the constant coughing, the blood clots, the stained handkerchiefs are heralds of death."

"But if I had known sooner, perhaps we could have arrested it."

"I didn't want to lose you. You have no idea how many Italian men leave their wives over an illness, a lost breast, gray hair . . ."

"Did you think I was like those men?"

"No, but I was afraid to take the chance."

He squeezed her hand and said, "You won't die! The doctors will cure you. They won't let you get away."

But she did die, and with her the fetus. Gregori mourned deeply, though his family, whom he had never contacted, knew nothing. He had feared that if his stepfather ever fell out of favor with Stalin, only distance could save him, the parched priest with an ecstatic thirst, and his wife. But death, which daily enters a thousand unsuspecting homes, rendered Gregori's precautions meaningless. In fact, the conjunction of Angelina's passing and Stalin's purges enabled the secret police to discover Gregori's treachery.

Shortly before Angelina had been sent to the sanitarium, Gregori had asked a catacomb priest about the efficacy of miracles. Told that a healer, Father Orlov, could cure consumption, Gregori had taken Angelina hundreds of miles to Totma, where the fatidic healer lived in a cave, with a pipe above ground to expel the fetidness. On the side of a hill stood the entrance, covered by an old rug. Angelina could hardly stand the odor of the pestiferous cell issuing not just from bodily waste and garbage, but from the old man himself, who had not bathed, according to rumor, for years. In the recess of one mud wall was a crucifix, several icons, candles, and a flat rock, covered with a red cloth, that supported a Bible. A kneeling mat lay before the stone. Here was where the mystic said his orisons and prayed for the recovery of the sick, but not before he laid his oily hands on the sufferer and anointed the ailing person's head. *Deus vobiscum.*

After the exorcism and healing rituals, Gregori carried Angelina through a driving rain to the horse wagon that had carried them from the train station. Her health declined noticeably on their return, and shortly, she was admitted to the sanitarium, where she inadvertently told one of the doctors about her experience in Totma, a disclosure that led the authorities to suspect Gregori, not of Fascist subversion, but of forbidden religious rites.

During their investigations, the secret police learned from Gregori's neighbors that he frequently entertained Ukrainian-speaking guests. The news confounded the NKVD. On further delving, they discovered that Gregori's visitors were all former Roman priests, and that some of them were rumored to still practice their faith in private. The agent in charge of the investigation reported to Comrade Sharok, who wanted to know how these Ukrainians could afford to travel to Leningrad, stay at hostels, pay for their meals, and yet have no visible means of support. "Find out more," he ordered.

Picking up Dominik Boretski, one of the Ukrainians, a frail and wizened man, the police confined him to an unheated cell, fed him greasy soup, and beat him with metal rods until he confessed.

When the NKVD showed Gregori the instruments of torture and the broken Boretski, Gregori told the secret police that he worked for the Italian secret service, in particular, the Propaganda Department, which supplied him with money and propaganda that came through the Serbian embassy. Comrade Sharok, pleased to have uncovered a traitor, was displeased to learn that his judgment of the man had proved wrong. An error of this magnitude could cost him his life. He was therefore inclined to have Gregori taken to Butovo or the killing fields at the Rzhevsky shooting range near Toksov; but after further thought, he decided a work camp would be crueler.

A month after Angelina's death, one year after his return to the USSR, Gregori found himself on a train for Arkhangelsk. From there the NKVD transported him to the fifteenth-century Solovki Monastery, in the Solovki Archipelago, just outside the Arctic Circle in the White Sea. The monastery's cathedrals, churches, and houses had been converted into a camp for prisoners. It was part of the infamous Gulag. Stalin, who had not forgotten his beatings from insensitive clerics during his seminary training in Georgia, thought it fitting that priests and others of a higher calling should be imprisoned in a former religious residence that passed most of the year in ice.

THAT WAY MADNESS LIES

Arriving early, Alexei slipped off his overcoat and paced the lobby waiting for Basmanaya. The checkered orange-blue linoleum and the furniture reminded him of clinics in Leningrad. Apparently, one factory supplied them all. The linoleum had escaped the floor molding and started to curl. Wherever he looked, he saw shoddy workmanship. Except for sports and ballet, which the Soviets excelled in, the country was hurting. Biology had been allowed to languish under the direction of that quack Lysenko. Psychiatry had been impoverished by the disparagement of the Vienna school and its replacement by the Bolshevik belief that once people were well housed and fed, mental illness would disappear. In fact, the proliferation of labor camps and denunciations had turned the country into an asylum inhabited by cowed citizens too terrified to speak their minds or ask innocently, "Can you tell me why my husband was arrested?"

The official Soviet policy of pretending that the country was nothing short of paradise meant that people who killed themselves were said to have died from accidents, disease, medical misadventures, or causes unknown. How could a great country, one that had produced Pushkin, Turgenev, Dostoevski, Chekhov, and Tolstoy, have made an art of prevarication? Had Pushkin not warned his countrymen about chimeras; had he not said, "The lie that elates is dearer than a thousand sober truths"? The Bolsheviks had turned Pushkin inside out and ruled the country shamelessly with self-serving deceptions, such as the belief that the USSR was heaven on earth.

In Ward One of the clinic, doctors treated outpatients and short-termers with general ills. Alexei strolled through the double doors into the ward, with its familiar sounds of alarm bells, buzzers, ringing phones, trolleys, shuffling feet, medical announcements, waiting-room patients, and commissars demanding immediate attention for themselves or their family. One such person, standing at the front desk and puffing on a cigar, was insisting on news about his wife's condition. She had been rushed to the clinic with appendicitis. Asked to snuff out his cigar, he reacted indignantly.

"Do you know who I am?"

"No," said the admitting nurse, "but I know that cigar smoke is not good for the patients. It carries into the rooms."

Undeterred, the man removed an enormous wallet and flashed a card. "Now," he said triumphantly, "you know who I am!"

The woman, who clearly had Caucasian blood in her veins and the temperament to match, told him to sit down with the rest of the people waiting to hear about family and friends. Waving the card under her nose, he asked peremptorily:

"Did you read it?"

"Whether you are General Tukhachevsky or Commissar Ivan Iashkov, you will have to wait for the doctor. When he arrives, I'll tell him you're here."

The end of Ward One led into a greenhouse, which Soviet doctors had built in the belief that patients who grow and tend plants are more likely to recover quickly. Peeking into the greenhouse, Alexei saw all manner of flowers and a gardener watering some ferns. He introduced himself to the man, who identified himself as Lazar Exter, an exile serving five years for a punning joke about Stalin. His long hair, freckled face, sunken eyes, and thin waist—his belt, secured in the last hole, hung down like a tongue—made Alexei think of the grave digger's scene in *Hamlet*. Was this Yorick come back to life?

Judging from the health and variety of the plants, Alexei could see that Lazar loved his flowers and had received training in horticulture. For a few minutes, the men stood and chatted; then Lazar led Alexei into the humidity shed, virtually an enclosed world of ferns and mosses and mushrooms and orchids and ivy that gave the shed the feel of a womb. On one of the potting tables rested a hot plate and teapot. Lazar offered Alexei a cup of herbal chai, but the doctor declined; he would shortly be meeting the director.

"Not a bad fellow," said Lazar, "but a bit of a buffoon."

"And Dr. Leshin?"

"An officious *putz*." Alexei stared. "A Yiddish word for prick."

"Useful."

"If you call Leshin a putz, he'll know what you mean."

"How often do the patients stroll through the greenhouse?"

"It depends. First of all, they have to be ambulatory or have a wheelchair. I've detected a pattern. The greater the depression or sadness, the more often they visit."

"Can you tell me why the mental ward has so few patients?"

"They come in waves, though I've never seen the ward completely full. Mostly they stay for only a few months, sometimes longer. I know why you ask, but the authorities act as if it's a state secret." He removed some dirt from under his nails. "Maybe it is."

Alexei whispered, "Are there any listening devices here?"

"No place to hide them. Put one in a pot and it'll get soaked."

"Do you know the woman in Ward Three, Rissa Binderova?"

"One look at her and you'll never forget." He blew a kiss to the air. "What a *punim*. That means face."

"I gather she's striking and clever."

"Both! A few months ago, she showed up with an attendant to look at my hothouse orchids. She quoted Pushkin, though not quite exactly:

'And eager lilacs everywhere

Lend flush and fragrance to the air.'

I took that as a compliment and thanked her."

"Can you tell me anything about Dr. Chulkaturin?"

"He didn't stay long and left in a hurry."

"And the previous doctor?"

Lazar shook his head as if to say, I can't discuss it.

"I think I know his name," said Alexei, "even though it seems to be unmentionable. A military man, right?"

"Army. But he's returned to his unit. I have my own theory why, but I'd rather keep it to myself. This much I can tell you," he said peering around. "The fellow created quite a problem for Basmanaya."

"Through a friend," said Alexei, "I learned he took his medical degree in Moscow, then posted to the Red Army: a special branch of the secret service."

Twenty minutes later, Basmanaya rushed into the clinic and asked for the return of the folders. "We keep them under lock and key," said the director.

"Good idea," replied Alexei, thinking of the parenthetic sentence that had escaped Dr. Leshin's notice. "No need for me to see them again. I'm fully satisfied."

Basmanaya briefly disappeared into his office. The moment he returned, Alexei started for the stairs.

"I can see you're anxious to meet her," said Basmanaya. "Is it for medical reasons or personal?"

"Why do you ask, comrade, when you know that I have neither met the woman nor seen her?"

"True, but others have, like your former professor in Leningrad, Dr. Chulkaturin." Basmanaya, knowing that Alexei had studied with him, had hoped to elicit a reply, but Alexei said nothing. So Basmanaya settled for directness. "Surely you know the man?"

"Yes, he is a famous doctor and teacher."

"I understand the *famous* physician was a mesmerizing speaker."

Alexei assumed that Basmanaya's information had come from Oblomov through Lena. Although she had indicated that she would be courting danger if the authorities knew about the notebook and its sale, in a country where denunciations won people promotions and medals, Lena's word, like that of so many others, was clearly for purchase.

"As a matter of fact, he was a spellbinder. Whenever he spoke, the auditorium was so full that latecomers had to stand at the back of the room. I always made it a point to arrive early." They had reached the second-floor ward. "And what of your impressions? After all, he worked here at the clinic."

"He left under a cloud, but I'm not at liberty to discuss it."

Alexei disingenuously asked, "Did he ever treat Rissa Binderova?"

They were now approaching the door to her room. Basmanaya stopped and replied, "I suggest we let sleeping dogs lie."

Whom was Basmanaya trying to protect: Dr. Chulkaturin or the clinic? For an instant Alexei wanted to ask whether the director could tell him more about Dr. P., but refrained lest Basmanaya think that one of the patients had revealed a confidence.

With a shaking hand, the director unlocked Rissa's door and swung it open. There sat a woman fingering a flute. For all her dishevelment, she was as beautiful as Pushkin's famously stunning wife, Natalia Goncharova, who cost him his life. Could this woman, a transfixed Alexei wondered, be equally lethal?

Although wearing a cheap apron over a peasant blouse, with her legs covered in coarse black woolen stockings, she could not disguise her harem eyes and sensuous lips. Mediterranean in coloring, she blended the best of the Sicilian women and the Greek. How her family had settled in Russia would, Alexei decided, be his first question. But before he could speak, she feigned playing the flute and, without looking up, asked, "Did you hear that? It's Mozart's Flute Concerto in G Major, the opening measures. Whether awake or asleep, I can hear those notes. The only way I can stop the ringing in my ears, and then only briefly, is to actually play the notes myself." She wet her lips and then played.

Tinnitus and earworm were not foreign to Alexei. A professor in medical school had said that some people hear a constant ringing in their ears, some an occasional ringing, and some hear music or a voice or a particular sound. The professor had recounted how a young student who loved American jazz had been induced by his friends to attend a classical concert to hear "good music." A pianist was playing a Mozart piano concerto, and the andante movement utterly arrested his mind to the point that he could never escape the haunting notes. Instead of turning the young man into a lover of fine music, the sound in his ears only reinforced his dislike of the classics. He tried every remedy—medical, herbal, and mechanical—to rid himself of the omnipresent Mozart. Although the music would retreat into the background when people spoke to him or other sounds commanded his attention, the background became foreground as soon as the other competing sounds disappeared. Finally, out of desperation, he requested that a doctor cut his auditory nerve. He said he would prefer deafness to the ceaseless sound of the music. The doctor cut the nerve, and the man lost his hearing, but the sound continued. It was embedded either in the auditory cortex or the neural system. Perhaps this explained why in spite of Soviet indoctrination, the old faiths persisted.

Alexei removed from his briefcase some sheet music and placed it on her bed. She gazed at the music and then, for the first time, at him. He smiled, but she turned back to Basmanaya and remarked, "I thought it was forbidden."

Confused, the director sputtered and mouthed an untruth. "Dr. von Fresser wasn't told. Therefore, we'll just pretend that it never happened."

"And Dr. Leshin?"

Her mentioning the lurking Leshin upended Alexei's plan to ask about her parents. Instead, he suggested a way to evade Leshin's authority. "You can memorize the music," he said, "and then return it. Leshin won't be any the wiser."

"It might take a few days."

"Then you had better get started."

"A man after my own heart, one who doesn't let a rule stop him from doing what's right." She played a few notes on her flute.

"When I return for the music, would you like me to bring more?" Basmanaya tried to object, but Alexei ignored him and said, "Miss Binderova, if I bring other works will you let me help you?"

She replied sincerely, "How could I resist?" She played again.

"Who are your favorites?"

"Vivaldi, Bach, Handel, Mozart."

"Done. I will talk to you again in three days."

Locking the door, Basmanaya insisted on knowing what Alexei hoped to achieve with the music. "She's mad. Believe me. Dr. Chulkaturin tried every therapy, but they all failed."

"In which case, why keep her isolated? She'd fare better in the company of others."

"She's a danger to the state," said the director emphatically, "and don't ask me to explain. It's all classified."

"There can be only one explanation. She is privy to information that could prove embarrassing to somebody. But who?"

"Keep asking such questions, and you'll end up in Kamchatka. I am warning you. This woman is poison. Stay away."

"What I can promise you, Leonid, is that in three days she will appreciatively play her flute and agree to cooperate." He clapped the director on the back. "Trust me."

Basmanaya sighed, realizing that he had become part of an experiment in mental reclamation that had yet to run its course. "Three days, you say, but I have a feeling that this is just the beginning of something larger."

Putting his arm around Leonid's shoulder, Alexei responded, "They picked the right man to run this clinic, perspicacious, persevering, and patient. I can already see your name in the medical annals."

Unfortunately, Dr. Leshin, having been told by an officious nurse about the visit, asked Alexei why his orders had been ignored.

"Unless you mean to imprison her here," said Alexei, "I feel that she deserves the best that we can do for her therapeutically. In fact, she was very forthcoming. Ask Director Basmanaya."

Shaking his head so rapidly that his jowls swung like twin pendulums, Basmanaya said, "I saw it with my own eyes."

"Rubbish!" exclaimed Dr. Leshin. "How would you know? If I'm not mistaken," he growled, "you're nothing but a functionary. I forbid any further contact with the patient!"

Had Dr. Leshin politely told the director that he wanted an end to their contact with Rissa Binderova, Leonid would have complied. But Leshin's having said that he was nothing more than an apparatchik offended him. Had he not worked his way up from emptying bedpans to the directorship of the clinic? In the Soviet Union, equality and accomplishment mattered. For good reason, then, he felt insulted. He remembered what Miss Binderova had said about breaking rules for the greater good, and as long as Alexei was there to take the blame, he would sneak him into the patient's room. In the meantime, he would transfer the officious nurse and stand watch for Dr. Leshin.

The next day, Basmanaya let Alexei borrow the key to her door—for an hour. Anxious to begin, Alexei took the stairs two at a time. Rissa was playing the music. He sat down beside her and listened. Although no expert, he was familiar enough with the classical composers and top-flight performers to know that Rissa was gifted. He waited to speak until she had finished.

Returning the sheet music, she said, "I've already committed it to memory," and then, like a child eyeing a possible present, asked, "What's in your briefcase?"

"Your favorites, as well as the Brahms Flute Concerto."

"It always moves me to tears."

"Besides music, does anything else affect you so deeply?"

"Memories."

"They bring us home."

"And yet we're told to forget."

"Why is that?" he asked.

"Because some people regard memory as a form of conspiracy. They tell us that the past is over and we should look to the future. I think such people can live from day to day only by forgetting."

"But only by remembering do we have a possibility of learning who we are," said Alexei, who fully intended to engage in Freud's talking cure to release whatever memories were tormenting her. "Tell me how your family came to settle in Russia."

Though not surprised that her parents had migrated from southern Europe, he was shocked when she told him when.

"My family came from Sicily at the end of the twelfth century, after the great scientific and poetic age turned to war instead of words. So my ancestors have lived in this country longer than most of the monolingual midgets who now govern it."

"Besides Russian, what do you speak?"

"Yiddish, German, Polish, Ukrainian, French, and English. I can also read Latin, Greek, Spanish, and Italian."

"Let me guess: Yours was a wealthy family with private tutors?"

"There were only two of us, my brother and I. He died in the Civil War, killed by the Red Army who found him in the company of the White Guard. In fact, he had been captured, but that didn't prevent the swine from killing him for being on the wrong side of the line."

"You're wasting your talents confined to this room."

She laughed and flapped her hands over her head. "Then open the door and let me fly away."

As before, her costume was unusual: Turkish puff pants, a rainbow Ukrainian tunic, and a red beret. A yellow scarf hung from her neck to her knees. Was she trying to look Bohemian?

"I understand you like riddles," said Alexei.

"Because I am one, and, if I'm not mistaken, you have come to unriddle me." She played a scale on the flute. "Right?"

"Frankly, you don't seem a riddle to me."

"Tell me, then, who am I?"

"Rissa Binderova. Your family came from Sicily."

She interrupted by putting a finger to his lips. "I appreciate your wit, which those boring Bolsheviks lack. You realize, though, if the floor nurse finds you here, she'll have you removed. Dr. Leshin's orders. She makes her rounds in the mornings and late afternoons. Those times that one actually needs her, she can't be found. She regularly takes her pleasure with one of the orderlies."

"She's been transferred."

Rissa gazed at him with dark, bewitching eyes. "Riddle one.

In a meadow teeming with bugs,

There Liudmila lies on a rug.

A Chernomor shorn of his beard

Is dressed in white and terribly feared.

Who is he?"

"Are you saying that you were taken from the clinic?"

"I just told you."

"Chernomor?"

Rissa picked up the flute and without resort to the sheet music played several notes from Vivaldi's A Minor Flute Concerto, breaking off suddenly.

"How's that for a hint?"

"I confess, I'm not fluent in music." He watched in utter fascination as her luscious lips fluted another musical phrase. "I need your help," he said, "give me more of a hint."

"Riddle the second.

A medical man in a spanking white coat

A stone in his trousers, a gun at my throat,

Come tell me this riddle, and I'll give you a groat."

Alexei mused for a minute and shook his head. Rissa again played, this time from the sheet music he had brought her, Handel's Flute Concerto in G Major.

"I give up. What's the answer?"

"Haven't you read my files?"

"The clinic has either hidden or destroyed them."

She resumed playing the Handel—rapturously.

✶

From his window, Alexei could see a full moon, and, as he often did in winter, he chose to walk in the cold, silver night. He intended to look at the river, but he never arrived. Instead, he found himself drawn to the theatre, where mostly young people were streaming into the auditorium. He followed them and took a hard wooden seat. Billed as a poetry reading, the event featured three local actors who had volunteered to read the poems of Pushkin, Blok, Akhmatova, Pasternak, Mandelstam, and Tsvetaeva. In no time, every seat was taken and the aisles filled. Alexei looked around hoping to recognize the young man who had accompanied him on the train from Leningrad, but couldn't identify him among the grim-faced secret agents in the audience who tactlessly peered out of the corners of their eyes. These men—and some women—made no effort to hide. When others clapped and cheered, they remained immobile; when others laughed, they never smiled. The young listeners obviously knew the police had come to watch them, and yet they eagerly gave voice to their enthusiasm, yelling the names of their favorite poems and requesting that some be repeated. Here, in Alexei's estimation, was to be found the best of Russia, the lovers of language and thought who valued their country's literary traditions.

A man resembling Mandelstam sat in the second row, and the woman next to him recited every poem in unison with the actor. Alexei asked the young man next to him:

"The two people in the second row: Are they the Mandelstams?"

"Yes," wheezed the boy, reeking of nicotine. "Osip and Nadezhda. Sitting next to them is Anna Akhmatova."

"*The* Akhmatova?"

"The very one. When word got out that Anna and Osip would be here tonight, the exiles rushed from every cellar and garret. I wouldn't be surprised if some of the people here can't even read, but they love to listen to poetry. My own favorite is Marina Tsvetaeva."

When Alexei mentioned Pasternak, the lad said, "Too dreamy for me. I prefer poetry of feeling to descriptions of woodlands and meadows."

One of the actors, as slight as a whisper but with the resonance of a prophet, read some of Akhmatova's poems, which elicited excited applause. He asked her to stand. She bowed to the audience. In response, the people rose to their feet and cried their delight.

He introduced Mandelstam, now exiled to Voronezh, and then quoted from Osip and a deceased Russian poet, Nikolai Gumile. "'Words devoid of precise significance,' our beloved Mandelstam says, 'are a perversion of language and have a bad smell. Many people have talked of such dead words.' No doubt he was thinking of Gumile, who writes, 'Dead words smell badly. These

words are terrifying because they show the extent to which people have renounced the chief quality that makes us human: the gift of speech and thought.'"
Deafening applause.

A pale actress with too much lipstick read next. She chose lines from Tsvetaeva that Alexei felt frighteningly apt.

"How is life with simulacrum,
For you who've trodden Sinai . . . ?
After Carrara marble,
How's life with crumbling plaster?"
She continued:
"Be honest: are you happy?
No? In trough's shallowness
How fare you, darling? Worse?
As I do, with another?"

Returning to his attic, Alexei thought about the woman he'd married and the one he now wished for instead. Natasha and Rissa were both strikingly handsome. The first had courage and craft, like her mother, and a compassionate heart. He had known from the start the list of her virtues; he had also known her principal defect. She lacked the coruscating intelligence that would make him want to talk to her as well as love her. After coitus, he would roll over and feign sleep. What did they have in common? Their conversations focused on family and friends, people and things, never ideas. She was uneducated, and no matter how he tried to convince himself that her warmth and wiliness made up for her absence of wit, he could not escape the fact that he found her dull. How well he remembered the night before his marriage, an evening spent with several of his medical-school chums. They had praised Natasha's pulchritude and comeliness, but not a word had been said about a beautiful brain. Like Pushkin, who had a premonition of disaster the night before he wed, Alexei had shook with apprehension. Natasha could satisfy his aesthetic and sensuous longings, but not his need to live a life of the mind. As a man of integrity, he had felt honor bound to marry the young girl to whom he was betrothed. Yes, "girl" was the right word. It took but a few weeks of marriage to realize that passion could not substitute for companionable minds. She was a provincial; he was not.

He often thought that had he called the marriage off the night before, he would have shown more honesty than saying yes to a contract that he felt he could never honor. Although the village might have thought poorly of him, his friends would have understood. Then why had he not excused himself from a commitment that he knew he'd regret? The simple answer was family, his and hers. In their provincial way, his mother and father had come to admire Natasha's peasant skills, to say nothing of her looks. She was unpretentious, kind, self-effacing, hardworking, and malleable. It was her malleability that made her subject to all kinds of mistakes. The last person to talk to her always came away the winner. She could not handle competing ideas. Hence, the balance always tipped in favor of the last voice she heard, even when that voice was not the most logical.

Natasha's family comprised the other side of the equation. Her mother doted on her and had planned since the day of her birth to see her well positioned. Natasha would not make a disastrous marriage with a drunkard. To the contrary, she would marry a man of means, dress well, and travel in educated circles. Alexei fit the description. And had not her stepfather, a good man, slapped him on the back and told him that Natasha would make a good wife? He had even walked Alexei through a flowering meadow to dilate on the virtues of an honest woman, such as he had married. To dash the hopes of two families was more than Alexei could bear.

During their time together, Natasha had remained unsophisticated. Perhaps their separation would help. One could hope; one could tutor her, as he had, but he feared that no magic could turn chaff into grain. For all the Soviet crowing about a classless society, finally one's rank was determined not by property and money, but by education and intellect. Rissa was a noblewoman, his wife a pretty toy.

Feeling the need to see Rissa not once a week but every day, he showed up the next morning to the surprise of Basmanaya, who reluctantly turned over the key. But instead of going directly upstairs, Alexei passed through the clinic, exited a back door, and hastened to a locksmith. When he entered Rissa's room, he again sensed her magnetism, a combination of loveliness and lyricism.

"Do you know why I've come back today?"

"To bring me more music."

"No, to try to bring you relief."

"Am I then to assume that you know why first the resident doctor was sent away and then Dr. Chulkaturin?"

"I know the second physician but not the first. Let me guess. His initials are VGP. Is that right?"

Like a flower at nightfall, Rissa folded her bloom. She hugged her knees tightly, buried her face in her arms, and refused to answer. A moment later, she fell back on the bed in a fetal position and began to keen softly.

"Help me to understand, Rissa. I've been told nothing." He touched her arm gently. "The story must come from you."

She closed her eyes. Alexei fruitlessly tried to coax her out of this state. At last, he left her room. Returning Basmanaya's key, he walked home pensively to study one of his medical books. The next day, he called on the other patients. This time, he decided to speak to them individually in the small examining room, with its desk, padded chair, and one wooden bench. He started with Helena Schmidt and then interviewed them in the same order as before; but this time, he deliberately tried to antagonize them, in the hope of eliciting a disclosure that might explain some hidden motive or essence for their behavior.

"You represent yourself as a deviationist, an oppositionist, but I think you are actually working for the secret police."

"Then you are a fool," came the reply.

"Fools often speak wisdom."

Helena shouted, gesticulated, and slammed her fist against the desk, saying, "Would you have me cultivate a respect for the state rather than for what is right?" She then stormed out, cursing Alexei.

In turn, Benjamin Federov, Arkady Gorbatov, and Sviatoslav Sarkaski responded angrily to his charge of their working for the secret police; each fulminated and shook a fist, and, curiously, each responded with similar protestations about his being a fool, and the same line, "Would you have me cultivate a respect for the state rather than for what is right?" Coincidence? Surely not. But he had no facts or files to explain it.

Intuitively, he felt that the answers to most, if not all, his questions lay behind the locked door. Predictably, he now found himself persona non grata in Ward Two. The patients refused to speak to him, an indication that his time in the clinic would be short. He returned to Rissa's room clandestinely, late at night, and discovered her playing Bach. A small table lamp created a pool of light. That afternoon, he had taken a tram across town to buy her several pieces for solo flute. She barely raised her head from the music to acknowledge his presence. Her long, dark hair hung loosely around her face, as she intently repeated measures and phrases to master the Bach. He sat on the bed and silently watched. Eventually, she looked up, and he handed her additional pieces of sheet music.

"Thank you. During your absence I've been thinking . . . about you . . . and the others."

"What others?"

"Have they told you yet why I'm here?"

"No."

"I've said nothing . . . kept my silence. If they ask . . ."

"I will tell them that you have been no help at all, that you are incorrigible. If you want me to say worse, I'll oblige."

"I'm fearful."

"Of what?"

"Punishment."

"What can they do?"

"Send me to Kolyma."

"You seem to have blat. No one else has a private room."

"There are reasons, but don't ask for them."

Alexei gathered that she knew people in government or in some influential family. Although the Soviets denied it, the old landed gentry still had some sway. "If you can have your own quarters, why can't your friends arrange your release?"

"You really are an innocent. The Soviets use every form of persuasion available to them, from aristocrats to ignorant peasants. Although you don't know it, they are using you now."

"I am merely trying to restore your peace of mind."

"I see: render me docile and malleable. It won't happen."

"No, I want to drive out your fears."

"Impossible."

"Can't we just talk?"

"We are."

"About why you are fearful."

"It's too complicated."

"Has any doctor ever given you sodium pentothol?"

"What's that, a secret Soviet potion that induces paradise?"

"It's a favorite Russian drug, a kind of truth serum that helps to free repressed memories. You talk and I listen."

"And once you tap into my memories . . . what then?"

"If you make peace with your past, it won't poison the present."

She paused and looked around. "You know that at this moment the Soviet cockroaches might be eavesdropping. But even if they are, what do you propose?"

"There's a new theory about the scrutiny of words."

"Psychoanalysis."

"Literary analysis."

"Words, words, that's all theory is. People need bread, not theories. In Russia, thinking has engendered a plague. Once, our country was green with promise; now, it's dead and mourning."

Alexei touched her hand. She tensed, then relaxed, and let his fingers remain resting on hers.

"The preservation of our memory is in words. Whether we intend to or not, we reveal ourselves in our speech. Farmers talk one way, professors another. A good doctor treats his patients' words as clues that require close reading to arrive at an accurate diagnosis. The sodium pentothol can make it easier for you to remember words."

Her expression bespoke both doubt and concern.

"You want words, I'll give you words. Riddle the third.

I met a doctor constructed of stone.
I met a doctor when I was alone.
I met a doctor who counseled 'gainst fear.
I grimly refused to issue a tear.

How could a doctor be fashioned of stone?
How could a doctor be deaf to my tone?
How could a doctor counsel against fears?
How could a doctor take refuge in sneers?

A doctor sans shame has bone made of stone.
A doctor sans grace takes Rissa from home.
A doctor sans clothes exhibits his spear.
A femme in a field is flooded with fear."

Shortly after six o'clock the next morning, Basmanaya's phone rang. Dr. Leshin had called to curse the clinic director.

"The man on duty, last night, said Alexei entered her room. Are you trying," Leshin shouted, shaking the phone like a rattle, "to get us both posted to the outer reaches of Russia?"

"He must have a key."

Leshin repeated mockingly, "'He-must-have-a-key!' Of course he does. Any imbecile could deduce that."

Basmanaya swore without conviction. "Damn it, I forbade him."

"A year in a work camp might do him some good."

"Or a military assignment."

"How many times do we have to repeat this exercise?"

"Are you saying we're at risk?"

"You are twice an imbecile. Of course, we're at risk! From the first signs of trouble, I told you to bug her room and record every word. No, you had to be softhearted and just let her be."

"Do you suppose he is trying to psychoanalyze her?"

"You're the director of the clinic, not me!"

"Andrei, you must admit that I did recommend she be sent away."

"What, so she could spread rumors through every camp in the country? I was right: better to keep her locked up."

"Psychoanalysis," Basmanaya mumbled. "I hate the word. Why is it the things we hate have so many syllables? Psychoanalysis! Six syllables. If you break it up into two words, 'Psycho,' and 'analysis,' then the longest word has only four syllables."

"You really are an imbecile. What's your point?"

A confused Basmanaya had lost the thread. "My point about what?"

"Breaking it up into two words."

"I just thought it worth mentioning."

"Leonid Basmanaya you come from a good family. You have a kind wife, with relatives in Moscow. Act the part!"

"My apologies."

"The last two physicians were charged with immoral behavior. What will this one be charged with?"

"Why not the same thing?"

"Your problem, Leonid, is that you suffer from a lack of imagination. What if every time I stole, I stole the same things? Don't you think the repetition would be noticed and prove my undoing?"

"But you wouldn't steal, doctor. So it's a moot question."

"Leonid, I am going to murder you!"

"I was just trying to help."

"Then keep still." After a disquieting pause, Leshin continued, but deliberately and subdued. "When a man sentenced to internal exile for political activity inimical to the state violates the terms of his exile, he is subject to imprisonment—or worse."

"Alexei will say he's a doctor with a right to see the patient."

"Ah, so in that thick skull of yours, there is actually some semblance of thought."

"In school, my teachers said I was quite clever."

"That was the old Russia, where the teachers were all blind. Now the schools have Soviet teachers who can recognize fools."

"The trouble is: He hasn't done anything wrong."

"Not yet, but like the others, he will. That's why I want him to continue seeing her, and I want a microphone installed in the room."

"I see. He'll gain her confidence, maybe more, and then . . ."

"We'll have access to both her words and deeper feelings."

Basmanaya shook his head at the phone as if Leshin could see him through the receiver. "Andrei, I still think we ought to send her away. May I speak my mind?"

"That shouldn't take very long."

"I remain convinced she's a threat, a danger to me *and* the clinic. That's why I recommend exile."

"By keeping her here, we rule the roost. Once out of our control, she could bring down on us the chistka. At the first sign of trouble, those damn purges spring up like mushrooms. Bug her!"

Alas, Rissa's room had been recently plastered, and a patch would draw notice. Unless a listening device could be planted in a light fixture, Basmanaya would have to think of some pretext for fixing a wall. Did Leshin have any ideas?

"You always have some excuse, Leonid. Just move her to the visitor's cottage. She likes gardens." Lapsing into sarcasm, he said, "With the sewer line next door, she'll have plenty of water. Besides, the cottage is completely wired. What we can't hear," he laughed sardonically, "we'll write off to silent love."

"The reason for my caution is, well, that if the listening devices were discovered and the clinic's work came to light . . ."

"They won't."

"But if they did, in your capacity as chief medical officer . . ." Basmanaya chose deliberately not to finish his sentence, hoping to induce the right response from Dr. Leshin.

"I'd step in."

Sighing with relief, Basmanaya added, "You know, Andrei, you really are quite a good fellow. So it's understood?"

"If a problem arises . . ."

"We dismiss the doctor for unprofessional behavior."

"Like our military friend and the professor."

"Precisely."

Told that she and her belongings would be moved to the cottage that very day, Rissa chose to wait in the humidity shed of the greenhouse. Alexei found her there, under the watchful eye of a woman attendant, whom he sharply directed to leave. He then retreated to the pharmacy and collected from Comrade Lvov a syringe and a vial of sodium pentothol. When he returned, Rissa was admiring some exotic orchards, glorious in their different coloration. Alexei removed his vest in the heavy air and sat watching Rissa fondle the petals.

"What better place to talk," he said, "than in the Garden of Eden. And you, like Eve, can lead me astray."

"I—I don't know," she said without turning to look at him.

"What's the matter?"

She failed to reply.

On the potting table, Alexei put a Costa Rican orchid and some bay leaves. He told Rissa to inhale the aromatic leaves while staring into the heart of the flower. With her permission, he injected the drug and told her to say whatever word came into her head in response to his prompts.

"For example, if I say black, you're likely to say white. Fat, skinny. Tall, short."

She shook her head and slowly sunk to the ground, where she sat glassy eyed from the drug. Alexei sat next to her.

"Courting."

"Candy."

"Inside."

"Outside."

"Meadow."

"Stream."

"Violets."

"Violence."

"Picnic."

"Grass."

"Ward Two."

"Informers."

"State."

"Secret."

"Mayflies."

"Sex."

"Pistol."

"Forehead."

"Click."

"Fear."

"I'll shoot."

"Rape."

Alexei took her hand. "Viktor."

"Podol," she screamed, and vomited.

Alexei kneeled beside her and stroked her hair. "You're safe now, Rissa. It's over. You'll never again have to relive that pain."

Rissa stared at him with dilated eyes as mournful as mist. Then she pressed her cheek against his and cried copiously, mumbling, "Never again, never again."

A bell rang in the clinic, signaling an emergency. Rissa reached up with one hand as if the sound were palpable and she could seize it. "No, it was a cow bell," she said. "A farmer was leading his cattle to pasture."

★

Alone in the cottage together, except for the listening devices, Rissa told him what she'd discovered: that Ward Two was a training area for spies placed in mental hospitals, where they would be privy to the confidences of "politicals" confined as insane.

Alexei, incredulous, said, "Informers, all of them!"

"Who is not an informer? I swore to be silent, and here I am telling you."

"They do it for a privileged life."

"And I in the service of what?"

"I'd like to think love."

When the listening devices revealed that Alexei knew about the "training program," Leshin and Basmanaya agreed that he too could never be allowed outside the premises. Alexei merely asked that his clothing and books be moved to the cottage.

"They both love classical music," said Leshin sneeringly. "Then let them lie in the beautiful silent music of a padlocked cottage."

Basmanaya cackled. "He said that in Russia the sane are jailed and the insane go free, so we've given him what he wants."

The two men, for professional and voyeuristic reasons, regularly eavesdropped on Alexei and Rissa. Although they heard sonorous flute music, they also heard, to their surprise, talk about plays and poems, operas and ballets. Alexei and Rissa discussed the artistic masters, mostly agreeing, sometimes not. They exchanged political opinions and were consonant in their belief that the individual mattered more than the state. The lovers were often mute, ostensibly finding in silence a fonder language than words. Clearly, garrulity suited neither of them, but the fullness of ideas did and, the listeners concluded, the satisfaction of touch.

Once while making love—yes, this too was overheard—Alexei said, "In the years ahead, will we remember all our yesterdays? Time forgets, but memory is forged in remembrance."

Rissa's sad reply, though murmured, was also recorded, "If we live . . . and even then one is never truly free."

The last time that Dr. Leshin spoke to Alexei, he said, "Would you like us to tell your wife that you have taken a mistress and have initiated a new life— all for love?"

"What would you, an opportunist, know about love?" said Alexei.

"Insults, insults, they mean nothing. And as for love, it is merely a rush of blood, an ephemeral fever that inflames a certain appendage, and, in fact, a madness that temporarily blinds one. So you are in the right place, after all, Alexei von Fresser, a mental institution for the criminally insane."

For his own sadistic reasons, Leshin did indeed tell Natasha about Alexei's infidelity. She cried bitterly and prayed to the Virgin Mother to touch her husband's heart. Her own "larks," as she called them, she dismissed, knowing that they lacked the force of feeling. After all, to survive in the USSR, everyone whored. She consoled herself by invoking the New Socialist Order, where men and women could cohabit without benefit of marriage, and where divorce did not make one a pariah. Women were free to make choices and not suffer social stigmas. If Alexei wanted to enter into a dalliance with some crazy woman in a mental institution, he was free to do so. Similarly, she was free to take men to her bed.

And yet, she was provincial enough to believe that marriage was made in heaven. Suddenly, she wanted to embrace Alexei and beg him to love her. They would start anew, he tenderly stroking her hair, and she leading his hand to her bosom. They would have children, and they would move to the countryside and live happily into old age.

All of these thoughts Natasha wrote her husband in letters resonant with passion, her newly acquired voice. But Leshin intercepted and cruelly used them to upbraid Alexei.

"Love is not coitus," said Alexei, "but a meeting of true minds."

Leshin laughed, "Spare me your sentimentality. A hard penis has no conscience."

ONLY THE PITILESS

Although Dimitri's desire for another man frightened him, he couldn't suppress his love for Yuri Suzdal. At first they had retreated to Yuri's apartment and merely kissed, but not before Dimitri had carefully studied the flat for hidden microphones. The inherent tenderness of both men led to gentle touches and finally sex, which they found immensely gratifying, but also terrifying. They knew that if Dimitri's superiors discovered their relationship, executions would follow. The charge would be that Dimitri's special status made him privy to secret information that he undoubtedly passed on to Yuri. No proof of passed messages or coded cables was necessary. Homosexuality earned one the firing squad.

To make matters worse, in 1936, Genrikh Yagoda had been replaced as the head of the secret police, renamed Narodnyi Kommissariat Vnutrennikh Del (NKVD), by a man with a savage temperament and a maniacal outlook, Nikolai Ivanovich Ezhov, the bloody dwarf. Owing to his influence, Soviet party members were now, a year later, required to replace their membership cards with passports, which were far more difficult to obtain and dangerous to forge. The chistka, employed periodically to cleanse the party of malingerers, malcontents, and impostors, now became both a party-revival campaign and a hunt for enemies. The previous desultory purges, often harmless, evolved into full-scale terror directed against anyone deemed an enemy of the people. Ezhov's "war" employed the slogan: "Under current conditions, the inalienable quality of every Bolshevik must be the ability to detect the enemy of the party, however well he may be masked." In particular, the Ezhovshchina, "the Ezhov business," sought to purge "Formers," that is, social aliens: people from the wrong class who were trying to hide their former identities, like priests and kulaks and royalty and White Guards and Tsarist officials. Stalin had ordered Yagoda shot, a signal that a new ruthless order was replacing the old corrupt one. Besides, Yagoda had a Jewish background; Ezhov did not. When Natasha had asked her brother which dignitary would be moving into Yagoda's dacha, Dimitri couldn't be sure, though he assumed the new chief of the People's Commissariat of Internal Affairs would receive the prize. Would he also, Natasha wondered, inherit Yagoda's pornographic films and handsome library?

The Ezhovshchina made Dimitri's work all the more precarious—and morally hateful. Whereas before he merely reported people for misbehavior that earned them a slap on the wrist, his reports now could lead to a person being tortured or exiled or shot, or all three. But if he failed to find traitors, his superiors were likely to accuse him of collaboration, a charge that could lead to his immediate discharge or arrest. An NKVD agent was judged by the number of denunciations in his dossier. In desperation, Dimitri sought to transfer to guard duty in the Kremlin or surveillance at the railroad station. He applied to work in the passport office. He even offered to take a demotion and work as a chauffeur to one of the Kremlin courtiers. But in every instance, his request was denied, and, in fact, the more he tried to disengage himself from spying, the more he hurt his own case. Although he couldn't explain why all his requests were refused, he guessed that the cause was Razan's position as Stalin's barber. Had he not recommended him? And as long as his father-in-law regularly held a razor to the Boss's neck, the NKVD would want to hold one to Dimitri's, obliging him to prove his loyalty by engaging in the unsavory work of the secret police.

At first, Yuri had no precise idea what services Dimitri rendered the NKVD. Rounding up party laggards sounded harmless enough. But with Ezhov now in office, Dimitri felt compelled to tell his lover what his work exactly entailed. He even graciously volunteered to disappear from Yuri's life, but the hairdresser said that their fortunes were intertwined. As frightened as he was by Dimitri's revelations, Yuri merely counseled caution. Dimitri suggested they no longer travel in the same taxi or sit together at the theatre. Meeting for a vacation in Odessa was impossible. They would have to confine their trysts to Yuri's apartment, and they would have to enter and leave at different times and through different doors. Even though Dimitri had not found any listening devices, they agreed to speak sparingly when they met. The two felt certain that the Ezhovshchina, with its diligent eavesdropping and letter opening, couldn't last. But for now, they decided that if Yuri's neighbors inquired about Dimitri's visits, the hairdresser would say that Dimitri and he met to play chess; and if anyone should knock at his door, their clothes lay at the ready, as well as a chessboard with the pieces placed to suggest a game in progress. The men had even agreed on which side of the board to play, black or white. Visitors appeared infrequently, but when the superintendent or postman or occasional neighbor materialized, Dimitri would spring to the table as Yuri answered the door. On the wall hung a large-framed portrait of Stalin.

Secrecy came naturally to Dimitri—it was his business—but the sneaking about began to wear on Yuri, who broached the idea of their leaving the country. So alarmed was Dimitri that he could hardly sleep the whole night. Flight would bring down on his family the harshest of punishments; and if the two men were apprehended . . . he couldn't even entertain the awful consequences.

Once Natasha had told Dimitri of Alexei's behavior in Voronezh, her brother felt certain that his career had come to an end, a feeling reinforced by a summons from Ezhov, actually a handwritten note on official stationery from the dwarf, who requested a "private meeting." He had seen the midget at a distance, had heard of his reputation for callousness, and had seen hardened men tremble at the mere mention of his name. Anticipating the worst, Dimitri penned a farewell letter to his mother and left it on his cot in the Kremlin. He debated whether to take along his pistol. If he was condemned, he could shoot himself before the guards could manacle him. But then he realized that he would never be allowed in the presence of Ezhov while armed.

As Dimitri walked across the square to the house used by the secret police, birds sang and the azure air exuded the perfume of spring. The sunlight warmed the cobblestones and made the domes of Saint Basil dance with color. Only the surrounding redbrick buildings, which looked like oozing blood, hinted at the menacing ministry that stood just a few steps away from the Kremlin's architectural wonders. Dimitri regarded the scene as a telling juxtaposition: Beauty and the Beast. Almost immediately, he was ushered into Ezhov's office, where Dimitri had once conversed with Yagoda. The diminutive NKVD chief sat under a new portrait of Stalin and behind a large desk, several inches lower than normal, in a raised chair, lest those seated in front of him see only his head peering above the desk. Ezhov greeted him warmly, shaking his hand and pouring him a schnapps. Half a dozen files, each holding several folders, commanded Ezhov's attention. Making a great show of rustling through them, he exuded confidence, as if to suggest that whatever charges he wished to bring, the evidence lay before him.

"Ah, yes, here it is. Your father-in-law . . ."

Why did I ever recommend that damn Jew, thought Dimitri? I knew he was at the root of my summons. "Razan Shtube," he replied.

"A favorite of Comrade Stalin's."

"Really?" he said, lightly clapping his hands in relief.

"Quite so." Ezhov thumbed through some additional papers. "Your brother-in-law . . . now *he's* an interesting case."

Dimitri shook his head censoriously. "A fool."

"In Voronezh, he had a chance to redeem himself, but he chose to throw it away. Such a peculiar fellow. We haven't exterminated him because he presents such a unique psychological specimen. The attending doctor treats him like a microbe under a microscope."

"I thank Comrade Stalin and you for keeping him alive." Dimitri slightly bowed. "Perhaps one day he will come to his senses."

"Just for the record, the Supreme Leader prefers pariahs and distrusts those who have a pure party record." He tapped his pen on a blotter. "I wish for you to tell your sister's husband that he owes Comrade Stalin his undying loyalty, and that those who bite the hand that feeds them. . . . Well, you understand."

"Perfectly."

"Good." Ezhov held two fingers to his mouth, as if sealing his lips with the papal signature. "Perhaps it has not escaped your notice that we have kept you on in the secret police even though your family's record is blighted."

"I can never thank the Soviet state enough for its generosity."

Ezhov looked at his nails. "Why have you requested transfers?"

Prepared for this question, Dimitri answered, "Because I don't feel I have the qualifications for such important work."

"It takes only one quality: pitilessness."

Dimitri carefully considered his reply, one that would allow him to escape unscathed. "For our enemies there can be no mercy."

Ezhov nodded in agreement. "Good, very good." He opened one of the files. "Given our generosity in ignoring your family's record, we expect a favor." Dimitri agreed and waited for Ezhov's orders. "You are a friend of one Yuri Suzdal." Before Dimitri could respond, Ezhov held up a hand signaling that he had more to say, and that Dimitri could comment later. "We have reason to believe that Yuri Suzdal is a traitor." At that moment, Dimitri wished he had brought his pistol to kill himself. "Several people have denounced him." Ezhov studied the files on his desk. "He is a social alien with ties to the Trotskyites." Dimitri knew for a fact that Yuri cared nothing about politics and had no such connections. "We have intercepted letters between him and the Trotsky traitors." Suddenly Ezhov shoved across the desk a letter that Dimitri could tell in a glance had been forged, and not artfully. His lover was left-handed and his writing had a distinct slant, which this missive lacked. "How would you describe your friendship with Suzdal, and what can you tell us about him?"

Although the question sounded innocent enough, Dimitri sensed snares in the words. Ezhov had asked him to describe his "friendship" with Yuri, but was he using the word ironically, knowing the actual relationship between the two men? Was he implying that friends share the same political opinions? Perhaps he was being deliberately led to lie in defense of his friend. He pondered his secret life with Yuri. If he failed to mention that they were lovers, and if the secret police had proof of their homosexuality, he would immediately be placed in a cell.

Dimitri tried to buy time by staring at the large framed photograph of Stalin hanging on the wall behind Ezhov.

Ezhov removed the cap of his pen and scribbled a note, remarking, "You haven't answered my question."

Feeling sweat trickling down his neck, Dimitri pulled at his collar. "I know very little about him, except that he's considered one of Paul's best hairdressers."

"Is that all? What about the many hours you spend with him over the chessboard?" He opened a folder. "We have a letter here from the building superintendent. He says that on the two occasions when he entered Yuri Suzdal's flat, you and the suspect were playing chess."

At the superintendent's first appearance, he claimed to be testing the heating system. The second time, he checked the float in the toilet, leading Dimitri to warn Yuri that the super was up to no good. In fact, the moment the super had left, Dimitri studied the toilet to make sure he had not installed a listening device.

"The man will denounce you," predicted Dimitri.

"You've been in the spy service too long," Yuri had laughed.

"Do your conversations always revolve around chess or do you sometimes talk about politics, like the Five-Year Plan?" asked Ezhov.

"Yuri has no interest in politics or economics. What would lead you to think so?"

Ezhov raised one eyebrow to indicate his displeasure. "I ask the questions, not you." He opened another folder and in a flat voice said, "This letter comes from one of his customers. I will spare you the beginning and come right to the point. 'I said to Yuri Suzdal that the Five-Year Plan seemed to be revolutionizing Russia, and he said, "At what price?" 'I thought this comment sounded like Trotsky.'" Ezhov grinned. "The good citizens of this country, as you can see, never sleep. They know that our enemies are everywhere."

How could people protect themselves against denunciations, unless they remained silent, and even then what was to stop the malicious-minded from dipping a pen into their odious ink to write poisonous lies, perhaps for no other purpose than to settle a score or earn some tenant more space in his apartment building? He had seen denunciatory letters in which the writers, usually in ungrammatical Russian, complained that their neighbors had given them the evil eye, or cast a spell over them, or conjured up fatal fumes, or spoke with a Yiddish accent, or spent so much money that it must have been stolen, or punned on Stalin's name to make it sound like a swear word, or didn't stand when Koba's car passed through the neighborhood. Protection against such denunciations was impossible. In fact, whatever a person said was eventually used against him.

"Comrade Ezhov, I cannot dispute the letters in your files. They are there in black and white. But I can tell you that I have never heard Yuri Suzdal speak of our country in anything but patriotic terms. He avidly follows the progress of our chess champions."

"Chess champions be damned! The man doesn't even have on his wall a copy of your sister Yelena's mustache painting. I would have thought that in light of the talk it has generated, *you* might have given him one, though all the copies have now been recalled."

Dimitri knew only what Anna had told him: that Yelena had painted Stalin's mustache, that a great many people had requested copies, and that the original had been sold and then confiscated. When he had asked why, his mother had pleaded ignorance and described the Tatar who had come to her apartment, a man whom Dimitri vaguely knew. Perhaps from him he could learn the truth.

The look of surprise on Dimitri's face led Ezhov to soften his tone and explain. "The painting was not perfect, and though no painting ever is, we wanted her to paint another from a better photograph of Stalin than the one that she used. If you are thinking that our Supreme Leader is vain, let me assure you that he knows nothing of this matter. It originated with the secret police."

Dimitri guessed Ezhov was lying and that one of the tenants had reported Yelena, and that the "super" had said the Stalin portrait in Yuri's apartment was unflattering. At that moment, facing Ezhov, he decided that the NKVD knew virtually everything about everyone, and yet he told himself that he would never make public his love affair with Yuri. Call it old-fashioned honor, call it fear, call it the hope that here was one detail that had escaped the NKVD's attention, but he would not be the person to reveal their affections.

"We would like you to report back in a few weeks. Learn everything you can about this Yuri Suzdal, especially his political opinions. A Trotskyite in our midst is like a viper in our bosom."

In the square, Dimitri stopped to watch couples strolling hand in hand, people feeding pigeons, children with kites, and a few hardy men leaning against a wall and bearing their chests to the sun. He looked at the cobblestones underfoot and wondered what tales they could tell. For most people, life was a series of nested stories, told about family and friends. No wonder a juicy tidbit was valued; it briefly dispelled their drab existence. Sometimes the tidbit could even prove the difference between life and death, especially in a closed society. When people received a tip that the police would be arresting them, they often fled. Every country, every army, needed informers to succeed. A ragged cloud threw the square into a complex of shadows.

When Dimitri and Yuri rendezvoused next, they entered the apartment building, as always, at different times and different doors. But on this occasion, Dimitri stopped at the superintendent's office to beard him. Without so much as a word of greeting, Dimitri shoved his special leather wallet with its official NKVD badge and documents under the man's nose. The super immediately realized that his snitching had backfired.

"I didn't know," he sputtered. "You may be sure in the future . . ." But he had no chance to complete his apology because Dimitri scooped up his wallet and, with the sternest look at his command, stared at the super, who cringingly sunk in his chair. Once Dimitri felt that the man's humiliation was complete, he sneered and left.

As Dimitri recounted this experience, Yuri feared that it would make the super all the more determined to find some anti-Soviet behavior that could be used to denounce them.

"The humiliated are the most dangerous," said Yuri. "Chekhov frequently warned us not to strip a man of his self-respect."

"Chekhov was too full of pity. Ruthlessness is called for in some cases. The man won't be back!"

Before lovemaking, they ate a modest meal and sat down to play chess. With Ezhov's assignment oppressing his mind, Dimitri casually asked, "How did you spend your day?"

"As I always do, snip-snip."

"Lunch?"

"At the Metropol. Why do you ask?"

"Just wondering."

For several minutes, the men played in silence, Dimitri's eyes fixed on the board and Yuri's stealing an occasional look at Dimitri.

"You're not jealous, are you?"

"No, it's just that in these times we have to be extra careful about our meetings and companions." He waited a few seconds before asking, "Was it a man or a woman?" Yuri looked uncomprehending. "At lunch . . . whom did you meet?"

"Madame Ranevskaia. You know the woman. She once owned a famous orchard. It was appropriated for workers' bungalows."

"Oh, yes, a charming woman, but as I recall an indecisive one."

Dimitri was particularly gifted in his use of the bishop, while Yuri let his queen wreak most of the damage. What the men lacked in strategy they made up for in daring. Yuri had slipped in behind Dimitri's pawns and threatened to put his king in check.

"Not so fast, my sweet," said Dimitri, bringing a bishop to the rescue and compromising Yuri's queen.

"She frequently travels to France, and occasionally Sweden and Norway. Art business."

"Has she ever been to America?"

"If you mean the United States, no, but Mexico, yes."

Dimitri studied the board and then casually inquired, "What business interests would take her there?"

"She represents Diego Rivera and Frida Kahlo. Rich buyers in Stockholm and Oslo collect their paintings."

"Hm, I had no idea." Dimitri pondered how to introduce his next question. He had no wish to infuriate Yuri, so he snorted skeptically and said, "Have you heard the absurd rumor that the super-Judas Trotsky moved to Mexico to be near Diego Rivera's wife?"

Yuri looked at Dimitri with a pained expression. "No, I hadn't heard. Did that rubbish come from the NKVD?"

Dimitri feared that he had not been subtle enough, because Yuri emotionally began to withdraw, as if he sensed danger, answering Dimitri's questions in monosyllables. Suddenly Yuri dropped one of the chess pieces and forthrightly declared, "If you are working up to asking me whether Madame Ranevskaia has ever met Trotsky, the answer is yes. Now, does that make her— or me—an enemy of the people?"

How was Dimitri to answer? He could warn Yuri of the secret police's interest in him, but he felt certain that such a disclosure would bring an end to their affair. He could say that he wanted to know in order to better advise his friend. But that approach sounded suspiciously like one crafted by the secret police. The last idea offered the most protection to Dimitri, because if Yuri had secret contacts with the opposition—a possibility that Dimitri no longer regarded as utterly fanciful—Dimitri would have time to save himself, and perhaps even Yuri. Dimitri chose to answer indirectly.

"I wish I had the money to buy a Rivera or Kahlo. They are truly painters of the proletariat. Have you any idea what their canvases cost?" Yuri relaxed. Yes, Dimitri had sounded the right note . . . nothing threatening. "Our own museums ought to be collecting them."

"Diego has promised to make a gift of some of his paintings to the Soviet people. A brilliant painter and a magnanimous man. All our artists should be so generous."

At the end of the evening, Dimitri did not return directly to his room. He walked through the crepuscular square to secret-police headquarters, where he looked through the files for any reports on Madame Ranevskaia. He found several, all to the effect that her activities necessitated watching.

Taking it upon himself to follow Lubov Andreyevna Ranevskaia, Dimitri discovered that she had two daughters, both unmarried. Anya, the younger one, was an art history student at a Moscow institute, keeping company with a feckless young man, Peter Trofimov. Although a devoted revolutionary who often gave speeches about the need for unselfish labor, he could never complete his university courses. The report in his official files read that his passion for the people led the party to ignore his fecklessness, but that he should never be trusted with any serious work. The older daughter, Varya, seemed easily the most mature of the three women. Adopted as a baby, she was skittish, pale, and inordinately serious. Had Madame R. adopted the girl to prove her patriotism? Perhaps her deceased husband, or her billiard-loving brother, had sired a child out of wedlock. In any case, Dimitri decided to interview Varya.

They met in Neskuchniy Garden, next to a pond. Dimitri had represented himself as a historian interested in the story surrounding the sale of the orchard. And, in fact, aren't most investigators like historians, re-creating the past? He had often used this ruse to deceive the people he questioned.

After introducing themselves, they slowly strolled through the gardens, Dimitri casting a wary eye in case someone was watching him. As they spoke, Varya frequently stopped to admire or balance a bloom in her hand. She stood in front of the lilacs and enthused about their incomparable fragrance. At last, they settled on a bench and Dimitri, having asked numerous questions about the family's former estate, leaned back and, ostensibly to show himself a gentleman, said, "I trust that you have comfortable quarters in Moscow, at least large enough for your mother to hang her paintings."

"You know about the Diego Riveras?" Varya asked. "A great many dealers come to our flat."

"For my small collection, I use only one, Yuri Suzdal."

"Then he's actually a dealer?"

"Yes, why do you ask?"

"He and his friends never seem to talk about art. Then again, I can't be sure because they always retreat to the kitchen."

Dimitri tried to make a joke of this information. "Perhaps they are merely hungry," he teased, scooping a handful of pebbles.

"I get the impression that they have more on their minds than canvases and prices."

"Really?" he asked, grinding the pebbles underfoot.

"They often have with them printed material they exchange."

"Probably just auction figures. I know Yuri. He's always on the lookout for a good buy."

Varya picked up a small stick and drew lines in the gravel. "What do you collect?" Had she not added, "Still lifes, portraits, country or city scenes?" he might have stumbled.

"I particularly like river scenes."

"So do I!" said Varya enthusiastically. "You must see the two we have in our flat. Their bucolic settings calm me when I'm tense."

"Are they for sale?"

"In the art world, everything is for sale—at the right price."

By the time he walked Varya to the trolley stop, he had decided to watch Madame Ranevskaia's apartment. Dimitri befriended the doorman of the building directly across the street. Here he planted himself and spied through the front glass doors. His patience was rewarded when he saw Yuri enter Madame's apartment complex. At short intervals afterward, three other men followed, each carrying a briefcase filled, Dimitri assumed, with printed matter.

Trained to take surveillance photographs, Dimitri positioned his camera and captured the men as they exited, separately. Although he had a picture of Yuri, he also snapped him. Turning the film over to the secret police, he asked them to check each of the men. When the report came back, Dimitri was stunned. None of them, as far as the police knew, had been engaged in political activities. But they did have records for homosexuality and for having attended readings of Anna Akhmatova's poetry, she whom the writers' union had rejected and who had never received Stalin's official imprimatur.

Although Akhmatova moved freely throughout the city and country, escaping internment for some inscrutable reason, she had written poems that could have earned other poets twenty years in a camp. Dimitri had been shown some of her verses and could recite a few lines that he thought should have made her an enemy of the people:

Without hangman and scaffold
Poets have no life on earth

She had also penned, "All poets are Yids." So to Comrade Lipnoskii's mind, any organized reading devoted to her work had about it a political purpose.

Dimitri painfully decided that the next meeting between him and Yuri must be their last. He would accuse his lover of infidelity, a charge that, if true, would hurt Dimitri more sharply than any political transgression Yuri could make. The personal betrayal, however, could not be shared with the secret police, lest Yuri turn around and implicate him. He therefore decided that the only way to settle the score and assuage his hurt was to drive Yuri from Moscow.

"My dear Yuri," said Dimitri, returning from the bathroom and climbing back into bed after coitus, and after Dimitri had applied a special liquid to his eyes that elicited tears. "I can hardly bring myself to tell you," he cried, "but the secret police know about your meetings with friends at Madame Ranevskaia's apartment . . . and the poetry readings . . . and the printed matter."

"We merely exchange poems!"

"Please, Yuri, do not lie to me."

With shaking hands, Yuri angrily dressed.

"And now," said Dimitri calmly, "you need to leave Moscow before you're arrested. I can arrange it so that you have a few days before the police knock on your door at two in the morning."

Reaching for the doorknob, Dimitri intended to emphasize his displeasure by departing in dramatic silence, but his feelings overwhelmed him, and he turned to look at Yuri, who flew into his arms and whispered his thanks for saving him from arrest.

Several days later, when the dreaded elevator stopped at his floor in the early morning hours, Yuri had already left the city.

Ezhov's frustration with Dimitri sounded suspiciously like an accusation. Once again, Dimitri had been summoned to the chief's office. But this time, Nikolai Ivanovich, wearing American-made Adler elevated shoes, was standing just a few inches from Dimitri's face. "He must have been warned that we were watching him."

"If you are implying . . ." Dimitri paused, hoping that Ezhov would gainsay him, but the chief merely stared coldly. "Why would I have gone to the trouble to watch the apartment and take photographs of these men if I intended to let them slip through the net?"

"Is that what I said?"

The sneaky dog, thought Dimitri. "No, Comrade Ezhov, but you seem to be implying . . ."

"The difference between seeming and being is a chasm. Don't assume when you don't know." He briskly walked around his desk, opened a drawer, and removed a folder. "Here is your next assignment. I want you to report on the friendship between Yelena Boujinskia and Sasha Visotsky. The story about their crawling through heating ducts and eavesdropping doesn't ring true. I smell a plot. Root it out!"

"Root it out?" Dimitri repeated incredulously. "How?"

"Children respond well to the Morozov story. Perhaps you can even locate the photograph Yelena used to paint Stalin's mustache." Ezhov must have read in Dimitri's expression incomprehension, because Ezhov added, "Let me remind you, comrade, what the hero of all our Soviet schoolbooks, fourteen-year old Pavel Morozov, said when he denounced his father as a kulak: 'Stalin is my father and I do not need another one.'"

What Dimitri and virtually everyone else in the country had been told was that the Soviets had killed the boy's father, and that a group of peasants led by Pavel's uncle had shot and killed the zealous son. Stalin frequently mentioned Pavel as a model for Soviet youth, a child who denounced his father in the interests of the state, and the Morozov story could be found in hundreds, if not thousands, of books and poems. The numerous statues dedicated to him in public places stood as a constant reminder of the virtue of denunciations.

Sasha Visotsky's parents held managerial positions in the transportation department that entitled them to live in the house on the embankment. Their files indicated that they had been party members since their teens. No black mark had ever marred their records. Uncertain how to proceed, Dimitri asked the children's school director, who suggested that Dimitri introduce himself as a journalist interested in writing about Sasha's parents' heroic work. Dimitri and Sasha met during recess in a classroom usually devoted to the teaching of English. At their first meeting, Dimitri asked Sasha about bridges and roads, trolleys and trains, airplanes and cars. After several days, Dimitri, taking notes, slowly gravitated toward the prank in which Sasha and Yelena had taken part.

"I hope your parents weren't too severe with you." The boy shook his head no. "Good. Glad to hear it." Dimitri paused and handed Sasha a chocolate wrapped in silver foil. "I suppose they knew about your little game before it got you into trouble?"

He unwrapped the sweet. "No, it was Yelena's secret and mine."

"I admire children who can keep secrets. But didn't you ever tell them what you saw—without revealing how you knew?"

The boy screwed up his mouth and, after a few seconds, remarked, "Maybe once."

"Oh? That must have been fun. What did you see?"

"A man undressing. On his arm near his shoulder, here, I saw a tattoo that looked like a cruciform with two bars across it."

"What did your parents say when you told them?"

"To forget about it."

"They were absolutely right," he said making some notes.

The boy's expression changed. He cocked his head and asked, "Why do you want to write about my parents?" Then he unfolded his reading glasses and asked to read what Dimitri had written.

"I've only taken notes, but as soon as I have a first draft . . ." Sasha looked confused. "I understand you're studying French?" Sasha agreed. "It's what your teacher calls *le brouillon.*" The boy's face brightened with recognition. "Then you know what I mean. When I have the first draft, I'll let you read it."

Sasha put away his reading glasses and skipped out of the room. Dimitri remained, sitting alone among the empty chairs and staring at some English writing on the blackboard that he could not translate, having studied French and not English. It came from John Dos Passos's novel *The Big Money.*

"America our nation has been beaten by strangers who have bought the laws and fenced off the meadows and cut down the woods for pulp and turned our pleasant cities into slums and sweated the wealth out of our people and when they want to they hire the executioner to throw the switch."

Tormented by guilt, Dimitri hunched over the desk and buried his head in his hands, which smelled of a cheap, perfumed soap. If he reported the boy's words, he would be imperiling Sasha's parents for not reporting what their son had told them. If his request for a transfer had only been granted. He left the school and, instead of taking the tram, walked to the Kremlin, troubled by Ezhov's words. By the time he reached his room, he was telling himself how good it felt to be safe.

A week later, two families disappeared from the house on the embankment, one of them was the Visotskys.

In talking to Sasha, Dimitri had used the pseudonym "Ivan Nizhinsky" and had warned the boy to keep their meetings a secret. Sasha, however, always shared privileged information with Yelena. Although the boy never passed on the name of his interrogator, he had described the man, and Yelena shared these disclosures with Natasha, who immediately recognized her brother. On the day that Dimitri spoke to Yelena, he found himself confronting not only her but also his sister. A shocked Dimitri swore that the charade was in the service of quietly advancing Yelena for admission to the Academy of Arts. Who, after all, knew her person and passion for art better than Sasha?

Natasha had been around dishonest bureaucrats long enough to know their foul smelling words. "Rubbish!" she cried, to Yelena's amazement. "I am not Sasha Visotsky. What are you up to, Dimitri?"

The school director had arranged for them to meet in a lower-form classroom with undersized desks for the young children. How ironic, Dimitri thought, to be in a place dedicated to learning when the point of the current exercise was to enable betrayal to pass for patriotism. Dimitri had known bad moments before but nothing equal to being unmasked by his sister. As she sat facing him, he realized to his chagrin, that she was playing Antigone to his Creon, and that they were dueling over who takes precedence, the individual or the state. Like a great many apparatchiks, Dimitri partially justified his nefarious assignments by telling himself that his family was safe. But once his actions exposed his loved ones to danger, he was prepared to abandon the mission. Had Yelena been his natural sister and not his adopted one, he would have refused from the start. But Natasha's claim on his fidelity—the hell with the story of the Morozov boy!—mattered most. After the initial lie about the Arts Academy, he settled on an explanation that was partially true.

"This whole unsavory business, dear sister, has to do with Serjee, the Kremlin photographer, and the need for the government to remove from public display the pictures of Stalin's mustache based on Yelena's painting. Happily, the Vozhd would like her to paint another, from a different photograph, one that Serjee has taken."

"What was wrong with the first painting?"

"I honestly don't know."

Natasha asked, "Are you speaking as my brother or a policeman?" Both her withering look and her damning question indicated how well she knew his divided loyalties.

"A Very Important Person is especially sensitive about his mustache and the message it conveys."

Dimitri assumed from his mother's explanation that she was trading on the power of the paintings. He could imagine Koba publicly scorning the superstitious believers but privately believing in the magic of his mustache. He had known a great many Georgian men, and all of them seemed to feel that facial hair was inseparable from virility. The official criticism of Yelena's painting was that the mustache diminished Stalin's stature, though a rumor circulated that the painting portrayed an impostor. With Razan now in charge of barbering, Stalin would want to display his bushy Turkish cut in photos, and perhaps in a new canvas, that exhibited "the real thing."

"Are we meeting here," said Natasha defiantly, "and not in your office because we might be overheard talking about Stalin's vanity?"

Natasha's question provided Dimitri with a ready escape.

"You are exactly right."

"Then tell me," she said, putting her face just a few inches from Dimitri's, "what did Sasha Visotsky have to do with this matter?"

Before Dimitri could answer, Yelena cried, "Where is Sasha? I want to see him."

Unnerved by the child's entreaties, Dimitri reached across the desk and patted her hand. "He and his family are in a safe place."

Natasha, privy to the unscrupulous behavior of her superiors, and disgusted at the willingness of others to denounce family and friends, had no reluctance to say, "Where, in a work camp?"

"No, in a Crimean resort."

At that moment, Natasha felt sorry for what her brother had become—a functionary with midget morals. She would scour the archives for any information on him. The secret police always said that no one was innocent. Well, surely then, a file labeled Dimitri Lipnoskii existed. She was quickly learning the useful lesson that information is power and that damning information is absolute power. Once she brought her brother to heel, she would turn her attention to Alexei. Yes, she too had been faithless, but after her last tryst, the one with Kazimir Ouspensky, she had sworn that no hireling would ever again be her master. It was advantageous to let a member of the Politburo bed you, but a librarian, a man who had hardly been able to survive as a book publisher? He might be the head archivist, but she had already imbibed all his lessons. She could interpret as well as he a denunciatory letter, and hadn't she taken it upon herself to have sensitive documents microfilmed, spirited out of the archive, and hidden in the large stuffed panda that she'd bought for Yelena?

The panda had a seam running down the back so that when the stuffing began to thin, it could be refilled. Natasha had put the microfilm in muslin. After debating whether to tell Yelena, she had decided that she had already endangered the child enough by using her as a courier to steal secret documents. If questioned, the child could honestly say that she had carried papers for Natasha from the archives but had no idea of their significance or location. Natasha hoped that the filmed documents could be used as a bargaining chip to keep the child safe. She had slowly gathered compromising material on Yagoda, Ezhov, Malenkov, Molotov, as well as Stalin; she had even removed from the Archive of Literature and Art Isaac Babel's confiscated novel and some Mandelstam poems.

If nothing else, the sale of the literary manuscripts to a western dealer would bring a handsome sum. It wouldn't be the first time that banned Soviet writers were published in Paris and London and New York. To put money away for an emergency was always wise, especially if one knew that the secret police had their suspicions about you. Where to hide money presented an even more difficult problem than where to hide manuscripts. Western bank accounts were forbidden, and Soviet ones were subject to government scrutiny. No wonder people said that more pillows in Russia were stuffed with rubles than goose feathers. Of course, that remark pertained to those who could lay their hands on rubles; most people could barely afford a bowl of soup. Natasha and her family were among the lucky ones. They had more than enough to live on. Staying alive had become a practiced art that required a knowledge of when to remain silent, which was most of the time, and when to smile, laugh, cry, celebrate, and mourn. You never wanted to be privy to important information about others unless you had a mind to use it for your own selfish purposes, as Natasha did. Why denounce someone if there was no self-interest involved? In fact, the moment a person fell out of favor, you made sure to distance yourself from the pariah. Thus, people rarely had friends, only acquaintances, and they were usually tight lipped. How Akhmatova remained close to the stigmatized Mandelstams without being exiled to a work camp was indeed a miracle.

A few others also defied logic. How did the writer, Ilya Ehrenburg, maintain his right to travel freely in the west when he had initially been critical of the Soviets? Every intellectual and artist wanted to know the magic formula. In fact, it lay in two sources, Stalin's permission and Poskrebyshev's rubber stamp bearing the Boss's signature. When matters of state kept Stalin busy, his aide-de-camp had the authority to stamp papers ordering people to camps or to allow them to travel outside of the country. Poskrebyshev kept his famous rubber stamp locked in the top right-hand drawer. The key in Nikolaevich's pocket was attached to a chain affixed to his belt. Dimitri knew the desk drawer and enough about locks to know that it could not be easily opened. But even had he wished to sneak into the aide's office, it was guarded day and night. If the day came that he and his family had to leave the country, he would have to resort to the photos and labs of the secret police for visas and exit permits.

Dimitri offered to drive his sister and Yelena home, but Natasha wanted to be alone with her charge. As they walked, Natasha tried to explain to the child why Dimitri had asked to see her.

"Stalin has had numerous photographs taken of him, and the one that you copied does not, in the Supreme Leader's estimation, show his mustache to the best effect."

"I know *that!*" said the precocious Yelena. "What I want to know is why the mustache looks kind of different in some photographs?"

"Let's hope that his barber, our dear father, Razan, can remedy the situation with his tonsorial skills. Do you know the word?"

"Of course!" said Yelena proudly, pointing a finger at her throat. "He is an expert at removing tonsils."

"Yes," Natasha laughed, "something like that."

The next day a Kremlin courier, bearing a package, rang the buzzer to the Shtube apartment. Anna, alone at the time, opened the door, admitting a man who showed her his official credentials and introduced himself as Boleslav Dantonovich.

"I have with me," Boleslav said, "an official photograph of our Beloved Protector, Stalin. Autographed!"

He handed the package to Anna. She removed the white wrapping paper to reveal a smiling Stalin. Written at the bottom was the inscription: "To the Shtube family, Iosif Stalin." An envelope, taped to the wood frame, contained a brief note. "Please have Yelena study this photograph to paint another canvas of my mustache. I will be very pleased." Signed: "A Lover of the People."

A commission to paint another picture! Anna wept with joy. But she did not anticipate Yelena's response. "I would rather not paint the same subject twice. If I must, then I want to see for myself Stalin's mustache. It keeps changing."

When Poskrebyshev heard Razan's request that the child have an audience with the Boss, the taciturn secretary laughed so hard that he loosened a temporary filling in a recently drilled tooth. "Are you mad?" he thundered. "The Supreme Leader has little enough time for *you*, much less some adopted brat."

Outside of Poskrebyshev's office, Razan ran into the Kremlin film cutter, who, according to common knowledge, often doctored movies for Stalin's sake. "Which picture are you editing now?"

"*October*, Eisenstein's 1927 film about the revolution."

"I saw it in Brovensk . . . several years ago."

"With or without Comrade Stalin as the hero?"

"Is it hard to superimpose his face on the actor's?"

"We do it all the time with photographs, putting in some people and taking out others. Trotsky, for example, frequently disappears."

"Are the originals in the archives?"

"Yes, but only special persons have access."

Razan returned that evening to shave the Boss. But now, as he relayed Yelena's request, he wondered which Stalin his daughter would meet, the real or the false. He delicately remarked, "She's anxious to see for herself who you are."

The Vozhd's enigmatic reply brought Razan no closer to solving the mystery of the man. "As the protector of the people, Stalin must reflect their many moods and faces. He can exhibit the mischievous or the meek, the avuncular leader or the man of steel." The man in the chair lapsed into his third person lecturing mode, wagging the finger of his right hand. "Surrounded as we are by enemies of every sort, the Soviet people must learn, as Stalin has, to wear one face for friends and one for the wreckers. The more masks in the closet, the safer you are. Stalin learned that truth as a youth in Georgia. Just as you don't want to wear your heart on your sleeve, you don't want to show your true feelings on your face. The face is the window into a man's secret thoughts. Therefore, to confuse your enemies, you must learn how to appear one way and act in another. Most people betray themselves with a look. The Vozhd keeps them off balance and guessing with his various visages.

"Now isn't it true, Master barber, that you can change a man's appearance with your razor and scissors? Well, Stalin can do the same with a raised eye or a lowered one, with a closed mouth or an open one, with teeth showing or not, with a lip pulled up or down." He demonstrated. "And all these facial gestures are connected, like wires, to his thoughts. Every person has at least one facial gesture that sums up his myriad moods. For Stalin, it is his mustache, which he can make dance, sing, mourn, celebrate, condemn—all depending on the role he is playing at that moment in response to current events. You do realize, don't you, that events have a face? They express sabotage, collusion, falsity, defeatism . . . you see the point. What Stalin looks for in those around him is the face of loyalty and the belief in a new world to come. So keep in mind, Razan, that if you wish to survive, you must always wear the right face, as you would a frock for the right season had you served in the Tsar's court."

The barber knew, on pain of death, not to mention a body double. Instead, he praised Koba for his embracing people of all trades and nationalities. Then he sycophantically added, "Since Yelena is still a child, I would hope that you bestow on her your famous gentleness. But it's up to you which Stalin you want her to paint."

"Yes, of course." He reached for his calendar. "The day after tomorrow would be a good time. I'll tell Poskrebyshev to remind me. You never want to disappoint a child."

On his way home, Razan thought of all the children orphaned by the Soviets. Were those children not disappointed? Adoption, a poor attempt to assuage the effects of loss, may have made Koba's cronies feel virtuous, but the children felt the pain of absence. Hardly a day passed that Yelena didn't ask Razan to tell her what he remembered about her parents. When his scant information ran out, he concocted yarns that he feared would, like most lies, come back to haunt him.

The appointed day for Yelena's meeting with Stalin saw her dressed elegantly in a new outfit and, thanks to the hairdresser in the building, coiffed with curls. Even her imported Italian shoes, bought at the embankment store, radiated respect for the Boss. Although Razan had advised that Koba preferred common clothes, Anna had proceeded without Razan's knowledge. No child in her care was going to appear before the Supreme Leader in anything less than the best. When Razan objected to the cost, Yelena sat on his lap and said, "Please." He couldn't say no.

In keeping with the special day, Razan called for a cab to take them the short distance to the Kremlin. The cabby told Yelena how beautiful she looked and Razan how fortunate he was to have such a lovely daughter. In her glowing state, Yelena proudly and easily passed through the Troitsky Gate, managing to elicit smiles from the guards inside the wall. Yes, thought Razan, she will acquit herself very well. The real test would be to impress not Stalin but Comrade Ugly. If Yelena could impress him, she might well be asked back.

So familiar had Razan become that as he made his way to Stalin's quarters, he rarely had to show the armed guard his official pass. For this special occasion, he requested that a guide be allowed to escort Yelena and him through the Kremlin's glittering rooms. The request approved, the guard indifferently led the way. Yelena especially liked the Hall of the Order of Saint Andrew, Peter the Great's Throne Hall. The gilded pillars and doors, the Tsarist monograms and crests, the regional crests, the parquet floors, and the ten bronze chandeliers persuaded Yelena that she had entered a fairyland. Her reluctance to leave came as no surprise.

"Is *this* where you work!" she exclaimed.

"Not in this room or the other splendid ones, but in a cramped office. You'll see."

On their way out of the hall, she kept looking over her shoulder as if to keep the image fresh in memory. "We've been studying Peter the Great in school. I can tell you all about his wish to westernize the country."

Razan chuckled. "Later," he said, and led her to Poskrebyshev's office. He sat at his desk stamping papers.

"Ah," he said, looking up. "At last we have the honor of meeting the young Rembrandt."

Yelena cheerfully replied, "I'm a girl, not a boy."

"Quite so," said Poskrebyshev, who actually showed the trace of a smile. "What is it that fascinates you about Stalin's mustache?"

"It's so emblematic," she said precociously.

Poskrebyshev chortled. "Where did you learn a word like *that*?"

"At art school. Everyone knows Stalin's mustache."

"Then why have you requested a meeting to see him? Aren't the millions of photographs in the country enough for you?"

"Which photographs? They're different."

Poskrebyshev's face darkened. He once again became Comrade Ugly. "I have no idea what you mean. Perhaps your father can explain."

Before Razan could speak, Yelena blurted, "I want to paint the real Stalin's mustache."

The child had unwittingly verbalized a state secret: that Stalin was more than one man.

Razan could feel the ground shaking beneath their feet.

"Nonsense, Yelena!" said a terrified Razan. "Photos simply differ. Right, Nikolaevich?"

Stalin's devoted servant coldly said, "Before the child leaves the premises, I want you to take her to the lab for fingerprinting and a head shot."

"Of course," replied Razan, trying to sound unconcerned. "Now can we see the Glorious Leader?"

"I'll ring, but you'll have to stay here."

The attending guards led Yelena into the small room Stalin used for barbering. Koba, seated on his divan, patted the cushion next to him and gestured for Yelena to join him. The child and the Boss chatted amiably about her school and her lessons, which Stalin seemed to endorse. But then he digressed. "The seminary I attended employed force to educate the students. Beatings! Did you know that in Georgian one of the meanings of the word 'beating' is to educate?"

Yelena looked terrified.

"Don't worry, child, we reserve such means of instruction for hardened criminals." He briefly fell silent. "Can you imagine treating children in training for the priesthood like convicts? I have never forgotten or forgiven."

Yelena, unbidden, touched Koba's mustache. He recoiled. The guards sprang forward, but Koba raised a hand to ward them off.

"It's all right. I was just taken by surprise." Smiling at Yelena, he said, "Go ahead and touch the mustache. My daughter says it scratches when I kiss her. Do you think it's soft or silky?"

"Neither," said Yelena, fingering his mustache, "but I like it better than the one I painted. It's different."

Stalin's eyes turned unfriendly, and his tobacco-stained teeth came into view as he lectured, "My dear child, they are one and the same. Remember *that* and you'll always be Koba's friend."

The Supreme Leader lifted her onto his lap and gave her a hug. Then Yelena skipped out the door. Stalin called for Razan, who stood on the threshold. "Tell me, friend, who were her parents?"

With that question, this Stalin seemed to say that he was not the Supreme Leader. The real Vozhd would have known the fate of the Boujinski family. Or did this Stalin in fact know what had happened and was asking the question to mislead the barber? To protect the identity of Koba, any deceit or trick was allowed. If both Stalins pleaded ignorance, the real one would be all the harder to know. When Razan explained the fate of the family, this Stalin merely nodded. What would the other say?

Razan asked to be excused because the child had an art class and wouldn't want to miss it. As he had threatened, Nikolaevich Poskrebyshev had a soldier march Razan and Yelena to the laboratory for fingerprinting and photographing. The barber had been subjected to these indignities before, but Comrade Ugly insisted that the Kremlin needed up-to-date information. He snidely suggested that people altered their prints and donned disguises to escape the attention of the authorities. "No one," he said, repeating the line that was all too familiar, "is innocent."

Yelena's art teacher let her use the official photograph as a model for her class project, a painting of Stalin's mustache. The canvas took longer than expected because Yelena had recently been studying Dutch portraits and wished to capture the essence of the mustache in the detail of the hairs, creating a chiaroscuro effect. Benjamin Levitin, her teacher, suggested that she superimpose the mustache on the Great Hall of Saint Andrew, thus juxtaposing the power of Peter the Great and Stalin. When she frowned at the suggestion, he recommended that she paint two canvases, one taking for its background the hall and the other employing a neutral landscape.

"Let the schmuck decide for himself which he prefers."

"Schmuck?"

"A term of endearment," he said ironically, "but applied only to people who aspire to be wiser than the world."

"Aren't you going to tell me what it means?"

"No."

A moment later, Benjamin thought better of his reply, knowing that children go out of their way to learn the meaning of words, especially ones that are clouded in mystery.

"Forget that I ever said it." He clasped her hands. "Promise?"

"I promise."

When Yelena had finally completed both canvases, she neatly wrapped and tied them in shopping paper. Natasha collected her at school and brought her back to the embankment, where she proudly exhibited them for the family. The two women liked the one with the background of the ten gilded pillars of

Saint Andrew's Hall. Razan preferred the simplicity of a neutral background with only the black mustache filling the canvas. On the appointed day, Razan met Dimitri at the curb and, at Anna's insistence, let him take Yelena and the paintings to the Kremlin. As before, the child was greeted with smiles. In Poskrebyshev's office, they had to endure his stares, as well as those of the guards. At last, a light blinked on the chef de cabinet's phone, and he told them that they had permission to enter. But unlike her previous audience with Stalin, who had behaved kindly, this Stalin brusquely asked Dimitri to leave.

"I want to speak to the child alone, without you hovering about."

Dimitri handed the paintings to Yelena, kissed her forehead, and whispered, "Good luck."

Yelena handed Stalin her paintings. He roughly snapped the string and tore off the wrappings. His right hand held up one picture. She hoped that he would refrain from touching the canvas. To her eyes, his paw looked unwashed. Positioning the pictures on the floor against his desk, he stood at a distance, ostensibly evaluating their quality.

"I'm glad you painted two canvases. I then have a choice. But why two?"

The words came spontaneously. "Mr. Levitin said, 'Let the schmuck decide for himself which he likes.'"

"And who is this Mr. Levitin?"

"My art teacher."

Stalin continued to study the paintings at a distance. Finally, he stroked his mustache and said, "May I keep them both? I'd like to sample the reaction of others."

"Of course."

"Good, you may go now."

He shook Yelena's hand and closed the door behind her. Staring out the window into the garden below, he waited a few minutes before picking up the phone and ringing Poskrebyshev.

"Nikolaevich," he said, "your wife is Jewish. I just heard a word that sounds to me like Yiddish. If not, it's German. Call your wife and check. The word is 'schmuck.'" Pause. "How the hell would I know? Spell it any way you like, and call me right back."

The next day Benjamin Levitin disappeared.

STATISTICS

"I repeat: The death of one man is a tragedy, the death of millions is a statistic," said Stalin, as Razan applied talcum powder to the Supreme Leader's pockmarks. "I learned the lesson early that it is better to kill the country's enemies as a group than to try each man individually. But of course there are exceptions."

That night, Razan suffered terrible dreams. He awoke in a sweat. In a small town that looked like Brovensk, a statue dedicated to Stalin stood ready to be unveiled. When the sheet was removed, a slim rod about ten feet high held an enormous mustache, and nothing else. The people gasped. But the worst was yet to come. The mustache called his name.

"Razan, you pity all the people removed from the house on the embankment, all the suppressed you have personally known. Every one of them traitors! Ask yourself: When 'enemies' are led away, do your neighbors object? No. They tell themselves that nobody would dare to shoot others without conclusive evidence against them. If people are arrested, it means it was necessary. Also ask yourself why so many people willingly let themselves be arrested and later confess."

In his dream, Rubin Bélawitz, Razan's rotund childhood confidant from Albania, appeared and said those who confessed believed that for their own sacrifices to matter they had to support the party. It was beyond their power to admit that the great experiment had gone wrong. To further the work of the party, they even confessed to crimes they had never committed.

The mustache spoke again. "Production and crop failures mean only one thing: Enemies of the people not only exist but thrive everywhere. Believe me,

Razan, the Supreme Leader does not make mistakes. Others do. In any case, you can't make an omelet without breaking eggs."

The townspeople agreed, shaking their heads and muttering, "Death to the traitors." When Razan asked the farmers and factory workers why they denounced their neighbors, they admitted to settling scores with their bosses, taking possession of furniture and apartments they coveted, getting back at faithless lovers, and gaining entry to Communist groups by denouncing their parents.

The mustache said, "You have heard the word of the people."

Razan replied, "But how can you explain the hundreds of thousands languishing in jails for no legal reasons?"

Suddenly storm clouds gathered, and the wind blew violently. The statue toppled, and the mustache landed in a puddle of mud.

That evening, as Razan removed an offending hair from Stalin's upper lip, the barber asked, "And who are these maggots wrecking our country? By now the west ought to know how much you love the people."

At once Razan realized the statement's latent irony, but would Stalin? The Boss said nothing as Razan applied alcohol to his ears and lit a match.

Although consecrated by savage conviction, Stalin often assumed a gentle manner, using his pipe as a prop, or singing a favorite Georgian song, "Soliko," or inviting questions, all the better to disarm and identify his critics. "I see you are troubled, Comrade Shtube. How may I put your mind at ease? Ask me anything."

"Some of my neighbors . . . they work for the government and display your photograph. They seem harmless enough. Unlike fleeing kulaks, they have papers and permission to live in the city."

Stalin lowered his voice, a sign of danger. "No one is harmless, Razan. From plotters to priests, everyone has a secret life. In every heart, ventricles pump the Judas germ."

If Razan fell from favor, he knew that Poskrebyshev would love to see him and his family on a condemned list, which he could happily stamp "Suppress," a euphemism for liquidation. The barber quickly asked Stalin to tell him about his daughter, Svetlana, whom Razan extolled for her beauty and intelligence.

"Her copybook poems," said Stalin contemptuously, "are a bad imitation of Akhmatova. Poets!" Stalin complained. "I have to correct their meter and rhymes. They are all pretenders."

So the rumor was true. Stalin did edit verses before they saw print. Historians, of course, required a tight rein. Everyone knew that Soviet history had to conform to Stalin's view of its purpose and his role in it. But poetry? No wonder people said that before long the Boss would be comparing himself to Pushkin.

"Much of what currently gets scribbled is rubbish. I ought to know. In my youth, I wrote poems. A number of them were even published. But I do not claim for myself the exalted title of 'poet.' A good critic, yes. The trouble is that because the Soviet people love literature, innumerable poseurs call themselves poets."

Razan knew that you could die for writing a single unorthodox line or a politically incorrect metaphor. It was best to write nature poetry and not have to worry about a taboo subject destined to be airbrushed out of history. Boris Pasternak had learned that lesson.

"Comrade Shtube, we have often talked about safe topics, but we have made it a point, perhaps wisely, never to talk about any political figure." At this moment, Razan instinctively knew that Stalin was going to ask him whether he approved of the show trials. "Vyshinsky," he said. "Andrei Vyshinsky. From the point of view of the man in the street, people like yourself, how is our chief prosecutor regarded?" Razan had come close. Although most everyone inside the Kremlin knew that the confessions of the condemned during the show trials had been obtained through torture, Vyshinsky proudly declared that "confession of the accused is the queen of evidence."

In 1935, Andrei Yanuarievich Vyshinsky had been appointed prosecutor general of the USSR, and in 1936, he was appointed chief prosecutor of the Moscow treason trials. A year later, he still cast an ominous shadow across the law courts. His words were often quoted admiringly.

> I think it is clear to all now that these wreckers and diversionists, whether they be Trotskyites or Bukharinites, have already long since ceased to be politically in tune with the workers. They have turned into an unprincipled band of professional wreckers, disgusting diversionists, spies, and murderers. It's clear that these men must be rooted out and destroyed without mercy.

Stalin waited to hear Razan's judgment.

Warily, the barber said, "A good Bolshevik, a professor of law, and a rector at the University of Moscow . . . how could such a person not be highly esteemed?"

Stalin chuckled. "You Jews are all Talmudists. What you have just said can be taken, of course, to mean that any man with his qualifications *cannot* be well regarded. Is that not so?"

"You would make a good Talmudist yourself, Dear Leader."

"From whom do you think the Orthodox and Latin churches learned their catechisms: Saint Thomas Aquinas. And where did he learn his? I will tell you. Partly from Aristotle, but mostly from the Jews." He fondled his mustache and waited for Razan to respond.

"I am not as well versed in religion as you are, but I did not intend to answer in a compromising manner."

Stalin smiled. "Then tell me, what *do* you think of Vyshinsky? But before you speak," he muttered, "I will tell you my thoughts. The man began life as a Menshevik. I distrust his words, which he never uses in the service of reconciliation but only cruelly and vituperatively to score points against his opponents. Do you agree?"

"Words indeed can hurt rather than heal."

"But is he hurting our cause or helping it?"

"It depends on the situation," said Razan, inwardly cringing.

"I didn't know you were a relativist."

"Isn't every good Bolshevik?"

"Absolutely not! Bolsheviks, like Christians, know right from wrong." He held up a hand mirror. "Sin and goodness differ."

Razan tried humorously to dismiss the subject. "But as you said, Supreme Leader, I am a Talmudist."

Removing the barber's apron and tossing it aside, Stalin led Razan by the arm to his office window. "You see out there? At this moment, numerous assassins are plotting my death. I would prefer to share with those people what I share with you: mutual affection and respect." Razan beamed. "But misbehavior cannot be ignored. Study history, Comrade Shtube. I read it every night. Learn how great nations fail owing to treachery."

What Razan knew for certain was that Stalin at the February and March Plenum of 1937 had unleashed a ferocious purge of his own people. But the arrests had actually started in 1934, with the murder of Sergei Kirov, who headed the Leningrad Bolshevik Party. Some said that Stalin had ordered him killed for opposing Koba's wish to liquidate critics and kulaks, and for putting the Leningrad Party in opposition to Stalin. Dimitri Lipnoskii called Kirov's death "the seminal event" that unleashed Stalin's demonic spirit. Executions in the thousands followed, but slowly. Although Razan had no reason to doubt Dimitri's assessment, the barber had noted that the purges began in earnest right after the 1934 Night of the Long Knives in Germany. Hitler had decapitated those who might challenge his power. It appeared as if Stalin was imitating Hitler. Ezhov, no fool, knew how to endear himself to Stalin. He fueled the purges by exacerbating Stalin's native Georgian fears of conspiracy, insisting that even the most innocent-seeming people were actually spies, two-facers, and enemies of the people. No one was to be trusted.

As a precautionary measure, Stalin ordered all of Kirov's close Leningrad associates killed and most of the members of the Leningrad Party shot. From 1933 to 1938, the size of the party was cut in half. The years 1937 to 1939 were the worst. Every day, *Pravda* reported the names of "enemies of the people." Either a terrible germ had infected the country and was causing wholesale madness and slaughter, or the anti-Soviets, from Trotsky to the monarchists, had gained control of millions of minds, persuading them all to become wreckers. Potential assassins, according to Ezhov, lay in wait around every corner. If the dwarf was hoodwinking only the Vozhd, why did most of the Russian people believe that the country was indeed in the grip of a mass conspiracy, one that required the most ruthless countermeasures? Razan was told that in those two years, one million were shot and two million died in the camps. Were they all enemies of the people?

Razan, for whom seeing was believing, had recently begun to admit another source of comprehension: feeling. He was letting his thoughts grow from his gut. Although he had never seen a show trial, had never seen a so-called wrecker, had never seen people confess, had never seen Leonid Zakovsky's guide to torture, had never seen a person subjected to "French wrestling" (*frantsuskaya borba*), or the *zhguti* (the "special club"), or the *dubinka* (the truncheon), or the conveyor belt (constant interrogation), or sleep deprivation, he had seen—and felt in the pit of his stomach—Alexei Ivanovich Rykov's last moments with his daughter. One March day at dusk, while Razan paused at the front of his building, set to depart for the Kremlin, a black sedan pulled up at the curb. A minute later, Rykov appeared leaning on his daughter's arm. She led him to the car. He was dressed in a suit, tie, vest, and unbuttoned overcoat. The back door of the black limousine opened, though no one appeared. Rykov turned to Natalya. They shook hands awkwardly, said nothing, and then kissed formally, three times on the cheek. Rykov climbed into the car, which drove off toward the Kremlin. Natalya left the sidewalk and stood in the middle of the street watching the Black Maria disappear. Just before it turned the corner, she began to run after it. When she turned back, she was crying.

Razan clasped her in his arms, as she buried her face in his shoulder. She related her father's last minutes. "Once he heard, he asked me to look after mother. Her stroke occurred when the attacks on him became more ominous. 'Tell her I've gone for a walk,' he said, 'and telephone Poskrebyshev for the precise time. I want to dress properly. It won't do to appear disheveled, which is a sign of fear.' I called, and Poskrebyshev said, 'The car is on the way now.'"

No friend or member of Rykov's family ever saw him again. Tried and convicted, he died March 15, 1938. When Razan heard from Natalya that Rykov had kept a list of prominent Bolsheviks who had been suppressed, the barber copied it, later adding other names.

Although Razan wished no man or woman ill, he knew that many of the "suppressed" were merely dull apparatchiks, but others, like Kirov, exhibited an admirable independence of mind. Did they not know that entering the cage of a wild animal greatly increased their chances of being eaten? This truth applied to him as well, so by 1939, after his long service, all his senses were attuned to trouble, and his byword was caution. Instead of joining Stalin in telling stories or exchanging jokes, he rationed his words and excused himself from social events that at one time he and Anna would have attended. Even knowing that Stalin had a double, he still couldn't definitively prove, given the behavior of the man whom he barbered, whether this man was the real Vozhd. It was a mark of the man's genius that for all his identifiable characteristics—pockmarks, decaying teeth, stale alcoholic breath, withered left arm, pudgy fingers, bad leg, Georgian accent, and love of movies—he might be only a decoy. Who, then, actually engaged the world's leaders?

The entire Soviet apparat, and especially the State Security Division, pretended, of course, that Stalin was but one man. In fact, Razan never heard a whisper to the contrary. Of all Stalin's secrets, the closest held by the apparat were the names of his decoys. But unbeknownst to Natasha, she had the name and background of one among her purloined papers. It was embedded in Babel's unfinished novel, which she had microfilmed and hidden in Yelena's stuffed panda.

Razan decided that the crisis over Yelena's painting, followed by the confiscation of photographs depicting the work, had to do with Stalin's identity and affected Yelena's safety. His wish to protect Yelena became an obsession and, like Jean-Paul Marat's rash, had to be scratched. The question that Razan couldn't answer was whether the authorities wanted the official portrait to portray the real man or a decoy. He could see arguments for both sides. If an assassin had Stalin in his sights, all the more reason for promoting the fake over the genuine. But given the personality cult that Stalin reveled in, he would want his beaming face peering down on his beloved people from every poster and wall. But Razan's every attempt to discover the real Stalin failed.

Perhaps the answer was to be found in the Boss's love of movies. So when Stalin invited the barber to join him to see a film that Koba had commissioned—

a comparison of Stalin and Houdini, who had died in 1926—Razan agreed. He followed the Vozhd and his guards to an elevator, where they all descended into the Kremlin courtyard, proceeded through the old winter gardens, where the pruned stalks poked through the snow like skeletal fingers, and entered the Great Kremlin Palace. On Razan's first visit to the Kremlin, he had been given a tour of the yellow-and-white stone palace on the crest of Borovitsky Hill, but he had never visited Stalin's luxurious cinema built on the second floor. A musty smell pervaded the first floor.

"It comes," Stalin said with a smile, "from the rottenness in the west wing, where the imperial family used to keep private apartments." As if to prove his physical fitness, the Boss ascended the stairs two at a time and flung open the door of the cinema like a child expecting to find inside a delicious treat. His guards automatically took up positions on either side of the room, with the thinner of the two men positioning himself in a small alcove next to a table spread with wine and mineral water and cigarettes and cigars, as well as boxes of imported chocolates. A screen was mounted on the far wall and, in front of it, eight rows of padded chairs, one upholstered in plush, which Stalin took. So excited was the Boss at seeing the film that he never once offered Razan a drink or a sweet. The Vozhd even neglected to ask the barber to sit. When Razan, in deference to the Boss, retreated to a back row, Stalin said he wanted him within sight.

"Sit here." He patted the chair next to him. "I asked Eisenstein to produce it and have Isaac Babel write the screenplay. But Sergei refused and Babel, I learned, was in prison. Ah, these artists, they all want to be individualists instead of collectivists."

Razan felt sorry for the minister of cinema, Ivan Bolshakov. A pale retiring fellow, whom Stalin called Ivan or I. B., he was on call day and night, as was the projectionist, Aleksandr Ganshin, for Stalin's favorite entertainment. It was whispered that the Vozhd took his political inspiration from films. Before being suppressed, the writer who had lived on the embankment next door to Razan had said that Stalin ruled the Soviet Empire by means of "cinematocracy"—rule by cinema. At the time, Razan thought the comment ridiculous. But seeing the Boss's euphoria, he now wondered.

"I. B. is my minister of cinema," Stalin exclaimed, leaning back in the plush chair and resting his legs on an ottoman. "He behaves like a scared rabbit. Do you know why?"

"Do you mean why he's the minister of cinema or why he's scared?"

Stalin smiled. "His predecessor was an enemy of the people. I had him shot. Relax, Comrade barber!" Koba exclaimed. "I can see that you're nervous.

Ivan also translates the films for me, though I suspect he's not always accurate. At least that's what Molotov says."

"A good reason to feel scared," said Razan, "given the importance of words and where a mistake can lead."

Luxuriating in his overstuffed chair, Stalin stroked his newly trimmed mustache.

"Usually, after I have met in the little corner of my office with my advisors, we come here. For some reason, they always leave the first row empty. I find that strange, don't you?"

Razan wanted to say that perhaps his lackeys feared to seat themselves in front of him lest they appear presumptuous, but the barber said only, "Maybe they're all farsighted."

Stalin slapped Razan on the back and roared, "You really are quite a wit. A wonderful pun. I must remember it. Farsighted." He paused just long enough to cause Razan to worry. Then Stalin said in a voice so flat that it sounded monotonic, "Apparatchiks, yes-men, functionaries . . . that's all they are. Farsighted! They can't find the front row of a cinema or an idea even when I lead them."

As the silent film began, photographs of Harry Houdini and Iosif Stalin appeared side by side. Razan made a point of noting which Stalin photograph had been selected for the film. Subtitles explained the similarities between the two men: virtually the same height; physically strong; fluent in two languages; obscure immigrants who had known great poverty, Harry in Hungary, and Stalin in Georgia; book and signature collectors; crowd pleasers; adored and even revered; famous, and for essentially the same reason, their magical abilities.

In one frame, Harry and his father sat side by side at a workbench cutting neckties; in another frame, Stalin and his father sat side by side at a workbench cobbling shoes. As the screen changed to show Harry trussed and nailed into a wooden crate lowered by a crane into a river, Razan tensed. After a few minutes, Harry surfaced—free! Razan sighed. In the next scene, the barber watched Stalin escape from a Tsarist prison camp, tramp through the snow, take a sledge, board a train, and slip off as it slowed toward its destination, a railroad platform in Tiflis. Razan read the subtitle: "Both men escaped from every prison cell and shackle in the world. How? Through careful planning. They never left a single thing to chance, always looking after each detail."

In the next series of paired scenes, the admiring workers questioned first Houdini and then Stalin.

"Mr. Houdini, people say your chains are unshackled by angels. They say you can shrink and slide through keyholes, and that you can dematerialize yourself and pass through solid wood planks and stone walls. But you say it's all done by trickery and training. To us, it looks like you have supernatural powers! Who should we believe?"

Houdini answered, "America is needle and thread, backaches, and ten cents an hour. Believe me, I *am* special! Just think of all the people who aren't."

"Comrade Stalin, the people say that because you are beloved by the workers of the world, you embody their combined strength. Is that how you have managed to escape from imprisonment, make a revolution, suppress the enemies of the people, and bring prosperity to our great motherland? If you are not supernatural, then you are Herculean."

Stalin answered, "Capitalists and landowners want to crush the workers and rule the world. Yes, it takes great strength to overcome the bloodsuckers. But I will prevail, and the proletariat will rule!"

Near the end, in a scene Razan never forgot, Stalin and Houdini discuss socialism, though in reality the two men never met.

STALIN (*sympathetically*): Your beloved mother is dead, Harry.
HOUDINI: I adored her. She was my source of life and sustenance.
STALIN: Now you must believe in something else. I can help you.
HOUDINI: No! No! She was a saint. Without her, what else is there? I must defeat death and reach her. Otherwise I'm alone.

During Stalin's next speech, Houdini's mixed emotions—despair and hope—express themselves in anguished gestures.

STALIN: Not alone, Harry. The people are behind you. Together we can all create a better world. You and I together.
HOUDINI: I hate politics.
STALIN: We must show death that life is stronger. Socialism gives life and plentiful harvests. You can smell the fertility. The scent is in the air, Harry, and the wonder.
HOUDINI: You're trying to mislead me.
STALIN: Why would I do that? The people love me. You know that what I say is true. Just look at the Soviet paradise.
HOUDINI: I can't see it.
STALIN: Open your eyes. Don't resist, Harry. Heaven is not above but below your feet.
HOUDINI: Oh, Mama, what's happening to me? I'm being mesmerized.
STALIN: Your mother's dead, but I'm here. You need me. I embrace you, comrade.

Stalin holds Houdini in a bear hug.

HOUDINI: You're suffocating me!

STALIN: No, this is just the beginning. We can show death that life is stronger. You and I, Harry, through socialism: one mind, one body. It's all possible, Harry.

HOUDINI (*dazed*): When, mother, when will you return?

STALIN: Never.

HOUDINI: No!

He extricates himself from Stalin.

STALIN: You can't escape the truth. Socialism is the answer. It alone can conquer death.

HOUDINI: I don't believe you.

STALIN (*calmly*): Your mother's in her grave, Harry, but I am here.

As they watched the film, Stalin anticipated the subtitles, repeating them from memory. He even gesticulated as he spoke, ostensibly engaging in a dialogue with the silent movie. It appeared to Razan, from Stalin's subsequent comments, that he couldn't tell the difference between the movie and real life. He actually seemed to believe that he and Houdini had engaged in a conversation, and that he had convinced Houdini of the rightness of the socialist cause.

"A great man, that Houdini," said Stalin. "I can feel myself hugging him. A sad and unnecessary death, especially for a man who planned his every move. He wasn't ready. Houdini loved boxing and knew the sport inside and out. He had stomach muscles like iron. I know. I've read everything printed about him. But when a university student came backstage and asked for permission to test him, his pride wouldn't let him say no. It was all so stupid. Houdini was lying down. As he started to get up, the young man hit him before he could flex his muscles. Ruptured his appendix. He died several days later." Stalin reflected for a moment and then continued. "Now you know why I rarely let a person touch me. You are one of the few, the very few, so don't abuse the privilege."

On returning from a mission to Perm, Dimitri found a message to see Lavrenti Beria, whom Stalin had recalled to Moscow, with all his Georgian thugs, to head the secret police. With Ezhov, for no apparent reason, having fallen out of favor, Beria was appointed to direct the ministry of State Security, checking on the loyalty of Soviet officials. Headquartered in Lubyanka Prison, Beria had at his disposal brutal interrogators and prison cells. His office doubled as a torture chamber and a brothel; the latter he used for raping schoolgirls who were kidnapped by his bodyguards.

His receding hairline, large distinctive forehead, round face, thin lips, and pince-nez gave him the appearance of an intellectual. But his college education—he was trained as an architect—had not mitigated his ruthlessness. It was he, in his capacity as principal policeman in Transcaucasia, who had declared, "Let our enemies know that anyone who attempts to raise a hand against the will of the party of Lenin and Stalin, will be mercilessly crushed and destroyed." He had secured his place in Stalin's affection with his fawning oration, "On the History of the Bolshevik Organizations in Transcaucasia," which shamelessly distorted the truth and asserted that Stalin was the originator and sole leader of Transcaucasian Bolshevism. The Vozhd showed his appreciation by making Beria a member of the Politburo and one of his most trusted subordinates. Calling him "The Prosecutor," Stalin charged Beria with suppressing any signs of opposition, at home or abroad. Beria replied that every man was guilty.

Dimitri knew Beria only by reputation. A Georgian friend had called him a "butcher," and now he was sitting calmly at his desk peering through his pince-nez at Dimitri, who had no idea why he'd been summoned. As with almost all secret-police interrogations, a file lay open on the desk; but Beria failed to take into account that Dimitri had already mastered the tricks of the trade.

"Comrade Lipnoskii," said Beria, turning over several sheets of paper, "your record is good, but your family history should have earned you the death penalty under my predecessor."

"I fail to understand . . ."

"Don't interrupt. Your brother Gregori . . . we sent him to Rome to spy for us, and he came back a *shpik* for Mussolini. A double agent. He has been sent to Solovki." Beria used the revolutionary vernacular, the street word for spy, no doubt to show his personal contempt for Gregori. "When did you last speak to your brother?"

"It's been years."

"Can you prove that?"

As Dimitri thought of how to prove a negative, Beria tapped his fingers on the desk. Finally, Dimitri replied, "If you had intercepts or taped phone calls, you would have shown them to me. But you have nothing. And for good reason. My brother and I have long been estranged." He pointed to the file. "As you know, I despise his religious convictions."

"They'll beat those ideas out of him in Solovki. A wonderful irony, isn't it? As the Vozhd says, we use an old monastery to reeducate priests to the truth of atheism." Beria laughed and repeated, "A wonderful irony." He removed his glasses and, wiping them, said, "Normally, we take no chances. Most families would have been exiled for having a traitorous son. But you have been a faithful agent, and then, too, there's your stepfather. As long as he has the Vozhd by the throat, so to speak, we will believe what you say: that you and your brother hate one another."

Dimitri, whose cramped breath had tightened his chest, began to relax. But his relief was ephemeral. Beria turned a page and said with a feigned smile, "You can go now, but I want to see you tomorrow."

Ah yes, thought Dimitri, the wait-and-sweat technique. Let the victim leave and stew over the insinuations, in the hope that on his return, he will change his story and confess all. But Dimitri knew preciously few details about Gregori's activities and decided it was best not even to inquire. Silence, he told himself, never deceives.

Outside Lubyanka Prison, he passed the long line of family members waiting to inquire about their loved ones. They carried parcels of food, string baskets with books, and bundles of clothing. The question that all of them hoped to have answered at the front gatehouse was whether the person they sought was even in Lubyanka Prison. If not, where then?

Returning to his narrow room in the Kremlin, Dimitri picked up his well-marked copy of *Antigone* and remembered what the police instructor had said when he had distributed copies to the class of neophyte agents.

"The great social struggle of our age is the one between individualism and communalism. Of course, every person should share in the freedoms and fruits of a great society. But an excess of individualism leads to greed and a destructive self-reliance that ignores the plight of others. Communalism can be equally pernicious if it snuffs out individual creativity and impresses upon the people a detestable conformity. *Antigone* is the first great work of literature to engage this philosophical divide. Although the title refers to Oedipus's daughter, the play is really about Creon's struggle to balance individual rights against the needs of the state."

Dimitri turned to the words that his instructor had often quoted:

> You can never know what a man is made of,
> His character or powers of intellect,
> Until you have seen him tried in rule and office.

The next day, Beria stared at him coldly. "We have another reason to question you. The hairdresser Yuri Suzdal. You told him that he would be arrested unless he fled. He told us so himself."

Dimitri knew that interrogators make numerous accusations, proceeding from the rule that you can tell whether a person is lying if, one, he yells and shouts his innocence, and two, he never changes his language or alibi or excuse. Skillfully, Dimitri framed his excuses in different words and cited several alibis. Beria shortly realized that the usual interrogatives wouldn't work, and that he would have to try another tack. After exhibiting hardness, he now became soft: bad cop, good cop.

"I suppose, Comrade Lipnoskii, you know the joke currently making the rounds?" Dimitri shook his head no. "What's the highest building in Moscow? It's the Lubyanka Prison. Because from the top floor, you can see all the way to Siberia."

Dimitri forced a smile but couldn't bring himself to laugh.

"Not funny?" said Beria disappointed, immediately dropping the mask of cheerfulness and returning to what he knew best: hardness. "We have a photograph of you and Yuri Suzdal at the railroad station."

He handed it to Dimitri. But since the two lovers had never stood together on a train platform, either to leave on a holiday or for any other reason, Dimitri knew that the NKVD Photographic Department had used separate snapshots—ironically, perhaps his own—to juxtapose him and Yuri. The background railroad setting had been clearly staged. In fact, the forgery was so careless that the men were clothed for different seasons of the year, Suzdal, winter, and Dimitri, summer.

"Comrade Beria," he said, returning the photo, "you and I both know it's a forgery. Just look at what we are wearing."

Beria studied it a moment, bewildered, as if he'd failed to scrutinize it before, and then he barked, "The fools! They can't competently perform the simplest tasks." He smirked and added, "Comrade Lipnoskii, you are to be complimented for identifying shoddy work. You have just proved your worthiness for the most difficult assignment you have yet to undertake. We want you to conduct a full surveillance—mail, phone, personal contacts, taps, informers— to establish that Razan Shtube and his wife, Anna, are working for the Albanian government as Fascist spies."

Dimitri could feel along his veins a thickening anger, but before he could respond, Beria said, "What better way to show your loyalty to the country? And who has greater access to these people than you?"

His temper barely under control, Dimitri leaned his elbows on Beria's desk and said icily, "Someone has made a mistake."

An irate Beria, apparently having already forgotten about the picture, fumed, "You dare to call the work of the NKVD a mistake?"

"As fraudulent as the photograph."

"We have arrested a courier who entered the country illegally. He left Tirana last week and was uncovered in Voronezh, before he could make his way to Moscow. Among his papers we found documents incriminating your parents."

Beria reached under his desk, and a distant scream indicated that a prisoner was being tortured; or, more likely, that a recording from a previous interrogation was being played for Dimitri's benefit.

"I understand the point, Comrade Beria, I have used the same methods myself."

"The fact remains that we have apprehended an Albanian courier."

"Everyone knows that half the population of Voronezh are secret police, always willing to perjure themselves for promotion."

"So you have little faith in the NKVD?"

"I prefer my own senses."

"Then use them to expose Razan and bring us irrefutable proof of his conspiring against our Great Leader and the people. I don't care whether the evidence is true or false, so long as it is irrefutable."

Dimitri said sardonically, "Invented evidence."

"Comrade Lipnoskii, those who lack the discipline imparted by the NKVD spend every day improvising competence. You are not one of those. Your skills are now ingrained and natural."

How, Dimitri asked himself, had his stepfather fallen out of favor with Stalin? Perhaps, in fact, he hadn't but was merely another person close to the Boss who, for safety's sake, had to be suppressed. In Stalin's circle, familiarity bred more than contempt; it made one privy to Stalin's life, thus rendering the Supreme Leader vulnerable to anyone wishing him harm. Even if Razan was devoted to the Bolshevik cause, he had obviously become too familiar with the Vozhd and his inner sanctum. Virtually everyone close to Stalin eventually perished, and those who remained were each day more likely to disappear. But what if Razan had been stamped a pariah for another reason? The possibilities were almost endless. Perhaps he had inadvertently insulted Stalin, told a joke that was taken the wrong way, scared him by nicking his neck during a shave, talked to the wrong people, read banned books, viewed uncensored films, perhaps even credited Trotsky with contributions to the October Revolution. Dimitri would have to find out the reason for the trumped-up charges, but first he'd have to find an excuse to delay the investigation until he could fashion some plan to save his parents.

"I can see that you are mulling over your new assignment," said Beria. "Silence lends itself to different interpretations. It can be taken for consent, or can betray one's guilt, or can be a forewarning of conspiracy." He banged the desk. "What am I to make of yours?"

Dimitri played a card that the secret police normally ridiculed in others: personal feelings. "I find your information so shocking that I ask for time to digest it and decide how to proceed."

"In the event that you decide not to cooperate with us, let me remind you that on these very premises, we have a laboratory for testing poisons. You didn't know that, Comrade Lipnoskii, did you?"

"No."

"It's a new addition. My idea. We test our poisons on both animals and traitors." He removed a sheet of paper from his desk drawer. The stationery bore the NKVD imprint. "Let me read one doctor's report, 'We administered the poison in the prisoner's food. Although he was a healthy, strong man, he rushed about the cell as his stomach pains worsened. From his execrations against us and the Supreme Leader, it was clear that he understood what had happened to him. He ran to the steel door, blood pouring from his eyes, beating the door with his fists and his feet. He shoved his hand into his slobbering mouth, gagged, slid to the floor, and died.'"

Of course, Dimitri knew that Beria's description was intended to unnerve him, so he summoned his sternest look and posture and militantly announced, "Enemies of the people deserve worse."

This reply disconcerted the "prosecutor," who was, in light of the cunning of Dimitri's reply, all the more inclined to believe that Dimitri had told Suzdal to run away. Furthermore, the file in front of him suggested collusion. But for now, to silence his doubts, he stoically repeated his earlier command. "We want you to collect evidence that will enable us to convict Razan Shtube and his wife, Anna, for traitorous acts against the state. Do you understand me?" Beria stood. "If you wish to prove your loyalty to Stalin and the Soviet people, you will succeed in this task. If you do not, well, I have already shared with you the work of our secret poisons lab."

For hours, Dimitri aimlessly walked the streets, stopping periodically for a schnapps. By the time he fell into bed, he was thoroughly drunk and absolutely convinced that he would not betray his own family. What remained to be decided was how to proceed. Should he shoot Beria or poison him? As a secret agent, he too had access to some of the more baneful tinctures. But as sleep overtook him, he dreamed that he was flying. He had launched himself off a promontory, backward, as if doing a flip, and seconds later was airborne. Righting himself, he flew over the familiar Moscow landscape. Below lay the Kremlin, and the river, and Saint Basil's, and Red Square with its redbrick buildings and mausoleum, and crowds waiting to see the embalmed body of Lenin. That his entire family sat comfortably on his back seemed perfectly natural to him and, in fact, made him smile.

Sobriety returned to Dimitri accompanied by a fierce headache. He took his dream as an omen and decided that his next step would be to talk to his mother, whose common sense was anything but common.

They met in a stand of birch trees at the forested Izmailovo Park, arriving, as arranged, after dark and on different trains.

"Why did you want to see me alone? Is Razan in trouble?"

Dimitri ran his hand across his eyes.

Anna kindly said, "You used to make that same gesture when you were a child and found yourself in hot water. What's the matter?"

As she reached out to touch him, he stepped back and replied plaintively, "It's bad. Gregori is in prison, and you are suspected."

After Dimitri had recounted his meeting with Beria, Anna lit a cigarette. "Poor Gregori. I knew that one day his need to believe in something or someone greater than himself would ruin him." She inhaled deeply.

"Can you think of any anti-Soviet activity that my stepfather might have engaged in, even inadvertently?"

"Razan, anti-Soviet? He's an uncritical fool. Oh, he takes precautions, like everyone else, but underneath he trusts people. I've told him a hundred times, 'When talking to the Vozhd repeat how much you admire him.' But he thinks it's enough to tell Stalin how beautiful his daughter is. He says that she's his favorite, but I tell him to praise both."

"You're right. Stalin treasures adoration."

They walked in silence as Anna lit one cigarette after another, discarding them after only a few puffs. In the approaching dark, her lucubrations led her finally to say, "Although I can prove I didn't commit a crime, how can I prove I was not thinking about doing so?"

Dimitri nodded in agreement and added, "Anti-Soviet thoughts, though unprovable, are punishable. That's why the government engages in thought control: to prevent subversive ideas." Anna stridently laughed. "In fact, one has a much better chance of escaping the charge of a material crime than an abstract one."

Anna nodded and then made an astonishing suggestion. "Tell Beria that your parents are Zionists, and they've frequently said that Palestine is paradise, not the Soviet Union."

Coming to a dead stop, Dimitri turned and stared at his mother, fearing she'd lost her senses. "Are you mad?"

"If you have a better idea," said Anna, lighting her last cigarette, "tell me. If you don't, I suggest that we meet Razan in a safe place to talk. I'm sure he can tell us how to make it work."

The NKVD had begun to patrol the Moscow parks where people escaped to speak freely. As Dimitri and Anna left Izmailovo, they passed two men in raincoats whom Dimitri knew to be secret policemen.

"What if they ask why you were in the park with your mother?"

"I have the perfect excuse. Comrade Beria told me to use any means to uncover incriminating evidence against you and my stepfather. I was just following orders. But we cannot meet here again."

The next day, Anna suggested that Dimitri commandeer a taxicab in the name of the NKVD and slowly drive it through the city. They could speak freely in the car. Dimitri liked that idea, since he normally used one of the cab drivers as an informant; and his taxi, with its missing front grille and dented right fender, resembled the other worn vehicles. A borrowed cab would be easy to explain, and if stopped, readily explained.

As warm breezes carried the scents of August, Dimitri carefully removed the listening device in the overhead lining above the backseat and drove slowly around the Ring Road. Traffic was light.

"Mother says that you can clarify this zany idea of hers," said Dimitri.

Sitting in the backseat, Razan leaned forward and explained that given the number of Jewish doctors in Moscow, and given their reputation for competence, their departure for Palestine would be an immeasurable loss. "Not that they're thinking of leaving; they're not. But the mere suggestion of inducing them to leave, particularly in the name of Zionism, would drive Stalin crazy and get your mother and me sent to an insane asylum."

Dimitri nearly drove off the road.

"In all my life, I never heard such a lamebrain idea. Are you trying to get yourselves killed?"

"With all the talk in the west of anti-Semitism, German concentration camps, and pogroms, Stalin won't kill us. He'll arrest us. I know that much about the man from my barbering."

Touching her son on the shoulder, Anna said, "Have the secret police report that we belong in an asylum. You can then suggest we be sent to the same one as Alexei. From there we shall make our escape."

Dimitri shook with laughter. His eyes teared. "My dear mother, I have heard about some great escapades in my life, but this one tops them all. It simply won't work. I'll try, but you'll see."

"Palestine!" Beria bellowed. "A paradise!"

"They hope to persuade our Jewish doctors to leave the country."

Beria, who had been bent over his desk studying Dimitri's report, slowly lifted his head, adjusted his glasses, and hissed, "They are Zionist wreckers!" He paused. "It's nothing less than an attempt to sow religious dissension!" Beria ran a hand over his mouth to wipe away the foaming saliva. "The next thing you'll tell me is that they intend to parade in the October celebration dressed as Kaganovich or Molotov or as Stalin's double." But the moment he used the word "double," he withdrew it. "Forget what I just said. How could anyone try to be a stand-in for our Great Leader or want to parody him?"

"Agreed, but nonetheless . . ."

Beria paced between his desk and the window. He stared mutely into the street. The word "double," so fraught with recondite meaning, confirmed for Dimitri what he had long suspected but wouldn't dare utter: Stalin used political decoys. At that moment, he realized how great a danger Razan posed to Stalin, and why he, like the barbers before him, had to be removed, not to mention the pogrom that Stalin was putting in place. Now he understood what lay behind Beria's order to unearth damning evidence. But when the exhilaration of his insight had passed, he felt sick, knowing that only he stood between his family and a firing squad.

An irate Beria thundered, "We must create a *cordon sanitaire* around these conspirators. Find out who they are. If this Jewish plot spreads, it could prove lethal. The western press is already accusing us of anti-Semitism."

Without thinking, Dimitri replied, "Well, aren't we?"

Beria shouted: "Idiot! Don't you see the implications?" He rubbed his jaw. "Find the network. We must isolate the traitors."

Dimitri edged forward in his chair. "Comrade Beria, such a plot will be seen for what it is: preposterous. As much as I dislike betraying my own family, those behind it are obviously ill."

Beria studied Dimitri and, with feigned sympathy, replied, "I am disappointed in you, Comrade Lipnoskii. Don't you see the greater danger? Surely when you entered the service of the secret police, you were schooled in how peasants think." Dimitri nodded. "As you know, the people put more store in faith than in fact. Myths, legends, superstitions—this is the stuff of religion. Faith, not fact, captures the imagination, precisely because it is not amenable to proof. An exodus of Jewish doctors! What could be more dangerous than the belief that God was calling them home to Palestine? It would undoubtedly appeal to the enemies of the people, who would twist the meaning to their own purposes. Now go out and get me names, thousands of them—after all, they are merely statistics—and we shall rid our beloved country of this pestilence."

"Wouldn't it be best just to exile the barber and his family to Voronezh, and assign them to a mental institution? I know one."

"Out!" Beria roared.

Dimitri staggered from the Lubyanka Prison, followed by a police agent who made no effort to conceal himself. Dimitri had now become the servant of two masters, the state and his family. On the sidewalk, he mumbled to himself, "Antigone revisited."

PART II

PAVEL'S POLISH PELAGIA

Rain, heavy rain and autumn frost,
The nearing train meant all was lost.

And what of Pavel, nesting in Brovensk? His forge eventually suffered con-fiscation. On the military train's first visit, Basil von Fresser had counseled the citizens of Brovensk to resist, earning him, his wife, and eight other Ger-mans living in the town exile to an icy camp near the top of the world. Wisely, the villagers agreed that relinquishing ownership of their farms was the only way to prevent "resettlements." A few owners, however, had ignored the new laws, including Pavel, who had quietly continued to work outside the orbit of the collective, fashioning farm implements and fancy ironwork and artistic metal lattices. Efim Klimov, the one-eyed apparatchik the Soviets had put in charge, knowing nothing about ideology, retired to the inn, and left Pavel and his furnace untouched by Bolshevik theory. Comrade Cyclops, as the people called him, discharged but one chore. He regularly visited the telegraph office to collect his orders from the Central Committee of the oblast and relay them to the town.

In the middle of the night, a lugubrious train whistle signaled the second arrival of the ravening special army cavalry corps charged with nationalizing privately held shops. This time, the army seized the forge and compounded the injury by informing him that his brother was an enemy of the state. Pavel could be either exiled to a work camp to produce shovels and plows and scythes and hoes and axes—handsome scroll wall sconces and tapered metalwork were now a thing of the past—or enlist in the army and become part of the operation to "free" western Ukraine, western Belorussia, and eastern Poland.

The military captain, Antip Skoropodski, in charge of recruitment for the Brovensk area, had heard that Pavel was a skilled horseshoe player, a game that Antip adored. But after one match with Pavel, he knew that he had just met his regiment's future champion. Promising Pavel an easy service, Antip proposed that Pavel join the army in the capacity of farrier. In addition to forging horseshoes and caring for equine hooves, Pavel would play other regimental champions, whom Antip would challenge in his role as horseshoe impresario. Pavel agreed. Steaming off on the military train, Pavel and Antip traveled for several days before transferring to a westbound troop train bound for Ukraine and the Polish border. Before crossing into Poland, Antip and his regiment stopped in a small Ukrainian town for Antip to school new recruits—and to wait for the Germans to complete their conquest of western Poland. But the Soviets were surprised by the rapid German advance eastward and realized that they would have to field an invading army earlier than originally planned. Antip was therefore instructed, in his capacity as a *politruk*, political officer, to indoctrinate his soldiers not leisurely but in one week. The "special courses" might have sounded to sophisticated ears like rubbish, but to the majority of soldiers, illiterate peasants, the propaganda rang true. Suave and well spoken, Antip's physical appearance reinforced his message. He had dark lustrous hair swept back and parted in the middle. A courteous manner and a pleasant smile (he was proud of his good teeth) stamped him as a kindly man, and in fact, he was inclined to eschew draconian measures. But if necessary, he could be conniving and cruel. His only bourgeois sin was a liking for lilac cologne, with which he liberally doused his cheeks after shaving. Unlike most of his men, he sported no mustache, regarding the fullness of his upper lip as one of his more attractive features.

"You will be entering a bourgeois state," Antip lectured from the front of the classroom in a village school, a chalkboard in one hand and a pointer in the other. "We are entering Poland," he said, holding up the board with its hand-drawn map of the area, "in order to aid Ukrainians and Belorussians . . ." Antip paused. His orders from central headquarters were unclear. In the same directive, he was told to say that the Soviets were coming to help Poland in its war *against* Germany, and to explain that they were coming only to offer protection *from* the Germans. The directive had concluded with the command: "Just make the intervention of the Soviet Union plausible to the masses." Antip continued, "In our war *with* Germany, we wish to help Poland. Now, you may well ask: How can we help Poland? We can free the proletariat from the *polskie pany*, the Polish pans, the masters, who for twenty years have been drinking the blood of the poor. The peasants must be allowed to treat the pans as they please. We will distribute leaflets to the local population urging them to rectify the wrongs suffered at the hands of their class enemies: capitalists, landowners, officers, uniformed men, reservists, scouts, policemen, teachers, particularly school principals, and the parasite priests." Antip looked at his recruits and could read the shock in their faces. He therefore added, "Remember, their priests are of the Roman Church." His recruits relaxed. "And let us not forget to remind the victims of Polish rule that they have been ill used for years by those who staff the local administration: judges, public prosecutors, activists, prominent members of political organizations, church and government volunteers, landowners, businessmen, leaders of the community, and even state pensioners. All of them . . . *to jail!*"

Antip rubbed his smooth chin and debated whether to speak further of the leaflets, some of which called for assaults on the "enemies of the people" and their stooges with whatever was at hand—scythes, axes, pitchforks, ice picks, hammers, crowbars, shovels. One leaflet in screaming block letters said: "*PO-LIAKAM, PANAM, SOBAKAM—SOBACHAIA SMERT.*" For Poles, pans, and dogs—a dog's death. He wondered whether to suppress it. But thinking better of running afoul of his superiors, he concluded his peroration by saying, "I repeat then: We of the Red Army are here to assist in the national and class liberation of the people from under the rule of the Polish pans, the *beloruchki*, those with white hands." The group was by now growing restless, so he saved the sweetener for last. "Each Red Army man and woman will receive three hundred rubles to buy consumer goods in Poland. But do not think that just because the shops are overflowing with goods, the Polish poor can afford them. The ragged ones are relegated to eating turnips and tares."

Two days later, on September 17, 1939, Stalin ordered the Red Army to cross the Ukrainian and Belorussian borders into eastern Poland. Antip's regiment was to occupy the town of Rzeszów, situated on both sides of the Wistok River in the heartland of the Sandomierska valley. His orders: take control of the factories producing aircraft engines and cannons. Pavel rode in a canvas-covered transport truck on a crisp autumn day. So many refugees crowded the road that the convoy had to stop to allow them to pass. The river of people formed a classless society, all intent on survival. They traveled on every conveyance: carts, horses, donkeys, cars, trucks, motorcycles, sidecars, ox-driven wagons, bicycles, and foot. Pavel gawked at their unfamiliar dress and possessions. Some had left behind their businesses; some had abandoned their property; some had worked as merchants, lawyers, aldermen, journalists, doctors, teachers; some made no attempt to hide their Jewish roots and readily admitted their hatred of the Germans. The virtuous and the corrupt, the grasping and the brave, marched together down the road toward the Ukrainian border. The rich rode; the poor walked. Respectable ladies from aristocratic families escorted their delicate daughters, dressed in finery fit not for the dusty road but for the drawing room, and prostitutes with carmine-painted lips shared the equality of fear. Poets, pawnbrokers, princes, and pimps were all of a sudden all comrades. When the mass of people converged on Kiev, they would no doubt each make for the sector of society to which they belonged, the junk dealers to their fellow scavengers, the actors to the theatre, the homosexuals to the demimonde, the gendarmes to the police stations, the whores and procurers to the brothels. Even anti-Bolsheviks, some of them singing songs to the memory of Symon Petlura, the Ukrainian nationalist, were seeking escape from the Germans.

Once the regiment continued on its way, friendly crowds greeted the men with bread and salt, a traditional gesture of hospitality. The crowds were largely composed of young people from the so-called ethnic minorities: Belorussians, Jews, and Ukrainians. Before the German invasion, a third of the city had been Jewish, but when the Germans pulled out, as agreed, to allow the Russians to enter, two-thirds of the Jewish population had already been resettled in camps outside the city. Young Zionists, who had hidden from the Germans and were hoping for the best from the Russians, eagerly inquired about the prospects for emigration to Palestine. Antip and his Bolshevik propagandists had done their work well. Invariably, the Soviet reply was the same: that the new authorities would create Palestine for Jews "right here."

Bivouacked outside the city, the regiment grew restless a week into the encampment. A number of soldiers meandered into town and found temporary residence in private homes. Pavel intended the same, but on the outskirts of town, he spied a stunning young woman, with hair as blond as hay, wearing a bright apricot-colored cap. She passed through a wooden gate into a one-story wooden house, sporting bright green outdoor shutters, surrounded by a lush pasture. Pavel could see a single cow grazing on the grass. He followed the blond beauty and knocked on the door, unaware that he was seeking admission to the home of Madam Petukhova, a rich widow in the throes of death. Her husband had emigrated from Ukraine to Poland and had, until congestive heart failure admitted him to the cemetery, made a handsome living as a lapidary, trading on the side in diamonds and zircons. The young woman who had just entered the house answered his knock. Her name was Pelagia Petukhova, and, judging from the color of her hands and face and neck, she was clearly a *beloruchki*.

Pavel explained that he was seeking only a temporary stay before the Red Army moved to occupy those cities from which German soldiers were now withdrawing. Pelagia could not help but notice Pavel's blue eyes and sinewy arms. His muscles rippled through his clothing, and his speech was not crude. She could smell his sweat and found it not acrid but sweet. As he extended a hand of friendship to her, she noticed that he had long, delicate fingers. He knew no Polish but she spoke Ukrainian and Russian with ease, and even some German.

"We have an extra room at the back of the house," said Pelagia. "You will have to tiptoe. Mother is deathly ill. I fear that in the next day or two, I'll be calling the priest."

On the wall hung a crucifix, not an Orthodox one with three bars, but a single-barred Roman cross. Before the closure of the churches, Pavel had been baptized Orthodox, but felt that a person's religion was hardly worth fighting over; after all, had he not accepted his stepfather without protest? In his simple way, he had arrived at a Bolshevik belief: Religious rites separate people.

That night, he and Pelagia sat in front of the fireplace and exchanged family stories, the first step in their journey toward bonding. She found him sensitive and caring, inviting her thoughts and not bludgeoning her with his own, as former suitors had done. He paradoxically used his imposing physical presence in the service of a compassionate courtesy. She could see in the way that he touched an object, a figurine, for example, that a sensuous spring fed mind and body. Yes, here was a gentle giant, as such men were called.

She had been courted by many men, though she was never bedded by any. All of them seemed intent on gaining, at the same time, a beautiful woman and a dowry, perhaps even Krasula. As part of the decayed nobility, her family believed in suitors first speaking to the parents and indicating their expectations. Once her father had died, her mother became the protector of Miss Petukhova's reputation. Any young man wishing to pass into the family sitting room first had to tame the lion at the gate. Few young men had much to offer her other than rough manliness and a hard life, so older men began to pay her court. But these she found unsuitable. They had gnarled hands or wrinkled faces; they smelled of the field or garlic; they spoke ungrammatically or foully; they knew little Polish history and letters. To one suitor, she mentioned the name Copernicus. His reply: "Never met the man." Pavel was different. His tastes in architecture and furnishings were sophisticated, and, owing to his stepfather's influence, he had read some of the Russian masterworks: *War and Peace*, *Fathers and Sons*, and *Crime and Punishment*. Although he knew no other books written by Tolstoy and Turgenev and Dostoevski, these three alone enabled him to eclipse her other suitors, except for one young man, Zygmunt Frajzyngier, a Jewish schoolteacher who had come to the house once and, with the reluctant approval of Pelagia's father, taken her to see a ballet; but Zygmunt had died shortly after from consumption.

Pelagia's fascination with Pavel was also heightened by the eerie resemblance he bore to her younger brother, Blazej (Blaise), who had died from bulbar polio. The only son, he was beloved by his parents and sister for his sensitivity and interest in literature. The family was convinced that he would be a second Adam Mickiewicz, the famous nineteenth-century romantic poet.

"I like to think of myself as open minded, but I'm actually not," said Pavel, "especially when it comes to the woman I marry. I admit I want her chaste and faithful. Is that a terrible thing to say?"

Pelagia assured him that she expected the same of the man whom she married, and that he had no need to feel "bourgeois." "I find," she said, "that the most conservative people, like priests and landowners, are often the most likely to behave shamefully. They think they're immune."

Pavel told her about his dog, Mir, and how he left her with a friend in Brovensk. But as he and Antip boarded the train, he heard barking and saw Mir on the platform "calling him home." Pelagia shyly allowed that she too had a pet; it was the milk cow back of the house. She fondly called the *krowa*, cow, "Krasula."

"I raised it from a calf, and she never fails to give us a full pail of milk. Such a wonderful animal. She's a part of the family. My father so loved her that before his death, he fashioned for her a special padded collar with three small bells. And inside the collar, he stuffed good-luck charms and religious medals and talismans for long life. Papa was very devout."

They talked well into the night and, before retiring, innocently hugged. That night, Pavel never closed his eyes, watching for the morning light when he could again see the fair Pelagia. She, on the other hand, fell asleep immediately and dreamed of wearing her mother's white lacy dress as she walked down the aisle of her local church to be sanctified in marriage by the local priest, Father Henryk Jankowski, known for denouncing from the pulpit "fallen" women and Jews. In her dream, Pavel was standing at the altar waiting for her, while his stepfather, whom Pavel had disclosed was a "kindly" Jew, kneeled in the church garden before a crucifix, promising to embrace the true faith if Father Jankowski would allow him to stand as best man for Pavel. She found herself tormented by the thought of Razan Shtube holding such an exalted place at her wedding and woke with a start when she heard her mother cry out for help.

Madam Petukhova, a skilled seamstress, had long served the rich Rzeszów families, who admired not only her skills but also her speed. A wedding dress that would take a normal needle worker a month or more to make, she could complete in a fortnight. She had in fact made her own wedding dress that now rested in mothballs in the large cedar chest at the back of the basement. She had already altered the dress for Pelagia, her only living child, and hoped to survive long enough to see her married in it.

Pelagia sat at her mother's bedside for two days, as the poor woman slowly passed from lucidity to raving to a semiconscious state. Madam Petukhova had first discovered the lump in her breast fifteen months before, but she was too modest to allow the local doctor to examine a private part of her body. The tumor had grown so large that it had distorted her breast and caused the nipple to ooze a white liquid. On the evening of the third day, Madam Petukhova nearly died, not from cancer but from fright. Pavel, unfortunately, had not yet returned to the house from his daily routine. Pelagia answered a banging on the front door. In front of her stood a thief, Bronislaw Sadkowski, whose crooked face, scarred in a knife fight, mimicked his warped mind. He had been appointed by the Soviets to the role of militia commander for Rzeszów. Even though imprisoned four times for stealing and for taking speculators across the border into Hungary, he now worked for the Red Army requisitioning prized property.

"It's for the Soviet cause," he declared untruthfully.

Other thieves were also enjoying a new life under the Soviets, who employed the tortured reasoning that a prison record in a capitalist state indicated that a person had been either a class enemy of the bourgeoisie or its victim. Either one qualified a criminal to work for the Soviets. Thus, no crime prevented the Soviets from assigning custody of a city area to criminals. That many of the people appointed by the Soviets were recognizable to the locals as lawbreakers appealed to the Soviets' sense of delayed justice.

"I am also looking for pans," said Bronislaw, whose left eye drooped owing to his injury.

"Search the house. You won't find any here. But be quiet." She put a finger to her lips. "Mother is bedridden and quite ill."

Bronislaw rifled through the closets and drawers and chests.

"You won't find any pans in there," said a disgusted Pelagia, who knew Bronislaw for a thief.

A confused Bronislaw replied, "*Davai kushat* (Give something to eat). I am starved."

She found some blood sausage that he quickly devoured, ripping off a piece of bread to go with it. From his pocket, he produced a crumpled leaflet bearing the image of Stalin.

"Hang it next to the crucifix. He's the next thing to a God." She took a thumbtack and placed the leaflet below the cross.

When Pavel rapped on the door, she said, for Bronislaw's sake, "That will be my Russian friend, a Red Army officer with the local regiment. He is staying here."

Bronislaw turned ashen. Gently sliding the lace curtain aside, he looked out the front window and saw a uniformed man. "I'll leave through the back door."

In the few seconds it took for Pelagia to admit Pavel, Bronislaw had left the house, entered the pasture, and taken Krasula with him. Pelagia, on discovering the loss of her cow, screamed and ran to tell her mother, who nearly died in that instant. Pavel stood dumbfounded. Madam Petukhova closed her eyes and seemed to breathe her last. But minutes later, she opened her eyes and summoned enough strength to ask for the priest. Pelagia went for Father Jankowski at once. The priest brought his instruments for Extreme Unction, greeted Pavel, and asked to be alone with the good woman while he administered the last rites. Ten minutes later, he hastily exited the house.

Pelagia entered the room and, sitting beside her mother, held her hand. Madam Petukhova's face resembled a death mask. She looked to Pelagia as if she had passed from this world into the next. But the old woman lasted until late that night, and she managed a few last words, which came in short bursts.

"Papa hid all his best jewels in Krasula's collar. A small fortune in diamonds and some other stones. He said the Germans and Russians would search the house. The collar, he thought, was the safest place. I told Father Jankowski."

"Did he say anything?" asked Pelagia.

"He said he guessed that the hidden cache was worth enough to start a new life and build a small church in German-occupied Kraków." Pelagia went to the window and looked into the empty pasture; tears ran down her face. But given her "white hands" and the exalted positions that criminals now held, she waited for her mother's funeral to tell Pavel. At the grave site, in a steady downpour, Pelagia revealed the loss and the perpetrator. Pavel promised to track down both Bronislaw and the priest, even if he had to desert the regiment. Huddled together under Pelagia's umbrella, they returned to the house.

A geologist by training, Antip knew where to find different kinds of soil, knowledge he exploited when he ordered his men to truck in two kinds of earth for the horseshoe pitching court he ordered built on the west end of town. The Russian tank regiment he had challenged to a match was home to Serhiy Chumachenko, a man famous in the Red Army for his many tournament victories. He pitched his shoes on a low trajectory and landed them in an open position short of the stake, where they would slide into the post for a ringer. But to achieve this effect, he needed hard-packed soil. To put Serhiy at a disadvantage, Antip settled on potter's clay, which had to be kept in a moist and puttylike condition for use in the stake area.

Serhiy made it a point always to inspect the pits before agreeing to a match. When shown the hard-packed soil of Antip's pits, he happily agreed to a contest and a hundred-ruble wager, funded in part by the men in his tank corps. Anticipation ran high as the two regiments taunted each other. Both had their champions. Although Pavel's reputation preceded him, Serhiy knew that on hard pack he had no equal. The night before the match, Antip had his men remove the hard pack that they had originally used to construct the court, and replace it with potter's clay, which held the shoes fast.

Hundreds of boisterous, vodka-inspirited soldiers crowded around the playing area, running north to south. The pits at either end of the court were covered with tarpaulins because, as Antip explained, they had recently been raked, and he wanted to keep them pristine. Serhiy appeared to roars of approval, as his admirers parted in ceremonial fashion to allow him to make his grand entrance. Pavel, in the company of Pelagia, received a hug from her that elicited whistles and catcalls. His own regiment simply clapped. Both men had exchanged their uniforms for sweat clothes and sneakers, and each had his own set of regulation horseshoes. Antip asked for the prize money and placed it on a table in sight of all. As the two contestants swung their arms in circles and performed knee bends in preparation for the match, Antip directed two aides to remove the tarps. Serhiy stopped in mid-motion and turned the color of bleached bone. He saw not hard-packed dirt in the pits but wet clay. A good sport, Serhiy smiled and slightly bowed toward Antip in acknowledgment of his having been duped. Pavel, who knew nothing of the deception, shook hands with Serhiy, wished him well, and walked to the pitcher's box. Forty feet away stood a stake fifteen inches high with a three-inch forward lean, and four feet beyond the stake, stood a backboard. Serhiy would try to adjust his game to suit the conditions by throwing his shoes with more height, a technique that required a different motion and degree of strength. He knew, once he had discovered that the surface was clay, that he had little chance of winning. Although Antip chuckled at his own chicanery, he offered Serhiy the opportunity to reduce the amount of the wager, but Serhiy declined, lest he admit weakness in front of his regiment.

Pelagia watched from the sidelines, her hands clasped tightly, as if she held Pavel's fortune in hers. Having developed a fondness for this Russian soldier, she prayed for his success.

Serhiy pitched first. His shoe fell short of the stake, where it stuck. Pavel put his first shoe next to the pin. Serhiy's second shoe had enough loft, but the closed end hit the stake and the shoe caromed off to the side. Pavel's next throw was a ringer. And so it went. With Serhiy unable to bounce his shoes, he lost his rhythm and began to spray his shots. In short order, the match was over. A delighted Antip scooped up the prize money and pocketed it, having no intention of sharing the winnings with Pavel. Antip thought it reward enough to invite Pavel to dine with him that night. Besides, had it not been for Antip's enterprise, Pavel might well have lost. Pavel made no protest and merely asked that Pelagia be included for dinner, a request to which Antip agreed, having himself noted Pelagia's albino skin and nearly identical lustrous hair, her lovely legs and rounded chest. Pavel knew that he would have to act forcefully and soon if he was to keep the skirt-chasing Antip from transferring him to another regiment and pursuing the pretty Pelagia himself.

Who would transport the fair damsel to the restaurant became a point of contention between the two men. The commander insisted that Pelagia ride and not walk; and since he had a car and driver at his disposal, he would transport her, while Pavel went on foot. But to the chagrin of Antip, Pelagia insisted on accompanying Pavel so that she could "enjoy the lovely fall night and the autumn leaves floating through the evening's silver light." Although normally even tempered, Antip had little patience for being refused, and taking no for an answer put him out of sorts for days. Pretending to good manners, he bowed at the waist and invited both to use his car. But Pelagia had made her intention clear and was in no mood to change it.

A disgruntled Antip, heavily perfumed, was already seated in the restaurant and sipping his second slivovitz when Pavel and Pelagia arrived. Unable to disguise his annoyance, Antip blurted, "You're needed in Bialystok, Pavel, and though I don't like to lose you from the regiment, we'll just have to carry on without you. I should have said something earlier, but I didn't want to upset your concentration for the big match."

Pelagia stared at Pavel dolefully, but he squeezed her hand under the table to reassure her. In Antip's face, she could see a look of delicious triumph.

"When do I have to leave?" Pavel asked.

"By the end of the week. Tomorrow I have to tour the countryside. I'll be back in two days. You *sadis' i upravliai* (sit down and rule)." Pavel thought: Sit down and rule—I!

It took him only a few minutes to realize that if he was now in charge of the regiment, he could have the soldiers search every barn in Rzeszów for Krasula. But his thoughts were suddenly interrupted. Seated next to the restaurant window, the diners could view the dusty street. When Pelagia saw a flatbed truck with interlocking wood rails carrying five cows, she shouted, "Krasula," and flew out the door. By the time the men reached her in the street, she was in tears pointing down the road at the disappearing truck.

"My cow," she stammered, "she's on that truck. Catch the thief!"

Unfortunately, Antip had told his driver to come back in two hours, but Antip managed to commandeer a civilian car and to point the driver in the direction that the truck had taken. The delay, sadly, had given the thief enough time to transport the cow out of town and hide it in any number of barns or houses.

That night, Pavel had Antip sign a search warrant that granted him access to the local farms. By mid-morning, with Antip absent, Pavel issued orders to search all the barns in the area. But Pavel's precipitous action left the soldiers bewildered. How were they to identify Krasula from any other cow? Pelagia's definition hardly helped, except for the collar, which might already have been discovered and removed. Then, too, there was the reluctance of farmers to allow access to their barns. Pavel ordered his men to behave with the utmost civility.

The Polish farmers, justifiably suspicious of authority and famously conservative, were disinclined to show the cow hunters their barns. And for good reason: Barns held all manner of secrets, such as illicit stills, metal boxes with zlotys that had been kept from the tax collector, stolen goods pilfered from the Germans and Russians and rich farmers, silver crosses and goblets and holy books thieved from the local churches and synagogues and, in some cases, from the unsanctified graves of children born hopelessly crippled in mind or body. Barns were also the places of trysts and could therefore prove embarrassing. But word soon spread among the farmers that the cow hunters had no interest in stills and metal boxes and stolen goods. They were looking for a cow called Krasula, with a special collar. Good luck visited the cow hunters when a farmer's son who worked for the railroad disclosed that he saw just such a cow herded onto a cattle train destined for Kraków, where the Germans had colonized the city, rounded up Jews, and confiscated farm animals. Hence, cows were selling on the black market for handsome sums. The boy thought it strange that in place of a large cowbell or a simple leather strap, the animal had a special padded collar with three small bells. Did he recognize the man who had led the cow onto the train?

"Everyone knows the robber Bronislaw Sadkowski."

In promising Pelagia that he would find the cow, Pavel had threatened, if necessary, to abandon his regiment. The next morning, he boarded the train for Kraków, dressed as a farmworker. He worried that his lack of Polish might make him stand out. Passing from one car to the next, in search of a seat, he espied Father Henryk Jankowski slumped next to a window, his church garments wrinkled and stained. The priest gave him only a cursory glance. It was clear that he hadn't recognized him as the soldier to whom he had been introduced at the home of Madam Petukhova. Lucky, thought Pavel, and paid a man in overalls a few zlotys to give up his seat at the end of the car, where Pavel could observe the devious priest.

Pavel's mind wandered to Pelagia and their fond farewell. With Antip standing nearby, Pavel had hugged Pelagia and whispered, "I will write. Whatever address I give you, double the number and read it backward."

The size of Kraków would have overwhelmed Pavel had he not simply followed Father Jankowski, who seemed to know where to go and how to get there. By streetcar and foot, he shadowed the priest to a large holding pen, where just minutes earlier a black marketeer had sold Krasula to a traveling theatre manager who produced comedy skits. Both men watched as a middle-aged character, dressed in balloon pants, a silk shirt, a floor-length scarf, and a top hat, led Krasula, with collar intact, from the pen and down the road half a mile toward a tent erected in a field owned by Mr. Polanski, a farmer. Trailing behind, Pavel worried lest the priest lay rough hands on the thespian and make off with the collar. So he stopped the priest.

"You speak Russian?" asked Pavel.

"Some," replied a startled Father Jankowski.

"Do you remember me?" Pavel asked.

"We have met maybe. Where, who knows?"

"Madam Petukhova's house."

The priest recoiled as if from a venomous snake. Speaking in his broken Russian, he blurted, "What you knows has with me nothing . . ."

Pavel interrupted. "I am here because of the family jewels."

"Pelagia Petukhova," he replied falsely, "is my cousin."

The ensuing silence reminded Pavel of a cornered thief wielding a knife, as Father Jankowski used his stare like an augur to hollow out Pavel's innocent eyes. At last, the priest spoke, "Only the best interests of religion I have at heart. Madam Petukhova, she told me, on her deathbed, she wants for the fortune I should build a new church and buy . . . new priestly vestments."

Pavel wasted no introductions. He shoved a finger into the priest's chest. "Pelagia wants the jewels returned."

"They to her mother belong."

"And to her."

Father Jankowski retorted disdainfully, "And now trash—actors."

"Actors you plan to steal from."

The priest, who had spent his adult life imploring frail people for alms, knew better than to argue with this fellow molded in muscles. Besides, honey attracts more flies than does vinegar.

"We together work. You and me. Share."

Pavel took only a minute to conclude that the best way to keep an eye on this slippery priest was to join him at the hip. "Agreed."

Father Jankowski, a consummate rogue, knew that he could act as well as any performer. Years of inveighing from the pulpit against sinners and Jews and Communists and Orthodox Catholics had fine-tuned his delivery to the point of artistry. That evening, the two men attended the opening of *The Curse*, a skit scheduled to run for a week. The story was simple enough, and the cow played a central role, all of which Father Jankowski subsequently explained to Pavel. A wicked witch, in the form of an Orthodox Russian priest, turns a beautiful Polish girl, Celestyna (the celestial one), into a cow. The acting company, playing on the Catholic sentiments of the audience, also made clear that Celestyna represented Poland. Father Jankowski robustly applauded the message. The only way that the handsome Florian, Celestyna's beloved, could be reunited with his princess and make her human again was if the wicked witch, namely, the Orthodox priest, kissed the cow on the lips. The fun and laughter of the skit issued from how the witch was deceived into embracing and kissing the cow.

The actor who played the witch also took several other roles; therefore, Father Jankowski knew how to proceed. He spoke to the manager after the show and volunteered his services without pay to act the cameo role of the witch, thus freeing the regular actor to concentrate on his other parts. Although initially skeptical, the manager auditioned the silver-tongued priest and agreed to consult with the troupe.

Father Jankowski added, "All I ask is room and board. And should you ever be dissatisfied with me, I will leave without incident." Any fear the manager may have harbored was allayed when Father Jankowski explained, "I am a former priest, and in these perilous days, with the church under attack, I need to keep myself alive by one means or another. My savings are enough to support my other needs. I will be satisfied with a pillow to rest my head and a modest meal."

The manager consulted the company and, for their benefit, had the priest run through the role. A throaty huzzah said it all.

Father Jankowski quickly learned that the troupe's previous cow had been confiscated, then carved and cooked. The German officer in charge had described the steaks as delicious. In place of a real cow, the acting company had tried using a papier-mâché one but found it inadequate. The new cow was lodged in the Polanski barn and needed tending. When Father Jankowski and Pavel offered to assume responsibility for its safety, the manager accepted and counseled that if the Germans came, they should hide the animal in the woods.

Once the cow was put in trust of the two men, the priest observed that he was unaccustomed to sleeping in a barn.

"Let us therefore divide the spoils now, and I will stay at the boardinghouse with the rest of the troupe."

Pavel, who preferred to camp in the barn among the familiar smells of animals and straw, agreed and removed the collar with its three bells. Just as Madam Petukhova had whispered, the restraint was filled with valuable jewels, which the two men divided. But as neither man knew the true worth of the gems, the priest actually left with stones twice as valuable as those that Pavel kept back for himself. Returning the empty collar and bells to the cow, Pavel wrapped his cache in a large checkered handkerchief that he stuffed inside his money belt, and Father Jankowski put his in an old leather feed bag that he covered with hay.

That same evening, Pavel sat on a milking stool in the moonlight and wrote Pelagia a letter, telling her that he had located the "antique chair" that she wished to purchase. His only problem was which address to give her. Neither the tent nor the barn had one, but the boardinghouse on Wieliczka Street did. Pavel wrote, "It is easy to remember this street. Just think of the salt mine. The number is 32." Antip, trained in perlustration, opened and read the letter, copied the address, sealed the envelope, and foolishly handed it to Pelagia, upon whom he was daily pressing his attentions. He thought that the letter would make her look favorably upon him; make her think that he was not jealous; make her think, in short, that he was a gentleman. She disappeared the next day, taking the morning train to Kraków. With the Germans and Russians currently allied in the conquest of Poland, Antip decided to ask his German counterpart in Kraków to arrest Pavel and return him to the Russian sector to stand trial for desertion. If Pelagia agreed to his overtures, then Pavel would only be exiled, not shot. Antip felt good about his generosity.

Pavel told Ada Król, the multilingual lady who ran the boardinghouse, that if a young woman came looking for him, he could be found at the tent theatre. Her quizzical expression prompted him to add, "You need not think immoral thoughts. The woman in question is my Polish cousin, Pelagia."

Ada knew all about trysts. Her boardinghouse rang with the sound of bouncing mattresses and the sighs of sex. She had no objection to affairs: She just wanted to be paid extra for serving as a place of assignation. Not believing Pavel, she held out her hand. He, misunderstanding, kissed it—and she laughed.

"Nothing ventured, nothing gained," she said as she walked away.

That evening, Pelagia, who had been directed by Madam Król to the tent, showed up in the company of Pavel, who had taken the precaution of not entering the theatre until all the performers were onstage. Otherwise, the priest might have seen Pelagia before the show started and decamped with the cow. Pavel viewed the priest not as a holy man of the cloth but as a brigand. To his chagrin, Father Jankowski could see Pelagia in the audience. For her benefit, he threw himself into the part, giving it more passion than he had commanded before. So convincing was his performance that the superstitious peasants insisted that the evil priest be put to death. At the end of the skit, the benighted men refused to leave and demanded that the witch stand before them. To protect his actor, the director-manager was forced to explain that the skit was all fantasy, just make-believe. But one peasant, Kózka, remained unconvinced and vowed that the perfidious priest would pay for his evil deed.

Kózka, the diminutive name of a goat, had long been called that because his whiskers grew below his chin and down his neck. After a while, no one could remember his given name. His surname was Gorski, a family well known for their piety and for their producing absolute *wodka*, a skill that the family had learned from living in the "vodka belt": the crescent of north European countries from Russia to Norway. Kózka followed the priest to his digs. The round-faced, sanguine fellow carried with him a bottle of wodka, ostensibly as a gift for the wonderful performance turned in by Father Jankowski, who had no objection to making himself tipsy with one of God's finest creations, strong drink.

The priest greeted Kózka warmly. Few actors will speak ill of a fan or dismiss an admirer. They repaired to the priest's room, where the peasant asked him how he had become a witch. Father Jankowski, thinking that he was being asked how he came to be cast in the role, related his audition and the approval of the cast. The explanation merely confirmed for the peasant that the priest was a witch.

"If you convinced everyone, you must be one in the flesh."

"When I need to, I certainly can be," replied the priest proudly.

Kózka handed the bottle to Father Jankowski. "For you, the witch, the Orthodox priest who cast a spell over Celestyna and brought such terrible grief to Florian."

Glowing in his acting abilities, the priest recklessly said, "You have just described me. I am that person."

As the priest held the bottle to his mouth to uncork it with his teeth, Kózka asked the most astonishing question: "Do you think you could pose as a priest when you were really a Jew?"

"Easily," said the unsuspecting Father Jankowski, leaving the bottle unopened.

"Then how do I know you're not doing that now."

"Don't be silly," he scoffed. "My reputation for Jew-baiting is known all over eastern Poland."

The peasant, remembering Isaak the doctor, who had set the broken bone in his leg, replied, "What if I tell you I'm a Jew."

"Anyone can see that you're not."

"How so?"

"You haven't the money . . . or the sharpness."

Father Jankowski had meant "sharpness" as in money dealings, but Kózka took the word the wrong way.

"I am not stupid."

"Who said you were?"

"You did."

The priest, growing impatient with this impertinent fellow, thanked him for the vodka and tried to usher him out by taking hold of his shoulder. But Kózka shrugged him off.

"You priests wanted Poland without Jews," persisted the peasant. "Now, in the Russian-held sectors, we have Jews without Poland."

Father Jankowski was by now thoroughly confused by this disturbed man. "I thought you said you were Jewish. If you are, you ought to be glad that the Russians have invaded. If you are not, you should be out in the street killing Jews."

"And witches?"

To humor the poor peasant, the priest said, "Yes, and witches."

Kózka pointed to the bottle. "Well, are you gonna open it or ain't you?"

The priest removed the cork with his teeth and, having no table, put his Bible on the bed to steady the two glasses that came with the room. He then kneeled to pour.

Kózka quickly rolled up his right sleeve above the elbow, removed a razor from his pocket, slashed the priest's throat, and calmly watched. The priest gurgled like a kitchen sink sucking down the last water and slumped forward. Before leaving the room, Kózka looked around. He was surprised to find under the bed a horse's feed bag, a perfectly useful farm item, which he took as he left.

Two days later, Antip's letter arrived, accompanied by a bundle of fliers exhibiting Pavel's face and offering five hundred rubles for any information leading to the arrest of this army deserter "who is an expert horseshoe player, and who speaks no Polish or German and may be traveling in the company of a young woman, Pelagia Petukhova."

When Antip learned of the death of Father Jankowski, about whom he cared little, he attributed the murder to the work of the deserter Pavel Lipnoskii and raised the reward to six hundred rubles. The manager of the theatre troupe, short of money, approached the Germans and declared that although he knew nothing of the whereabouts of the miscreant, he could tell them all about the cow Krasula.

"What the hell do we care about a cow?" roared a German officer.

"It's missing. The cow had a collar with bells."

"And you conclude . . . what?"

The manager wiped his forehead. "Perhaps it explains the death of the priest and the sudden departure of the Red Army man."

The German officer stared at the poor fellow as if he belonged in an asylum. "My dear sir," he said, dripping with sarcasm, "from a missing cow's collar you have constructed a theory, perhaps one as great as Hitler's view of the master race. But yours explains a murder and a desertion. Brilliant, simply brilliant!"

"I was merely trying to explain why or how the two events might be connected. If you catch him, do I get the reward?"

The German officer, Franz Kupner, said nothing.

That night, Captain Kupner wired Antip in Rzeszów, assuring him that he would cooperate in every way possible.

Following country lanes and footpaths, Pavel and Pelagia led the cow toward the Rumanian border.

Stalin looked out his office window at a marvelous October morning slipping from the wet rooftops into the Kremlin grounds. November, with its long nights, was nearing. The Vozhd sighed and returned to his desk to complete the list of military leaders and defectors who were to be summarily shot. Under the letter "L" was the name Lipnoskii, a name that the Supreme Leader knew all too well. Antip Skoropodski had urged that a certain deserter be found and executed, Pavel Lipnoskii.

With the jewels that Pavel had taken for his share of the booty and the cow in tow, he and Pelagia felt confident that they could bribe their way across the Rumanian border and continue to Budapest. But although the eastern divide between Germany and Russia was porous, the Germans, trying to prevent Jews from fleeing south, had fortified the border with Rumania. Lacking German transit papers and visas, the couple approached the border guards cautiously. It was late afternoon, and the weather had turned brittle. Pelagia struck up a conversation with the German corporal in charge of the crossing. Although her command of the language was imperfect, she could make herself understood.

"We have lost our papers. We need to cross into Rumania."

The man, whose face had been scarred badly by smallpox, politely but firmly resisted. "Whose cow is that you have on a tether?" he asked. "All farm animals now belong to the Third Reich."

"She is a pet cow," responded Pelagia. "Where we go, she goes."

A young boy, obviously blind, was sitting in the small passport control hut. The son of the corporal, he asked if he could touch the side of the cow. Pelagia led him outside, guided his hand, and answered his question about the cow's name, Krasula. The father was clearly touched by Pelagia's compassionate treatment of his son.

"The boy likes to sit with me after school," said the corporal. "His name is Anselm. He has been blind since birth. The other children tease him. Have they no feelings?"

This question emboldened Pelagia to tell the corporal the truth: Pavel was wanted by the Russian authorities, and they had to escape into Rumania. Two other men, both German border guards, entered the hut. They inquired about the presence of the cow. The corporal assured them that he had the situation under control. He then led Pelagia outside the hut.

"They are dedicated Nazis. You must turn back now. The cow will only attract attention and slow you down."

Pavel nodded, and Pelagia said, "Take the cow for your son."

The corporal whispered, "Go to Kraków Glowny Station. You might just slip by in the crowd."

A massive relic of the Hapsburg Empire, the railroad station roiled with activity. Thanks to her beauty, Pelagia gained access to the stationmaster, Alfons Dudek, who, like many collaborators, tried to impress his overlords with his zealotry in detaining illegals. "We were robbed and lost our papers," she said, "as well as our tickets for Bucharest." She reached for her purse, hoping to pay in zlotys and not zircons. "How much will tickets cost us?"

"If you paid once, you ought to know," said the stationmaster truculently, suspicious of anyone wishing to leave the country and keen for the reward money that accompanied the arrest of a felon.

An unperturbed Pelagia smiled. "What with inflation, we gathered that the price of a ticket must fluctuate. Right?"

Dudek mumbled something about women. He then turned to Pavel and said, "Cat got your tongue?"

Always enterprising, Pelagia replied, "My brother is deaf and speaks with his hands."

She wiggled her fingers at Pavel and moved her hands up and down. Although they had not agreed beforehand to this plan, he behaved similarly, understanding at once that she was trying to keep him from having to speak.

"Too bad about your brother," said Dudek. "A muscular fellow like him would make a fine soldier."

Frightened that the stationmaster might report Pavel as a prospective laborer for a concentration camp, Pelagia blurted, "He's an expert horseshoe pitcher, and we're on our way to a contest."

Alfons Dudek ran a hand over his mouth. "I'll be back in a moment—with your tickets." He disappeared inside his office and rustled through some recent fliers. Sure enough, he had remembered correctly. There was Pavel's face on a yellow flier and a note that said he was accomplished at horseshoes. The stationmaster quickly telephoned the German lieutenant in charge of trains for his sector. But Dudek's prolonged absence had made Pavel and Pelagia suspicious. When the lieutenant pulled up, with two armed men at his side, Pavel and Pelagia had fled. Alfons Dudek defensively said, "They must have guessed that I support the Germans."

The lieutenant sniffed at Dudek's self-serving reply and ordered that the neighborhood and train yards be searched. Although the couple seemed to have vanished, they had in fact taken refuge in a half-empty freight car, where they hid behind crates of cheap glassware destined for Warsaw.

Pavel recommended that they remain in the car until it began to move. But the next morning, several men returned to load additional freight and discovered the couple lodged in a corner. Soldiers materialized almost immediately. The Wehrmacht, having been put on alert for fleeing Jews, Gypsies, defectors, Communist spies, and criminals, arrested the couple and quickly identified Pavel Lipnoskii, wanted by the Russians. As Pavel was led off, he knew he had a choice: either proclaim allegiance to the German cause, like so many Ukrainians and Belorussians, and thereby run the risk of being inducted into the Wehrmacht, or acquiesce in his return to the Russian sector. Pelagia was taken aside and questioned separately for having consorted with a Russian defector. Her captors felt confident that she was a Bolshevik or, even worse, a Polish nationalist.

When Pavel was brought before Bruno Kirk, the lieutenant in charge of Kraków's rail sector, the German held the flier describing Pavel and his horseshoe-pitching skills. He smiled knowing that the German civilian governor of the *generalgouvernement*, Hans Frank, loved a sporting match. Bruno telephoned headquarters to announce his prize catch. He then ordered his adjutant to bring them tea and biscuits. Bruno and Pavel spoke in Russian.

"Your reputation for pitching precedes you," said the lieutenant. "Hans Frank will be pleased to hear that you are at our disposal. Although chess is his passion, he has generously agreed to sponsor numerous athletic tournaments now that he has been made governor-general for the occupied Polish territories. In fact, he has personally sponsored Ernst Bauer, the Wehrmacht's horseshoe-pitching champion, and I'm sure he'll want to arrange a match for the benefit of the soldiers. His wife, Brigitte, also loves such events. I am certain she will want to be present in her role as 'queen of Poland.'"

Pavel puzzled over the phrase "at our disposal," which could have several meanings, like imprisoning him, putting him to use in some capacity, returning him to the Soviet sector, or killing him. But the lieutenant treated him and Pelagia with great courtesy, lodging them together in a Wehrmacht guesthouse. Although they were placed under house arrest, neither their persons nor their bags were searched. The first time they were alone, Pavel gave Pelagia the jewels that he had claimed for her share. But fearful that the Germans would eventually discover and appropriate them, she carefully wrapped the gems in an old woolen sweater, which she put in a box, and asked the guesthouse cook, Bianka, a proud Polish woman who resented serving the Germans, to mail the box to the main Budapest post office, addressed to Pelagia Petukhova, care of *poste restante*.

For two weeks, the couple lived comfortably in the guesthouse, until a match could be arranged between Pavel and the German champion. At Ernst Bauer's insistence, the courts had to conform precisely to tournament lengths and widths, and the pits filled with clay. Pavel, allowed to practice in the backyard of the guesthouse, where a court was hastily constructed on hard-packed dirt, was presented with regulation two-pound, eight-ounce horseshoes. Each day, irrespective of the weather, he practiced; and each day, Pelagia watched him, either from a garden chair or, in inclement weather, from the house. Even when unseen she seemed to make herself palpable. But tomorrow she'd be present at the match.

A crisp November day greeted the contestants and onlookers. Sunlight splashed the court like an egg yolk. Padded chairs were provided for the dignitaries, with Hans and Brigitte Frank seated front and center. An imperious woman, she was said to have launched his legal career and assuaged his fears about defending Nazis in court. Overdressed and pickled in perfume, she loved nothing more than a public event where she could strut and strike poses. Hans too fancied uniforms, titles, and public attention, but he was especially proud of his courtroom oratory on behalf of the National Socialist Party. He had famously proclaimed, "[The judge's] role is to safeguard the concrete order of the racial community, to eliminate dangerous elements, to prosecute all acts harmful to the community, and to arbitrate in disagreements between members of the community. The National Socialist ideology, especially as expressed in the party program in the speeches of our leader, is the basis for interpreting legal sources." Hans's newly conferred SS rank, *obergruppenführer*, had transmogrified his modesty into arrogance. He sat like a peacock in his freshly starched uniform, an iron cross hanging from his neck. Out of uniform and not dressed in medals, he looked common, with his bulbous cheeks, large forehead, doleful eyes, and slicked-down hair, except for a thin crest running down the middle of his balding head. Hitler's personal legal advisor, he had been rewarded with the governorship of Poland owing to his loyalty and his investigation proving that Hitler had no Jewish ancestry, as some had charged.

Like Stalin's functionaries, Frank had mastered the fine art of ingratiation. Even his sponsorship of this match had its roots in his wish to please the Führer, who wanted his governors to maintain the morale of the troops. When the two champions entered, Hans Frank stood and greeted them both, though he hugged only Ernst, a signal for the Wehrmacht, who initially composed most of the crowd, to voice an ear-shattering cheer, which they reproduced every time Ernst threw a ringer. A few claps sounded for Pavel along with a cry of joy from Pelagia, who left her hosts agape as she rushed into the arms of Pavel Lipnoskii and murmured, "I love you."

The players were evenly matched, though Ernst Bauer's ringer percentage was 72 percent and Pavel's only 64. But on any given day, a player can rise to the occasion and perform well above his average or succumb to an attack of nerves. What happened this day became part of Poland's history.

Word had spread through Kraków that a condemned Russian, with a Polish girlfriend, was to play a German from the Wehrmacht. Although German soldiers occupied the first ten rows of seating around the court, twice that many Poles stood in rows behind. They had waited for the match to begin— ten o'clock was the starting time—and then slowly gravitated to the campgrounds in the romantic belief that the arrest of the lovers meant that Pavel hated the Bolsheviks and Nazis equally and loved the Poles. Bauer was leading thirty-one to twenty-six by the time the Polish fans counted in the hundreds.

At either end of the court stood a judge, empowered to record the score and settle any disputes. Each judge was equipped with a stopwatch to make sure that the players, once they stepped onto the platform, delivered both shoes within thirty seconds. In championship matches, the first player to reach twenty-one points wins, but the contestants had agreed to a 150-point match. Neither pitcher spoke to the other, a courtesy that serious players always observed. Pavel stood behind Ernst and silently watched Bauer's deft and delicate wrist motion. The German's release, free of any jerks or hitches of the arm and wrist, displayed a precise throwing technique, one honed through years of practice. To reach 150 points would take countless throws. His economy of movement translated into a preservation of energy. After releasing the shoe, Ernst's hand followed through above his head gracefully. His shoes unfailingly rose to about eight feet, arced, made a three-quarter turn and, just before they crossed the foul line of the pitcher's box, opened and, like a pair of welcoming women's legs, received the stake.

Pavel thought of Pelagia and the coital embrace that they had yet to initiate. He looked at his hands and wished he could stroke her body tenderly. Bauer, too, had a sportsman's hands, with finely tuned fingers. In his youth, Ernst had played the violin and cello. But unlike Pavel's hands, the German's had not been steeled by a fiery forge. For Pavel to get back in the game, he would have to relax his grip. From the strain on his hand and wrist, he knew that he had been gripping the shoe too tightly. He was tense owing to the importance of the match, the setting, and the possible consequences. Once he told himself that his opponent was not Ernst Bauer but himself, he began to throw with more confidence. Although behind in the score, he knew that matches were won incrementally, a point at a time. He would have to cancel Ernst's ringers with his own, and to do so would take immense mental discipline. Pavel decided that besides loosening his grip, if he focused on his footwork, his consistency would improve. And so it did. He began to match Bauer ringer for ringer, winning points on shoes in counts, namely, those shoes that were not ringers but that fell within six inches of the stake. Bauer's motion became "hitchy," and when the men were tied at 140 apiece, the German's anxiety was visible. He sweated profusely, pulled at his collar, examined his horseshoes, took longer to mount the throwing board, lost the elasticity in his legs, and kept glancing at Hans Frank. Pavel read all the signs and grew increasingly confident.

Having won the previous point, Pavel started the next inning. His first shoe was a ringer, and the second spun off the stake, stopping two inches away. Bauer threw a ringer with his first shoe but missed with his second, which bounced off Pavel's shoe in count. Bauer mumbled to himself in annoyance. The great advantage to pitching first, of course, was that your opponent's shoe often caromed off yours. With the score now 141 to 140, both men had a hot streak. They each threw ten ringers in a row. But the effort seemed to exhaust Bauer, physically and mentally. His next two shoes were in count but not ringers. Pavel barely missed with his first shoe, which ran out of bounds, but collared the stake with his second. The score now stood 144 to 140. Bauer rallied—for the last time. He threw a ringer and a shoe in count. Although Pavel threw two shoes in count, both closer to the stake than Bauer's, the ringer eclipsed them. Score: 144 to 143.

In the next inning, the match came to a resounding and sudden end when Pavel threw two ringers for six points, and Bauer missed with both of his shoes. Final score: 150 to 143. The Poles cheered so loudly that the Germans ordered them from the field. A loss was one thing, humiliation another. Hans Frank shook Pavel's hand and gave Ernst Bauer a perfunctory click of his heels. The governor-general's displeasure was evident to all. Aryan athletes were expected to win. Jesse Owens had been an unfortunate exception. The German sports authorities had apologized for underestimating Jesse. It was a mistake not to be repeated. Bauer left quickly, and the crowd silently opened to let him pass. A minute later, he entered the backseat of a Mercedes and was driven off. Forcing a smile, Frank, through an interpreter, asked Pavel what he would regard as a suitable prize. Pelagia, standing at his side, prayed that he would say what he did.

"Two train tickets to Budapest."

"You do know," said Frank, "that Budapest will shortly come under Nazi occupation? Are you therefore sure," he added sarcastically, "that you want to take your Polish Pelagia there?"

"I'm sure," he said, smiling at her.

Tauntingly, Frank asked, "Not London or Paris or Washington?"

"Budapest."

"And you, my dear?" Frank said, gently touching Pelagia's arm.

"The same."

"Then Budapest it shall be. I will have someone drive you back to the guesthouse. You can pack tonight and leave tomorrow. A car will collect you in the morning. I will send my own driver. It's the least I can do for a Russian champion and his . . . mistress."

Pelagia's cheeks burned with shame, but she said nothing. To show her contempt for the governor-general, she embraced a sweating Pavel, thanked Lieutenant Bruno Kirk—"your hospitality has been much appreciated"—and merely nodded at Mr. and Mrs. Frank. She then joined Pavel in the official car that returned them to their Kraków guesthouse. Bianka had prepared a special meal in honor of Pavel's victory, and had somehow secured a bottle of good wine. She joined the couple at table and, having been unable to attend the match, listened to Pelagia's recital of it. When Pelagia told Bianka that she and Pavel would be leaving by train the next morning, courtesy of Hans Frank, the cook's expression radically changed. Her smiles fled, and a darkness came into her face.

"Which train?" Bianka asked.

"For Budapest," answered Pelagia.

Bianka said nothing further about the matter, but Pelagia could see that she intended, for some reason, to look into it. After clearing and washing the dishes, she quickly disappeared. The couple both had the same thought: When would they next have the chance to be alone? Retreating to the couch, they hugged and kissed, while a log burned in the fireplace.

Pavel whispered, "I am thirty-eight, sixteen years older than you. The age difference . . ."

She put a finger to his lips. "Shh. Age is no obstacle when two people love one another."

He kissed her passionately and carried her into the bedroom where they made love tenderly.

"You're my first," she said, "and I want no other. Let us marry as soon as we reach Budapest."

In the morning, Bianka woke them before their car was to leave for the station. The clock read a few minutes to five. "You must get out immediately. The train to Budapest is a 'special' train. You must not board it."

Pavel thought that perhaps Pelagia had mistranslated. He said, "The governor-general promised."

"Hans Frank can't be trusted."

"The Russians and Germans are allies," replied Pavel.

"Until they're not," said Bianka cryptically.

Pavel and Pelagia dressed. But owing to their lovemaking the night before, they had left their packing for morning. Although they hastily filled their valises, the delay was just long enough to allow two men to silently approach the guesthouse. The SS man who knocked on the door was not Bruno Kirk, the lieutenant who had kindly housed them. Abrupt and unflinching, this man, who also spoke Russian, ordered them into a car at the curb. The driver put their bags in the trunk and then resumed his seat behind the wheel, with the SS man at his side. Pavel and Pelagia sat in the back. Shades covered the windows. The car drove to a railroad siding. Through the front windshield, Pavel caught sight of a long line of people, with possessions of every sort, waiting to board—could it be?—cattle cars! Armed guards prodded the line of people with whips and police dogs. At last, the lieutenant spoke.

"You will be riding in a special car with padded seats and a lavatory. Our governor-general is a gracious man. But the car must be sealed to cross the border in safety. Partisan guerilla groups, passport control . . . you understand. If I'm not mistaken, Lenin returned to Russia in a sealed car. So we are extending to you, a sports champion, the same treatment that your Beloved Leader received. We have even decorated the car for your benefit—with pictures."

The driver pulled up next to the private train car, its windows eerily painted black. Removing a key, the SS man ascended the three high steps of the car, unlocked the door, and held it open. Pelagia boarded. Pavel, looking back at the station, saw standing under the porch roof, Bruno Kirk. He looked downcast. Their eyes met and for a moment remained fixed. Then Lieutenant Kirk turned and entered the station. Pavel climbed into the special car. He could hear the door being locked. To his surprise, he and Pelagia were not the only passengers. Several others were already seated: a scientist, an artist, a politician, a philosopher, and a female lawyer. He introduced himself and his "fiancée," Pelagia, who beamed with happiness and translated. Then they shook hands with the eminent company. On one side of the car hung a portrait of Lenin; on the other, Stalin. As it happened, the only empty seats were positioned beneath the latter's portrait. So Pelagia and Pavel sat under the Vozhd's haunting presence. At Pavel's urging, she asked in Polish, "Are you all bound for Budapest?"

The others looked at each other.

"Are you not," asked the politician, "being deported, like us, for working on behalf of the Bolsheviks?"

Pelagia briefly explained the circumstances that had brought the couple to this private car.

"I fear you have misunderstood," said the politician. "This train is not going to Budapest, but to Mauthausen concentration camp."

ESCAPE FROM PARADISE

"The Fascist Finns," said Stalin, baring his neck to Razan, as the barber prepared to shave off the lather and stubble. As usual, Stalin's bodyguards stepped forward prepared to stay a murderous hand, should the barber be so inclined. But Razan scraped the soapy remains onto the sheet, folded up the blade, and readied himself to singe the tufts growing from Stalin's ears. But before applying the Turkish Delight, he waited for Stalin to vent his annoyance with the Finns. "Molotov explained to them that all we wanted was a mutual security pact to protect us against attack from either Germany or the Entente. We offered concessions. But no, they feared that we had the same territorial aspirations as the Tsar. Fools! Now we will have to go to war with them for our own safety."

"But the German-Soviet Nonaggression Pact signed two months ago," said Razan, "made Germany our ally."

"They're not to be trusted. Look at Poland. The Germans have dismembered it. Estonia and Latvia and Lithuania signed treaties with us to guarantee our northern flank against Germany. Why not Finland? We even gave Lithuania the Polish city of Vilnius, as a reward. The Finns are being misled by Prime Minister Erkko, a capitalist rat."

"No doubt we'll win," said Razan ingratiatingly.

"And quickly. But we have to speed up our shipbuilding, add additional troops, cut forest roads to Finland, improve our supply lines and communications, and move our prison camp from Solovki."

Razan and Anna were now living on the edge of a precipice. The disclosure of Gregori's imprisonment at the Solovetski Concentration Camp, and the knowledge that the family had attracted the attention of the NKVD, meant survival would require immediate action. The fact that Solovki would soon be evacuated provided the catalyst.

After dinner, Razan made his familiar gesture—a hand on his mouth—to indicate that he wanted to speak to Anna outside. When he told her that Solovki would be evacuated sooner than they had expected, Anna observed, "Dimitri says that most of the guards in these camps are former criminals, so they're open to bribes. The danger comes from their treachery. They might take our money and then betray us in return for a government reduction in their sentences."

A policeman stood on the corner, his face occasionally turned toward them. She suggested they cross the bridge toward the Kremlin. The man followed. Razan stopped to blow his nose. Anna could see the sadness in his eyes.

"They certainly have a genius for turning family members against each other," he said.

"Dimitri says the order must have come from Stalin."

On learning about Dimitri's orders to spy on them, Razan had felt both furious and relieved. Anyone in the employ of the government knew that only a few survived—by mere chance. But at least those people slated for suppression had one consolation. They could stop dreaming and resign themselves to their fate. Except for those who took their own lives, few tried to escape. After all, where would they go and how? Travel by rail was virtually impossible, because guards patrolled the train stations and constantly checked papers. Every small town had its informers; big cities were safer. With any luck, one could get lost in a crowd, at least for a short time. But those who took refuge in Moscow or Leningrad haunts were eventually betrayed by opportunists or by friends who succumbed to NKVD pressure.

His mind mired in fear, Razan said, "Stalin says war with Finland is inevitable. Is that good or bad for us? My guess is the Finnish border is too dangerous. All those Red Army men massed there."

Anna glanced at the man trailing behind them and whispered, "I know a way to cross the border."

She fell silent and started back to the flat. The man passed, stopped, turned, and followed them toward the house on the embankment. As they approached the front door, Anna said enigmatically, "In the haste of war, confusion reigns." She took Razan by the arm. "We want to exploit that confusion."

Only later did Anna make herself clear. They would escape from the country not by seeking succor among the nationalities in the south, as she had originally planned, but by following the rifle brigades and tanks and planes and ships into Finland. "The troops will need nourishment and drink. We will provide both from a horse and a wagon. My mother made a profit this way during the Civil War."

Although she had a few ideas about how to free Gregori, she said nothing about Alexei in Voronezh. Razan suspected that she still resented his having left Natasha. At a small bistro on the outskirts of Moscow, Razan and Anna met Dimitri to discuss which of her plans had the best chance of succeeding. Over a goulash, he agreed to the idea of their escaping through Finland and told his astonished parents that he planned to take Natasha with him to Voronezh to free Alexei. He said that they should all meet in Petrozavodsk, where a friend of his lived in two rooms. Dimitri gave them the address.

But their carefully laid plans were interrupted by the secret police, who searched their apartment without any advanced warning, to the chagrin of Anna, Razan, Natasha, and Yelena, who were just sitting down to a dinner of herring and lamb-stuffed kishkas. The knock at the door sounded harmless enough, and Anna could see nothing amiss through the peephole, just two men dressed in dark overcoats, scarves, and black fedoras. Their credentials identified them as NKVD agents. Comrades Yermakov and Zlobin said that their orders to search for contraband had come directly from Beria.

"We are looking for shortwave radios," said Zlobin.

Anna smiled at the patent mendacity but offered them a plate of green soup, which they declined. Resuming her seat, she noticed Natasha and Yelena exchanging glances.

The men rifled through drawers and closets, opened stored luggage, removed the lids to saucepans and stewing pots, patted down the furniture cushions, went through Yelena's art supplies and toy box. Nothing! While putting on their coats to leave, Comrade Zlobin decided to take one last sweep of the apartment.

"My daughter has one of those," said Zlobin, pointing to the panda in the corner. "The store at the Moscow zoo, right?"

At once, Natasha knew to disown the panda. "My sister, Yelena, found it in a park a few blocks from her school."

"Yours looks slightly different," he said. He tossed the stuffed animal in the air, observing that it felt lumpy.

Natasha came from her chair, took the panda, and said, "Please, comrade, it belongs to Yelena. I see no need to treat it roughly."

"Unless you have something to hide," he said. Snatching it back, he undid the zipper, reached inside, and removed several muslin-wrapped spools of microfilm. "Ah, what's this?"

Natasha played the role of a betrayed wife who has just learned of compromising letters. "I am stunned! Microfilm in the panda!"

Yermakov, the less educated of the two agents, copied his comrade and held the film up to the light. "Mostly rubbish," he said, tossing on the floor Babel's unfinished novel and the Mandelstam poems. "Just some scribblers who must have thought they were writers."

Natasha quickly gathered up the spools, turned her back, and stuffed them down the front of her dress. Zlobin noticed nothing, so absorbed was he in a compromising film bearing on Yagoda, Ezhov, Malenkov, Molotov, and Stalin. He whistled through his teeth and, adjusting his glasses, said, "You won't believe what I've found! Sex, drugs, booze. Whew."

Awed by the documents that Zlobin had found, Yermakov stood reading over his shoulder. "Look at this one," said Zlobin, "an old Tsarist report about the Boss. Wow, in his youth the Boss was some lady's man. He even got a woman pregnant and left her behind in one of the camps. This stuff is dynamite!"

On the word "dynamite," Natasha signaled Yelena to help her clear the table. In the kitchen, Natasha wrote an address, put it under a plate, turned on the sink tap, and took Yelena's hand. Slipping into the foyer for their coats, they eased out the front door, leaving it slightly ajar to avoid the click of the latch.

Like youngsters reading their first salacious novel, the two agents salivated for several minutes over the films. Razan and Anna had by now also retreated into the kitchen, where they found the address and where the agents found them washing dishes.

"Where did they go?" demanded Yermakov.

"Who?" said Anna innocently.

"Your daughters," said Zlobin.

"Oh, they just stepped outside for some fresh air. You'll probably find them on the street, in front of the building."

The two agents scooped up the spools and left the apartment.

Razan pointed to the bathroom. He and Anna sat on the edge of the tub, as he ran both faucets to cover the sound of their voices.

"Where did they go?" asked Razan.

"Natasha has a girlfriend who lives near Gorky Street. She left her address."

"I feel sorry for the two men. They'll probably be shot."

"No doubt."

"And us?" asked Razan.

"My guess is we have only a few hours. You must get word to Dimitri. I will leave for Leningrad as soon as I can pack a bag. The rubles hidden in the lining of my blue dress come to a large sum, more than enough for me to attempt the impossible and for you and Yelena to get to Petrozavodsk." She dipped her hand in the water, touched his forehead, and made the sign of the cross. They embraced. Razan's eyes filled with tears; Anna remained outwardly unmoved.

But as they unclasped, she held Razan at arm's length and said, "Let me look at you to remember. It may be the last time."

Razan buried his head in her breast and cried unabashedly. Her skin exuded the appealing earthly scent that always excited him when they coupled. After a minute, he wiped his eyes and asked, "What should I do about Yelena?"

"Register her in school."

"In her own name?"

"You have no choice. That's how her papers are stamped."

"A forgery . . ."

"Not worth it. No one will recognize the name Boujinskia. I've already warned her to say nothing of the family. If she's asked, she will say that Dimitri's friend is her uncle."

"And her real family?"

"As far as she knows, they returned to Tashkent. Then she was adopted. But her new parents died."

"There may be more truth in that lie than in most."

"You mustn't grow dispirited. We'll survive." She touched his cheek. "Our savings are large enough to bribe our way to Finland."

Razan had to admit that the sum, though not staggering, was considerable, owing to Anna's having capitalized on Yelena's painting. "Where can we meet in Petrozavodsk?" he asked. "Some landmark? Dimitri said his friend frequently moves between apartments. Who would ever have thought that in the Soviet Union one had such freedom of movement or that so many apartments were vacant."

"I gather that he trades with other people like himself, even though it's against the law. As for our meeting, I have no way of knowing whether Gregori and I can escape—or when. The first chance you get make your way to Helsinki and register with the police. I'll do the same, as will Dimitri and Natasha. Pavel . . . who knows?"

"What if you're caught . . ." The words stuck in his throat.

She removed a knife from her bag. "If necessary I will use it. For my children—anything. I have killed before."

So great was the shock of Anna's admission that Razan nearly fell into the tub, now slowly filling as a result of poor drainage. He reached for the wall to steady himself. She could see in his face competing emotions: fear, disbelief, awe, contempt, sympathy.

"Pyotr was lying on his back in the creek bed when I found him. He was resting on a slab of ice, dead to the world."

"Really dead or unconscious?"

"I flipped him over, and he drowned." She could see Razan's throat muscles constricting. "I had good reason. He beat me and the children unmercifully. Whoring, drinking, lying—at these he was expert—but work? Supporting his family meant nothing to him."

A dazed Razan and a clearheaded Anna talked briefly about their life together, remembering tender moments and risible ones, and would have continued except that the tub had filled with water. The two looked at each other, remembering fondly bathing together, when three NKVD men burst into the apartment, looking ominously like black crows. They began immediately to disassemble the apartment, looking, they said, for hidden documents or microfilms.

"Anna and Razan Shtube, you are under arrest, accused of spying and of possessing state secrets. Take your overcoats and passports."

Razan insisted that they were both innocent. Ordered to enter the back of a green truck, with the word "Bread" printed in four languages on the side, they were conveyed in this "inconspicuous" NKVD vehicle to Comrade Beria's office. People in the streets stopped to look, knowing all too well that the bread truck delivered not a life-giving substance but death. As a result, the color green and the word "bread" had become odious omens.

A squinting Beria dispensed with all introductions and formalities. "Forget microfilms, I want to talk about your Palestine Plan. The details are unclear to me, but I know that the words are really an acronym for a secret organization. Dimitri has exposed you. Now tell me about the group, its intentions, and its membership." Later, Beria would reflect on the brilliance of Anna's explanation.

"Comrade Beria, you are right. Ours is an organization to resettle people and prevent prejudice. The uneducated believe in miracles, like those said to take place in the Holy Land. Who are the most likely people to engage in a pogrom? The ignorant. If we lack the means to educate all the people properly, then we must reach them through what they hold dear: their superstitions. The belief that God's first love, the Jews, have been called home by Him, will go farther to stem prejudice than Soviet laws. Just think of Loktev."

Beria, who liked to appear knowledgeable but could not at the moment place the name, said, "Of course, Loktev. It was some time ago. Remind me of the circumstances."

Anna pursed her lips to suppress a laugh. "Just last year he and the priest Father Vasily were apprehended for their stirring up the peasants in the Far East."

"Oh, yes, as I recall, they were . . . promoting religion."

"In a manner of speaking," said Anna, in full control of the exchange between her and the NKVD head. "If you remember, Loktev eerily resembled Nicholas II."

"I regard it as a great Soviet achievement that we killed the last Tsar of Russia and ended the Romanov line. Privilege," he said, waving his hand, "has been abolished and everyone's equal."

Anna ignored the propaganda and continued. "The uncanny resemblance of Loktev to Nicholas II gave the wily priest an idea. He would parade the look-alike through small villages and collect alms for the church by confiding to the peasants that the Tsar had survived and was waiting in the next room. Father Vasily would then parade Loktev before the group to the astonishment of the assembly. But one problem presented itself. Loktev was a retarded simpleton. So Father Vasily taught him to bow and retreat after repeating one sentence: 'Be brave, Russian people, God is merciful.' Then Father Vasily would lecture the people on the sanctity of the Orthodox Church and its need for financial support. At the end of his speech, he would graciously accept donations and lead Loktev to the next village."

"Yes, now I remember. It all happened under Yagoda, that fool. The priest was shot, but I don't remember what happened to Loktev."

"He was sent to Solovki, where he is serving a ten-year term."

"Which is exactly what I will propose for you two, if the Vozhd agrees. Your position as wife to the official barber won't help you." He banged his desk. "Stalin has already exiled the wives of many Politburo members; you will both go from my office to a prison cell."

He reached for his private telephone line to the Kremlin, and told the Boss whom he had arrested. After a long pause, he slammed the phone and said grudgingly, "The barber may go."

"And my wife?" asked Razan, extending an arm toward her.

Beria exploded. "Albania and Palestine be damned! Did she not create a religious cult from a painting of Stalin's mustache? Only an enemy of the people would exploit the Supreme Leader's person."

Clearly, Anna's "art gallery" had been denounced as a commercial ruse. What would the family do now?

Before being shipped to the islands of death, as prisoners called the Solovki Archipelago, Anna went through the indignity of having to remove her clothes, submit to a body probe for hidden "instruments," and spend a week in Lubyanka, where Razan, like a common petitioner, was allowed to visit her once, the first day.

Leaning over the visitor's table, Anna whispered, "I killed once. I can kill twice. If you can get Stalin to give me an office job, Gregori and I will escape—others have—and meet you in Petrozavodsk."

"I'll beg on bended knee," he said, eliciting a smile from Anna.

A few minutes later, as he exited the prison, two uniformed guards stopped him to say, "Poskrebyshev called," a statement that meant of course that Stalin was summoning him. As the guards shoved him into the backseat of a black limousine, he was sure that his once privileged position as the Kremlin barber had expired, and it would no longer stand him in good stead with the Boss.

Although Poskrebyshev sneered as Razan was led into his office by an elite NKVD officer, Comrade Ugly handed Razan the barbering bag that the barber always left with Poskrebyshev before exiting the premises. Razan was pleasantly surprised by Stalin's warm greeting, which for the moment remained a mystery, one that quickly needed solving if he was to save his wife. Koba requested a mustache trim, and as Razan applied his skills, he noted as always that Stalin balled his left hand and thrust it into his pocket. Afterward, Stalin and the barber retreated to the settee to talk about "family matters."

"A shame about your wife," said the Vozhd. "These things happen. Women just can't be trusted."

"Anna could."

"We had our reasons," said Stalin, reaching for his pipe.

"She's a good bookkeeper. And she writes a clear hand. If she could be assigned to an office, she could render the country a great service. Did I not hear you say that Solovki would operate until the advance of the Finnish Army made evacuation imperative? Anna can help, if only for a few months."

Stalin opened his tobacco pouch, packed the bowl, and sucked the stem. Razan remembered what Yefim Boujinski had said about an unlit pipe. He therefore took from his barbering bag a stick match, which he would have normally used to singe the hairs in Stalin's ears. He lit the match and reached across the settee for Stalin to light his pipe. The Boss stared warily at the barber; then he smiled and sucked the flame into the bowl, blowing a cloud of smoke in the air. Razan waited. When Stalin rubbed his mustache with the stem, Razan relaxed knowing he was temporarily safe.

To reintroduce speech and escape the stares of Stalin's omnipresent guards, Razan asked about Stalin's daughter, Svetlana. "She's such a beauty, and so clever."

But it was the wrong subject to broach, because it provided the Vozhd an opening to ask about Razan's daughters.

"Where are your Natasha and Yelena? I especially remember the little girl. Such a wonderful child."

"On their way to Georgia for a week's holiday."

"When did they leave?"

"The day before yesterday, by train."

Stalin went to his desk and picked up one of his many phones. "Get me the passenger list of all those who traveled by train to Georgia in the last two days. How long will it take?" He paused. "Well, that will just have to do."

"If I'm not mistaken," said a rattled Razan, "they may be motoring first to Voronezh."

"Whose automobile?"

"Natasha knows several government officials with cars. One of them— I don't know who—was driving there to visit family."

Stalin picked up the phone again. "Find out which of our people has left by motor for Voronezh." With a wide grin, he returned to the settee. "I just want to be sure that your family is safe."

Having no room to maneuver outside the question of daughters, Razan asked, "Did you ever take Svetlana to Georgia to show her around Tiflis and where you were born?" He hoped that in memory lay truth.

"I showed her the seminary where they tortured me and made me an atheist." Stalin put his pipe aside and, leaning back, engaged in what he liked best: sermonizing. "The presumed purpose of any religion, besides preparing our souls for eternity, is to make the earth, physically and morally, as hospitable as heaven. But how do we make the earth a paradise and mankind moral? The Jews thought that monotheism would put an end to the constant warfare among polytheists as to which god was the true one. But the Christians, who built on the Old Testament, earned Jewish contempt by lapsing into polytheism with their tripartite God: the Father, the Son, and the Holy Ghost. Once Christianity became the state religion, believers fought not over the end result—they all believed in a heavenly paradise—but on how to arrive at that glorious goal. In short, they fought over process and ceremony, or, as the churches call it, rites and liturgy.

"One church council after another, both Catholic and Protestant, argued about how to practice a particular religion. Should we emphasize baptism or the Eucharist? Should we hold Saturday or Sunday holy? Should we require confession? Should we impose a hierarchy between God and the people or allow direct worship? And so on, and so on. Do you know why these minor details became so important in church doctrine and politics? Because differences define people."

Was this the reason for Stalin's venomous split with Trotsky and others, and the awful purges? Was it to stake out his own claim to the unalloyed Communism? Any bacterium of difference, any atom of dissent, had to be extirpated. How else could one achieve purity?

"What I discovered," continued Stalin, "was that the Orthodox Church in one respect was right. It insisted that example was a language that anyone could read. And how was that example administered? Through punishment! The church taught through constant beatings, and worse. They burned heretics and nonbelievers at the stake, skinned them alive, disemboweled them, put out their eyes, and lopped off ears, noses, and hands. But although we find it abhorrent that the church countenanced physical abuse, the undeniable truth is that beating was the church's most effective cure for errant behavior and belief. It is the very means that parents use to cure their children of independence and assure that they will follow in the parents' footsteps. And so I condone beatings, severe ones, terrible ones, to eliminate heresy. Now do you see?"

Razan had asked about Svetlana and Tiflis and earned himself a lecture on how to instill obedience. But as long as Stalin focused on the past, Razan was safe in the present. "You suffered in Georgia, as all your biographers say, but you must also have some good memories."

"Not many. In Tiflis, behind the splash of colors and the sonorous syllables, every group maneuvered for political gain. The city was a seething pot of intrigue. No person was free of the taint of being a shpik." Stalin coughed and expectorated into a spittoon. "You'll never guess where I was first introduced to spying. In the seminary. The priests were always trying to expose our inner life and feelings. No violation of student privacy was too great for them."

Suddenly, Razan had a disconcerting insight. Stalin had, in his own way, turned the Soviet Union into a seminary, but with this difference: Koba had supplanted God.

"As a young man, to survive in Georgia, one had to understand *konspiratsia*. In fact, I would even say that konspiratsia explains the culture and soul of the Soviet Union, with its many nationalities and political groups and religious sects, all colluding and plotting." Expanding on the importance of rooting out conspiracy, he quoted approvingly a chilling sentence from Sergei Nechaev's *Revolutionary Catechism*: "All tender feeling for family, friendship, love, gratitude, and even honor, must be squashed by the sole passion for revolutionary work." At that moment, Razan concluded that in trying to choke out conspiracy, Stalin had choked out life instead. No wonder that an outraged Dostoevski had written *Demons* in reply to Nechaev's nihilism.

Stalin lit a cigarette and then resumed lecturing, presumably for Razan's benefit. But why? If the trouble was not Anna or her family, perhaps Stalin was merely trying to confirm his identity. But which one, the real or the counterfeit? And would they both talk in this manner? Razan listened closely for a misstep that might give a clue.

"We need order—*poryadok*—at any cost. Even if we have to spy and open people's mail. Every shpik engages in *perlustratsia*. And why not? All these sacred intellectuals are nothing but traitors. I hate them. Mandelstam was one of them, a *predatel*, who satirized me in verse. His punishment will serve as a warning to others."

Thinking the meeting over, Razan thanked the Vozhd for his "immeasurable insights" and prepared to leave. But before he could reach the door, Stalin replied coldly, "Comrade Shtube, do not counterfeit. You have no talent for it. Bring your daughters to the Kremlin. I wish to speak to them. If you try my patience, your wife will be assigned to hard labor."

Bravely, Razan said, "I will need two gate passes for them."

Stalin picked up a desk phone and ordered one for Natasha Shtuba and the other for Yelena Shtuba. Razan corrected him.

"Natasha von Fresser and Yelena Boujinskia."

Stalin repeated the correction to Poskrebyshev, smiled, and said, "It's done!"

He now knew why Stalin had let him remain free. Ironically, his liberty was limited to betraying his daughters. As he pondered his plight, he wondered what hidden meanings lay in Stalin's words "It's done." Koba was famous for making statements that he later claimed meant one thing and not another. What was "done"? Anna's assignment to a desk job, the issuance of passes, the betrayal of his daughters, his own fate? And didn't "done" mean finished, completed, settled? He couldn't think of a single thing that was accomplished, except for the two passes that he would collect from Poskrebyshev. Perhaps even more worrying was the word "It's." He had heard no antecedent; he couldn't think of a reference point. "It's" was singular and had to harken back to some subject. Which *one* did Stalin have in mind?

Walking to his apartment through the snow gave him time to sort out his thoughts, all the while listening to the footsteps of his government shadow. What if the tail chose to perch outside his door; how could Razan then reach his daughters? Instead of proceeding directly to his flat, he made for the barbershop, ostensibly to talk to Kasarov, the corpulent Cossack in black boots and Turkish fez trailing a red tassel, with whom he exchanged haircuts. Behind the shop were a storeroom and an unguarded door that opened on the loading dock at the rear of the building. Here he maneuvered his steps. Once out of sight, he made his escape.

Just as Anna had said, her daughters had taken refuge with Natasha's friend, whose family owned a house so dilapidated that the authorities refused to requisition it, even though positioned only two blocks from Gorky Street. He knew to be careful. Entering a restaurant, he ordered a meal, and left through the kitchen. Leaning against the wind, he finally arrived at the address on the note, a cellar apartment. A short, pretty, blond woman answered the door, Resonia Zeffinoskia. Razan introduced himself. A moment later, Natasha and Yelena appeared, both of them dressed and shod warmly against the cold of the basement and the damp earthen floor. Water dripped from a pipe wrapped with a rag. In the sole window, under the low ceiling, a geranium struggled to survive. The seedy and dated furniture had probably been purchased during the reign of the last Tsar. Razan thought of Tirana and his parents' house. Was there anything so sad as a faded and torn brocade that was once lovely?

Before Razan could say a word, an excited Natasha blurted, "Stalin has a double! I know. It's in Babel's novel."

Razan, who had long kept the secret of the political decoys, asked Natasha what in particular the manuscript said.

"It's unfinished, but it's about a man with an iron hand who rules a small mountain kingdom in Georgia. Babel describes him as having a droopy mustache, pockmarked face, bad teeth, and a limp. He even gives him a pipe. When the man is exiled to Siberia, he pays a look-alike impostor to take his place. One of them spends a few days in Balagansk with a Jew, Abram Gusinski. Which one is unclear."

Playing the devil's advocate, Razan asked Natasha a series of questions. After all, in the Soviet Union, one could never be sure of what was real and what was not. Even the idea of the "Soviet" changed from one day to the next. First, it was rule by the proletariat, then rule by the Politburo, and currently rule by one person. To know the truth was virtually impossible. Unlike a scientist whose belief proceeds from knowing, a Politburo commissar knows from believing—in the Vozhd. What did Babel or Natasha or Razan or anyone else really know? Nothing lent itself to proof, especially since facts were always being revisited and truth revised; for example, although the world thought that an American discovered the North Pole, Stalin declared in 1936 that the real discoverer was a Russian, Otto Schmidt.

"How can you be sure it's not just a fiction? Babel earned his bread making up stories."

"As soon as this manuscript was confiscated, Babel was arrested and Gusinski was shot. I saw the papers myself in the archives."

Razan patiently explained, "For the sake of argument, let's say Babel is right. And let's say a double actually stayed with Gusinski. How does one tell them apart?"

"The decoy, according to Babel, has a circumcision and Stalin does not."

"Strange," Razan said, reflecting on his time in the Kremlin. "All the years I have been shaving the man's face, listening to his voice, trimming his beard and mustache and ears, I have never seen any part of him unclothed. He takes great care to hide his body. Hmm."

"What are you thinking, Papa Shtube?"

With an eye on Resonia, whom he felt, like everyone else in the country, must be treated with suspicion, he replied, "Let us say some madman discovered the real Beloved Leader and killed him." Natasha raised her eyebrows, not at Razan's suggestion of an assassination but at his diction. Beloved Leader indeed! "When has the killing of a country's leader ever led to anything other than mass retaliations and the murder of innocents?"

"What are you saying?"

"I am asking whether knowing Stalin has a double really matters?"

Natasha was silent.

"If Stalin should die, a double could turn out to be worse."

Now was not the time to disclose private thoughts, not even in the presence of family. In some ways, family members were the worst. They caused loved ones to let down their guards and say forbidden things. But once they possessed confidential information, who could predict how they would behave, given the rewards they might reap?

"I am thinking," said Razan slyly, "that Babel is being fanciful. I remain unconvinced. After all, what if Stalin had himself cut?"

Resonia added, "If both men behave abominably, as you have suggested, Comrade Shtube, it's a Hobson's choice."

The barber mused. In the devious world of the Soviets, most of the commissars were interchangeable; they were merely distinctions without a difference. Razan smiled wordlessly at the blond curly-headed Resonia, put his arm around Natasha, and led her aside. "Besides the novel, which you've read, have you ever seen any official archival documents with details of Gusinski's Siberian exile? His death won't tell us anything, but his life might."

"We have Gusinski's statement to the secret police. He pleads friendship with Stalin and begs for permission to write Koba. And he recalls an ice fishing episode they shared."

At once, the barber dropped the subject of a decoy, handed Resonia a roll of rubles, and asked her to take Yelena to Gorky Street to buy a number of items. When Resonia and Yelena had left, he told Natasha that he had cause to believe that Dimitri couldn't be trusted.

"I know what you're thinking, and for a long time, I agreed. But in the archives, I could find no trace of treachery. In fact, Dimitri has been to this apartment before and never revealed its location."

"That was then; now is now. When you stole secret papers bearing on Stalin and his henchmen, you committed a capital crime. Koba will no doubt see in the theft a conspiracy and will order the arrest and torture of everyone involved, starting with Dimitri. The confession a man makes under torture is, sadly, often self-serving."

"What you are saying does not sound like my brother."

"Let's hope I am wrong." He spoke in short breaths. "To escape, I will need your assistance." He handed her a piece of paper. "It's all written down here. Memorize the details and then burn the note." He pecked her on the cheek and hugged her goodbye. As always, she slightly stiffened her back; after all, Razan was not her real father. Stepping outside the apartment, he paused in the cold air to consider what Natasha had told him. His head was a carousel of ideas, going round and round, up and down. He buttoned his coat and pulled on his cap in readiness for the wind. After a few steps, he stopped. A smile lit up his face. He had been struck not by a celestial flash of light but by the obvious. Abram Gusinski's ghost would provide the means to unmask the real Stalin.

The taxi coming slowly down the street, with its front grille missing and its right fender dented, looked ominously familiar. He was certain that it would hold Dimitri Lipnoskii.

THE HAUGHTY BARBER

Standing in the shadows, Razan watched the cab stop a few doors away. Yes, Dimitri would not want to come too close and risk having someone inside the basement apartment see him approach. As the cab driver pulled away, Dimitri mounted the curb and stood on the sidewalk straightening his military coat and hat before facing his sister. Turning into the building, Dimitri found his path blocked by Razan, who grabbed him by the lapels, and pushed him against the wall.

"You filthy denouncer!" said Razan. "You scum. You maggot."

Although Dimitri's mouth opened, he was so surprised by Razan's attack that he momentarily lacked the power of speech.

"Your mother's been sent to Solovki, and you are here to betray your sister and Yelena. You misbegotten son of a great lady."

Finding his breath, he gasped, "What are you talking about?"

"At our last interrogation, Beria told us everything," he hissed through clenched teeth, while tightening his hold on Dimitri's lapels.

"Told you what?"

"That he learned from you about the religious fervor attending your mother's painting sales. You called her a religious zealot."

"Lies! All lies!"

"Then why did you come here?"

"To tell Natasha that I've made arrangements for us to flee to Voronezh," he declared, disengaging Razan's hands from his coat.

"To collect her unfaithful husband? A likely story."

"But a true one."

"I don't believe you."

"To have him back she will forgive all."

"Let's just see!" Razan pushed a pliant Dimitri through the front door, down the hall, and into the basement apartment. "I want to hear it in her own words. Only then will I believe you."

Natasha started to throw her arms around her brother's neck, but remembering what Razan had said, she froze and then let her arms fall to her sides. With his heart beating abnormally fast, Razan spoke clumsily, sputtering, "He says . . . Dimitri . . . you have forgiven Alexei and he has a plan to take you to Voronezh . . . and you will have no objections, even though Alexei's been faithless. Can that be?"

"I still love Alexei and had no idea until this moment that Dimitri wanted to get me to Voronezh. I am delighted. Overjoyed."

"But you are to take Yelena and leave for Petrozavodsk."

Although Natasha loved Yelena dearly, she had, in her excitement, forgotten Razan's note. "I am sure that once Alexei and I have a chance to embrace and confess our wrongdoing, we'll be reunited. I've dreamed it ever since I heard . . ."

"But how can you be sure," Razan asked, "given what he's done?"

Dimitri interrupted. "We could all be arrested at any moment. We must hurry."

But Razan, convinced that Dimitri intended only to deliver his sister to the secret police, hurried to remark, "I have serious doubts that you can be trusted. And who better than I ought to know?"

"Insolent man," Dimitri said, making no attempt to hide his disgust. "For Natasha's sake you must trust me. Here is what I propose," and he laid out his plan, which was at odds with Razan's. "Let us not trip over pride," said Dimitri. "I can see how to reconcile our different ideas. The important thing is to escape."

Natasha interrupted. "Aren't you forgetting something, Dima?"

Her brother's jaw tightened. Secret policemen didn't err.

"Papers, Dima, papers! We need transit visas and passports—with photographs and official stamps!"

Dimitri replied with immense satisfaction, "All taken care of. Secret police files and labs have many uses."

Praying that his stepson would not betray them, Razan returned to the house on the embankment, where he had agreed to wait until he received Dimitri's signal: twelve white roses. That same evening, Razan went to see Kasarov and asked the barber if he could store his belongings with him. Of course. Together, the two of them, using the freight elevator, removed the Shtube family's valued possessions—clothing, books, personal letters, Anna's jewelry, and his matryoshka doll—and moved them to Kasarov's flat. At the back of his closet, Razan had found a terrifying object: a plaster bust of Stalin. Was this an NKVD joke? A warning?

The day that the white roses arrived, Razan filled an inexpensive vase with water, placed the flowers inside, and gave them to Kasarov's wife, Ada. In his gorgeous Petrovich overcoat, Razan rode the elevator to the main lobby, where he could see at the front entrance two men and a green bread truck. Reversing direction, he entered the busy barbershop and, with a wink, asked Kasarov if he could look over his backroom supply of facial ointments. He then opened the door to the loading dock, where trucks, as always, stood waiting to deliver their wares. Some drivers were just leaving. He asked for a lift.

"My leg," Razan said, affecting a limp, "won't allow me to walk very far."

The obliging truck driver dropped Razan around the corner from a rag shop that also sold used clothing. The owner, a Czech violinist, Cerny Michl, had immigrated to the Soviet Union shortly after the Civil War. Although his hands were no longer nimble enough for concertizing, Cerny would sit in his shop and play haunting Czech folk tunes and, occasionally, for the enjoyment of friends, a Dvorak concerto. Razan had often been attracted to the music. To show his appreciation, Razan never left without first buying some *shmatte*, rag, that he brought home to Anna's dismay. A tall, thin man, with sad eyes and wisps of hair over his ears, Cerny often wore the very clothes that he eventually traded or sold. Razan regarded him as a Dickensian character, and was quite sure that one day the shop, with its clutter, would suddenly combust. Wearing Petrovich's Gogolian masterpiece, which Comrade Michl had often admired, Razan offered to trade it for two items: a small greatcoat and an enormous brown, satin-lined gabardine greatcoat that Anna had urged him to buy, and that had hung in the shop, unsold, for several months. As Razan spread his coat on the counter, he said, "Have you ever . . ."

Cerny interrupted. "The greatcoat you want . . . do you know who once owned it?" Before Razan could reply, the cunning shopkeeper, dusting it off, said proudly, "Marshal Ouspenski. *The* Marshal Ouspenski who commanded a glorious division against the White Army."

Razan had never heard of the man and knew that Cerny was merely touting the name and fame of the coat's former owner to make it appear the equal of Petrovich's incomparable creation. The barber said nothing, waiting for Cerny to show his cards.

"I'll trade you Marshal Ouspenski's coat for yours. Even."

Razan tapped Cerny on the hand and replied, "Play me a Bohemian melody, one that captures the spirit of rascality."

The shopkeeper, not deaf to the allusion, took up his violin and played. "There! Are you satisfied? It is a song of a young man who has been cheated out of his inheritance."

Razan laughed. "It would take two greatcoats to equal the one that I have just put before you. It was cut and stitched by the great Petr Petrovich, the finest tailor in Asian Russia. Khans and imams come to him for their robes."

Comrade Michl answered, "You know the story of Mr. Zote, who dreamed of a cashmere coat, but went home with an angora goat?" He chuckled. "No deal! Nothing!"

Razan replied, "You call my coat *nothing*?" With this feigned indignation, he swept up the coat and turned to the door.

"Not so fast," called Cerny. "Where is your sense of humor?"

"Just don't Ouspenski or Zote me. I'm here to bargain, and I know the worth of my wares."

"Perhaps another melody on my violin would take the sorrow from your face."

"I'm in a hurry, Cerny. Some other time."

"One should never be in such a hurry as to miss the chance to hear Dvorak." He whispered, "To you I can say this: Some people believe in Stalin, but I believe in music, and in meadows, and in the melodies that Fritz Kreisler plays."

When Razan left the shop he had in his possession two greatcoats, Marshal Ouspenski's and one worn by Colonel Posner, a midget of a man, who had fought nobly for the Reds outside of Kiev. The coats were stuffed in a cloth shopping bag and secured with a shaggy hemp cord. By a circuitous route, Razan made his way to Resonia's apartment. Here he opened his bundle and began, almost immediately, to instruct Yelena in how to walk in a commanding fashion, as if she were a diminutive military officer. For hours they practiced walking side by side, with Yelena matching the distance of his stride and the motion of his hips, until she could imitate his every step and movement.

He then prepared for their departure by cosmetically aging his face and Yelena's. With both wearing their greatcoats, Razan pocketed a loaf of bread and chunks of cheese, took the black bag with its stethoscope and other medical gear that he had bought on the black market for a staggering sum, and led his daughter out the back door of the safe house near Gorky Street. At a public phone, he called in sick for work; he then waved several rubles to hail a cab, because taxis often ignored military personnel, who could claim free passage for reasons of state. A block from the station, they exited the cab and entered the train sheds, where half-naked, sweating men in goggles and full leather aprons worked with acetylene torches, sledge hammers, files, and grinding wheels to keep the rolling stock in repair. The shed smelled of fire, and sparks flew like comets. A friend of Dimitri's, in charge of milling, had agreed to let Razan and Yelena wait in his cramped office for the arrival of the sister and brother.

The day before fleeing, Dimitri had begged Lavrenti Beria for an audience, which the butcher granted when he read Dimitri's note claiming he had found incriminating evidence about his own family. Beria liked nothing more than to see children and parents dismember each other. They met in a room with a two-way mirror, so Beria could watch the interrogation of a particularly recalcitrant pawn of the west, who was being flogged with a rubber truncheon. A signal lesson for Dimitri. "My mother, as you know, has already revealed herself as an enemy of the people and has been justly exiled to Solovki. My stepfather seems devoted to Stalin."

Beria unfolded a new handkerchief and blew his nose. "Really? I am delighted to hear you say that Razan is a Soviet patriot. He has cut my hair more than once, and his Turkish barbering is exquisite."

"But my sister, Natasha, has betrayed the state with her theft of secret documents, as you no doubt have heard." Beria's fulsome lecherous look spoke for him. "If you will have your office issue an arrest warrant, I will bring her here to Lubyanka Prison, as soon as I can discover her hiding place. You can personally quiz her."

Beria smiled. "I hear she's quite a beauty."

Dimitri, knowing Beria's weakness for pretty women, added, "She also likes powerful men."

Beria sprang to his telephone and ordered that an arrest warrant be issued immediately for Natasha von Fresser.

The plan had taken shape as Dimitri had hoped. He left the prison with the warrant and, winding his way through alleys and gardens, made his way to Resonia's basement apartment, where his sister hugged him with a hunger born of initial distrust.

"To reach Voronezh safely," he told her, "we have to act quickly. I have volunteered to help the secret police apprehend defectors. Just do as I say."

At the train shed, among the hissing trains and bustling workers, they rendezvoused with Razan and Yelena, who were sipping tea and watching the fiery scene outside their door. Dimitri, as good as his word, passed along transit visas and passports, fresh from the police lab, listing the barber as a military doctor and Yelena as his aide.

A grateful and excited Natasha exclaimed, "Dimitri's plan worked. We are traveling by truck to Voronezh." She hugged Yelena, sweetly telling her to look after Razan. Smiling at her stepfather, she said, "And you must take care of our dearest Yelena."

Razan clasped the brother and sister, bent their heads to his chest, and held them silently, as if cradling two infants.

As the siblings extricated themselves and made for the door, Yelena shouted after them, "Good luck, Natasha. Good luck, Dimitri." Then they were gone.

Razan's thoughts turned to Petrozavodsk. Could this unnamed person to whom Razan was to deliver Yelena be trusted? Who was he? With no way of knowing, he had to hope that Dimitri's friend would not denounce them. Under the most propitious conditions, bribing friends to hide one put numerous people in danger, increasing the risk that they would denounce the lawbreakers. For the moment, the success of all the parties depended on their papers. Since the days of the Tsar, the Russians had loved government documents and come to expect ukases. What was more persuasive than an order with an official stamp?

Moments after Razan and Yelena entered the gloomy train station and passed through the doors to the platform, lights suddenly illuminated a huge overhead picture of Stalin that seemed to validate the many police crowding the platform in search of defecting soldiers and spies. Amidst the tumult and smells, a guard barked, "Your papers and tickets!" He took one look and scoffed, "Why is an old man like you heading for the Karelian front?"

"I want to do my part," said Razan. "I am a doctor, as you can see from my papers, and he is my assistant."

"What kind of doctor? My father is a thoracic surgeon."

"Ear, nose, and throat."

The guard waved them through, pointing to platform number four, where a train sat eerily silent. Walking side by side, as they had practiced, Razan and Yelena made their way to car number twenty-two, and, as Razan had choreographed, walked to their seats. The hard part lay ahead: keeping his coat buttoned for the duration of the trip to hide the money bags strapped to his body. For her part, she dared not take off her coat in the men's lavatory lest she reveal her sex and her age. Although the press of bodies in the car made the air stifling, they sat in their greatcoats, appearing to be disciplined Soviet soldiers.

At last, the train pulled into Petrozavodsk. As Dimitri had directed, they took a cab to the White Sea building block, a complex that resembled a dozen others. At apartment 449, the man who answered the door identified himself as Yuri Suzdal. His two rooms, once occupied by a Soviet official, now lacked the simplest amenities, like a loo. A communal one in the hall, with strips of newspaper for toilet tissue, served the entire floor. Lightbulbs dangled from electrical wires. The elegant wallpaper, seen now only in spots, had been used by previous tenants to light the stove. The plastered walls exhibited numerous scrawls, some of them literate, some not. One person had written a joke: Three men were imprisoned. The first said that he was jailed for supporting Bulganin. The second said that he was jailed for voting against Bulganin. The third said, "I am Bulganin." The poor bricking admitted winter drafts. Suzdal led them to the rear and a small coal burner that made bearable the area around it. In the other room, the ice-caked windows prevented one from seeing outside. Razan had no intention of staying long. The plan was for him to deposit Yelena with Dimitri's friend, whom Razan now knew as Yuri Suzdal, and to take the next train to Moscow. For safety's sake, Yuri would shortly be moving. He handed Razan his new address. As Yelena settled into the alcove set aside for her, Razan gave Yuri enough rubles to sustain both of them for several months.

"How have you been living until now?"

"Before I left Moscow, Dimitri arranged through a noble friend to find me temporary quarters. Yes, this place is bad, but you should have seen the first one. Dimitri also arranged for me to have working and traveling papers." Yuri laughed. "They come right from an NKVD lab. Such irony! Papers, though, will get you only so far, but Dima's advice proved invaluable. He said, 'Your initial impulse will be to distance yourself from the beast—the government and police—but that puts you on the outside. You have a better chance of surviving if you enter the belly of the beast. From time to time, the beast looks inward and devours its own with purges, but most of those people ostensibly pose a threat to the Vozhd. Usually the beast is looking outward, to the west, to its borders, to its restive national groups.' So I applied at the government-run housing bureau for a job as an assistant hairdresser. If the police were trying to find me, I figured the last place they would look is inside the Department of Housing. I've been working for a kind woman, Ekaterina Kirova. When she can, she gets me extra work on the side. Her husband found me this place and arranged for Yelena to be enrolled in a state school. As you recommended, she is registered under her own name."

Taking Yelena in his arms, Razan held her fast, kissing her head. He knew how scared she must feel, even though on the train, he had repeatedly explained, in whispers, why she had to stay in Petrozavodsk, and how important it was that she not draw attention to herself and keep her own counsel.

To make her feel less apprehensive, he said to Yuri, "I'm sure that you could do wonders with Yelena's thick locks."

Seeing Yelena's unease, Yuri gallantly bowed. "Your Highness, whenever you want your hair done, I am at your beck and call."

The barber stayed but a few hours, long enough to persuade himself that Yuri would gently care for Yelena. Clearly, Dimitri and Yuri were lovers. Before leaving, Razan asked the former hairdresser whether he knew of their intent to cross the border to Finland.

"I know that's your hope, but how you plan to achieve it, especially now, in time of war, I have no idea."

"The entire family will meet here. Until then it is premature to talk about plans."

Razan barely reached the Moscow train in time. He sat looking out a window contemplating the next step. He opened his wallet, counted his rubles, and chuckled to himself. Anna had squirreled away plenty. Money would not be a problem. As the train rumbled along, he saw an occasional flickering candle in some cottage. He wondered what their lives could be like, and he remembered a Chekhov story with the line: "We do not see and we do not hear those who suffer, and what is terrible in life goes on somewhere behind the scenes." Razan buried his face in his greatcoat and softly cried, thinking of Anna.

All through the night, he hardly heard the snoring passengers as he planned his movements. He would present himself at work to the astonishment of Poskrebyshev, but to the understated delight of Stalin, who no doubt had already prepared for his barber a bed of nails. While shaving the Vozhd, he would ask him about his exilic days in the company of Abram Gusinski. If Stalin's answers proved his identity, Razan knew how to act; but if the man failed the test, and if it turned out that the real Koba and his personal barber had all this time remained out of sight, Razan would most likely be arrested and immediately liquidated. If Razan could be granted one wish, it was that the man he shaved would be Iosif Vissarionovich Dzhugashvili.

As the train shifted and shook, and the mighty steel railroad wheels beat a steady rhythm—"to Moscow we go, to Moscow we go"—he puzzled how he could carry into the Kremlin a razor that could pass for the real one. Closing his eyes and substituting the sound of "to Moscow we go" with "a way must be found, a way must be found," he conceived an audacious plan. What did he have to lose? His life already hung by a thread. He would take Rubin's wood-carving of his razor from Kasarov's apartment, where he had stored it. If one of the guards discovered and confiscated it, he would say that he had intended the replica for Stalin as a gift.

At the Moscow train station, he was stopped at a checkpoint, showed his travel pass, passed through the sullen crowds waiting to purchase a train ticket, and reached the street, where he entered a cab. At the embankment, he entered by way of the loading dock and learned from Kasarov, at work in his barbershop, that roosting in the lobby was an NKVD agent. Instead of taking the elevator, he walked up the eight flights of stairs and was greeted by Ada Kasarova, from whom he retrieved his wooden knife and his nested doll.

Returning by way of the freight elevator, he exited not on the main floor, lest a policeman spot him, but in the basement, where it took him a moment to acclimate his eyes to the dark and find the light switch. At least twenty wooden pallets lay on the floor covered by tarpaulins and secured by ropes. He untied one and lifted a corner of the canvas. To his amazement, he saw plaster busts of Stalin, row after row, in the dozens, just like the one he had found at the back of his closet. He could only presume that they had been delivered for distribution to the apartment residents. The monomaniacal madman was making certain that his people worshipped no other gods, and that his inescapable person stood always before them. The sole Father from whom all life flowed, he could not abide the idea that his form did not lodge in every home, and of course every Soviet citizen's heart.

Was it not enough that the Stalin stain could be found everywhere in the country? The Vozhd's reply would be: I can never rest. With over a hundred nationalities and dozens of religions, I have forged a nation, but always the threat of dissolution and insurrection lurks. I have supplanted the old myths and given the people a real Garden of Eden, not just a fairy tale. I have replaced the old Mosaic laws with just ones. Deuteronomy is no more germane today than our worshipping the sun. I have cast out the old proscriptions and idols and have replaced rule by the priests with rule by the people. I have created a new world, one that eclipses the biblical creation.

The barber had the urge to find a hammer and break all the busts, but given that they numbered in the hundreds, that task would have taken more time and effort than he had to spare. And what if someone in the floor above heard the noise? Instead, he removed one of the busts, wrapped it in some old newspapers he found in a corner, and ascended the stairs. As he expected, on the main floor he saw several policemen patrolling the area. One was pacing in front of the barbershop, his escape route. Walking up to the man, Razan handed him the bust and said, "Everyone should own a bust of Comrade Stalin." The stunned policeman, distracted by the gift, stared at the bundle. "Remove the paper," said Razan. Accustomed to orders, the man peeled away the newspapers, while Razan passed through the shop to the backroom and the loading dock. By the time the policeman could collect his wits, Razan was nowhere to be seen.

In the last few minutes, it had begun to snow. All the better, Razan thought, as he walked toward the Kremlin through the wetted streets, the flakes on his face would sharpen his senses. He smiled at the people pulling scarves and hoods around their heads to protect themselves and hastening to retreat indoors.

After signing the visitor book at the Troitsky Gate, he submitted to a pat down inside the fortress. The replica of the razor rested in his breast pocket where it could be seen easily and not treated as contraband. One of the guards removed and admired it. "For our Beloved Leader," said Razan. The guard glanced at Razan's pass and assigned another soldier to accompany him to Poskrebyshev's office. In the old days, his pass had entitled him to make his own way to the Senate Building. Comrade Ugly had obviously lost no time in issuing different orders. As they walked toward his office, Razan inconspicuously shifted the wood carving to his pants pocket.

When the barber entered, Poskrebyshev's jaw dropped, and though he wished to revile Razan, nothing but gasps escaped from his mouth. He immediately reached for the phone.

"He's here," the aide sputtered. "Shtube." Pause. "Yes, the barber." Pause. "He gave no explanation."

Putting down the phone, Poskrebyshev opened the closet where the barber's bag was stored, and removed it. "Five minutes," he said. When Stalin rang, the two guards, as usual, led Razan into the inner office. The aide-de-camp then activated the microphone in Stalin's office to listen. At first, he heard nothing, and for good reason. The Boss stared at Razan and silently waited for the barber to trap himself. But Razan, counting himself a dead man, simply waited him out. The clock ticked. No one moved. The second hand circled the clock four times, and still not a syllable was uttered. Stalin signaled the guards to put the barber's bag on the divan and to leave. Razan knew that Stalin was at his worst when alone, because then no witnesses could report his brutal behavior. Removing a pistol from his desk drawer, he handed it to Razan. Still he said nothing. The barber felt that if he didn't get to a bathroom, he would soil his pants, but to excuse himself would be a sign of weakness. Although in his fear he could virtually smell his own urine, he clenched his teeth and remained mute. The man whom Razan had barbered for so many years seemed unnerved by the void, and flinched first.

"You have a choice," he said. "You can do it or I can."

"What if I turned the gun on you?"

The Boss laughed robustly. "It's not loaded. Do you think I am fool enough to hand my enemies a loaded pistol?"

The word "enemies" told Razan all that he needed to know. "If this is the last day of my life . . ."

"It is."

"Allow me the honor to give you a last Turkish haircut and trim."

"In light of the circumstances, I'll forgo the shave."

Stalin phoned Poskrebyshev to send back the paladins who would hover over him while the barber snipped and singed. It was then that Razan made the switch, planting in his bag Rubin's wooden razor.

Razan put the apron on his client and began trimming the man's mustache and hair. With his life already forfeit and nothing to lose, Razan began asking leading questions about Georgia in the hopes of finally determining the identity of the man in the chair.

"I've been thinking about your experiences at the seminary in Tiflis," said Razan. "You have often said the place was bestial."

"We called it the Stone Sack. But once we left the cursed halls and rooms and stood on the front porch, we could see wonderful Yerevan Square, with its jumble of Muslims, Christians, and Jews. The mixture could be explosive, particularly on the bustling side streets with their narrow lanes and alleys, where goldsmiths clanked their hammers in open workshops, and pastry cooks sold their sweets, and bakers hawked their flat loaves prepared in clay ovens. Here too were spies and assassins. Betrayal has a universal language: money. After the seminary, when I took to the streets, the Okhrana found me, thanks to a paid informer.

"We'd meet in the houses of friends or at a remote inn. But our favorite spot was the Svet Restaurant on Trading Street. One night, as I was coming out, I saw two men standing across the road. They began to follow me. Their presence could mean only one thing: I had been denounced. Some bastard had saved his own skin by conspiring against me. I tried to run, but I had a lame leg. The police easily caught me. I remained in a Tiflis jail for several weeks before being sent to Siberia. It was not the first time."

The barber put away his scissors. Applying alcohol to the Vozhd's ears, he lit a match and, as the guards closed in, immediately extinguished the flames with a towel. "Have I ever once burned our Beloved Leader?" asked Razan.

"And lucky for you, haughty barber."

As Razan removed the apron and folded it up—he always shook out the hairs later—he asked, "Did you not once say that for a few days in Balagansk you lived with a Jew, Abram Gusinski."

"I don't remember mentioning it," Stalin said, "but why does his nationality matter? You Jews are all the same. Clannish." He then changed the subject. "Have you heard any anti-Stalin jokes lately? As you know, I enjoy them immensely. Besides, in humor we discover the serious concerns of the people."

Razan would have to walk gingerly through this minefield.

"Did the exiles in Siberia make jokes?"

"All the time," said Koba, leaning back in the chair.

"About each other or the Tsar?" asked Razan.

"Mostly the government. I remember a fellow who had gone mad in the camp. He would walk around saying out loud, 'Why do we say about the Tsar, "our brother" and not "our friend"? Because one can choose one's friends.' Then he would chuckle. He thought it the funniest joke in the world. He wrote it down on a piece of paper and stuffed the paper in his mouth—and choked on it."

"If you'll forgive me for saying so," said Razan, helping the Vozhd from his chair, "it sounds like the humor I grew up with."

"It does have that cosmopolitan flavor."

Of late, the Boss had been calling Jews cosmopolitans, which was intended pejoratively, because he regarded them as a race apart, one that refused to integrate into the so-called national identity.

Casually, while collecting the tools of his trade, he asked, "Did Gusinski share that kind of humor . . . maybe when you were ice fishing together?"

Suddenly, the Vozhd went from his chair to a phone, where he pressed a button, waited, said, "Information!" and then disappeared into Comrade Ugly's office, followed by his two guards. During their absence, Razan thought of every conceivable torture he might be subjected to as punishment for prying into Stalin's early life. When the door opened again, only the two guards appeared. They told him to collect his bag and coat, and led him out of the office to an elevator.

Leaving the Senate Building, they wordlessly traversed the square and entered the Armory Building. A bald supervisor with elegantly manicured fingernails met them. Expecting the worst, Razan was delighted to discover that the man behaved in a perfectly courteous manner. His assistant, a hard-faced Kremlin soldier in a starched uniform, resembled most security men, humorless and silent. The supervisor opened a logbook and asked Razan to sign in. "With your ID number," he added. "The reason?" asked Razan. "A mere formality," replied the supervisor. The security man led the barber down a flight of stairs to the dank armory basement. He then removed a ring of keys and opened a closet. Razan stood terrified as the soldier handed him a porcelain chamber pot with a stained wooden lid and a blanket. Taken to a windowless room with a narrow iron bed and a thin straw mattress but no pillow, Razan knew that these few amenities were far more than most prisoners enjoyed. The soldier swung the metal door shut and locked it. As he had promised, the supervisor gave him dinner that evening and waited outside the bathroom before Razan was jailed for the night.

Strangely, Razan felt no fear, perhaps because the authorities had not removed his belongings, in particular, his barbering bag with the wooden imitation and his steel razor. Exhausted from fear, he fell asleep quickly. His mind was a riot of dreams that dissolved into two, which he never forgot.

On the other side of the wall, just inches from where his head lay, he could hear Anna's bed creaking and her soft, regular breathing. A locked door separated the two rooms. He rose and whispered through the keyhole, but she failed to respond. Back in bed, he heard the clicking of heels. Razan returned to the keyhole and smelled the pungent lavender cologne of Lavrenti Beria. Muffled voices followed and then, loudly and clearly, Anna said, "It was a sad childhood, since you ask. My father was unknown to me. My mother worked at an inn, as a housemaid, where the carters drank cruelly and had their way with the women. Perhaps one of them is my father. I married a farmer to escape from the daily violence and drunkenness—and from my mother. She was the innkeeper's mistress. He beat and humiliated her until the day she died of consumption. My husband swore he had money. He lied. He introduced me to scenes of debauchery and shame, bringing home other women. I could hear their love moans downstairs while I lay in bed above. Suffering and weeping and degradation were my companions. I tried to hang myself, but life was stronger than death. Even while choking, I fought to loosen the rope. After that experience, I swore to protect my children and stand between them and their father who took great pleasure in using a knout. A tradesman came through town with a grindstone. He was sharpening old knives and selling new ones. I bought a blade with a serrated edge that could easily slice a man's throat. From that day forth I was a free woman."

The keyhole gave Razan a good view of Beria, who comforted her by gently stroking her hair. She turned her face upward and smiled. It was then he tried to force her head down to his groin, unbuttoning his pants and insisting that she "suck him like a pump." When she resisted, he tried to throw her to the floor to rape her. She bit and scratched. With one hand, Beria drew a pistol; with the other, he gave her a sapphire. She feigned submission. As he slid off his pants, she grabbed the gun. A shot rang out. Beria lay dead. Razan restlessly tossed on his iron bed. Pavel, wearing a leather apron, was pouring molten metal into forms that, after cooling, issued as busts of Stalin. When he had finished, he took each bust, placed it on his anvil, and shattered it with his sledgehammer. But as the pieces fell to the ground, they sprouted like weeds in the shape of miniature Stalins, each sporting a bushy mustache that covered his mouth and accented his yellow eyes, until the entire floor of the forge was forested with Koba heads.

Razan woke with a start.

In the morning, the supervisor guided Razan to Poskrebyshev's office. The aide was just putting his desk in order, sorting papers and signing a few important ukases. Razan was told to wait. With a diseased smile, Poskrebyshev said, "Look around. It will be the last time you pass through here—or the inner sanctum."

One of Poskrebyshev's phones blinked a red light, the cue for Stalin's guards to accompany Razan into Stalin's office. On entering, the barber expected to find the Boss waiting for him. But the office was empty. Who, then, had given Poskrebyshev the signal to send him in? The guards seemed not at all surprised by the vacancy of the room. Razan, having no other choice, fell in with the charade. He opened his bag and prepared to shave the Boss.

ANNA ON THE BUBBLE

Spared the indignity and suffocation of being packed into a Stolypin wagon—railcars that transported prisoners on shelves, not seats, inside of wire cages—Anna was shackled to three vicious, foul-mouthed women, all condemned for murder. Her initial impulse was one of repulsion, until she reminded herself that she too had taken a life. To keep her equanimity, she revisited her marriages, first to Pyotr and then to Razan. Her thoughts seemed to come in rhythm with the rails. Pyotr had muscles, and a trade, and a rudimentary knowledge of reading. Clickety-clack. He'd paid her court, asked for her hand, swore his fidelity. Clickety-clack. She was not marrying for love, but for security, and for strong children. His forge, his seed, his strength, in return for her care. Clickety-clack.

On their wedding night, he had shown her no gentleness, even though she was willing. He took her brutally and slapped her face to establish, he said, his rule over the family. Then children came. The commotion of kids and the ever-increasing need for more money had turned Pyotr to vodka. An ugly drunk, he would beat her and the children after carousing at the inn. When his hands began to shake and his work to fail, he put Pavel in charge of the forge and sent Anna into the fields to sow and harvest while he drank himself stupid. How often had she dreamed of him dead? A thousand times a day would be vastly shy of the mark. So when God intervened and led her to the place in the creek where he lay on his back among the rocks and ice in the water, she felt as if a supernal force had directed her to turn him facedown. Yes, she was utterly convinced that the impulse and courage to do what she did had come from above. A squeal of brakes interrupted her thoughts. The train had stopped at a watering station. Thirty minutes later, clickety-clack.

Then God in his goodness had brought her Razan: a gentle man, an honest man, a skilled barber. What mattered that he was a Jew? Did he not treat her kindly, and silently endure her children's taunts? His lovemaking may have lacked the lustiness of Pyotr's, but his tenderness was equally romantic. He valued her advice and even sought it. She was more than an equal; she held in his eyes an honored place. How many Russian women in Solovki would have her incentives to flee? She would take Gregori with her. The thought of joining her family, leaving the country, and making a new life with a treasured husband would inspire her inventive mind to discover a way off the island. Nothing would hold her back. Whenever the government orders came to completely evacuate the islands, she and Gregori would be ready. As the train rattled toward Kem, she knew that to succeed she would need cooperation, which could be bought with the gold coins she had secreted vaginally and the jewels pleated into her hair.

At the moment, a full bladder was more real than her imagined escapes. To reach the pail at the end of the car, she had to drag three other women down the center aisle. Their jailer, refusing to free any of them from their collective chains, delighted in seeing the women huddle for privacy to urinate or defecate. That night, as the odorous car echoed with stertorous breathing, the train halted amidst a grinding of brakes and hissing of steam. The prisoners were uncaged and ordered to exit the train, though still a few miles short of their destination. Torrential rains had washed out a section of track.

With the guards roaring like mad bulls, the chained prisoners were led into impenetrable fog and made to walk the remaining distance to Kem. The mud in some places reached to their ankles. Finally, the rain dissolved into a drizzle as fine as water dust. But this respite was interrupted violently by a hurricane wind blowing out of the north; the cracking treetops brought to mind demons crying out in the night. They passed several huts with iron roofing that rattled like metal snakes. By the time they exited the desolate forest and made their way into Kem, a bare village except for one pretty church, Anna had experienced levels of hell that Dante ignored: first on the train, where humans lived in suffocating quarters so unsanitary that they wished for release through death, and then in the town, where the wind broke wooden window frames that showered splinters into the roadways, and dislodged chimney bricks that flew through the air like shrapnel. As she looked out to sea, she saw that several fishing boats had lost their sails and been swamped. Two of them, right before her eyes, sank to the bottom of the bay. When, she wondered, would their corpses wash ashore?

Herding the women from the Kem Transit Camp to the boat for the short trip to Solovki, the guards hurried them along with whipping sticks and addressed them as "whore," "bitch," "cunt." Some of the women thieves, trying to assert their dignity, yelled at the prostitutes, "We may steal, but we don't sell ourselves," to which the prostitutes answered, "At least we sell what belongs to us, not stolen goods." Fortunately for Anna, she found a place on the deck and escaped being consigned to the hold, where the women had even less space than on the train. In the distance, she could see the white fortress walls, stained rust-colored by rain, of the Solovki Kremlin. Many of the onion domes had been removed and replaced with roofs that resembled cowsheds. Soon she would see the neglected gardens and canals, the decaying walls and broken windows. Even from the sea, the monastery looked forbiddingly grim, the perfect locale for unspeakable crimes. Built from cyclopean stones, it resembled a giant sarcophagus that would hold the dead after Armageddon. Its design—sharp contours and squares—exuded solidity and convinced the onlooker that here resided power, that here ruled a stern and merciless god called not Jesus or Stalin but "pitilessness."

On the dock of Solovki Island, Commandant Trubetskoi and Chief Warden Ponomarev, in black boots and tunics, their sartorial homage to Stalin, met the prisoners.

"Some of you," said the commandant, hitting his leg with a baton, "will wade into the sea and gather seaweed from the shore. The water is bitterly cold, but it will harden you and prepare you for camp life. Some will go out in large boats to gather the weeds from the sea bottom with long hooked poles. Some will preserve the seaweed in piles and ferment it onshore, weather permitting. If we remain here until spring, some will scatter the piles so the seeds can adequately dry. Some will prepare it for burning. The ashes, containing iodine, will be poured into a well. Later on, they will be taken to a factory at the Solovki Kremlin and processed."

The commandant nodded toward his chief warden, who added, "Those of you on the seaweed detail will regard yourselves as lucky. The others among you, because of your offenses, will be assigned to fish for herring, tan leather, make bricks, dig for salt, and bury the dead. Anyone who fails to obey will be exposed to the elements: in winter, the cold and snow; in summer, the mosquitoes. Now, how many of you can read and write? Anna Lipnoskaya, step forward. We understand from your papers that you can do both."

As Anna moved out of the line, several men and women followed, insisting that they too were literate. Everyone knew that office work was less taxing than physical labor. But, unlike the volunteers, Anna also knew how to use an abacus, a skill that led the camp authorities to assign her to keeping the books on iodine production. Led past the administration building, she noticed, even at this late date, that the flower bed in front of the camp administration building contained the outline of an elephant, a visual pun. "SLON," the Russian word for elephant, was the acronym for "Solovetski Special Purpose Camp." Her bookkeeping position entitled her to shared quarters in the old Saint Petersburg guesthouse, where her room was larger and more comfortable than were most, and contained a small wood stove, a luxury provided to few. After her jailer escort had left, her roommate, Lydia, a thin and wrinkled girl still in her twenties, with hair the color of goose feathers, told her that hundreds of *zeks*, camp prisoners, lived in old dugouts, stifling barracks, and unheated monastery cells.

"Prisoners," said Lydia in a hushed voice, one that most zeks assumed lest they be overheard, "are often mutilated by sadistic guards with whips, chains, pliers, needles, and other sharp objects. During the summer, the unruly zeks are tied to a stake near the woods, where the millions of insects—mosquitoes, black flies, biting ants—eat them alive. Beware 'Sekirka,'" she said, passing her hand under her chin and across her neck to signify death. Although Anna pressed her, she refused to elaborate. Not until Gregori returned from Anzer Island and was stationed on Sekirnaya Hill, Poleax Hill, did she learn about the punishment cells in the two-story cathedral, where men and women prisoners were brought for infractions that ranged from serious to trivial to sit all day on a single pole, no more than twelve inches around, suspended across the width of the narrow church and raised high enough so that one's feet could not touch the ground. For the zeks to maintain their balance demanded not only dexterity but also strength. If they fell, the guards either beat them or tied the poor inmates lengthwise to a log, which they rolled down a flight of 365 steps carved out of a steep slope next to the church. Already starved and emaciated, the prisoners reached the bottom unrecognizable.

"You do know," said a defiant Lydia, "that some of Russia's greatest intellectuals have lived and died here: scientists, artists, poets, mathematicians, philosophers, historians, engineers. To endure in this hell, I tell myself that I'm lucky to be among such famous company." She said nothing about Stalin's picture over her bed.

A day later, Anna took up her job in the administration building, trying to make sense of the financial ledgers. Bookkeeping in Solovki was worse than inadequate. Inmates changed names, kept frozen bodies under their beds to double their rations, fixed the books so that ten pounds of seaweed became twenty, and lost countless items between the lines of debit and credit. A competent accounting of prisoners, even a sloppy one, would have connected Gregori Lipnoskii and Anna Shtuba. In fact, Anna kept waiting for some official to mention her son. But Gregori's name never surfaced; hence, she was forced to ask, sotto voce, if anyone knew his whereabouts. She soon learned that he had been assigned to attend the sick and dying on Anzer Island, a short distance from Solovki, though in bad weather a harrowing boat journey. By means of a bribe, she managed to transmit word to him that she was now on the main island working in the accounting office. His reply: He hoped shortly to find an assignment, like his current one on Golgotha Hill, caring for the dying. Priests and doctors, for good reason, worked side by side. When medicine failed the body, the priests cured the patients' souls.

During her first days on the island, what struck Anna, besides the incompetence of the authorities, were the ever-present wind, the absence of below-zero weather, and the quiet. "The White Sea," said Lydia, "is warmed by the Norwegian Current, a northern arm of the Gulf Stream." Twenty degrees Fahrenheit Anna regarded as balmy. Although she had arrived on the island in the midst of a storm and a turbulent sea, on the succeeding days, the water seemed barely to move, and the absence of waves created an absolute silence. "Had you come during the summer and not in October," said Lydia, "you'd marvel at how easy it is to see to the bottom." Even now, peering into the sunless sky and inky water, Anna could understand why monks had settled this area. The stillness promoted contemplation. How hateful that the reverential Solovki landscape should have been obscenely violated by torturers. If only the world knew; or would the world's preoccupation with its own comfort blind it to cruelty, as was the case with Maxim Gorky, who had years before come to this island prison and then failed to tell the truth of what he'd experienced?

Near the arched gate to the monastery stood a huge sign: "Life has become better. Life has become happier. I. Stalin."

The unseasonable calm, however, ended abruptly, as violent winds assailed the monastery walls, raced among the graves and the uncut cemetery grass, and howled down the dark passageways, compounding the cold of the monks' cells that the Communists had turned into jails. Each night, Anna doubled the blankets and imagined the past that Lydia invoked, until she could hear the moans of the dead. Her heart trembled. She envisioned men kneeling before a crucifix praying for release from the sickness and pain of the flesh. In her dreams, she saw monks with pallid faces staring through window gratings out to the salt sea and envying birds freely swimming in the air. From their eyes fell silent, bitter tears. Miraculously, the monks faded and in their place stood prisoners, languishing, withering, drying up. She wondered: Do they, like the monks, hear the doleful tolling of the bell? John Donne's words came to her, the ones her ex-priest often quoted, "Never send to know for whom the bell tolls; it tolls for thee." Even though Lydia had shown her, on the monastery portals, representations of the miracles that took place in this frigid hell—fish falling from the sky to feed the monks, the Virgin Mary driving the enemy to flee from these sacred precincts—Anna knew that untimely death waited for everyone on this cursed island.

No sooner had she started making sense of the account books than the labor force started to dwindle, slowly being sent on barges to Kem. She smiled knowing that the best time for her and Gregori to escape was in the confusion of retreat. For six months of the year, the White Sea was frozen, but not thick enough to permit a sled to traverse it. Patches of open water could be missed in the raging snowstorms and in the black winter nights. Then, too, one could not ignore the bitter frosts and mists that befogged the sea. No, escape would not lie across the icy sea; it would have to come from a precise knowledge of the camp: from knowing that the frozen, dead zeks buried underfoot, their fingers, hands, elbows, legs, and heads sticking out of the snow, would be staying behind, but not the NKVD corpses.

Anna quickly learned the geography of Solovki—the woods, the clearings, the marshes—and the vocabulary of the verminous camp. To survive in the camp, one had to know prison jargon and how to use it. Years later, she still had her notes.

The camp prisoners, both men and women, were generally divided into two groups: the criminals (*urki*) and the politicals, who were disparagingly called "counterrevolutionaries" or "enemies of the people," even though most of them were farmers and industrial workers. The criminals mercilessly preyed on the politicals, whom they hated even more than they did the despised camp officials. Criminals roamed the camp freely, enforcing the rules of their overlords. They served as jailers and guards, observing no moral code except their own. To show their contempt for "normal society," they defecated, urinated, masturbated, and fornicated in public. The greater the outrage, the greater their pleasure.

Anna quickly saw that the criminals had formed themselves into a class society with strict rules. At the bottom were rapists and petty thieves, such as pickpockets; at the top were bank robbers and murderers. The bosses were the *pachans*, who ruled those below them, meting out jobs, punishment, and favors. Each class had its own tattoos, most of them sentimental, "I'll always love my beloved mother," or obscene, "Girls, suck my cock." But the pachans inked their chests, stomachs, and backs with eagles, sunrays, hammers, anvils, copulating couples, and the faces of Marx, or Lenin, or Stalin, mostly the last.

Unlike the general camp diction, the criminals had their own crapulous slang, *blatnoe slovo*, or thieves' music, which included a number of Yiddish and Hebrew words, no doubt owing to the Jewish gangs in Odessa. The criminals also had their own way of walking, in small short steps with legs parted slightly, and they paid special attention to their dress and caps. A peak folded up or down or worn toward the back all conveyed a special meaning, a code that Anna shortly cracked.

The Stukachi, the stoolies, came principally from the Tsar's former officers in the White Guard and from the ranks of the priests. For the smallest gain— an extra bowl of soup, a crust of bread, a night with one of the women prisoners, a heavy blanket—they would inform. A good many of them served as jailers, never missing a chance to prove that they could be more brutal than the wardens, who came from the criminal class. Despised and distrusted, these former soldiers and criminals, prisoners themselves, saved the government money by policing the others. This practice, first tried in Africa by the colonial powers, was now being copied by the Soviets and would subsequently be perfected by the Nazis. The prisoners, though, were far from helpless. On more than one occasion, an informer lured into the woods never returned; and in the matter of *tufta*, the Stukachi could often be bribed. Every prisoner had his work norm, whether for tanning, or fishing, or gathering seaweed. The norms were inhumanly high and therefore impossible to meet. Failure meant whippings and possibly death. To circumvent the authorities, the prisoners would put, in the bottom of the holding pits, rocks and logs, and cover them with mud and sticks. The day's work would be piled on top of the tufta so that it appeared that the day's norm was met. Without this deception, no work team or individual could possibly have harvested the allotted amount. The fact that men outnumbered the women and children ten to one meant that females could easily trade their bodies for favors. Abortions were therefore frequent and jealousy rampant.

Anna's comeliness did not go unnoticed. Her first day at work, Comrade Monty Vessalikovski, the adjutant in charge of the accounting office, put his hand on her shoulder and tried to run it down the front of her frock. She grabbed his wrist, turned, and said sweetly, "Where is the blat?"

Tall and strikingly handsome, Monty cut quite a figure but for one imperfection. His black head of hair stood straight up, as if electrified. Cropping his hair would have prevented this effect, but he believed that his hair was one of his most seductive features. The Vessalikovski family had immigrated from Sofia, Bulgaria, to Moscow, where he had attended a technical institute and specialized in hydrology. Monty's father, a shoemaker, treated his son as an avatar, and his mother regarded him as a Soviet hero only one degree below Stalin. At his laboratory job, he strutted about like a commissar, refusing to speak to inferiors and taking credit for work that others performed. In time, his vaingloriousness proved an assassin to his ambitions. His comrades accused him of being an enemy of the people, an accusation not far from the mark, and applauded when he was led off to the train for Solovki. Put in charge of repairing the island's old irrigation canals, he regarded himself as superior to those who had to wield axes and saws and poles. Made a jailer and then an adjutant, because of his willingness to inform, he used his position as assistant to the chief warden to justify wearing his former laboratory uniform and have his way with the women. When his eye fell on Anna, she concluded that she could put his bachelor serpent in her service.

"A quickie," she told him, "is for peasants. When the moment is right, we will have time to indulge ourselves in a proper bed without fear of interruption."

Although Monty reluctantly agreed, his desire and passion grew more insistent. Whatever Anna wanted for herself, he supplied, particularly smoked foods, which figured in her escape plans and which he stole from the official larder. Each "gift" that she received earned Monty a teasing peck on the cheek. Sometimes she would even show him some leg. Envisioning the day of their consummation, he made plans. A fire would be blazing in his log stove. She would slowly undress in front of him, or perhaps he would undress her. It all depended on which would better intensify the moment. He would have on the table next to his bed a bottle of red wine and two glasses. The door, of course, would be safely secured. A candle made from beeswax, not a cheap, smoky taper, would sit at a distance on top of his clothing chest. The light would cast a shadow, creating a romantic mood. Although he had never married, before his exile he had enjoyed numerous lady friends; the camp women he bedded he regarded as *deshovkee*, whores. His one concern was that before he could have his way with Anna, the camp would be evacuated, a process that had begun slowly in the summer, even though prisoners were still arriving daily. He never could understand the logic of the Gulag. But as the evacuation gained momentum, so did his passion. He therefore decided to have Anna as soon as he could. One evening, with everyone gone from the office, he threw her on the tufted couch and, treating her like a camp criminal, possessed her roughly. She knew better than to resist or cry out lest she invite his displeasure, with a consequent loss of privileges: food, firewood, footwear, and fabrics. But she swore to herself that Monty would pay dearly for his thirty seconds of excitement. No one hurt Anna freely; Pyotr had proved that truth.

The next day, she deceitfully told Monty how great had been her pleasure, and she asked him to help bring Gregori back from Anzer Island to work in her section. Imagining nights of bliss, Monty persuaded the chief warden to do as Anna had asked. Gregori's first attempted crossing failed; the winds drove the boat onto the rocks, and he had to wade ashore through the freezing water. It was not until several days later that Anna's bearded son stood before her looking like an old man, with his lined face and bloodshot eyes and gray hair. After Monty left the room, she embraced Gregori and wept, running her fingers gently over every crease in his face.

"At least," she said, "you're still alive."

He kissed his mother's forehead and took her hands in his. "One of the founders of this evil camp said, 'We have to squeeze everything out of a prisoner in the first three months—after that, we don't need him any longer.' You see the result."

"But you proved him wrong," she said kissing his eyes.

"Because of God's goodness."

Anna failed to reply. Although steeped in the Bible since childhood, she was inclined of late to think like Razan and nearly said, "Where was God in the first instance, when they were turning this religious retreat into a ravening death camp?"

At Anna's suggestion, Gregori requested a transfer from the infirmary, where he briefly served under the watchful eyes of doctors and nurses, to the cemetery crew. The dead, his mother had told him, are less inclined to inform. Equally important, winter burials were virtually impossible in the frozen ground. So the crews did little except stack cadavers in pits and pilfer their belongings. It was this fact that inspired Anna to jettison her previous plan for escape and to embrace a new one. Knowing not to trust anyone, not even her son, she kept her ideas to herself. She smiled at the thought that Solovki had led her to a perfect definition of hell: a place of complete and total silence, devoid of the human voice, because words can always be used against one. The famous biblical passage from Mark came to mind: "For what shall it profit a man, if he should gain the whole world and lose his own soul?" And what precisely did informers gain? A morsel of food or a piece of blanket that kept them alive long enough for their jailers to exact a few more hours of labor? In the end, one person would turn in another for an additional bowl of *balanda*, prisoner's soup, called "Dark Eyes" and made of foul-smelling salted fish. Or perhaps the soup that day was "Mary Demchenko," concocted of rotten beets. Or maybe the extra ration was a "pie," a small piece of black moldy bread. Any old scrap would do.

Understandably, the importance of food to a prisoner could not be overvalued, nor the power of bribes; but what Anna quickly learned was that the jailers, especially the criminal ones, valued more than money the telling of fabulous tales. At Solovki and the other so-called special purpose camps, storytelling had saved more prisoners from death than had rubles, which the jailers could steal whenever they chose. A well-fashioned tale, replete with exotic embellishments about faraway lands, peopled by magicians and maidens, silk merchants and emirs, flew their ready imaginations from the prison to the tents of Turkey and the jewels of Jerusalem. Once a prisoner had earned a reputation as a gifted storyteller, instead of his being cursed and beaten as a counterrevolutionary, he could expect a hot biscuit.

Since her arrival, Anna had heard that the old Solovki Theatre, disbanded in 1929, had once occupied the vestry of the Assumption Cathedral, and that the space was currently the province of criminals and non-politicals who used it for storytelling. One evening on her way back from work, as she crunched her way through the snow and sea-scented air, she detoured into the vestry. A man was just finishing a ghoulish tale. She paused, not intending to stay.

"Having agreed on their plan of escape, the two men lined up the food, asking a third man, a young one, to join them. After traveling through the woods for a day and a half, they made a shelter from tree bows, dug a pit, and lit a small fire. The innocent, new to the camps, had no idea what was in store for him. Apparently, he'd never heard the old rhyme:

Above the 65th anything goes,
Especially torsos, legs, arms, and toes.
Above that cold, bleak, frozen parallel,
Hunger leads to cannibalism and hell.

"The dupe asked when they were going to eat—and what. The other two men looked at each other. Now was the moment. Seizing the dumb ox, they slit his throat and cannibalized him. But they made one mistake. After eating their fill, they cut off the remaining pieces of flesh and stored them in their knapsacks. Caught the next day, the two men had hoped to escape the firing squad, but when human flesh was found in their packs, they were executed on the spot for cannibalism most foul."

The storyteller then asked a man in the audience, named Loktev, to accompany him. A ragged simpleton, who looked disconcertingly like Nicholas II, shuffled forward with an accordion and said, "Be brave, Russian people. God is merciful." Then he pounded out a tune, while the storyteller hoarsely sang,

"Uncle Vania played the squeezebox;
On the squeezebox he liked to play;
Once he played it in No-Man's zone,
And right away they did him slay."

The storyteller repeated his refrain, and the two men returned to their seats.

Instead of applause, the performance was met with silence, as the prisoners reflected on the truth of what they had just heard. Anna interrupted. She rose and asked for permission to tell a story. If she could win over these people, she could escape all the more easily. But no one in the vestry could ever remember a woman storyteller. The pachan in charge, surprised by her daring, said that the theatre was the preserve of the non-politicals, and that she was not welcome. But the women in the audience insisted Anna be heard and ushered her to the modest stage, where she told the following folktale in a resonant voice, enriched by a colorful diction:

In old Calcutta, a haunted princess lay dying in her bed. Each hour, her condition worsened. Her father, a rajah, wearing a crown encrusted with rubies and diamonds and pearls, offered his daughter's hand in marriage to the man who could deliver her from death. Abhay, a young apothecary of humble origins, came to the rajah's fabulous palace, with its Turkish rugs and crystal chandeliers, and volunteered to save the beautiful princess, Ashavari.

"You come from a lower class," said the rajah.

"But I know the herbal secrets of the highest caste."

"Do you not fear death?"

"As much as any man, but from the rumors that I've heard, I think your daughter is suffering the poisonous effects of visitations from an evil source."

"But how would such a person find entry in my house?" asked the rajah. "I keep all the windows and the doors securely locked."

"And the cellar?"

"The crypt can be reached only from inside the palace. It holds the caskets of our noble ancestors and trunks of ancient finery."

The young man begged permission to enter the vault. He made his way with a lantern down the marble stairs. At the bottom lay the acquisitions of several lifetimes. Lifting the lids of eleven leather trunks, he saw garments made from silks and satin, bolts of Egyptian cotton, rolls of pure white linen, and lengths of English lace. "Nothing here," he said, and closed the lids. Then he came upon the caskets, seven, eight, nine of them, all with silver lids. One arrested his attention because of its enormous size, thirty feet around at least. It stood apart, close to a granite stone in the floor fitted with a ring. He raised the casket lid and saw an enormous head, resting on a satin pillow, severed from its rotting body. It spoke to him mysteriously. "We were once brothers in arms. But his ambition drove him to madness. He could find pleasure only in death, so he set his mind on poisoning the world."

"Even Princess Ashavari?" asked the young man.

"Yes, I am her cousin. When she refused to marry me, I joined forces with the murderer, but quickly saw the error of my ways. When I disagreed with him, he stole up behind me with a scimitar and cut off my head. He enters the palace from beneath that granite stone."

From the unquiet head, Abhay learned that the murderer, a dwarf, limped and sported a black mustache that hung to his waist. His hiding place, an ancient sewer, ran from Calcutta to Georgia.

"Each night, when he emerges, he steals to the princess's bedroom and removes from his purse a vial with a toxic dust. Then he reaches his arm round the door and shakes the vial. Ashavari," he said, "is slowly dying from the poisoned air."

Abhay promised to protect her, for he knew about toxins and poisons, both of which he used in his work.

The disembodied head closed its eyes, and Abhay shut the lid. Returning to the rajah's sitting room, he told the sorrowing father that he could cure his daughter by hiding behind her bedroom door, but that he would need a blade sharp enough to split a hair. The rajah objected to a single man entering Ashavari's room but at last agreed and gave him a weapon forged by a famous sword maker in Damascus.

That night, Abhay took up his post and closed his eyes not even once. Exactly at midnight, the door opened. An arm reached into the room, a stunted arm. Abhay raised his scimitar and, just as the arm was about to sprinkle its vile dust, cut it off near the neck. The man howled like a dog and fled, leaving his arm and his vial with its poisons behind. The man's screams awakened the entire palace. Showing no fright, the servants were drawn to the cries, and the rajah, finding his daughter safe, was joyfully speechless.

"If you wish," said Abhay, "I will show you Death," and he held aloft the severed arm with the hand still grasping the vial. "The fiend will not come again, and your daughter will soon recover. I know the antidote for this poisoned dust."

Just as Abhay had predicted, the fiend had forever fled from this innocent house and, when scented summer flowers bloomed and golden bells sounded from the palace belfry, all of Calcutta knew that Abhay and the Princess Ashavari were wed.

So pleased was Comrade Monty Vessalikovski by the applause Anna received—for he had been seated in the back row, keeping an eye on the thieves and pimps and murderers—that he acceded to the criminals' wishes that one of the authors among the remaining prisoners write a comedy to mark the end of their stay in Solovki. Monty, seeing no harm in the request, agreed. What he didn't say was that since his superiors liked to laugh, he could ingratiate himself with Trubetskoi and Ponomarev, and earn a promotion.

"After all," he told Ya Mazarov, the author, "we will be leaving the islands shortly. The least we can do is have a final chuckle. You needn't worry about me looking over your shoulder, though I do expect to be acknowledged as the impresario. One thing: Be sure to make the skit humorous at the expense of the enemies of the people."

Mazarov, an intellectual, a writer, and a director, had in 1917 devoted his professional life to the propaganda brigades: the freight cars reconfigured as miniature theatres that brought didactic plays to the railroad sidings of distant provinces in the service of teaching the unlettered how to behave in a socialist Utopia. He had aged considerably since his confinement at Solovki and was plagued by ugly boils. His crime? He had, by earning the affection of the actors, vexed the unpopular commissar in charge of his brigade. In addition, he had written, without formal permission, a booklet on the most effective ways to bring literacy to adult populations. The apparat regarded the pamphlet as lacking in Bolshevik orthodoxy. Ever since the first days of his exile, first at Kolyma and now at Solovki, resentment had raged in his breast. In light of the proposed evacuation, he decided not to pinch caution. But to protest the inhumanity of the camps proved daunting. How would other writers have reacted? Most, he decided, would have written drivel, though some would have died rather than compromise their dignity by praising the camps and the Politburo. He wanted to bear witness and write words that would tell the truth, not lies. For years, he had been prohibited from writing. Now was his chance, undoubtedly his last. Tovarishch Vessalikovski had selected him to write a skit. But who would perform it? The formal closing of the theatre in 1929 had been accompanied by a night of slaughter, in which the camp guards had shot hundreds of intellectuals and artists, including the few actors still at hand. Ya Mazarov would write his masterpiece, and go out in a blaze of bawdy.

Anna Shtuba found herself involved not because she had anything artistic to contribute but because Monty had commissioned the skit while she was bending over the debit-and-credit columns trying to disguise the many false entries resulting from tufta. He had told her to assist Mazarov in any way that she could. When Monty, full of smiles, had left, Ya Mazarov pulled up a chair and said, "I was present during your recital of the sick princess. You are to be congratulated on your storytelling abilities."

Although pleased to be praised, Anna arched her back and leaned away from Ya, who reeked of stale tobacco.

"I need three people," he said, "prisoners who can fathom a satire and also keep their own counsel. Any recommendations?"

After Ya had left, Anna weighed his needs and saw that although a number of prisoners could meet the first, hardly a soul could meet the second. A few days later, Mazarov, puffing on an evil-smelling, hand-rolled cigarette stuffed with dried seaweed, asked her to type the first draft of his skit.

She read the manuscript that same night and couldn't sleep, troubled by the thought that she was privy to an anti-Soviet parody. If she failed to notify the authorities and, in particular, Monty, she would almost certainly be punished and Vessalikovski shot. As much as she desired the latter, she wanted no part of the former. But how was she to proceed? To tell Monty about the skit would condemn Ya Mazarov, whom she admired for exhibiting the courage to write it. Perhaps the actors would refuse to read it aloud or the authorities would conveniently intervene. Mazarov, she decided, was suicidal, and she would plead that having been ordered by Comrade Vessalikovski to assist Mazarov, she had no choice but to obey.

When Mazarov came to her office for the script and the copies, she asked him to step outside. Throwing a coat over her shoulders, she followed him into the cold. Shouting into the wind, she said, "Why did you write it? You have endangered your life."

"I will tell you," said Mazarov. "We prisoners are like dogs. You can intimidate a dog, to a point. But if the dog has a need to growl, nothing will stop him, not even beatings. The same is true of the Russians. You can cow them into obedience, but eventually they will resist. This is my way of growling. Grrr!"

Anna decided that the night of the performance would start the countdown toward escape. From Monty, she had obtained enough smoked meats to sustain her on a long journey; from Gregori's stripping of the dead, she had collected threadbare jackets and boots, which she unstitched and then reconstructed, fortified with adequate padding. If they ran out of supplies, they would have to use her few savings to buy from the peasants. In the days leading up to the performance, she suffered Monty's repeated sexual assaults to gain additional rations, such as a loaf of bread and a sausage. But with each violation, her pity for Monty eroded. She would be merciless.

When the evening of the performance arrived, Tovarishch Vessalikovski entered the vestry in the company of all the high camp officials, including Commandant Trubetskoi and Chief Warden Ponomarev. Monty wore his finest clothes and, with his boots shining and his chest festooned with tin badges extolling Communist glories, he glowed like a tinseled Christmas tree. Everyone stood as the camp masters took their seats in the first row; then Monty bustled about to see that all the stage props Mazarov had requested were in place.

Coarse candles, made especially for the occasion, lit the room, and the guttering wax exuded an oily smell that reminded Anna of those cheap churchmen who used to sell their good tapers and replace them with cheap ones. The flickering shadows on the wall brought to mind shadow puppets, which she had once seen in a traveling show. At the front of the vestry stood an open ladder with a piece of wood projecting from the top. At the end of it hung a puppet, manned by a zek perched on the ladder. A short distance away stood two empty chairs, facing each other. Monty returned and approvingly looked at the full house.

Mazarov strode down the aisle, positioned himself in front of the audience, and said, "Our skit, commissioned by Comrade Vessalikovski is called "The Truth Puppet." I beg your imaginative indulgence to think of this space"—he gestured to the area behind him—"as the interior of Comrade Stalin's Kremlin office. The doll hanging from the wooden arm we are calling a Truth Puppet."

This was the cue for two criminal zeks to enter and sit in the empty chairs. Each carried a script that Anna, having no carbon paper, had typed from first to last. At once, she realized Mazarov's strategy. By inducing criminals to act in the skit, he had radically reduced the chances of their being shot. The criminal zeks rarely feared official punishment, since they composed the majority of guards, behaved the most ruthlessly, and ran their own government within the camp. Mazarov stood up.

"The two men facing each other are the late, unlamented Yagoda and our Infallible Leader, the bringer of happiness and prosperity. We trust his mustache does him justice. Yagoda cannot see the Truth Puppet because it hangs behind his chair. Now for our skit."

Bowing, Mazarov took a seat in the front row.

STL: You seem worried this evening, my friend. What is it, Genrikh?
YAG: Well, to tell the truth, I am worried about my assistant, Beria.
STL: He isn't ill?
YAG: No, it isn't that. It's about his habits. I hate to say so, but I suspect that Beria simply cannot tell the truth.

(*zek laughter*)

STL: That's not unusual for a secret agent.

(*zek laughter*)

YAG: The trouble is that occasionally I need to know the facts, and I'm never absolutely sure that what Beria says is reliable.

STL: Well, my dear Genrikh, I can set your mind at ease.

YAG: How so?

STL: I believe I have the means, right here.

YAG: What do you mean?

STL: Owing to the latest invention of our great Soviet scientists, I now have an infallible means of telling the truth from a lie.

YAG: Comrade Stalin, I never dreamed that our scientists had made such remarkable strides.

STL: Oh, my dear fellow, in the matter of thought transference, progress has been remarkable. You think the radio is wonderful. Well, our scientists have studied thought waves and have achieved results that will surprise the world.

YAG: I surely would like you to put Beria to the test.

(*cries of delight*)

STL: Nothing easier. Their latest invention is called the Truth Puppet.

YAG: How does it work?

STL: It is so delicately attuned to the waves of human thought that it can instantly detect a lie.

YAG: You mean that this puppet can tell a lie from the truth? (*Yagoda shakes his head in disbelief*) How?

STL: Any lie immediately imparts itself to the delicate mechanism of the puppet, which starts to dance.

YAG: Remarkable.

STL: And the greater the lie, the wilder it dances. It is a Soviet masterpiece. No family should be without one.

YAG: That is the very thing I need. Are you sure it will work?

STL: When a lie is told, the puppet dances.

YAG: Is it currently working?

STL: No, why would I wish to test you?

The puppet dances.

Tell me, Genrikh (*he pulls his chair closer to Yagoda's*), before you kept this appointment, where were you?

YAG: Shopping for a new overcoat. I saw a most gorgeous one, made of camel hair. But I didn't buy it.

The puppet doesn't move.

STL: Strange.

YAG: What's strange?

STL: Why, it's strange that you didn't buy the coat. No money?

YAG: It wasn't that. It's just that when I thought of all the poor people who have so little, I couldn't bring myself to waste money on luxuries.

The puppet doesn't move

STL: (*in an aside, he says*) I knew it wouldn't work. (*to Yagoda*) Meet anyone you know?

YAG: Yes.

STL: Man or woman?

YAG: Vera Brusilova.

STL: Did you have lunch with her?

YAG: Yes, at the Metropol.

The puppet dances.

STL: How very strange. I had Poskrebyshev phone the restaurant, and they told him you hadn't been there.

Yagoda wipes his forehead with a handkerchief.

YAG: That's absurd. The waiter even said it was a nice day for ducks.

The puppet dances more.

STL: Why should he say, "A nice day for ducks"? It isn't raining.

YAG: I don't know. I distinctly remember him saying, "It's a nice day for ducks."

The puppet continues to dance.

STL: It's no use. I know you were not at the Metropol restaurant. Now, where were you?

YAG: To tell you the truth, Supreme Leader. I was at the Stray Dog.

STL: With Vera?

YAG: No.

The puppet dances.

STL: And yet Beria told me that you were, as you originally said, with Vera Brusilova.

YAG: Why, Dear Koba, should you wish to cross-examine me in this way?

STL: Because I know you're lying. Now I want the truth.

YAG: Well, if you must know, I was with Vera.

The puppet stops.

STL: At the Stray Dog?
YAG: Yes.

The puppet dances.

STL: No, you were not.
YAG: Well, I didn't think there was any harm in going to my apartment.
STL: Your apartment. What were you doing there?
YAG: Nothing.

The puppet dances excitedly.

STL: Nothing. You mean to sit there and tell me that you took Vera Brusilova to your apartment and you did nothing?
YAG: We talked about movies and books. I didn't think anything of it.

The puppet dances violently.

STL: So that's the way you act. I work my fingers off for our beloved people,
and you are at your apartment with Vera Brusilova doing nothing. You
expect me to believe that? Well, let me tell you that I know that every
word you've uttered is a lie. Every time you told a lie, the Truth Puppet
danced. It was switched on.
YAG: I think that's an underhanded trick to play on anyone, Supreme
Leader. Anyway, my lies are only little white ones. How about you? I
suppose you always tell the truth.
STL: I never told a lie in my life.

The puppet falls to the ground with a bang.

(great hilarity)

Commandant Trubetskoi, who himself a second before had been con-
vulsed with laughter, rose and stonily ordered his apparatchiks to follow him
out of the vestry. "And that includes you, Comrade Vessalikovski!" But his
departure, with his underlings close behind, did not put an end to the laughter,
not then and not later.

By morning, a rumor had swept through the camp that Mazarov and Vessalikovski would be shot. The commandant was waiting for official approval
from Moscow. Anna knew where the rumor had started: with the teletypist,
who normally kept his own counsel about most of the communications between the camp and the Kremlin. But in matters of death, he almost always
leaked the bad news, either out of hope that the condemned would try to

escape or from a sadistic delight. No one knew which. Perhaps he understood that when the camp was evacuated, he had little chance of leaving alive.

The executions of Monty and Ya took place on a Saturday night. The camp prisoners, standing in the cold and blowing on their stiff hands, watched as guards led the two men to the shooting wall. Here they were told to undress, an act of public humiliation. Strangely, Mazarov was smiling, while Monty showed absolutely no emotion, mechanically removing his clothes. Mazarov removed his jacket and sweater and pants. Standing in his underpants and shirt, he was told to remove his shoes and socks and the rest of his clothes. He slipped off his shoes, socks, and underpants but not his shirt. With his genitals showing and his feet planted in the snow, he suddenly broke into song. But instead of the official paean of praise for the Supreme Leader—

> Today and forever, Oh Stalin be praised
> For the light that the planets and fields emit.
> Thou art the heart of the people, the truth and the faith
> We're thankful to Thee for the sun Thou hast lit!

—he sang:

"Today and forever, Oh Stalin be damned
For the light of learning and freedom you've squelched.
You art the death of the people, the lies and the hate
We've been taught to applaud whenever you've belched."

Caught by surprise, the commanding officer was slow to order the soldiers to take aim and fire. That brief stay of execution gave Mazarov a second to lift his shirt, revealing a sketchy tattoo from his neck to his navel of the head of Stalin. He had obviously asked one of his talented cellmates to ink the face on his torso upon hearing that he'd been sentenced to death.

The soldiers paused. How were they to proceed? Prisoners were shot in the chest and heart, with the commandant applying a bullet to the back of the head for emphasis. To shoot a picture of Stalin, albeit a tattoo, would be heretical. Commandant Trubetskoi was at a loss. He huddled with Chief Warden Ponomarev, while the two condemned men shivered in the Arctic wind. A few minutes later, the commandant announced that Monty would be shot execution-style behind the head, as befitted a military man, and Mazarov would be hanged on the morrow, as befitted an "artiste." As the single shot rang out, Mazarov was ushered back to his cell for a one-day reprieve.

On leaving the killing ground, Anna went straight to her office, where she kept in a filing cabinet not only her food cache but also her vial of strychnine, the one that Gregori took from the infirmary and that she, for a modest bribe, would now smuggle through her criminal friends to Ya. In the morning, the actor appeared to be sleeping. The guards, unable to wake him, called a doctor, who could find no heartbeat or pulse and therefore declared him dead of a cardiac arrest, no doubt brought on by the fear of hanging.

Monty's body, brought to a pit for cold storage until workmen could dig a proper mass grave in which to dispose of the dead, suffered the indignity of Gregori's hands stripping his laboratory uniform and medals, and of the priest's scalpel filleting the Romeo for food to sustain Anna and him during the period of their flight. The idea was Anna's. Revenge, she told herself, takes many forms and pleases different palates, but none would be so gratifying as the moment a hungry person devoured the flesh hacked from Monty's bones.

In the following days, Anna acted quickly. The Russian high command had ordered the evacuation accelerated, fearing that the Finnish Army would over-run the Karelian peninsula. As the prisoners began to dismantle the island's machinery and crate it for storage in the holds of the cargo ships arriving at the island with increasing frequency, Anna exploited the confusion and her clerical position to organize her escape and Gregori's. She typed transit letters on camp stationery, validated them with Monty's official notary stamp, and rifled the money box. She requisitioned pine planks for the construction of three coffins, one of which would hold the yards of stolen camp files. Years later, in Helsinki, it was reported that after the island was abandoned, the Finnish Army had discovered the coffined archives and had shipped them home for deposit in a top-secret government vault.

With the retreat came the grisly business of disinterring the dead. Al-though the graves of religious anchorites and Christian saints were not dis-turbed, the coffins of recently deceased former Soviet officials and spouses were shipped to the mainland. Resting in the cathedral on Poleax Hill, the boxed bodies would, on arrival in Kem, be sent by train to their families for reburial in family plots. The responsibility for this transfer fell to Gregori, whose mortuary duties included Sekirnaya Hill. After Anna had finally re-vealed her plan, Gregori dutifully followed her orders. Using a few of Anna's jewels, he bribed several criminal zeks from his group to open a couple of coffins and dump the bodies into the sea. The men then brought the empty coffins to the camp for transfer to the mainland; but before the transfer took place, Gregori, now dressed in Monty's altered clothes, took up residence in one coffin as Comrade Uspenskii, and Anna in the second coffin as Comrade Savvatii's wife. Their belongings and food supplies accompanied them inside the boxes. Monty's flesh traveled with Gregori, even though the priest had resisted at first. Both coffins were nailed shut, put aboard a cargo ship, sailed to Kem, and loaded on a train for Leningrad, while their fellow prisoners, less lucky, were being transported west to Yagodnoe to work in the gold mines.

The two stowaways had packed chisels to escape their wooden tombs. Once the train was en route, they pried themselves free, retrieved their belongings, and shifted the freight so that their coffins were buried from sight; yes, they used the word "buried" and laughed about it. After Anna packed their knapsacks with clothing, food, and the chisels, she prayed for the train to stop at a small village, where the stationmaster would unlock the doors to the freight cars. They could then make for the woods. At last, their train halted. When the doors to the freight cars slid open, the stationmaster's initial surprise at seeing Gregori and Anna leap from the car was exceeded only by his awe of Gregori, who was wearing Monty's clothes and who ordered the poor man to transfer them to one of the passenger cars. The waiting ticket holders looked at them as interlopers, no better than seat stealers. Prying eyes were always cause for alarm, but at least the train was miles closer to their destination, Petrozavodsk.

"We were assigned to guard this car only so far as . . ." said Gregori, looking around for a sign identifying the name of the town.

Anna saw it first. "Segezha!" She also saw a pile of wooden crates on the railroad siding and several men who she assumed were waiting to load them. She nudged her son.

"Now," Gregori ordered, "load the crates and seal the cars. We will continue our journey by hard coach, though we deserve better."

The stationmaster sputtered, "But, but, all the seats are taken."

"Then put on two more," said Gregori, "in the vestibule of one of the cars. We must get to Petrozavodsk."

Anna smiled. She had never seen her "religious" son so forceful, so authoritarian. Prison had hardened him. Of course, the uniform and medals helped, as did the papers bearing the Solovki seal that he was now waving under the stationmaster's nose. In short order, two folding chairs were produced and placed in a vestibule, where he and his mother were unlikely to be overheard. Once the other passengers realized that they would keep their seats, they visibly relaxed and, as peasants often do, offered to exchange food. Shamelessly, Anna traded her store of human flesh for pirogies, not telling the people why the meat tasted so strangely sweet.

"You are a terrible sinner," Gregori whispered to his mother.

"A means to survive."

"How will you ever be able to stand before the throne of God?"

"How will He ever be able to explain Solovki?"

LET THE INNOCENT ESCAPE

Where to stay in Voronezh presented a problem. Dimitri and Natasha couldn't register with the police for housing, lest they be arrested. If they approached any of the political exiles in the city for space, they would more than likely be disappointed. The exiles lived poorly themselves and were constantly watched. Living quarters in the Soviet paradise depended on one's status. Without enough rooms in the cities, and without the papers that allowed one to stay outside a city's precincts, people were forced to rent unheated cubbyholes, at the mercy of truculent managers, who were often paid informers, always ready to denounce the smallest infraction. So, any rented space was a gamble that might require a quick departure. The brother and sister found two second-floor rooms in a shabby wooden house built in the previous century, when it had exhibited some grandeur. The house was presided over by a drunk, Arkady Zumanski, and his wife, Vera, a practiced virago. The couple received regular police notices alerting them to enemies of the people. Dimitri and Natasha had yet to be listed, a boon that allowed Dimitri to use his papers to identify himself and his sister as members of the secret police engaged in undercover work for the NKVD. After all, wasn't the community overrun with wreckers? That the two police investigators had chosen the Zumanski house from which to conduct their activities came as no surprise to Arkady and Vera. They simply assumed that their good name in the NKVD books had led the authorities to recommend their house for lodging.

Mrs. Zumanskia had a voice coarsened by smoking, and a cough reduced to a wheeze by leathered lungs. She wanted her guests to know that her forebears were aristocrats, with connections to the great Nikolai Gogol. Although she could not quote a single title from the great man's works, she lorded her lineage over her husband, a simple man who took pleasure in drink and refuge in the barn among his prized pigs. Arkady, round as a barrel, with flaring nostrils and pinkish skin, spoke in grunts, as if out of breath. He had a penchant for jokes, though his wife seemed to hate laughter, which she likened to the sound of the "lunatic prisoners" she had more than once seen led through the streets. How, she wondered, perhaps with some truth, could one laugh in this world? To keep an eye on her husband, she made sure that all of her guests knew that they could expect perks—an extra chop, a second glass of vodka—if they caught him misbehaving. His jokes had apparently riled the police, though they had done nothing more than reprimand him. Fearing that she would lose the NKVD's custom, she had warned him that he could be jailed for risible tales. His response to his overbearing wife? A joke! "Why would the police want to arrest me? I'm not a Communist or a Jew."

The first evening in Voronezh, Natasha wanted to hasten to the mental ward to see her husband.

Dimitri asked ironically, "Which one? The more exiles, the more insane asylums. It's simple Soviet arithmetic."

"The one reserved for the commissariat and special cases. At least that's how Alexei described it."

"I suggest we leave the boardinghouse, walk for a few minutes, and return."

"Why?"

"You'll see."

After unlocking the door that opened on the wooden stairs behind the house, they exited the front door, bidding Vera goodbye. She stood on the porch and watched them turn the corner. A few minutes later, they quietly ascended the outdoor steps at the back of the boardinghouse, eased open the door to the second floor, and tiptoed to their respective rooms. Here they waited until, as he had predicted, they heard footsteps. The person paused at Natasha's room but after a second continued to Dimitri's. As the handle turned and the door slowly opened, he steadied his service pistol. In the dim light, he could make out an arm reaching around the door for the wire to the light switch. Wielding the butt of the gun like a hammer, he brought it down on the person's arm. Vera screamed and fell forward against the door and then to the floor. As she writhed in pain, Dimitri turned on the light, nearly causing her to faint from fright.

"What are you looking for?" Dimitri asked angrily.

Cradling her arm, she moaned, "It's . . . it's expected of me."

"I am myself a member of the secret police."

"Yes."

"Didn't I already show you my papers? NKVD."

"But . . . but . . ."

"No buts. I could arrest you and have you sent to a camp. Now leave this room and never again enter it or my comrade's until we have left. Understood?"

"Yes, of course. It's been a mistake . . . I can assure you that I will never . . . you must forgive me. But who will pay for the doctor to set my arm if it's broken?"

Dimitri put a few rubles on the bed. "For your pains. And just remember: Spying is a dangerous business."

When the brother and sister left the house later, they did so in full confidence that Vera would not be rummaging through their rooms. So distraught was she, and in so much pain, that without her husband's knowing it, she raided his vodka chest and poured herself a full glass that she downed in three gulps. That night, when Arkady climbed into bed next to her, she was snoring like a regular sot.

The two Moscow scofflaws easily found the clinic with the help of a friendly trolley conductor. They circled outside, fearful that their names might have already been forwarded to the security detail. Walking around the complex, they noted exits and entrances, including the security guards at the iron gate that opened into the garden, the site of the cottage. Dimitri could see several ways to enter the clinic, but felt that each had its drawbacks. Ideally, he hoped not only to avoid detection but also to have Alexei in tow. If that meant killing Alexei's mistress, so be it. Nothing was too extreme to maintain the integrity of the family.

Riding a trolley car back to the boardinghouse, they whispered.

"You won't forget the stratagems and jargon that I taught you in the truck coming down here? Every secret policeman uses them."

"Don't you remember Galatians?"

At nine years old, she had recited all of it by heart and won the church memory contest.

"We ate well that night to celebrate," he said, recalling with satisfaction the roast pork and salted cucumbers. "You did pack the uniform I gave you?"

"I even had Resonia alter it."

She had also packed old clothes that would fit in with the other poorly dressed people, like those in the trolley, and a few dinner dresses that she could not bear to part with. But had her fastidious brother done his homework and manufactured all the necessary papers?

Taking her hand, he gently said, "Yes, but we must act quickly." He knew that in two days they would have to meet their prearranged driver, who would be moving them north.

The following morning, Natasha entered the clinic dressed in a police uniform that had once belonged to a former NKVD code breaker, a woman, dying of lung cancer, who had gladly bartered it for a pail of potatoes and two loin chops. Dimitri had decided that given the Soviets love of medals, he would pin a few of his own on her chest. At the front desk, she asked the clerk to summon the director. Leonid Basmanaya appeared shortly. She knew the Marxist catechism for questioning prospective criminals. Dimitri had told her to use it on the director. The formula was really quite simple. The presiding officer proceeded on the basis that it is not what the person has done that determines guilt or innocence, but who the person is. The good Marxist interrogator always looked for clues in one's biography. If Basmanaya could be made to sweat, she felt certain of success.

Natasha introduced herself as having come from Moscow to conduct a chistka in the Voronezh area to root out passive party members.

"In this clinic," Basmanaya proudly declared, "you will find only active party loyalists, like myself."

"I'd prefer if we talked in your office."

"Of course."

The clinic director settled into his desk chair, picked up his phone, and told his assistant, "No calls!"

Without being asked, Natasha seated herself on Leonid's leather couch, one of the perquisites of his position. She removed a pad and pencil. "Tell me, Comrade Basmanaya, about your own background."

"I was born in Kharkov and went to school in Kursk."

"Your class, comrade, what class are you from?"

"I first studied epidemiology and then hospital administration."

Folding her arms, Natasha said, "Please, comrade, do not pretend to misunderstand me. From which social class did you come?"

"I've already been cleared. My record is spotless."

"Just answer the question."

Basmanaya looked around, as if hoping to be saved. From a drawer, he removed a tin of mints, offering one to Natasha. She declined. "My father fashioned wooden toys," he said. "Nested dolls were his specialty. He was a master of the art. His work was widely sought."

"By royalty?"

"I can't be sure."

Natasha smiled skeptically. "Hmm, I wonder."

"About what?"

"Your uncertainty."

"His matryoshka dolls went mostly to shops. Did royalty patronize those shops, who can say?"

"Please, comrade, don't toy with me!" She liked her own pun. "The poor can't afford rich playthings. Did you live in a house?"

He knew not to volunteer any information. Speaking to Leshin was one thing; the police another. Silence never betrayed. "Yes."

"Servants?"

"We had a young girl who helped with the chores."

Natasha faithfully copied his words, which might prove useful in freeing Alexei. A nervous Basmanaya wiped the perspiration from his forehead and popped another mint. He could smell his own acrid sweat. "So you had one servant," said Natasha, making a show of noting that fact.

What Leonid said next derailed Natasha's well-planned catechism.

"My mother was dying of tuberculosis and needed help around the house. She had been a teacher. Chemistry. In a secondary school."

"I'm sorry."

"Anything else?"

"I'll be brief. Your wife?"

"Surely you know she manages a state shoe factory. Is it not in your papers?"

"Sometimes our information is dated. Family origin?"

"My grandparents lived in Arkhangelsk. They were furriers and traded with the trappers."

"So they were in a commercial business," she said, making further notes, "which they undoubtedly lost in the Civil War." Before Basmanaya could respond, she asked, "Which side were they on?"

"Initially the Whites, but when they understood the democratic reforms the Bolsheviks wished to introduce, they donated their life savings to the great cause."

"Why didn't you finish medical school?"

Basmanaya smiled, aware that his answer would serve him well.

"The Whites burned down the college."

"The swine! Sorry to hear that."

She would soon have to ask the most important question of all. But she'd wait just a little longer.

"So," she said, "you changed your field of study to medical administration. I assume you attended a state school."

"Yes, it specialized in administration of all sorts. In those days, the country desperately needed managers and directors and engineers to help organize the mighty Soviet projects being launched."

"We still need them. Tell me, comrade, how would you describe your current profession? Yes, I know that you're the clinic director, and I'm aware of all the good work of the clinic . . ."

A surprised Basmanaya blurted, "Even our spy program?"

Natasha paused to absorb what she'd just heard. The clinic was engaged in secret government work. If Alexei was a part of it, she and Dimitri would find extricating him from this place far more difficult than they had imagined, and fraught with far greater danger than would attend the abduction of a civilian physician. With an incurious look, she pretended that she had known all along about the clinic's work. But she still hadn't learned whether Basmanaya could provide the key, literally and figuratively, to the door behind which Alexei was held. Delay was no longer possible. She had to ask now.

"I need to inquire about one of your patients, Alexei von Fresser. His work, I imagine, is proving . . ." She deliberately paused in the hope that Leonid would supply the details. He did.

"Unsatisfactory!" declared the impetuous Basmanaya.

"Just as I expected. At least we can take satisfaction that he's not part of the . . . secret work."

"Absolutely not! The man's a madman. Why do you ask about him?"

"We have unearthed a plot. At the moment, I'm not at liberty to discuss it. You will just have to trust me. His file, please!"

While flipping through the pages she discovered that all the rumors were true. Alexei had distinguished himself as a doctor and then disgraced himself with a patient, one Rissa Binderova. He had chosen to cohabit with her on the grounds of the clinic, and the authorities had, in effect, encouraged this arrangement by housing them in the garden cottage, which was thoroughly bugged. The file even included selected wiretap recordings, most of which Natasha found to be tiresome, though she did pause over the ones bearing on the sexual congress of the two patients.

"Comrade Basmanaya, in light of these files, I wish to see Alexei von Fresser."

"Now . . . here . . . in the office?"

"At once. It is urgent."

Leonid rang through on his phone to the security guards. "Please bring to my office Alexei von Fresser." Pause. "Yes, from the cottage." Pause. "I know I promised, but tell him I won't disturb him again."

Natasha requested that she meet him alone. "If we confront him together, he'll undoubtedly try to divide us and sow distrust."

Basmanaya grinned as he exited, thinking that this young woman had been in the company of government types long enough to know all their trick questions and tactics. Lest he be suspicious, she asked that he leave the door open. When Alexei entered, he peered at Leonid's desk. For a moment, he thought the room empty, failing to see his wife sitting to one side on the couch. She spoke first and in a manner that suggested she was wary of the room being bugged.

"I suggest, Comrade von Fresser, that you choose your words carefully and hear what I have to say."

On seeing his wife, Alexei was initially dumbstruck. He looked around helplessly and then joined her on the couch, but at a distance. She studied his eyes for some hint of his feelings, and he wondered whether she saw the guilt in his face. For safety's sake, she would have to talk in a coded language. From the files, she knew all about his love nest.

"The Moscow office," she said, "would like you to accompany me."

"Why?"

"To right some old wrongs. The NKVD is prepared to give you a second chance. We would have to leave by tomorrow."

He shook his head no and nervously slid his hands up and down his legs, from thighs to ankles. An observer would have thought that he was massaging himself. And perhaps he was, in a way. The guilt he felt made his body feel like a twisted rope; and her presence merely tightened it more.

He studied his feet. "I can't leave my patients."

"From what I understand you have only one."

"She needs me."

"And you, her! We are offering you a chance to start again."

"It would be irresponsible, a violation of my medical training."

"Comrade von Fresser, you are living the life of a parasite." She tapped her pen on her pad. "The state supports you, and what do you give it in return? Can you answer that question?"

"If I save only one person . . ."

"For whose sake: hers, yours, the state? We cannot be selfish about these matters. I urge you to reconsider."

"Ever since I started treating this patient I have been considering what is best for all concerned. The decision has not been an easy one. In the end, the state is very likely to liquidate us both. And yet . . ."

"What if the NKVD generously offers to rehabilitate her as well? That is, she can come with you. What would you say then?"

Alexei found himself stuttering. "Well . . . I'd . . . I'd . . . have to ask her."

Natasha looked around. She had no confidence in the security of Basmana-ya's office. "Can we speak privately outside?"

"Of course, but it's cold."

"I see you came here from your cottage in an overcoat. Wear it!"

He led her to a side door that had a thick window looking out on the winter-blasted garden. For a moment, they stood silently watching the sun disappear. As they stepped outdoors, a small, white cloud appeared in the gray canopy and shone with a suffused phosphorescent luster. It seemed rooted in one spot, even though the wind had picked up. Was it her imagination or did the cloud suddenly fracture and flicker, sending streaks of red and yellow fire in different directions? Natasha and Alexei stared at the sky. Then the glowing cloud vanished; in its place, a large dark cloud moved in from the north, each second growing darker. Natasha put great store in omens and suggested they find a place inside the clinic to talk before the appearance of more celestial signs. Alexei teased her about which sign to credit, the pyrotechnical cloud or the black one. But she knew that this world merely prefigures another, and that God sees the truth, but waits. Since the greenhouse was the safest place in the clinic, he led her there and then to the shed, though with serious misgivings, because it had been the sacred site of Rissa's recent road to recovery. Alexei introduced his wife to Lazar, who was privy, like everyone else, to the doctor's living arrangements. He therefore excused himself, leaving the couple alone.

At first, neither spoke nor moved. Suddenly, Natasha threw her arms around her husband and began to cry. He stood with his hands in his pockets, not for lack of feeling but a surfeit of embarrassment. When she put her mouth to his, he returned her embrace. The moment for both was made fecund with memory. As she swore her love, he could not help but admire her bewitching face, with its lustrous eyes and faultless skin and sensuous lips. She was still a beautiful woman, though her former carefree behavior seemed to have abdicated to weariness. Perhaps in his absence she had become the woman he wanted.

"We can start over again," she whimpered into his ear. Before he could reply, she flooded him with words. "We can go away. Finland. We can have children. An Ivan and an Alexandra. Your namesake." She put her hands on his cheeks, her desperation now palpable. "My dearest, my darling, my sweetest, my husband beyond all compare. I will cook your favorite dishes for you. We will sit by the radio and listen to music. We will play cards and go dancing and take the children to the park. You can teach them to ski. You can have your own study. I won't interrupt you. You'll have your interests, and I'll have mine. I promise never to complain that your nose is buried in a book. If you want to see operas and concerts, you'll hear no complaints from me. I know how much you like chamber music. Go with your friends. I won't protest. You'll be glad to learn what I've been doing. I've been reading about the famous artists. Yelena got me interested. We can go to museums, and I can tell you all about Rembrandt and the other Dutch masters. I like them best. The modern painters leave me kind of cold. What about you?"

But even if he had cared to reply, he had little chance, because she again suffocated him with her caresses and a flood of words. "We can walk hand in hand on the boulevard. Look at the shops. While you enjoy yourself at the bookstalls, I'll try on shoes. Restaurants! Helsinki has good ones; at least that's what mother says. I'm sure you'll be able to work in a hospital. We'll find an apartment. Pick out the furniture and drapes and kitchenware. You can have your own reading chair and a floor lamp that hangs over your shoulder like a tired tulip. You are smiling. 'Tired tulip' is something I read in a magazine. I thought it was cute, don't you?"

While she happily outlined her plans for their future, he grew weary of her sweetness and banal expressions. Her professions of love painfully brought to mind her unimaginative habits, her commonplace interests, her prosaic remarks, "I think it will rain today," and her puerile questions, "How do you suppose Lyubka Grigoryevna can afford a pink parasol on her pension?" And just as dull people form a fraternity, imagination binds people fond of ideas. Alexei had learned that a union of minds was a treasured enjoyment. Natasha would never understand what attracted him to Rissa; it was not her fascinating looks and musical gifts, but her infinite intellectual variety. If only Natasha knew how sick he was of the universal nattering, the fecklessness, the stupidity, and his need for the pure oxygen of inventiveness. Our lives, he wanted to say to Natasha, are too short not to spend them in lively company. And yet, Alexei lacked the will or the insensitivity to visit upon her any additional hurt, and therefore reluctantly agreed to the plan of escape, even if Rissa refused to leave also.

By the time they had left the greenhouse, Natasha had made it clear that Dimitri would come for them the next day and that they should be ready. As Basmanaya approached, the husband and wife formally exchanged parting remarks. Once Alexei was gone, Natasha asked Leonid for Rissa Binderova's file. Like any woman in Natasha's position, she was particularly interested in seeing the photographic record, as well as the written one. What did this woman look like, this siren who had captivated Alexei? She assumed that they would shortly be meeting, but for the moment her vanity made her want to see if Rissa was as comely as she. Basmanaya produced a file with photographs and written reports. Natasha could see at a glance why this woman was worthy of her husband's attention. But of greater interest than Rissa's lovely face was the typed file, which began: "Her grandmother, unnamed, had an affair with Tsarevich Nicholas II in 1886. The affair ended before he was crowned, but the child of that affair was the mother of Rissa Binderova, who may prove to be a useful pawn in our dealings with the west, particularly Great Britain, where the late Tsar still has royal relatives."

Thanking Basmanaya for his "invaluable help," Natasha left the clinic feeling that God had shown her competing omens, with truth triumphant. She couldn't wait to reach the boardinghouse to tell Dimitri what she had learned. The woman they planned to free, Alexei's current paramour, was none other than the granddaughter of Nicholas II's Jewish mistress. A western expression came to mind. She would repeat it as soon as she relayed her news to Dimitri.

"Put that in your pipe and smoke it!" she said, feeling as if she had found the Tsar's grave.

"But I never smoke," Dimitri replied coyly when she repeated the phrase. "You've confused me with the Vozhd," he said, immediately worried that such a comparison could earn him ten years in a camp.

"Isn't that amazing, though: the granddaughter?"

Try as he might, Dimitri couldn't see how this information strengthened their hand.

"Don't you see," she replied, "with your training, you could forge a letter from the British government requesting access . . ."

"You're mad! One trip to the clinic and you return infected with brain fever. Where in the world would I find letterhead stationery and an envelope with the royal seal? I have no such equipment here."

During this conversation, Natasha had been lazing on his bed. She noticed a floor vent that allowed warm air to rise from the first floor to the second. Vera and Arkady's room was just below his. Touching a finger to her lips, she pointed to the vent, which Dimitri inspected. She had good reason to worry. Dimitri quietly crept downstairs and waited in an alcove off the parlor, from which he could overhear anyone using the wall phone. Just when he thought his vigil in vain, Vera passed through the parlor, looked around, and dialed. Dimitri listened.

"Yes, a matter of national security. I told you: two of our boarders." Pause. "Z. Zumanski. This is not the first time we have turned in a report." Pause. "Arkady's my husband. He works in the Department of Sewers." Dimitri came up behind Vera and put a hand over her mouth. With his other hand, he snatched the phone.

"This is Arkady Zumanski. My wife is rather excitable. What she calls national security is nothing more than some unruliness. You know, too much kvas." Pause. "My apologies." Pause. "Of course we know how important your time is. But women . . . you understand. Excitable." Pause. "Thank you, comrade. It won't happen again."

With a sudden jerk, Dimitri pulled the wire out of the wall. He removed his hand from Vera's mouth. Leading her back to her room, he made her sit. She said nothing, too scared to talk. Natasha arrived. Dimitri paced and revised his plans. For a long while, no one spoke. He had originally thought to enter the clinic in the guise of an inspector general with orders to evaluate the premises for cleanliness. But having overheard that Arkady was with the sewer works, he now had a new idea: if possible, approach the clinic from below, and escape the same way. He was waiting for Arkady to return to determine whether Voronezh's network of sewers would work in his favor. One hour passed, and then a second. Dimitri's patience exhausted, he asked Vera where he could find Arkady? Her answer supported his own surmise, the local tavern, "Ivan's Oasis." He removed his service pistol, showed Natasha how to remove the safety, and told her to shoot Vera if she so much as got up from the chair.

"I have to pee!" protested Vera.

Dimitri spied a chamber pot under the bed. "Use this," he said.

"In front of you?"

"I'm leaving. Remember, Natasha, shoot her if necessary."

Ivan's Oasis reminded Dimitri of the Brovensk Inn, which saw more of his father than did his own family. Arkady was slumped over a table at the back of the smoky, dark bar, but still conscious. At an adjoining table, a soldier slowly slipped out of his chair and rolled under the table, asleep. Dimitri brought a bottle of vodka from the bar and stood it on the table in front of Arkady, whose head slowly rose and whose eyes went from dark to light.

"Why aren't you at work?" asked Dimitri.

"Goretski's taking my shift."

As Arkady reached for the bottle, Dimitri stayed his hand. "Not until you explain how the sewer system works. It's a police matter."

"What's to explain? A sewer is a sewer."

"Yes, by any other name it smells the same."

Arkady opened his mouth of decayed teeth and smiled. "I like that. Say it again so I can remember it. The boys will laugh themselves silly over that one."

"First tell me about the system. Where does it run, which ones have walkways, and where are the manhole plates? I want the layout for the whole western part of the city."

"Only a few places have walkways."

He again reached for the bottle, but Dimitri moved it away.

"Draw me a rough map," said Dimitri, removing a small pad and pencil from his breast pocket.

Arkady could see the NKVD seal on the leather cover of the pad and forced himself into a semi-sitting position. He took the pencil and sketched a spiderweb.

"Which of those tunnels services the commissariat clinic?"

Arkady scratched his head with the pencil and then circled a spot on his diagram. "Here," he said and, taking the bottle, poured himself a full shot of vodka, which he tossed back with one gulp, followed by a sigh of satisfaction.

"Where on the grounds of the clinic does this tunnel surface?"

Arkady poured himself another drink. Dimitri's dismay was apparent. He didn't want this sot passing out. "No more 'til we're done."

"The manhole plate's in the garden. But to open it you need a special wrench key."

"Does the tunnel at that point have a walkway?"

"A short one."

"I assume you have a wrench key."

"Why all these questions? Since when do you care about sewers?"

"Only the ones with walkways. Prisoners use them to escape."

Arkady, for the first time, sat upright. "Really? I had no idea." Dimitri could see that Arkady was already scheming. "A person could make some money leading them through the sewers."

The trap was now baited. "Yes," replied Dimitri, "and the police are prepared to pay you to lead these people to us."

"You've got yourself a deal. Starting when? And where do I meet them and take them?"

"I'll handle that." He moved the bottle and took a sip for himself. "Tell me, where do the black marketeers congregate? That would be a good place to make wholesale arrests, which would earn us both a chest full of medals."

"South of town, two kilometers after the brick factory. You'll see what looks like an abandoned church. In the basement, they do business, mostly at night. And behind it, anything on wheels is used to bring in and take out the goods. But you didn't hear it from me."

Dimitri patted him on the shoulder. "Be ready to leave tomorrow morning, at eight, you and I together. Here, keep the bottle and have another drink, but if you're not sober by morning, I'll bring charges against you as a wrecker."

Miraculously, Arkady's inebriation dissipated and he said with clarity, "Only one more drink, and then I'll set out for home."

"Oh, by the way, your wife told me to pass along the message that she would be staying with a friend for the night."

Arkady grunted, "Probably that busybody Marfa Kubin."

As Dimitri hastened back to the boardinghouse, he marveled at how well fear worked as a teaching tool. The two women were sitting just as he had left them. He ordered Vera to grab her coat, take a last pee in the communal lavatory in the hallway, and accompany him.

"Where are we going?" she asked, fearfully eyeing the pistol that Dimitri retrieved from his sister and holstered.

"Just dress warmly."

Taking a trolley to the south end of town, they walked to the once thriving church of Saint Gregory's Holiness. From the outside, the shell of the church looked abandoned. It was not until one started picking his way through the ruins that the muffled sounds of life could be heard under the flooring. In the cellar, Dimitri found stands exhibiting every kind of ware, from cigarettes and perfumes to sugar and petrol. Vera surveyed the scene, her face hardly able to disguise her rapacity. Dimitri led her out the back door of the cellar and into the parking area. After several inquiries, he found a truck driver heading for Kiev. The man was delivering boxes of Cuban cigars, stolen from a military convoy, and picking up metal barrels of cooking oil. He was driving a battered GAZ-AA delivery van, modeled on Ford's Model A truck. For a generous ration of rubles, the man agreed not to let Vera exit his truck until they reached Kiev. To try to make sure that the man would keep his word, Dimitri traded on his NKVD credentials and told him that the woman was being secretly exiled—hence his use of a black marketeer—and that whatever she said would be lies. If Dimitri heard that the woman had not been delivered safely to Kiev, it could well cost the driver his life. To emphasize the seriousness of the matter, Dimitri copied the driver's license number. As Vera climbed into the cab, loudly protesting her innocence and Dimitri's villainy, he shoved money into her lap, enough to silence her until the driver had pulled onto the road and departed. Dimitri grinned as he walked back to the trolley, thinking that he'd done Arkady a great favor.

The next morning, Natasha remained at the boardinghouse while Comrade Zumanski, in rubber overalls, and Dimitri, in dungarees, took a bus to a point near the clinic, where they descended into a sewer. The tunnel exhibited skilled brickwork, including a walkway that ran a short distance along the center channel, which carried sewage to a pumping station and then to a purifying plant. Both men snaked their way to the manhole plate in the garden. While Dimitri stood at the foot of a steel ladder, Arkady climbed it, removed a wrench, opened the latch, and pushed aside the manhole plate. Dimitri flew up the ladder and raced to the cottage. Before he could knock, the door opened and Alexei yanked him inside, handing him a note that read: "I've been expecting you. Don't speak. The cottage is bugged. I told Natasha I would go with you. Rissa refuses to leave."

Dimitri looked around for this person whom he knew only by name. A second later, she materialized. The image that came to Dimitri's mind was of some miraculous goddess rising from the sea or of a Helen launching a thousand ships of Ilium. He found himself breathing deeply to dispel his lightheadedness. Perhaps, after all, he was not doing Alexei a favor. But that wasn't the point. He was here to assist Natasha. And yet, he could not, as before, regard Alexei with hate. In fact, he envied him, except for his imprisonment. Perhaps imprisonment was the wrong word. What could one say about a person who chooses to die for beauty or for love? Such a person was outside the pale, transcended the mundane, defied conventional morality, and justifiably so. For a moment, he wished that he preferred women to men, and that he and Alexei could change places. Rissa extended a hand to Dimitri and whispered, "Tell her to love him as I have." She then hugged Alexei and disappeared.

Alexei took his knapsack and followed Dimitri through the grim garden to the sewer. They both scampered down the manhole. Arkady locked the plate and quickly guided the two men to an abandoned steam tunnel that intersected the sewer and terminated near the river, where the men emerged a few yards away from a neglected shipbuilding dock that dated from Peter the Great.

A skeptical Arkady took Dimitri's money but felt compelled to say, "If anyone questions me, I'll have to say you forced me to do it."

"Agreed."

The three men returned to the boardinghouse. Dimitri intended to reach Natasha first, to warn her not to say a word about Vera. But Alexei immediately embraced her, more from relief than from love.

Arkady toured the house, returned, and said, "You told me Vera went to stay with Marfa Kubin. But she still ain't returned."

"All she said was she'd be spending the night with a friend."

"Strange. I think I'll walk over to Marfa's house. She has no phone," he said, proudly adding, "It takes blat to have one," not realizing that his own had been rendered unusable.

Natasha, Dimitri, and Alexei never saw Arkady again. By trams and buses they made their way to the city limits, where by prior arrangement they waited for a driver to collect them at the sports center. Inside the round and spacious foyer, with its large window facing the street, a caretaker sat on a folding chair, warming his hands in front of a small electric heater.

"Unless you've come for the cross-country ski training, the center is closed. The heat won't get turned on until spring."

"Do you mind if we wait here for our ride?" asked Dimitri, removing his gloves and rubbing his hands. "The man should be along shortly."

"Which way are you going?"

"Moscow," Dimitri said, winking at Alexei and Natasha. They had agreed beforehand to let Dimitri do most, if not all, of the talking.

As the minutes ticked away, the caretaker folded his newspaper and began to study the three strangers whispering in the corner. Even though he couldn't see how well they were dressed, he could tell from Dimitri's greatcoat and Natasha and Dimitri's fur jackets that they were a cut above the average worker. Why, then, didn't they avail themselves of the Moscow train? He hadn't heard of any exiles on the run, though anyone living in Voronezh would not be surprised by such news. In fact, in this city of political prisoners, the citizens were constantly being urged to report any suspicions they harbored owing to dress, an unpatriotic word, a Stalin joke, an unduly large group, and in general anything out of the ordinary. It was this last category that prompted the caretaker to ask a few questions before he decided whether to phone the special police responsible for the registration and surveillance of exiles.

"No buses from here," he said. "How will you get to Moscow?"

"A friend is picking us up," Dimitri replied.

"An official car?"

"A truck."

"The roads are spotted with ice. You military people?"

To end the questioning, Dimitri said, "Contraband. We are tracking black marketeers." He put a finger to his lips, a gesture familiar to all Soviets. "We have a tip. Shh, not a word."

Hoping to distract the caretaker, Alexei asked, "May I have a word with you?" The caretaker shook his head yes. "That black wart you have above your ear needs looking into. If I were you, I'd have it removed and biopsied."

"You a doctor?"

"Yes."

The sister and brother looked at each other incredulously. The police would now know which road the escaped doctor and his companions were taking. Dimitri quickly added, "A doctor of forensics. He studies evidence in criminal cases."

The caretaker looked disappointed. "My mother mentioned the mole. Here I was thinking you were a real doctor."

"Have it checked," repeated Alexei, as Dimitri gently guided him back to the corner.

"Not another word!" Dimitri exhaled through clenched teeth.

The caretaker excused himself, but whether for a telephone or a mirror tormented the escapees. Before the man returned, a truck stopped in front of the center. The group scampered out the door and into the front seat.

"There isn't enough room for everyone in the cab," said the driver, introducing himself as Mikhail Artemev.

"As soon as the center's out of sight," Dimitri replied, "one of us will move to the back. The caretaker was suspicious."

"Isn't everybody in this country?"

Mikhail fitted the role of a truck driver engaged in the business of transporting stolen goods. His short, muscular body, his large, scarred hands, his grim expression would have given any policeman pause before ordering him out of his van. He spoke with a Caucasian accent, having grown up in Ossetia. His devil-be-damned attitude was typical of mountain men, and he seemed to take pride in defying the authorities. "Unless they shoot me," he said, "no law is going to keep me from doing what I please. A prison camp!" he said scornfully, "they sent me to one in Kazakhstan. I was back driving these roads in under six months."

At a stand of beech trees, he idled the truck and reached behind the driver's seat to remove a pillow and a ragged blanket. Although the weather was frigid, one of the men would have to ride in the back. Dimitri volunteered. He untied the tarpaulin and squeezed in between boxes of caviar and vodka. Mikhail apologized for the rough quarters but said he had no objections if Dimitri dipped into the roe. They would spend the night at a boardinghouse deep in a stand of fir trees.

"It caters to truckers. In other words, the people who run it can be trusted. You and your cousin here," said Mikhail, referring to Alexei, "can trade off every hour. I don't want you freezing to death and me having to bury you."

"What if the police stop us?" asked Dimitri.

"They won't!"

From his comment, the escapees deduced that the police were "on the take," and that the boardinghouse was a local safe house for thieves and black marketeers.

By the time the truck passed through K_____, Dimitri and Alexei had frequently exchanged places and were exhausted by the effort to keep warm. Mikhail pulled into a wooded area with a sandy road that led back to an old-style Russian log house with shiplap siding, painted red to imitate a brick surface, and three-paned T-windows. The scrollwork over the windows had obviously been carved by a master, though the colors, yellow and orange, had badly faded. Several trucks were parked in the trees. Mikhail knew one of them and remarked, "Stepan Borschak is a good fellow. He'll have plenty of stories to tell us."

The overseers of the lodge, the Medvedevs, disclaimed any political interests but passionately followed Russian chess. In the sitting room, a cherrywood table held an inlaid chessboard with ivory pieces. The board dated from the eighteenth century and had been passed down through the family, which counted among its members a number of distinguished players, though no grand masters. Behind the table and chessboard stood a ceramic Scandinavian stove that emitted enough heat to make the fireplace superfluous. Four truckers arrived just to take dinner: whitefish, potatoes, and cabbage. Dimitri later observed that the meal, though not gourmet, was filling and the company jolly.

The tradition at the boardinghouse was that after dinner the guests told stories, followed by chess. Stepan Borschak limped from a bullet in his hip. In his late forties, he had fought in the Civil War on the side of the Reds, not for ideological reasons but because the girl he loved was a devoted Bolshevik. When she left him, he turned to womanizing, stealing, drinking, and embellishing stories that he heard on the road. Whatever the original plot, he managed to turn it to his principal interest: betrayal.

Tonight, he regaled his listeners with a tale of infidelity. A strong, young peasant woman married a rich old man, Skortsov, whom she soon cuckolded with a young stable boy. Promising money and property, she induced him to kill her husband. But after the transfer of deeds, he started wooing another woman. One day, the couple was on the same boat as this woman, for an afternoon cruise on the Volga. When the husband started winking at his girlfriend in front of the passengers, his wife went to her, feigned friendliness, embraced her, and threw her into the water. A second later, she followed. Before anyone could come to the rescue, both women had disappeared from sight.

Natasha found the story repellent and asked Alexei to join her upstairs, but he preferred to play chess. In a pout, she ascended the stairs to her room. At the top, she called provocatively to Alexei, "I'll be waiting." Washing herself at the basin, she slipped under the quilt, convinced that Alexei would momentarily join her. But after several minutes of staring at the green walls and white molding, she fell asleep, wearied from the exertions of her journey. She dreamed that the woman who threw her rival into the river made it to shore and, several years later, returned to the estate where she found her young man now married to another buxom blond. When her faithless husband entered the stable to saddle his favorite horse, he found it poisoned. Cradling the head of the animal, he cried copiously. The horse opened its eyes and said, "You forgot all my love and the numerous times that you mounted me." Then the horse died.

The next morning, Natasha found Alexei's side of the bed untouched. He and his knapsack were gone. When she knocked on Dimitri's door, he was already dressed. She ran to him in tears. Dimitri said nothing. He sat with his eyes fixed on the floor.

"You know something about Alexei," she prompted. "Tell me."

At last, Dimitri looked up and forced a smile. He gave her his chair, and he sat on the bed. "Alexei left for Voronezh. One of the truckers who stopped for dinner last night was on his way there. Alexei and I talked, but I couldn't persuade him to stay. He said, 'I don't think we don't love each other, but ours can be only a dull, stale, tired bed.'" She heaved with emotion. Dimitri hugged her as he would a child, and with a finger tenderly removed the tears from her cheek. "As much as I care for you, my dearest Natasha, I really wonder whether you could ever love him as she has."

THE WORST CUT OF ALL

Stalin returned unattended. He apologized with two words for his previous day's retreat and for Razan's confinement: "State security." He sat at his desk and silently pored over some papers.

Although this man looked eerily like the Stalin whom Razan had been barbering for years, he had larger ears and skin craters, more of a paunch, and dyed hair. Where had the man who'd picked up the phone and said "Information!" disappeared? This person walked like Stalin, one moment shuffling and the next striding briskly. He exhibited the same gestures, particularly the way he stroked his mustache. His accent was unmistakably Georgian. And his left hand was likewise curled. Perhaps the other man, to whom Razan felt attached, was a double, and this man was the real Koba. If so, Razan would have to start anew. Fawning mattered most, as well as eye focus, because diverted eyes betokened guilt for a former crime, and staring signified plotting. Razan agonized. If he was mistaken, to compliment the "new" Boss might rile the old. How then could he signal this man that he could see the difference between him and the other without offending either? Or perhaps he should say nothing. But if he pretended not to see any difference, and if this man was truly Iosif V. Dzhugashvili, he might be sowing the whirlwind. Stalin's paranoid eruptions cowed the bravest soldiers, even generals. To negotiate the emotions of the Stalin whom he regularly trimmed and shaved was one matter, but how to handle this one was another.

The Vozhd's attention again migrated to the documents on his desk. A moment later, he looked up. "What were you talking about?"

"Ice fishing and Comrade Gusinski," answered Razan, noting that Stalin had not said, "What were *we* talking about?" He treated the shift in the pronoun as an opportunity to ask, "What happened to Gusinski?"

The Boss pointed to Razan's barbering tools. "Put them back. No haircut today." He fingered his mustache. "Gusinski found it amusing to show up the stupidity of Gentiles. I resented Abram's making jokes at the expense of the people. It's class hatred."

The only way this man could have known about Gusinki's humor and ice fishing was to have lived with him. Or had he spent the previous evening being briefed by the secret police? Razan needed to know absolutely whether this man was the real Vozhd. An innocent life was at stake.

"How long did you remain with him?"

"Long enough to see all the superstitions he followed, with the prayer shawl and head cap and rags he wore under his clothing. I tried to lead him out of his darkness, but he resisted."

"In those days, under the Tsar," said Razan, aware that Stalin could have been familiar with Jewish religious habits, "religion was a form of resistance."

"And yet so many of your people still believe in God."

As if seeking approval for his atheism, Stalin stared at Lenin's portrait, just long enough for Razan to pack up his utensils. With Rubin's carving safely in the bag, he pocketed the real razor.

"What time of year did you stay with him?"

"You are very curious about my youth."

"Because you are the Supreme Leader."

"I lived with him in the fall."

"Do you know the autumn holiday of Sukkoth?" asked Razan.

Stalin lit his pipe, exhaled a blue cloud of sweet-smelling smoke, and answered Razan fiercely. "Know it? I sat with Gusinski in a hut outside his cabin. We ate there for that damned holiday. I haven't thought of the name for years until you just mentioned it. The winter had come early, and the rain was unceasing. But Abram insisted on building a hut for the holiday. I told him he was mad. I said we should stay inside. The weather was filthy . . . just awful, but he insisted on our eating in that ramshackle hut."

Razan felt certain that this man, who knew every particular about Gusinski, was the genuine article.

"Do you still feel the same about Gusinski, now that he's dead?"

"Why would I change?" Stalin replied gruffly.

Razan, taking this statement to mean that all Jews were on the executioner's list, stalled for time by asking about the Houdini film.

"I've shelved it for the time being."

"Is it true that *Old and New* is to be reissued?"

Stalin studied him for a moment, but sensing no ulterior motive on Razan's part, said, "Why don't you join me, and we'll watch it together. Afterward, we can decide how to end our relationship."

Picking up one of his desk phones, he ordered the projectionist, Aleksandr Ganshin, to prepare the movie, and a guard to lay the table in the alcove. "It will take a few minutes. In the meantime, I have a few questions for you. At grave's edge, a man should be candid."

"You can be sure of my sincerity."

"Why didn't you bring your daughters here as I ordered?"

Stalin's pipe was not drawing well. He tamped down the tobacco, removed the stem, and reached for a pipe cleaner.

"You're mistaken, Dear Supreme Leader. I came when I thought I would find you in . . . at night. At first, Yelena had gone off with a friend, and I couldn't find her. But then she returned."

"Did you have any trouble at the Kremlin gate?"

"No. Once they saw the passes, they waved us through. But the office was guarded and locked."

"And yet none of the security men remember seeing you."

"Strange. Natasha and I even lingered, feeling your presence and accomplishments in the building."

Blowing through the pipe stem, he screwed it into the bowl and pointed the unlit pipe at Razan. "You expect me to believe that fawning horseshit?"

To Stalin's astonishment, the barber laughed. "Of course I didn't think you would believe me. But I wanted you to see that I could lie as well as those other functionaries who constantly anoint you with their oil."

Stalin cackled and lit his pipe. "I like that, Razan. You are underneath it all a good fellow. The truth is refreshing, though too much of it can ruin a good appetite. Don't you agree?" Drawing deeply, Stalin talked as smoke issued from his mouth. "So why have you returned, knowing the danger?"

"I hoped to appeal to your well-known compassion and mercy."

The Boss laughed so hard he excited a coughing fit. Reaching for his handkerchief, he asked, "How many years have you worked in the Kremlin? I never knew you had such a wry sense of humor." He paused and his eyes narrowed. "Where is Natasha?"

"She wanted to visit her husband, Alexei, in Voronezh."

"Is that where she's gone?"

"Went. She arrived at the clinic, met her husband, and left shortly after."

Stalin puffed and stared at Razan, who said nothing. "Why would she depart so quickly?"

"She's on her way to Tashkent."

"How do you know, Comrade Shtube? We have tapped your phone and read your mail—and learned nothing. So I repeat: How do you know?"

"A friend brought me the news."

Stalin howled like a wounded animal. "I don't believe you! But in the Lubyanka, they will extract the truth." Then, as if he had not just told the barber that he would be tortured, he jovially pointed to the door and exclaimed, "I want you to meet your replacement."

"As a matter of pride, may I ask: Was it because of my work?"

Stalin shook his head no. "I asked my inner circle. They said your hand is as steady as ever, no burned ears, no nicks with the razor or scissors. But what matters is not who casts the votes but who counts them. It has always been my habit to bring in new people and exile the old. Familiarity breeds betrayal. But just to show you how much I trust your judgment, I am inviting you to observe your replacement. If you find him wanting, I will interview someone else. But don't think that you can keep saying no to stay alive."

Stalin liked to see people grovel and beg for mercy. Razan would not join their ranks. Since Stalin wanted the barber to witness his successor, he would do so with a cheerful demeanor.

"You can watch from my couch. His name is Temuri. Georgian. No more Jews. You and Pauker were enough. Time for one of my own."

A moment later, in response to Stalin's pressing a buzzer, Poskrebyshev admitted two guards and a large, swarthy man with stubby fingers, unlike Razan's long, graceful ones. Without a word, Stalin mounted the barber chair and sat silently while the man pinned a sheet over his torso and wrapped white gauze around the Supreme Leader's neck. Deftly, the new barber shaved his face and singed the ear hairs. To Razan's expert eye, the man had done a commendable job, and Stalin seemed pleased. As the new barber reached for the wet and dry towels, Stalin addressed Temuri for the first time.

"Your family works a small farm in Georgia. Do they ferment the grape juice and skins in a large amphora, a *kvevri*, or in vats?"

"Kvevri. Like our grandparents, we bury them in the soil, with just the necks sticking out. Then we cover them with an oak lid, seal them with clay, and bury them in a mound of dirt."

"And when you dig up the fermented *saperavi* grape wine is it not densely red and cool?"

"Yes, and stains your lips like blood."

Stalin raised one finger to signal Temuri to continue his barbering. The Georgian applied the hot towels to the Boss's face and then dried the skin, filling the craters with a tan talc. Unwinding the gauze and removing the sheet, he departed with them in one hand and his barbering tools in the other.

"Is he your equal?" asked Stalin, smiling at Razan.

But Razan knew better than to praise his own skills at the expense of another, particularly since one could never be sure of what game Stalin was playing. He loved nothing better than to pit people against each other. Razan's silence induced Stalin to speak.

"According to Molotov and Malenkov, he doesn't have your skill, Comrade Shtube. But Temuri is not unskilled. His is by no means the worst cut of all. Besides, I can excuse a little peasant crudeness in one who makes Georgian wine and plays backgammon and who knows the Alazani valley with its orchards of walnut trees and vineyards of saperavi . . . do you understand?"

Of course he understood. The subject wasn't philosophy. Stalin, as he often did, had invoked his memories of Georgia and a bucolic life that he'd idealized. No reasoning on the part of Razan could compete with Stalin's Utopian memories.

"Razan, there's nothing like a countryman, don't you agree? I think you call them 'landsmen.' In fact, you have been one to all my people here in the Kremlin."

Yes, Razan too had fond memories, but for now, if he wished to succeed, he had to think of his next step, not the past. He excused himself and went to the bathroom. When he returned, Stalin said, "Come, let's watch *Old and New*. Nothing puts me in a better mood than a film."

In the outer office, Poskrebyshev took the barber's bag, rustled through it, glanced cursorily at the carving, and closed the lid. With a nod toward Stalin, he put the bag in the closet and turned back to his desk. The Boss placed a hand on Razan's shoulder and marched him down the red-and-blue carpeted hall to the elevator. This time, Stalin's guards followed.

As they entered the cinema, Koba signaled to a soldier in the alcove and ordered, "Pour the barber a cup of tea and flavor it with honey. I'll take mine with jam and the Armenian brandy. Grab the chocolates and don't forget the spoons."

From beside the steaming samovar, the guard dutifully took two *podstakanniki*, silver holders, for the hot tea glasses, handed each man his cup, and extended to Razan an open box of chocolates.

Stalin stroked his mustache and said with obvious satisfaction, "Think of it as your last supper."

"To your health," said Razan raising his cup. He then sipped his tea.

Stalin laughed and signaled the projectionist to roll the film.

For several seconds, the viewing theatre was thrown into darkness. If Razan had anticipated this blackout, he could have acted. But now it was too late. Perhaps at the end of the film he would have another chance. In darkness, he could sow light.

Stalin took his regular armchair and Razan sat slightly behind him, as Koba poured a half teaspoon of the Armenian brandy into the tea, stirred it, and said, "Sit next to me. You know I don't like anyone at my back."

"I was just trying to position myself to see the film as you do, from the same perspective."

During the film credits, Razan wondered, as he had so many times before, about the shifts in mood and personality attributed to Stalin. One minute, he was said to be all gentleness, the next, fierce as a tiger. For the first time, Razan fully realized the degree of acting required of Stalin's doubles. The barber closed his eyes and briefly imagined that the impersonators had been trained by no other than the brilliant Yiddish actor and director of the Moscow State Jewish Theatre, Solomon Mikhoels. Razan's mind drifted to the night that he had seen Mikhoels in his most famous role, King Lear. Virtually every Jewish Muscovite bragged about that performance, whether or not they had seen it. If Solomon *had* trained Stalin's shadows . . . the idea was absurd . . . such improbabilities rarely occurred . . . but if it were true, perhaps the death of Stalin would free the doubles to exhibit the same humanitarian values as Mikhoels. Did not the actor believe in Lenin's idea of encouraging nationalities to pursue their own cultures under the umbrella of the Soviet state? How better to guarantee a flourishing Russian community of artists?

To settle his nerves, Razan requested more tea. When he tried to take another chair, one nearer the door, Stalin ordered him back to his previous one. The screen flashed montages of ignorant peasants blind to mechanization and progress, dark to the mud and the flies. Always the flies.

"Did you know," said Stalin, "I didn't meet Eisenstein until he was making this film. It was originally called 'The General Line.' I suggested he call it 'The Old and the New,' and contrast poverty and abundance. Tell how the latter had resulted from land reforms. Then I told him to sweeten the ending. After all, you have to leave the people with more than flies and shit. They want to see love."

"A Jewish proverb says that truth matters more than love."

Stalin placed his hand on Razan's. The barber thought that this gesture was a preamble to the Vozhd lecturing him. But Stalin ignored the proverb and talked about the film, which mattered to him dearly.

"In the first cut, Eisenstein sentimentalized suffering. I said, 'Sergei, given what we have done in our times—the resettlement of the bloodsucking kulaks, the class warfare, the constant unmasking of enemies of the people—show the world the face of our enemy, but through the pathos of ecstasy.'"

On the screen, Razan watched as the opening scene unfolded: springtime. The peasants are tending their fields and engaging in their usual pursuits. The heroine enters, Marfa Lapkina.

"She's not a professional actress," said Stalin. "Eisenstein auditioned a great many women for the part but finally settled on an amateur. In the movie, he used her real name."

"She's quite attractive."

"One day, she stopped coming to the set. Some old women had told her that the film cameras were like X-ray machines: that they could see right through her clothing. She was devoutly conservative and insisted that the only person who would ever see her naked was her husband. Not until Sergei proved to her that the cameras did not show her undressed would she return."

"Since you mention appearance, permit me to ask why all the fuss a few years ago about Yelena's painting and the photographs made from it?" Stalin stared at him balefully. Razan pretended levity. "Come now, Boss, all condemned men deserve to have at least one of their questions answered. Besides, it's probably my last."

Baring his bad teeth, Stalin smiled coldly. "But in this case, for reasons of security, I can say only that she painted the wrong man, and that the people might have formed erroneous impressions about the face of their Vozhd. You can imagine what a problem that would have caused among the superstitious and the unschooled."

Razan boldly hazarded, "Are you saying that she based her painting on a photograph of a decoy?"

"I hate disingenuousness, Razan, though you Jews are famous for it. The people should always have before them the face of the real Stalin, not the mustache of an impersonator." He sipped his tea and brandy. "There, I've told you! By the way, Dimitri should never have talked to Serjee. The poor man took fright and poisoned himself." Stalin reached for the brandy and, ignoring the spoon, poured a hefty draft into the tea. "If you are wondering why we let Dimitri live, it's because he was useful to us as a *domestic* spy."

"Is that how you learned about Yelena's painting?"

"Razan, think! Every buyer was a potential denouncer. And when the state offers rewards, we always have more than enough takers."

"In that case, your denouncers have been duped. The original painting celebrates the mustache, as you said, of an impersonator."

"If you wish to provoke me, you are too late." He sipped. "What concerned me equally was that your wife was behaving like a nepman and a purveyor of religious relics. She sold the paintings on the pretext that they were the equal of icons. You know I condemn religion; relics are what remain behind of the *dead*. I rather be adored in life than in death."

Stalin pressed a button on the arm of his chair that told the projectionist to increase the background sound. The barber smiled; the louder the sound the less chance of Stalin being heard. The Supreme Leader reinforced his tea with brandy, and turned to Razan.

"You seem lost in thought."

"I was told that when you changed your mind about collectives and decided to force them on farmers, Eisenstein had to alter his film. Do you ever regret your decision?"

Stalin answered brusquely. "Not about the farmers or the film!"

Given his danger, Razan chose to follow Anna's advice and shower Koba with flattery, his requisite oxygen. "I meant no insult. Quite the reverse. I think your decision has proved prophetic." He would have continued with the encomia, but he suddenly felt ill. His head swam, and his stomach screamed with pain. An instant later, he guessed the tea had been laced with poison, a favorite Soviet form of death. If Razan hoped to achieve what he had set out to do, he would have to act now, before he died or was paralyzed.

"It has," Stalin continued, "made possible the advances in our country and its modernization. One day, people will look back and say, 'The Vozhd had it right. Individual ownership promotes greed. Cooperation is the necessary first step to a perfect society.'"

Stalin relaxed and shifted his position. Now fully facing the screen, he pointed and began commenting on the forthcoming scene, in which, a state agricultural officer addresses a village meeting and urges the peasants to form a collective. So intent was Stalin on prefiguring this scene and succeeding ones, he forgot that the projectionist would have to change reels. With the theatre plunged into darkness, Stalin continued to describe the coming events and failed to see the ones nearest at hand. As Razan reached for his razor, the fire in his gut exploded and his tongue bulged like an inflated toad. All he could think of was how to assuage the burning coals in his belly. Then came a shortness of breath that he couldn't relieve even with quick inhalations. He wished for a blast of cold air to sweep clean his intestines. If he could have reached down his throat and pulled the slimy snakes out through his mouth, he would have done so—anything to stop the burning. At that moment, he knew for sure that he had been poisoned and would shortly die.

Stalin never once glanced at him, nor did the soldier who had poured his tea and honey, the very person who had obviously poisoned him on orders from the death lover. Razan's hands swelled and a fever quickly engulfed his face. In a few seconds, he felt so hot that he wanted to tear off his skin and wished for an ice bath to cool the oven in his forehead and cheeks. His gums bled; his eyes oozed; his nose ran; his saliva felt like lava. He couldn't move his tongue; it felt paralyzed and inflated by pus. He squeezed it, but no infection issued forth. Convinced he would die in the next few moments, he willed himself to remove the razor from his pocket. But he couldn't control his hand because he'd suddenly been struck with chills. His body shivered and teeth clicked. With his left hand, he tried to stop the palsy of his right hand. What use was his razor now? His bowel screamed that it needed evacuation; otherwise he would defecate in his trousers. His sphincter muscle seemed to have quit working. He could feel diarrhea seeping out of his anus and staining his pants. If he could, he had to escape the cinema; but he refused to leave until he had completed his mission.

When he felt the awful need to vomit, he clenched his teeth, rose unsteadily, and slipped in behind the Vozhd. With all his remaining strength, he steadied his shaking hand, swiftly jerked the Vozhd's chin up and back, and drew the razor across Stalin's throat, jaggedly slicing through the bony trachea and the esophagus, and cutting both carotid arteries and the jugular vein. To force the bleeding wound closed and to make it look as if Koba had dozed off, he shoved Stalin's head downward and pulled up his collar. Before the projectionist relit the screen with the next parts of the film, Razan staggered out the door and, fully expecting the guards to give chase, fled not outdoors, but indoors, into an office closed for the evening, Ivan Fursei's, one of the few with a private lavatory. He dropped his soiled pants, and, while defecating into a white porcelain toilet, puked on the floor. To expel the bane of the poisoner, he forced his fingers down his throat, gagged and vomited repeatedly, until a river of green slime seemed to issue from every orifice.

Minutes passed. Where were the guards? Why hadn't he heard the tramp of boots and alarms? Surely, the security officials, after failing to locate him on the Kremlin grounds, would be checking the offices. But no one entered. When he felt strong enough to wobble down the hall, he stood, bent at the waist like all the subservient janitors glad to have a plum job in the Kremlin, and made for the west wing—the royal apartments—where he threw up again and secreted himself in a cedar-lined armoire. His original plan had been to remain in the palace until Koba's Myrmidons had left, and then exit the building by one of the tunnels that ran under the palace to the other side of the river, an escape route that the Tsar's courtiers used after their assignations in the royal suites.

Before crawling into the armoire, he noticed a faded fresco: Christ raising Lazarus. Two days later, when he awoke from a comalike sleep tortured by the garish dreams that visit the ill, he barely found the strength to climb out of the wardrobe and stand. It was dark outside, night. Ravenously hungry, he knew of only one place to find nourishment—in the cinema. Even if he had to gorge on candies, sugar was better than nothing.

In his lightheaded state, he shuffled to the cinema, wondering about the absence of bells tolling for the dead Vozhd and about the palace's empty halls. Perhaps at this moment, a government funeral was taking place in Red Square with all the Kremlin officials attending. Outside the cinema, he sunk to his knees from weakness. In this position, he saw no light under the door and pressed his ear to the space. A second later, he heard the humming sound of a projector—or was it a buzzing in his head? Persuaded that Stalin's funeral was in process, he wondered who would dare at this moment to watch a film. If the projectionist, Aleksandr Ganshin, was in Red Square for the speeches, who was running the camera?

Hand over hand, Razan climbed the steps to the projection room and quietly entered. Ganshin, to Razan's shock, was staring out the glass window at the screen and chuckling. The barber crept in behind the large projector and sat on the floor. Ganshin would have found it difficult to spot him because he was wedged up against the wall between the camera and a stack of reels. From this position, Razan could barely hear the soundtrack. Although curious to know who was sitting in the theatre, he'd have to wait until the film ended and Ganshin, who liked to snack, left the booth. Was it a mirage or did Razan actually see a cup resting on a chair, and an uneaten biscuit? Bewildered, he kept coming back to the question: What functionary would be watching a film during Stalin's funeral? It would take a brave person—of any rank or relationship—to be in the cinema now. Unless . . . unless Stalin had been buried the day before and Ganshin was now showing footage of the event. But if so, why was he chuckling? Perhaps, in the safety of the booth, he felt free to laugh about the man who had made his life a misery, not just owing to Koba's whims, but also to Svetlana's, she who famously made demands upon her father, particularly in the matter of his arranging with the jovial Aleksandr Ganshin to show whatever movies struck her fancy.

In his cramped, airless position, he began to feel nauseous. He would have to stand, even if it meant risking his safety. Rising on wobbly legs and steadying himself with one hand against the wall, he could glimpse the screen, but not the audience. Tarzan was swinging from a vine through the jungle and bellowing for Jane. A favorite of Stalin's, Tarzan made the Supreme Leader think that through force of personality, strength, and the right words—the knowledge of how to speak to the unruly and illiterate peasants—he could gain majesty over Russia, just as Tarzan had become king of the jungle.

Suddenly, Razan remembered his neighbor's comment about cinemato-cracy: that Stalin seemed to find more political wisdom in Tarzan, dressed in a loin cloth, thumping his chest, and summoning the forest animals with his cries, than in the ideas of Marx and Lenin. But when the old theories failed, as they so often did, Stalin tinkered with them instead of reaching for new and better ideas. Originality and inventiveness meant taking chances, perhaps even temporarily loosening his grip on the reins of power. He had, in short, no blueprint to overhaul the country, one that would enable him to change in midcourse in the face of disaster. It was not that he lacked disci-pline; he was an efficient killing machine. Each day, he composed lists of the condemned, only occasionally granting a petitioner a reprieve for his or her abject abasement. His taste for blood was insatiable, but not owing to the logic of revenge, though he could spout Marxist doctrine on that subject for hours. The reservoir of his life was fed by the springs of personal bitterness and impotent religious hatred. He could suppress the Orthodox Church and all the other faiths in which people put their trust, but he could not extirpate them from the human heart. The thrall of other theologies, inculcated long before he came to power, had forged stronger chains than his hatred for seminaries and prying priests.

When Stalin asked himself the question that he knew others around the world were asking—to what end are you sacrificing family, friends, relatives, neighbors, the goodwill of nations, your health, your sanity?—he always had the same answer: the welfare of the proletariat. And yet, when his beloved people acted as individuals, aspiring to a better life, he suppressed them with accusations about conspirators, wreckers, spies, saboteurs, and anarchists. In the most corrupted moral terms—equating goodness and stability, justice and denouncements—he promulgated draconian decrees, spouted bromides about the happy country, and promised that paradise lay just around the corner. But millions, though not all, could see through the slogans and the Communist jargon to the poverty of thought below.

At the conclusion of the film, Ganshin took his cup and went downstairs. Razan ate the biscuit and watched, as the minister of culture poured himself tea with a splash of brandy and reached for a chocolate. Letting his gaze roam over the audience, Razan could see who was present: Zhdanov, Kaganovich, Molotov, Mikoyan, Khrushchev, Beria, Malenkov, and . . . he rubbed his bloody eyes certain they were wrong. What he thought he saw was a robust, chuckling Iosif Vissarionovich Dzhugashvili. Although he could make out only the back of the man, he knew the contours of the head, the gestures, the voice, the laugh, the uniform, and the authority he exuded. Admittedly, the man he had barbered for years had mastered the same characteristics, but

Razan felt certain he'd killed the real Vozhd. Why, then, did he not hear the Kremlin bells, sirens, alarms, and a call for a day, a week, a month of national mourning? If Razan had identified the man below correctly, the man who had ruled Russia since 1929, then the Court of the Red Tsar had closed ranks and decided that in light of the numerous threats the country faced, Koba's death would have to be kept from the people and treated as a state secret, in which case a decoy would serve as a figurehead, and the country would be ruled by a Troika: Khrushchev, Malenkov, and either Molotov or Beria. No, Razan must be hallucinating. Such a decision would be more brazen than the shooting of Tsar Nicholas Alexandrovich Romanov, the Empress Alexandra Feodorovna, and the children. Besides, if the real Stalin were dead, why were the men below so serene? Did their smiles reflect their delight that the barber had slit Koba's throat? Beria was standing in front of his colleagues, his palm outstretched, as if imploring them. Razan turned on the speaker in the projection booth and listened.

"If I may be so bold, Supreme Leader, I advise that we say nothing of this security breach and immediately elevate another decoy, one who will be as current as the former, right down to watching your favorite films and reading history." Beria nodded toward Stalin, a clear invitation to respond.

"Comrades," said Stalin, turning to the others and partially revealing his profile, "I want all the traitors connected with this heinous plot exterminated. Now you see that what I have been saying about our being everywhere besieged by enemies is true. Our beloved Russia is assailed on all sides by vipers who would have us believe that one party member is as good—or as bad—as any other. But the government is not a stock market or the law of the jungle. Just as Tarzan rules his domain, the Politburo is the holy of holies of the working class. It must not therefore be confused with a stock market, in which you bet on one group or another. As Leninists, our mutual relations must be built on trust, and must be as clean and pure as crystal. These words I have read a thousand times in Lenin's writing. There should be no room in our ranks for conspiracy and intrigue; no room for factionalism. Lest the people hear of this outrage and lose confidence in our leadership, let us, as Comrade Beria advises, conduct ourselves as before. Until one of the remaining doubles can be fully trained, I shall remain out of sight."

Stalin's apparatchiks congratulated him heartily.

For all that this man had said, for all that he had spoken like Stalin, Razan still believed that he had killed the real Vozhd, and that the apparatchiks around him were now playacting. But to what end? For his own mental health, he reasoned that the man who had just spoken to his henchmen was a decoy. If only

Razan could explain the charade, he might be able to stop shaking. Had he put too much trust in Koba's remembering the Gusinski episode? Decoys, as he had feared, could always be taught the smallest details. Razan had even heard that some people could read a book once and remember every word in it. What if Stalin's doubles had such photographic memories? No, Stalin was dead!

A hunched man, prematurely aged and wrinkled by illness, left the Kremlin through the courtiers' tunnel and emerged on the other side of the river. Unable to walk any distance, he hailed a taxi and fell into the backseat, but not before stuffing a handful of rubles into the cabby's hand. Through the rearview mirror, the driver could see that Razan was near death.

"I know an unlicensed doctor," said the cabby, "a Jew struck from the official list for some religious reason. If you have no objections, I can take you to him."

Razan shook his head yes.

The doctor's office was a wretched train car in a fetid alley, behind a block of apartments. Razan waited while the cabby knocked on the door. A slightly stooped man, with a white mane of hair and binocular glasses, led them inside. The car was divided by curtains into three parts: for living, eating, and working. The privy stood outside, in a shed. "I've been poisoned," said Razan. With one glance, Dr. Shapira agreed. Asking no questions, he helped Razan to a cot and went right to work, administering a combination of medicinal and herbal purges. A bucket stood at the ready. Within minutes, Razan started to vomit. After the last two days, he thought that he had nothing more to disgorge. But he discharged the same hateful green bilious liquid. The doctor forced him to drink some bitter red fluid, followed by several glasses of near-boiling water. A sedative put Razan to sleep for several hours.

When he awoke, he could hear Dr. Shapira behind the curtain talking to another patient about an infected sore. Razan deduced from the advice the doctor dispensed that he was a capable physician. When Razan had a chance to observe the man's appearance and dress, he saw that Dr. Shapira had full lips, a prominent gold tooth, and cheeks marked by deep ravines. His watery blue eyes radiated sadness, as if they had resided for too long in the house of suffering. Although the physician looked older, his taut, smooth neck muscles, suggested he was no more than fifty. His hands moved with the practiced skill of a pianist's, as he raised Razan's eyelids, felt his stomach, tapped on his chest, and tested the nerves in his extremities.

"You'll live," said Dr. Shapira, "but not as before. You'll never sit down to a full meal again. I have no doubt your stomach is scarred, which will mean eating small portions several times a day."

Rocking back and forth, Razan resembled the flickering candle that Jewish supplicants imitate. His persistent hope, of course, was that the candle remained lit. Before he died, he felt compelled to tell his family what he had witnessed. Thanking the doctor for his help, Razan asked him about his own situation.

"It's really quite simple. I used to have a thriving practice in Moscow among Jews and Gentiles alike. But when the Soviets found out that I was an observant Jew, they put me on the forbidden list and told all my patients to find a different physician or suffer official displeasure. What does 'official displeasure' mean? Loss of job, apartment, passport, ration card? You tell me."

Razan had been around Poskrebyshev and the apparatchiks long enough to know that the phrase meant lackeys flourished and that the independent-minded suffered. Talent and skills had no value in a society that used conformity to grease the wheels of comity.

"You are not strong enough to travel," said the doctor. "In the apartment house across the alley, a Mrs. Tubina will look after you for a few rubles. She'll even wash those stained pants of yours."

"How long before I can travel?"

"At least a week, maybe two."

Handing the doctor more rubles than Dr. Shapira requested, Razan asked him to make the arrangements. The doctor returned shortly.

"Everything's set. You can decide the rent between you. She has a generous soul. Very religious. Orthodox. Also very nationalistic. Watch what you say, and you'll be perfectly safe."

Razan leaned on Dr. Shapira as they made their way across the alley, into the building, and up the stairs to the third floor. The elevator had stopped working years before, and no one knew whom to call to have it repaired. The small apartment held all her possessions and those of her children, now living in far-flung oblasts. The sitting room, with its sofa bed, had barely an inch of space on the walls, which were covered with numerous icons, candle braces, framed family photographs, plates, a clock, a calendar, two pictures of Nicholas II and his family, and one picture of Patriarch Tikhon. A shelf underneath supported a small oil lamp flickering in its gold chimney. Ragged rugs and runners barely covered the splintered floors. The mohair red-and-green furniture, replete with doilies, pillows, and dolls, had become unsprung years before. The side tables and windowsills held statues, plants, a Victrola, chipped cups and saucers, dirty ashtrays, a punch bowl filled to overflowing with old letters, wax flowers, a music box, lamps, several pairs of old spectacles, an antique slide viewer, magazines, a small radio, and ceramic figurines of everything from dwarves to dervishes.

Razan took up residence on the sofa bed, and Mrs. Tubina handed him a linen sleeping suit, pleated in front, to wear while she washed his clothes. A chain smoker, she offered him a cigarette. He declined and asked if she had any stationery. To his surprise, she produced good quality paper, currently hard to find, a small writing board, and a turquoise Sheaffer pen with a fine golden nib. He thanked her, leaned against several pillows, positioned the board on his crossed legs, wrote three words—"My Dearest Yelena"—and then paused. Not having written a proper letter in at least six or seven years, not since he and Rubin, for no apparent reason, had quit corresponding, he now realized that writing, like barbering, was a skill, and that without practice, one loses the knack. He closed the pen. Hours later, he finished it, well aware that letters leaving Moscow were often opened and read.

After leaving you and our good friend, I returned to Moscow and my job. Although, as you know, relations between my boss and me were somewhat strained, on my return he greeted me warmly and even invited me to join him to watch a Tarzan film from his private collection. You and my boss have at least one thing in common: You both love Tarzan. Before the film started, he kindly gave me tea and honey and chocolate. Such a generous man! At the end of the film, we mutually agreed it was probably time for him to find someone else to fill my position because I want to spend more time with my family.

I would have joined you already but unfortunately I took sick and am now staying with a friend, an old person who lives in a cluttered house. Among the clutter is a music box you would love. When you open the pink lid, which is inlaid with mother-of-pearl, it plays familiar passages from Glinka's Ruslan and Liudmila. Whenever I hear the music, I think of evildoers meeting their just ends. Just such a man, notorious for his cruelty, had been living in the city and was recently murdered. I happened to witness the terrible scene. Someone came up behind him with a knife and then suddenly, the man was lying on the ground bleeding. I expected to find this violent crime reported in the newspapers, but the next day and the following, I looked and found nothing. I now begin to wonder if maybe my illness prevented me from seeing clearly, or maybe I just had a nightmare. You know how the Russian people put great store in dreams. If it was a dream, I hope I have since awakened and am not sleeping now. Because if I am still asleep, then I am not actually writing you a letter. I am only imagining it.

Isn't that idea amusing? Tomorrow, what shall I think of today? That I did not write the letter or that I did? It matters to me because I so want you to know about me and to know I will be coming home soon, even if I have to walk the whole way. How awful it must be for people who don't know whether they have done or said one thing or another. Even worse is when you know, and others deny it or misrepresent your deeds and words or completely ascribe to you things you never did. But in this great country of ours, that kind of deception could never happen. Our Vozhd loves us and provides protection against the wiles of this world.

I must rest now. My head is hurting. As I said: I can't even be sure I am writing to you. To persuade myself I'm awake, I press the pen to my forehead and run my hand along the edge of the stationery, which has cut my finger and caused it to bleed. To prove what I say, I will sign this letter with a bloody thumbprint.

Love,
Your father.

Razan waited two days before asking Mrs. Tubina to check the letter for spelling and mail it. She faithfully went to the tobacconist's stand, bought a stamped envelope, enclosed and sealed the letter, and put it in the postbox.

When she returned to the apartment, she insisted on telling him a story that corresponded to his own uncertainty about dreams and reality. The owner of a large estate behaved cruelly to all his help. Two young stable boys, recently whipped for some infraction, swore revenge. They dug a large pit in the woods that could easily hold the body of a large man. One of the boys then went to the master and said he had found a large hole, and asked the master to follow him to determine its function. The other boy hid and lay in wait for his chance.

Suspecting nothing, the owner accompanied the first boy to the edge of the woods, saw the hole, scratched his head, and said he had no idea how it got there or its purpose. The boy brazenly said, "It belongs to you. Like everything else around here, it's part of your estate." The owner scoffed, "I don't need it," and the boy replied, "But, sir, of course you do." By now impatient, the owner said the lad was talking nonsense, and it was time to return home. "What I am saying, sir, is that this hole has been dug for your grave." The owner unfastened his belt to thrash him, but the other boy leaped from the woods with a knife and stabbed the owner. Before shoving his body into the hole, they decapitated him, as a sign of their hatred.

They buried his head in a separate hole, a small one, which they dug that same night in the courtyard. But every morning when the two boys arose, they found the head aboveground, not below, and no matter how deep they buried it in the courtyard, the next day it appeared on the surface, undecayed and bearing a smiling countenance, as though it had enjoyed every second of its hateful life and end. The boys decided to bury the head in the woods, but in the morning, as before, it appeared in the courtyard. They buried it miles away, and the same thing happened. They threw it in a river, they packaged it and mailed it to Sweden, they paid a man on his way to the Baltics to drop it in the sea, but always the head returned to the courtyard, whether a day later, a week, or a month. The boys could not destroy it. Eventually, the young boys went mad and had to be hospitalized.

So ended Mrs. Tubina's tale.

"What is the moral of this grisly story?" asked Razan.

"Only the Lord has the power to give and take life, and those who usurp the Lord's power are destroyed by madness."

That night, lying on his sofa bed, Razan smelled the unpleasant odor of stale tobacco. Dead cigarettes. One of Mrs. Tubina's overflowing ashtrays lay a few feet away, under a copy of *Pravda*. What the world needed, he thought, was a means to bury dead ideas. He rolled over and patted the pillow, hoping to sleep, but he lay awake thinking of the old woman's tale, and detesting the dreadful odor.

TO THE FINLAND STATION

After a fortnight, Razan's strength began to return. It was time to make his way back to Petrozavodsk. He paid Mrs. Tubina for her sofa bed and her care, embraced her affectionately, thanked the good doctor, shoving into his hand a great many rubles, and taxied to the train station. He had in his wallet the visa that allowed him free passage. As he paid the cab driver, he noticed a group of policemen in front of the terminal; they were stopping travelers and checking papers. Perhaps the NKVD had finally been notified of Stalin's murder. He entered through a side door, where he encountered only one soldier, and casually displayed his transit visa. But lacking a ticket to Petrozavodsk, he could not afford to wait a day or more, until seats became available. As the train for Petrozavodsk prepared to depart, he paced the platform, but all the doors to the passenger cars were closed and locked from the inside. Porters, though, were still loading baggage and crates. One car held horses. He remembered the Ukrainian death trains transporting soldiers and their mounts, and of course, the cattle car that he had taken to Kursk. As a soldier gripped the ring on one side of a Pelham bit and led a horse up the ramp, Razan grabbed the other side of the bit and continued into the cattle car. Before the soldier could question this civilian, Razan removed his transit visa and said, "Equine and livestock inspector. Special detail."

The soldier, either from the shock, or the fear of official-looking papers, secured the horse and backed down the ramp, as the barber pretended to examine the animal's lips, gums, and teeth.

"You know how susceptible to disease they are," said Razan.

The soldier merely nodded and proceeded to bring aboard another horse, which Razan also inspected.

"This one has periodontal problems," said Razan falsely.

"What's that?"

"Gum disease. I'll travel with the animal to Petrozavodsk and see to its care."

"We have an animal tender. He's just down the way in the canteen having a cup of tea."

The barber grabbed several rubles from his pocket and asked the soldier if he would be so kind as to bring him a bottle of cheap vodka when he returned with the tender. If the man was a veterinarian, Razan was in some danger. The tender, a middle-aged peasant, had a high forehead, black hairs growing out of his nostrils, a round face, bloodshot eyes, and a bulbous red nose. As the man approached, Razan could smell the liquor on his breath.

"No one told me that an inspector would be examining the horses," he muttered. "Which office are you with?"

Knowing how Russians loved authority, Razan said, "Agricultural, naturally. And you, where are your credentials, comrade?"

The young soldier was already securing the door of the cattle car. Before the peasant could answer, Razan clapped him on the shoulder and handed him the vodka.

"It will be a long trip. You'll need some refreshments."

"Yes, sir!" said the man, doffing his cap respectfully.

"When that one's empty, we can always find more at other stations along the way."

The man smiled broadly, revealing a dark cave, except for a few teeth in a state of advanced decay. He looked at Razan, blinked his besotted eyes, and gladly accepted the bottle. For the entire trip, the men barely exchanged ten words, as the barber plied his companion with cheap vodka during the journey from Moscow to Petrozavodsk. When the doors slid open and Razan faced a phalanx of soldiers, his first reaction was that he'd been discovered. But since no one immediately stepped forward to clamp him in irons, he boldly strode down the ramp, passed through the wall of soldiers, and melted into the city. What his sleeping companion said when awakened from his drunken stupor can only be guessed, though one can imagine him looking around for the man who had miraculously and unselfishly given him the elixir of life.

The apartment to which Yuri Suzdal and Yelena had moved was in a block of decaying concrete buildings that Yuri disparagingly called "Stalinist Modern." Cracks had already begun to appear in the outside walls, and chips of cement lay on the sidewalk, as if the buildings were slowly shedding their skins. The hinges on the front door stuck. Razan had to shoulder his way into the lobby. The elevator wasn't working, and the filthy hallway smelled of cat piss, kerosene, and fried foods. He walked up two flights of stairs and stopped to catch his breath. The hall lights had burned out, making it difficult to negotiate the maze of corridors.

Suddenly, a door opened and a heavy, gray-haired woman, bent at the waist, as though her spine, like a sapling, had been bowed in a storm and had never recovered, peered through spectacles that rested against a wart on the end of her nose. "Who are you looking for?"

Arthritis, Razan thought, as he replied, "Mr. Suzdal."

"Down the hall," she said, "third door on the left."

He rang. Nothing. He rang again. The peephole in the door slid open and a raspy voice asked, "Yes?"

"It's me, the barber, Razan Shtube."

The person behind the door closed the peephole, and for at least half a minute, Razan waited, hearing nothing, not even a footstep. Then suddenly, the door was flung open, and Yelena threw herself into Razan's arms. He pulled her into the apartment, asking nonstop about their health, safety, warmth, food supplies, clothing, rent, school, and everything else he could think of, including whether they had received any news from Natasha or Anna.

"Nothing," said Yuri, "though I did hear from Dimitri. He calls the corner phone box every Friday at six a.m. I spoke to him today."

"Did he say anything out of the ordinary had occurred?"

"Just that he and Natasha had reached Voronezh and met with Alexei. I gather the meeting was unsatisfactory. Alexei has chosen to remain behind."

"Any other news?"

"Radios all over the country have been out of order. They say it has something to do with the frequency."

Did this mean the Politburo had decided not to reveal the Vozhd's death and let a double behave as if nothing had happened? In the Soviet world, everyone had to march to the same drummer; adversity could never take place, and certainly not the assassination of Stalin.

"Try the radio now."

Yuri obligingly switched it on. A man with a Georgian accent was speaking slowly and softly. He identified himself as "your Vozhd." Razan kneeled and listened closely to the accent and cadences. To interpret Soviet arcana took a good ear, one that could decipher double meanings and intonations.

"Comrades, just as we adore Lenin, we should equally adore the current architects of our socialist society. We should give thanks to the Politburo for steering the country into a triumphant future. I look to the Soviet press to play its part. I look to our authors to write biographies of our brave revolutionaries, extolling past and present exploits. Too many of our people view the government's glorious efforts in a negative light. Instead of celebrating our historic victories, they belittle our constructive achievements. Instead of saluting the Soviet genius of leadership, they carp and conspire. I beg you to treat critics and disbelievers as deliberate maligners set on sabotaging the socialist revolution by blackening the leadership and doing everything possible to make the Politburo fail. Though they wear the mask of loyalty, wreckers and enemies of the people are everywhere trying to undermine our good works. They are in our very midst and at our own breasts. Those who are plotters be warned: I know your identities and will crush your conspiracies."

Although the speech lacked any explanation for why the speaker was giving it—what was the context?—and although Razan wished he had stronger evidence to go on, he felt that he had just heard official confirmation of a major disruption in the Kremlin, either bearing on Stalin or on a new purge. The voice sounded like the man he regularly barbered, but then given the NKVD's technical tricks, who could tell?

Yuri turned off the radio. "What's he been blathering on about?"

Razan said cryptically, "Let us hope that some people die the death they deserved."

Although firing squads daily shot black marketeers, whom the government called capitalists or "parasites," they provided a supply of illegal goods throughout the country. Traveling mostly on back roads and at night, they used any vehicle they could cobble together from used parts or could steal. Of course, some goods were more in demand than others, and thus more risky to transport. Dimitri had schooled his mother on this point, and had told her that she'd be better off waiting a day or two than riding in a truck carrying petrol or heating oil or much-needed military ammunition and hardware. The impending war with Finland made the life of black marketeers all the more precarious and, when they succeeded, all the more profitable. They had no qualms about who bought their contraband; one man's money was as good as the next's.

Reviled in government newspapers, the outlaw capitalists supplied goods that were not on the shelves. Unlike the government, which promised with each new economic plan to meet the needs and satisfy the tastes of its citizens, and failed, the black marketeers smuggled into the country both luxury items and necessities, such as western cigarettes and pharmaceuticals. Those who could afford to buy contraband merchandise ran the risk of discovery. If some envious guest reported that Mrs. So-and-So was serving caviar, the secret police wanted to know where, and from whom, she had purchased it. Smuggled goods, therefore, had to be kept under wraps. Fancy clothes, perfumes, exotic foods, banned books—all of these could lead to the buyer's arrest.

To be on the safe side, Anna and Gregori had left the train at Voznesenye and continued their journey in a black-market truck that stopped at a doss-house. The driver, Maikov, would be going south and said that they could cover the final distance with an old friend, Roman Karkaus, who often made the trip north. Karkaus's vehicle stood in the parking lot. A seedy-looking fellow with half-closed eyes and a wispy mustache, Karkaus drove a Ford Model T welded to a two-wheeled, covered dray. At the moment, it held Russian tea. His destination: Petrozavodsk. Maikov introduced his passengers to Karkaus, whose tongue, owing to his unquenchable thirst for vodka, floated free as a fish.

"I can tell you're escapees," said Karkaus to Anna and Gregori. "I could turn you over to the secret police and earn a reward. But I despise the bastards. The least you can do is buy me a drink!"

"I'll do more than that," Anna replied. She paid his bill.

Before Maikov had driven south, she had shown him a piece of paper and had asked, "Do you know this address? What landmarks should we look for?"

"The road will split. Go to the right toward the lake."

"And the other way?"

"Stay clear of that road. It leads to the political offices and police station."

As she crunched through the snow to Karkaus's vehicle, resembling a hermit crab, she told Gregori what Maikov had said. The motor wheezed and coughed before falling into a regular rhythm. Huddled in the back of the "Russian Ford," loaded with boxes of tea from Georgia and Ceylon, she and Gregori shivered. Even though heavily loaded, the vehicle lacked traction. The two riders leaped out and pushed, freeing the hostage tires from the icy tracks. Once on the road, she murmured, "I don't trust this man, Karkaus. Did you hear what he said about turning us in to the police? He'll betray us and collect the reward—and then give the cops a few crates of tea."

"We can always resort to the Solovki solution."

Anna grinned. "Exactly!" How good it felt to have her son enter the orbit of her world.

This time of year did not allow for much light, but Anna made it a point to lift a corner of the tarpaulin behind the cab to watch the highway and street signs. She nearly missed the split in the road that Maikov had mentioned because it was unmarked. Expecting a major junction, she took a few seconds to realize that the divide they'd just passed was the landmark—the forked roads. Karkaus had taken the left one. She immediately lifted the tarpaulin and banged on the cab. Karkaus slowed the truck and lowered his window.

"Why all the banging?"

"Gregori is ill. Stop for a minute so he can relieve himself."

Karkaus parked the truck next to a stand of birch trees. Fifty yards down the road stood a line of buildings, their lights winked in the dark. With electricity in short supply, offices were often lit with kerosene, or white gas, or coal oil lamps. Anna sighed with relief that they had stopped before reaching the buildings. Both mother and son armed themselves with their chisels. Then Gregori hopped out of the truck and disappeared into the trees, while Anna climbed into the cab to wait with Karkaus. Several minutes passed. Karkaus began to complain. Anna told him that it was better that Gregori vomited in the forest than in the truck. After five minutes, Karkaus insisted that she check on her son.

"I'll wait here," he said.

But she knew not to leave the truck, lest he drive off without them and contact the police, who would undoubtedly initiate a search. "Let's go together. Maybe a wolf or a bear attacked him."

Karkaus muttered that he'd been a fool to take them along, but when he saw that Anna, pleading fear, refused to move without him, he grabbed a tire iron and leaped out of the cab. Following Gregori's footprints, they entered the woods. With Karkaus leading the way, Anna followed. She heard the snap of branches before she saw Gregori coming toward them, with chisel in hand. Karkaus spun around and saw that Anna also held a chisel.

"What is this, some kind of trap?"

A second later, Anna moved forward and pointed her chisel at Karkaus's neck. "You missed the turnoff back there. You were going to denounce us to the secret police and collect the reward, you swine. Now just drop the tire iron."

Karkaus did, and pulled at his mustache. To the surprise of both his captors, he replied, "Yes, I was going to betray you."

"Didn't we pay you enough?" asked Gregori.

"Are you so poor that you need to collect twice?" Anna added.

"I spit on money," said Karkaus, removing the rubles Anna had paid him and throwing them in the snow. "Money can't free a man's soul. It can't buy independence. I use the money to bribe border guards, customs agents, and local police so that I can travel where I want and sell what I want. Take your money. I agree that I intended to act like a scoundrel. My returning the money will make us even. But killing me will do you no good. I overheard you in the back of the truck. You want to cross into Finland. Karkaus can lead you. Do you know what my name means? It's Finnish. My parents were Finnish. I speak Finnish. It means 'Mr. Escape.' My family has always had a knack for wriggling out of tight spots. I can lead you across the border. By yourself, you're bound to get caught."

Anna mulled over Karkaus's words. He had a point. She had done business with scoundrels before. They were usually more imaginative than they were saintly. And to escape required not decency but deception. If this man could take her family across the border on the wings of a lie or a hoax, she had no objections to their making common cause. But she knew that obsessed with his own independence, he wouldn't hesitate to act in his own interest. He would therefore need to be watched.

"We'll use your truck," she said. "My intention is to work our way to the border by selling, to soldiers at the front, tea and anything else we can get our hands on."

"I suggest biscuits and beef, which are always in demand, as well as cigarettes and vodka." He smiled at her crookedly. "You realize we're talking about stealing from government stores."

"A fool, Comrade Karkaus, I am not."

Karkaus shook his head with obvious satisfaction. He loved nothing more than to travel in the company of rascals. On more than one occasion, he had given rides to pilgrims and priests. Those pious types drove him to drink with their talk about heaven and hell, piety and prayer. He liked a juicy adventure, one he could repeat over herring, cucumbers, and strong "Moscow water." Travel through the Karelian peninsula would certainly have its risks, particularly since profiteers, even on a small scale, were easy game for the Bolshevik faithful. But soldiers with their mouths and their bellies pinched by hunger were unlikely to object.

"Back in the truck!" she ordered, and picked up the tire iron. "You know the city. We need a place to stay long enough to round up some goods and to allow me some time for a personal errand."

The worst part of town was home to brothels. In one of them, the madame rented her old friend and customer Karkaus a back room, which she immediately furnished with three cots. The flaming red hair of the woman, Mrs. Pestova, had come right out of a bottle of peroxide and contrasted with her plastered ivory makeup and purple lipstick. But even all the paint could not hide her wrinkles and turkey neck. She had a smoker's throaty voice, a persistent rumbling cough, and the yellowed eyes of a drunk whose liver was already exhibiting the effects of alcoholic poisoning.

For a few extra rubles, she allowed the locked shed in the back to house Karkaus's vehicle and possessions, whether obtained legally or illegally, and she made available a tarpaulin to protect them from the leaking roof. Their meals they took on the next street, at a greasy kitchen. If they wanted to bathe or wash their clothes, they could do so in the brothel, for an extra charge. She reminded the party that they were lucky to find a place as comfortable as hers, now that the city was overrun with refugees fleeing the war.

"All the better," said Karkaus. "The more people milling about, the harder for the government to find us."

Once Lake Onega froze and boats could no longer dock with their supplies, trains became the principal supply route for materiel. Anna asked Karkaus whether it was safer to pilfer from a dock or a railroad siding. He moved his cheeks from side to side as if gargling and replied that each had their strengths and weaknesses. The docks were unfenced, not so the railroad stockyard. But the docks were in plain sight, and the railroad mostly hidden from view. What they needed was a good pair of wire cutters and a moonless night. For both, they had to wait a few days. In the meantime, Anna, needing to find Yelena and Razan in Petrozavodsk, inquired about the address of the local educational ministry, and paid them a visit to ask which school Yelena Boujinskia was attending. She knew to act discreetly lest her questions invite suspicion. When she talked her way past the first desk, she arrived at the office of the registrar, a Comrade Brik. A large picture of Stalin looked down from one wall.

"When my sister died last year of septicemia," said Anna, "working in a military hospital, her husband volunteered for the war against the Fascist Finns and sent the child to live here in this city with an uncle. Now my brother-in-law is missing in action." She paused to let the implications sink in. "That's why I'm here."

"Boujinskia?" you said.

She spelled it for him, sniffled, and dabbed her eyes with a small handkerchief.

"Ah, yes, State School Number Four."

"And the head of the school?"

She listened intently. Comrade Kuznetsova. Minora Kuznetsova. The last words died on Brik's tongue: "Students are encouraged to follow in the footsteps of our Soviet heroes."

"Thank goodness for that," said Anna saluting. "We've had enough of the old-school values. It's time for the new."

The registrar smiled and accompanied her to the door.

Standing outside State School Number Four, she waited until the bell sounded and the children poured into the street. Even from a distance, she had no trouble identifying Yelena as she skipped down the steps. Anna followed her undetected for three blocks, until Yelena parted from her friends and proceeded alone.

"Ye-lay-na," Anna cooed, as she had a thousand times in the past.

The child pivoted, stared, and hurtled down the sidewalk. They clung together and only, after a long spell, reluctantly disengaged. "Papa said you might never return!"

"I was lucky," Anna said, "and I have a surprise for you." The child looked at her expectantly. "No, it's not a toy. It's something better. I have come to Petrozavodsk with my son Gregori, the one I told you about, who lived in Leningrad and was then transferred to the east. Now you have only one more to meet, Pavel, since you already know Dimitri."

"And Natasha?" the child expectantly asked.

"She'll be joining us soon."

"Promise?"

"Well, my dearest one, I will almost promise. Remember: There's a war. Travel is difficult. She is coming with Dima."

The child pressed her cheek against Anna's stomach and gripped her mother's sides tightly. "Don't go away again. I want us all to be together."

"Where is your father? Surely," she said in mock horror, "he has not abandoned you!"

She took Anna's hand. "Follow me."

The two of them walked several blocks, with Anna carefully noting the neighborhood and how to find it again. When they arrived at the apartment blocks, Anna told herself that the brothel had more charm than these Stalinist slabs. The inside of the apartment building was even worse than the outside. Offensive smells assaulted her nose, among them the odor of offal. Apparently, the plumbing had frozen, and the sewers had backed up. Yelena said that they were waiting for a workman to repair the system. Anna knew what that meant: The system would be down for quite a while. All the more reason to act quickly and pilfer the wares that would sell. Then they could make good their escape across the Karelian peninsula.

Razan was not at the apartment. He had gone to a nearby shop to buy a newspaper. He avidly followed the reports about the war and the evacuation of Solovki. Admittedly, the news about the prison camp was scant, but by reading between the lines and speaking to refugees from the northeastern front, he was able to learn that the camp had been virtually abandoned and the prisoners moved. He was determined to wait at least a month for Anna, even though the weather was worsening and Petrozavodsk was being evacuated. Before taking Yelena out of school and putting his transit visa to the test, he swore to keep vigil for his absent wife. Unlike Anna, who had set her heart on crossing into Finland, he had come to the conclusion that the attempt would be perilous and, even if successful, costly.

As he unlocked the door to the apartment, he heard Yelena and Yuri talking. He smelled pea soup. The child was asking whether Yuri would join them. Join them in what? Escape?

"Not without your uncle Dimitri," said Yuri, stirring the soup.

Had Yuri just heard from Dimitri? Razan quickened his step. On seeing Anna, he slumped to his knees, covered his head with his hands, and cried like a puling infant into the tattered rug. She gently raised him to his feet. They hugged fervidly, as if to keep each other from disappearing. This scene was so affecting that Yelena began to cry, and then Yuri. Only Anna remained dry eyed.

"You Russians are all the same," she said teasingly. "You cry on any occasion."

"Any occasion!" said a tear-faced Razan. "I am witnessing a miracle: someone who has survived Solovki."

She smiled appreciatively and added, "Gregori, too." Razan's incredulous look invited explanation. "We are staying a distance from here, at an unsavory place, but a safe one. So don't ask me to move in with you. I am with Gregori and another man . . ."

A disconsolate Razan murmured, "Another man?"

"Let us just say a Finnish business associate who knows Karelia. I will explain later. For now, it is important I get back to Gregori and Karkaus—that's his name—they are expecting me. I'll be gone for a few days. If I don't return, inquire at Mrs. Pestova's house on Ulitsa Dzerzhinsky number twelve. But if you go, you'll be shocked."

Yuri knew the address because the street housed not only heterosexual brothels but also a homosexual one. He looked away and smiled at the thought that the founder of the secret police had his name on a street of whorehouses.

"You won't even stay for dinner?" asked a disappointed Razan.

"There will be many dinners in our future, but not tonight. I have work to do."

Yuri's interest was now piqued. What did "work to do" mean? Not as a prostitute! "Mrs. Shtuba," he began, intending to ask her if she was employed by Mrs. Pestova, but then thought better of it. Instead, he simply said, "I hope Mrs. Pestova treats you well."

Anna, quick to detect the nuance, replied, "My son and I, as well as our Finnish guide, live in a back room with three cots. It makes for a good place to hide. Wouldn't you agree?"

Yuri had to admire the way Anna had deduced his meaning. "Yes, I think it's a splendid place. Better than here."

"My point exactly," she said, and kissed Yelena and Razan goodbye, hugging Yuri, to whom she whispered, "Thank you for all that you've done. I shall never forget."

"But," exclaimed Razan, "I have so much to tell you! All of it important . . . strange but true . . . I think."

Anna took his face in her hands. "We will have the rest of our lives to talk. And the first thing you must tell me is why you look as worn as a Solovki zek. You're not yourself."

"That is part of the story."

She reached for the door. "When we are alone . . ."

He retreated to the sitting room and collapsed on the couch from emotional exhaustion. Yelena put a pillow under his head. He thanked her and, once again, wondered if he had actually killed the Supreme Leader? Perhaps Anna had done him a favor by saying they had the rest of their lives to talk. He was still not convinced—absolutely convinced—that recent events had occurred as he thought. That is, he believed that he had killed a man he considered the real Stalin. But had he, in his poisoned state, truly killed Koba, someone else, or a chimera? Did the scene that he'd witnessed from the cinema booth actually take place, and if so, had he overheard a live conversation or one that he dreamed? What constituted proof in a world where lies and stratagems formed the basis of government and survival?

The man on the radio had said, "We should give thanks to the Politburo for steering the country into a triumphant future." Did "steering the country" mean that the Politburo would now be the governing power, and that Stalin was dead?

Anna had said he was not himself. She was more right than she knew. His stomach had atrophied; his hands shook (when he had tried to give Yuri a haircut, he lost control of the scissors, and wouldn't dare try to singe ear hairs); his sleep was tortured by dreams of death and dying; his powers of concentration were slipping, making it difficult to sustain his attention long enough to read a novel, resorting now only to poetry; his feet shuffled; his sight, which had always been acute, was now dimmed, though he had not yet ventured out to buy new spectacles; and he worried, frankly, that his sexual health had been diminished or even lost, since he no longer had nighttime erections. Given his state, Anna would find it hard to believe that he had slit the neck of the Vozhd, and yet he felt the need to relate what he thought to be true.

At the core of all human beings are certain stories. Whether they issue from fact or fancy, they make us, in large part, what we are. Even in old age, people still talk about their youth. Soldiers retell war stories. Fire and phosphorus burn in their brains. Our memories, which constitute a life, mark us indelibly. Razan was convinced that he had slit a man's throat. But convincing Anna might take some doing. Although no man or woman ought to live burdened with a story that cries to be told, he feared that his would be dismissed as the phantasm of a sick mind. He therefore decided to wait until Finland to speak, since preventing the death of his family in the forest came first.

That same night, Anna and her two companions surveyed the supply depot at the railroad, where military goods were stored before being trucked to a base outside the city. Karkaus then drove them to what looked like an abandoned house. Entering through a cellar door, they were stopped by a burly fellow. Karkaus whispered some code or password, and the sentinel admitted them to a lighted room that was a beehive of black-market activity. At long wooden tables, made from sawhorses and planks, thieves displayed merchandise of every kind and haggled over each sale. Karkaus bought three black woolen masks, a filtered flashlight, a sharp knife, and a chain cutter strong enough to make short work of the railroad fence.

For several days, the three stayed out of sight at the brothel. On the appointed night, they drove to the railroad yard, waited for the watchman to pass, and then crawled through the hole Karkaus cut at the base of the fence. Instinctively, Karkaus knew which piles to plunder. Anna removed the tarps and put the stacked boxes within easy reach of the two men, who raced back and forth with the contraband. They knew they had one hour to remove all their booty, at which time, the watchman would return. While the men spirited the goods through the fence, Anna positioned herself where she could easily see anyone coming. At last, she too left the yard.

With Karkaus's vehicle piled high with boxes, he had little room to drive and no space at all, with the front seat piled high, to carry passengers. He told Anna and Gregori that he would meet them back at Mrs. Pestova's shed.

"We go together or we don't go at all," said Anna.

"You don't trust me?" said Karkaus, looking injured.

"Would you trust me?" she replied.

"Absolutely."

Anna snorted skeptically. "Gregori can take the tram. I'll sit on your lap while you drive."

"How will I see?"

"Over my shoulder."

The prospect of sitting on this thief's lap didn't please her. As he tugged at his mustache, she could imagine his thoughts. If he got fresh, she still had the chisel, which she conspicuously displayed and then stored in her purse. The vehicle tipped and swayed on its return journey. Twice, Roman Karkaus thrust his hips in a suggestive manner. The second time, Anna reached down and pinched him.

On the following day, they sorted the goods and reorganized the truck so that it would seat two, Karkaus and Anna. Whoever joined them needed to walk. Only when the truck was packed and ready to depart did Anna reconnect with her family and introduce Gregori and Karkaus to the others. Razan had developed a nervous rash, convinced that Anna had either been killed or been abducted by some Finn whom she called Karkaus. But not wishing to look like a jealous husband, he had refrained from finding the address she had given him. If her absence continued two days longer, he would go. When everyone met, Anna surveyed the group to see whether points of friction arose. None did. Karkaus behaved well, and Gregori made quite a hit with Yelena, regaling her not with stories of saints, as Razan feared, but with the details of his and Anna's escape. Yelena particularly thrilled to hearing about trading human flesh for the real thing, though Anna had wanted Gregori to omit that part of the tale. Even Razan and Gregori seemed glad to embrace, perhaps because Solovki had caused the priest to doubt and to dampen his enthusiasm for proselytizing.

Karkaus was impatient to set out the next day or two for the border, but Anna insisted that they wait for Dimitri, who had told Yuri during their last coded telephone conversation that he and his sister would be visiting their ailing mother in no more than a fortnight. So began the wait. In the meantime, Yelena continued to attend school, Razan and Anna took walks along the frozen lake, and Yuri, when not occupied with hairdressing, joined Gregori and Karkaus in innumerable games of poker, a card game that Gregori had learned in Solovki, Karkaus from a westerner, and Yuri from the other two. The stakes were counted out in signed scraps of paper, to be reclaimed with real money once they reached Helsinki.

Days passed as the group waited for Dimitri and Natasha. Would they ever arrive? Had they been arrested? The clock ticked and nerves frayed. Finally, Anna said that they would wait no more than another three days. The decision, of course was hers, since they were her children. But always practical, Anna knew the longer the wait, the greater the danger. To reduce the chances of a neighbor reporting this group that regularly met in Yuri's apartment, she and Gregori and Yuri returned to the brothel—to wait. Karkaus was resigned, though anxious, and Gregori chafed.

"If you and I could escape from Solovki," he said to his mother, "what does it take for Dima and Natasha to get here from Voronezh?"

Anna knew that Gregori had never felt close to either Dimitri or Natasha, and that he much preferred his older brother, Pavel. She also knew that he was a man of deep resentments, one well suited to be a priest, owing to his uncompromising need to purge sin from the world, albeit sin as he defined it. Razan had once told her that Gregori and the Vozhd shared some of the same traits. When she had objected, he had pointed out that for all Stalin's professed atheism, it was an open Kremlin secret that just as religion had made him, he was determined to remake religion.

A day before Anna's deadline, Dimitri and Natasha arrived. Their journey had left them haggard and weary and underfed. Not wishing to revisit unhappy memories, they left most of their travails unspoken; but one Dimitri recounted.

"By every vehicle and conveyance we traveled eastward. I calculated that if the police were looking for us, they would look north or west. At the city of Kotlas, where we arrived after an all-night drive in the back of a truck, we boarded a bus for Velsk. But all the main roads west and north had roadblocks. Our bus was stopped. Fortunately I was not wearing my uniform."

Natasha anxiously interrupted. "Dimitri, remember a child is present." She swept up Yelena and held her tightly.

Yelena responded, "A lot of my classmates have seen their parents taken away. I'm not afraid."

What kind of world is it, thought Razan, where children take for granted the arrest and deportation of parents? Yelena had witnessed the disappearance of her own. He did not want her to become inured to pain and insensitive to loss. But how else could a child survive?

Dimitri began to pace, clearly weighing his words. "Well, two very nice Red Army men had blocked the road with their car. They boarded the bus and ordered everyone off. They were searching for deserters and checking papers." Dimitri leaned down and said to Yelena, "Do you know what a deserter is?"

"Our teacher said they're people who do not love their country."

"Perhaps," replied Dimitri, "but some of them aren't able to fight. They have to look after families or maybe they're ill. I still had my service pistol; it was stored in my bag. When the Red Army men asked to see my papers, I removed the pistol and pointed it at them. 'What does this mean?' one demanded. I told the two men to walk ahead of me into the woods."

"You didn't shoot them?" asked a transfixed Yelena.

"Kill them, no. I would never do such a thing," said Dimitri. "I took their guns and ordered them to walk deep into the woods before they turned around. One Red Army man objected and started toward me in a threatening manner, so I put a bullet in his foot."

"You shot him?" exclaimed Yelena.

"Just nicked him enough to make him behave. He was all right. Then I took their car keys, and Natasha and I drove off in the police car. But we knew that we wouldn't get far, because the Red Army and police would be hunting us down. We drove north and hid the car in an abandoned barn. From there we hitched rides until we reached the east side of Lake Onega. We walked the rest of the way. It was bitterly cold and the southern approach to the city is being patrolled. We found shelter with farmers—we paid them—and walked by night."

Not until some time later did Razan learn that Dimitri had killed the two men. But by then, much had changed.

Once dinner was over and the dishes put away, Karkaus laid out his plan. In small groups, they would travel southwest to the now Soviet-occupied town of Pitkyaranta, situated south of the Finnish city of Sortavala, their hoped-for destination. Though under constant bombardment, Sortavala was on the Finnish side of the peninsula. If movement north proved impossible, with any luck they could cross into Finland via the "Road of Life," frozen Lake Ladoga. They would meet in Pitkyaranta. Karkaus would transport Yuri in the Model T. Lacking travel documents, Karkaus could say that he lost them, and Yuri could show his; but Karkaus assured the others that given his knowledge of the countryside, they would be safe. A few days later, the Lipnoskii and Shtube families, toting packed bags and dried food, started on foot toward Pitkyaranta. Along the way, they came upon numerous ghost villages, in which they found refuge. From nearby streams, they collected water, heated it, and took make-shift baths. In the fields, they dug up buried tubers and rationed their food.

Karkaus and Yuri, having managed to avoid the numerous patrols, arrived first and located an abandoned farmhouse with beds but no mattresses. When Anna and her family finally reached Pitkyaranta and rendezvoused with the two men, they all sheltered there temporarily, until Dimitri could bribe an officer to give him a paper certifying that Razan Shtube and his party of seven had permission to procure firewood north of Lake Ladoga and peddle food goods to the Red Army. After resting for several days to husband their strength, they slowly followed the military road toward the front lines, as Anna and her children, in collusion with Karkaus, sold food, drink, and tobacco to weary Soviet soldiers, who gladly paid the reduced prices on offer. But even at the lowered rates, the family was swimming in rubles.

A few miles north of Pitkyaranta, a foot patrol stopped the slow-moving vehicle and the others, like tinkers, tramping closely behind. Razan showed them the official paper, stamped and signed by the local commandant, and Anna, armed with a box of cigarettes that she had removed for herself, offered the soldiers a smoke. When asked the price of the cigarettes, she told him, using the standard jargon about the fatherland and the harvest and the patriotic war, that she could not charge more than half, even if she suffered a loss.

The party could see that escape across the frozen lake was impossible with the presence of Russian patrols and tanks and field artillery. So they followed the forest until the Model T could barely move through the snow. When the vehicle finally stuck fast, Karkaus declared that the party was too large to negotiate the war zone and make it to safety. "We will have to split up," he said. Anna refused to leave the vehicle, with all its stolen goods; and her children refused to leave her. It was therefore decided that Razan, Yuri, and Yelena would make their own way through the woods, and the others would keep to the road and follow behind the Soviet troops. As Natasha hugged Yelena and cried, Razan tried to persuade Anna to join him, but her indomitable mercantile spirit prevailed. She argued that they would need the money in Finland, that she could guarantee her safety by having something valuable to trade or sell, and that Karkaus and her children would protect her.

"But the paper with permission to cut trees is in my name."

"Keep it," she said. "We'll meet not in Leningrad but Helsinki, at the Finland Station." The irony was not lost on him: The latter station was the place of Lenin's return to Russia. She then walked into his arms. As they held each other, Yelena hugged Anna.

"I no sooner find you than I lose you," Razan murmured. "Will it always be this way?" She held him all the closer. Had he not been persuaded that Yelena was safer with him, and that the fewer the people, the faster they could move, he would have found parting with Anna unbearable.

The party of three left the main road and followed a minor one, where the snow was untrammeled. Still weak from having been poisoned, Razan depended on Yuri and Yelena to carve a trail. They walked for several hours, until it began to storm, and Razan admitted that he couldn't continue. The woods were dotted with the cabins of hunters and fishers, most of whom had taken lodging elsewhere to avoid the war. Coming upon an occupied two-story log cabin, they knocked. A hunter, Teodoro Tomski, answered the door. His shoulder-length hair, heavy beard, and thick eyebrows brought to mind some mythic Yeti. Tomski took one look at Razan and knew he would have to house these strangers, a kindness for which Razan rewarded him generously, though Tomski asked for little. The hunter supplied them with bundles of straw for their sleeping needs and a large chamber pot. "Better an indoor pot," said Razan, "than an outdoor privy." Tomski had only a few extra blankets. With the wind whistling between the uncaulked attic logs, they slept in their clothes and sweaters and coats to ward off the cold, all the while waiting for an end to the storm. In truth, Razan was glad for the rest. To wash, they melted snow and heated it in large pots, which they poured into a miniature bathtub. At night, by a kerosene lamp, Yuri read Russian fairy tales to Yelena from her favorite book. The hairdresser and child, in their dependent needs, had become emotionally joined.

On the third night, with visibility near zero from blowing snow, a soldier thumped at the door and said his lieutenant wanted to speak to all the men in the house. Tomski, Razan, and Yuri left the cabin and showed the lieutenant their papers. Teodoro produced a resident hunting permit, Razan the document that permitted logging, and Yuri, to the barber's surprise, a medical deferment that declared him unfit for medical service because of partial blindness in his left eye. No doubt, Dimitri had authored his lover's release.

"Can you tell me," said the lieutenant, standing in a greatcoat under a fir tree, his squad of soldiers in the background, "why I see no piles of wood next to the house—or a cart to carry them back to town? The people in the city need wood. What is your explanation?"

Razan indignantly answered, "I've been waiting for my drunken helper, Jacov Gerstein. He was to meet us here with horse and dray."

"A German?"

"A Jew."

"The lazy dog."

The lieutenant followed the men into the house. On seeing Yelena, he inquired about her presence and demanded to speak to her alone.

"She's my daughter," said Razan. "She has done nothing."

"I just want to ask her a few questions."

Razan watched from a window. What he could see only in pantomime happened as follows:

"We're looking for deserters," the lieutenant said, "and I'd like to know more about the 'girly man.' Is he really blind in one eye?"

Yelena, sensing the need to protect Yuri, boldly replied, "He can hardly fry eggs. Yesterday, he fell down the stairs."

The officer hitched up his belt. "You haven't answered me."

In the peremptory manner of Anna, she responded, "You have no right to question the loyalty of a man whose eye was injured while serving his country." With Gregori's Solovki stories fresh in mind, she added, "He was a prison guard on a train, and some zeks attacked him when the train stopped to take on water."

"Is that what he told you?"

"Yes."

The lieutenant spat. "If they had shot those zeks in the first place, we wouldn't have to feed the bastards." He warned that he could check Yelena's story by seriously grilling this Yuri Suzdal. "But I trust you."

Praising Yelena for her cleverness, he told her to go inside and get warm, turned on his heels, and kicked a pile of snow as he left with his squad.

She waited and watched the man fade into the fog. Shivering, but not from the cold, she thought of her parents and her many prayers for their return. At that moment, peering into the wooded darkness, she knew that she would never see them again. Razan and Anna had treated her well, and she them. Even so, she hoped that one day she and her parents could board a train for Tashkent. Perhaps because her current direction was north and not south, she had murmured, "Goodbye."

For a small bribe, Teodoro Tomski arranged to have Razan, Yelena, and Yuri driven north. The price the hunter quoted might have been higher had Tomski not seen Yelena stand her ground with the lieutenant. He admired her courage. But Tomski warned the barber that he would be entering a no-man's zone and at any moment could be killed by a shell launched from either the Finnish or Soviet side. Razan said they had no choice and waited for the guide. Shortly, a small sleigh arrived, pulled by a chestnut Finn horse, which Pekka, the smuggler, explained was capable of pulling heavier loads than many larger draught-horse breeds. An erstwhile farmer who had spent time in Leningrad and spoke an accented Russian, Pekka knew horses. He called himself by just the one name and refused to offer his last. When he talked, his false teeth clicked. A cigarette drooped from his dentals, and his fingers were badly stained with nicotine. He was missing part of one ear and wheezed when he breathed. His face was badly scarred from pox and his nose resembled a large boil that begged to be lanced. He spoke little as he drove horse and sleigh through the forest, neither scraping a tree nor finding himself in a drift. To pass the hours, Yuri sang folk songs and whimsical ditties of his own composition.

> *A Russian bear broke from the woods,*
> *Stealing all of Yelena's goods,*
> *Including her family and home,*
> *Her canvas and oils and comb.*
>
> *Cheerfully she settled the score*
> *By drawing his face as a boar;*
> *She called him not Teddy but toad,*
> *And drew his hat as a commode.*

Although Pekka stopped for his passengers to relieve themselves, no one ate. They had to cover a certain distance by nightfall if they were going to reach a safe house in the woods, a place that Finnish smugglers used. The same would be true for the second and third day, if they were to reach Sortavala unscathed. Trails used by trappers and smugglers were the only safe way into the city; but once in Sortavala, hardly anyone was safe from the artillery shells.

In the dark, they reached a long, low hut used by outcasts. The main room had a dozen bunks, but no mattresses; a second room housed the kitchen. An outside privy was a two seater. The smugglers cooked their own food, so Pekka had brought smoked reindeer, bread, and carrots that turned limp when defrosted. Candles and kerosene lamps provided their light. Razan heard more Finnish being spoken than Russian. As Yelena undressed for bed, a drunken Finn accosted her. Before Razan could react, Pekka held a knife to the man's throat and told him that he'd slit his windpipe if anything happened to the child. The man staggered off, swearing incomprehensible words.

Each night, they slept at cabins similar to the first, havens of smugglers and thieves. On the last day of their journey, they stopped shy of Sortavala. The sound of distant guns and the smell of cordite gave Razan pause. Perhaps they should stay outside the city. Through the trees, he could just barely make out what looked like a bunker, half buried in the ground. Pekka suggested that it might be a good place to spend the night. When they left the sleigh, the snow-drifts reached Yelena's waist. The structure was a massive multilayered block-house, elaborately fortified with logs. Razan guessed that it was part of a line of bunkers called the Mannerheim Line and had been constructed at this point for a good reason: Sortavala was within striking distance.

The exiles hunkered down in the shelter unable to sleep, while shells screeched overhead. A few fell near them, but caused no damage. All night the guns thundered. Toward morning, as a single plane flew low overhead and strafed the area, five Finnish soldiers burst into the bunker and leveled their rifles. Pekka immediately explained the situation. The head of the Finnish patrol asked about the man slumped in the corner: Yuri. One of the plane's bullets had tragically found its way into the bunker, splintered, and hit Yuri in the forehead. A slow trickle of blood ran from his wound, between his eyes, down the bridge of his nose, and into his open mouth. Yelena screamed. A soldier kneeled next to the hairdresser and felt his pulse. Yuri was dead. The same soldier sadly remarked that the frozen ground would not permit a proper burial. Yuri would just have to lie in the dark woods, carrion for crows.

Unable to bear the thought, Yelena begged that they make some effort to bury him. In deference to the child, the Finnish soldiers detonated an explosive in the woods that left a small ground crater, and helped lay Yuri to rest.

While Yelena and Pekka whispered their own religious words, Razan mumbled Kaddish, "*Yisgadal v'yiskadash sh'mayh rabo.*"

Yelena found a large stone that she placed at the head of the grave and wrote a note that she placed under the stone. "Yuri Suzdal was a kind man, a good man. If you find him in summer, please dig him a proper grave. He deserves to lie in peace."

Once the Finnish soldiers returned to the bunker, leaving Yelena and Razan alone, she asked him to help her build a Golem next to the grave. He had often told her the story of a giant molded from mud. In the unquiet forest, with shells whistling overhead and trees thrashing the air as if trying to erase the obscene graffiti of war, Razan feared that any prolonged stay in the woods would increase their danger; but she insisted, reminding him that it was he who told her about the Golem's protective powers. Reluctantly, he agreed and helped her roll a snowball into a larger one, then a second, and a third. She stacked one on top of the other, until she was satisfied that the figure stood at least seven feet tall. Employing her artistic skills and Razan's penknife, she cut a piece of ice from the hardened roadway and sculpted a face that unmistakably resembled Yuri's. When she had finished, an imposing Golem stood facing south, the direction from which the forward Russian scouting party would be making its way. Declaring her work good, she trudged back to the bunker.

From Kremlin chatter, Razan knew that the Russian military was composed mostly of illiterate men who believed fiercely in the power of myths and omens and superstitions. Now that the Golem was in place, the barber hoped that when the advance party approached and saw this creature with a human face, the soldiers would bolt. The commander, of course, could always order them on pain of death to hold their ground. A few hours later, a single shot rang out, but no other. Razan imagined the course of events outside the bunker. The commander had shot the Golem to prove to his men that they had nothing to fear from a snowman. But the harm had already been done. The report of the gun had announced the arrival of the regiment's advance guard—and the Finns stood ready. As the Russian soldiers made their way toward the fortification, the Finns opened fire with machine guns and then leaped from the bunker to mop up with pistols. No one doubted that the Finns had guts and grit—*sisu*—when it came to fighting. The Russians had been able to discharge only a few feeble shots before the Finns killed the stragglers and wounded.

That same night, the guns of Karelia fell mostly silent. The Finnish soldiers, attuned to the rhythm of war, used the lull to retreat. Pekka took the occasion to drive Razan and Yelena to the main checkpoint, situated on the southeast edge of the city, where he had more than once deposited Russian exiles. He chatted with the soldiers for a minute, and, instead of merely declaring Razan and Yelena as escapees, he announced impetuously that they had transit visas, which they then felt compelled to produce. The soldiers asked why the Soviets would allow the barber and his daughter the freedom to travel and ordered them to report to Sergeant Isto at the main refugee headquarters. Pekka, regretting his words, apologized and drove to the building, where he insisted on accompanying them inside to stand witness.

Sergeant Kai Isto studied the transit visas and asked, "Why would the Soviet government allow *you* to leave the country when they deny transit to most everyone else?"

Razan debated whether to tell him how the documents had been obtained but decided to hold his tongue because the story seemed too improbable. Besides, whatever their source, the documents were valid in every detail. "I was the official Kremlin barber, responsible to Poskrebyshev and Stalin's inner circle."

"You shaved Stalin?"

"I don't know."

Sergeant Isto looked confused. "Don't know? If you, the person staring into his face, don't know, then who does?"

"The secret police. Stalin has doubles."

The sergeant leaped from his chair and exclaimed, "Is that true?"

"Absolutely."

"I must call headquarters to tell them. Is there any sure way to tell them apart? We have to be certain whom we are dealing with."

The desire to blurt out that the real Stalin was dead would have obliged him to explain how he knew, a moment in time that still remained obscure owing to the effect of the poison on his capacity to recall events clearly. "It would be erroneous to say they look exactly alike." The sergeant listened. "The man who I think is the real Stalin has larger ears and skin craters than the decoy I knew, and dyed hair. Also, worse teeth."

"You can actually prove that you were the official Kremlin barber?" Before Razan could respond, Sergeant Isto added, "We could use you in Helsinki—right away."

Pekka, who had known nothing about Razan's former position, gaped in awe. Finally, he gasped, "I can only tell you this, sergeant, he is a good man, and the child . . . a wonder."

Kai Isto, a student of languages, said that the general Finnish military staff had heard rumors that the Kremlin barber was a Jew, from Albania. Before he could continue, Razan spoke to him first in Yiddish and then in Albanian.

"To hell with the transit visas, I must get you to Helsinki."

"And the child?" asked Razan.

The sergeant smiled and said ironically, "If she's yours, I trust you won't leave her behind."

Pekka removed all the bags from his sleigh, shook Razan's hand, and hugged Yelena. The barber shoved a handful of rubles into Pekka's hand and muttered, "For all your good work."

Pekka laughed. "I nearly caused your arrest." Then he boarded the sleigh and left the same way he had come.

"Only a fool would fail to exploit a pause in the fighting," said Anna, as she urged Karkaus to try one more time to move his car and follow the advancing Russian soldiers. But with the wind constantly shifting, as soon as the infantrymen beat a path through the snow, a drift covered it. Karkaus repeatedly backed up and tried to ram his car through the snowdrifts, eventually immobilizing the Model T. He threw up his arms and declared he could drive no farther.

"Disengage the dray," she said in frustration. "We'll pull it and leave the car."

Karkaus and his dray had been long-standing partners. He felt that to break the weld and disconnect the dray would be the same as lopping off a limb or relinquishing his pocketbook. "And the car?" he asked. "Do we just leave it here?"

"No, we free it and pay you your share. Then you don't have to risk your life in the war zone." She quoted him a number.

He scoffed. "The goods are worth twice that."

"You're the one who's been selling them at half their value. Now you want to double the price. Let's not quibble. I'll split the difference with you."

Karkaus pulled on his frost-encrusted mustache, stamped his frozen boots on the ground, looked back over his shoulder toward the safe geography behind him, and said, "Done!"

She wet her fingers and, like a greengrocer, counted out the cash. He took a hammer and broke the weld. With some effort, the party turned the car around, and Karkaus disappeared down the road. That he had to be pushed out of numerous snowdrifts on his way south caused him less pain than those who were pulling the dray had to endure. Fashioning harnesses out of rope, Dimitri and Gregori, like horses, pulled it, with Anna and Natasha sitting atop.

Although the dray proceeded slowly, Anna's business flourished. She sold her goods with remarkable ease and bought others from the soldiers, all too willing to exchange a watch, a fob, a handsome belt buckle, an extra pair of boots, or a uniform taken from a dead comrade. The army mess cook generously stole food from his larder for a turn in bed with Anna. And why would she not accede to his lust? She had witnessed the example of Monty. To survive, all is permitted, with one exception: No one was permitted to touch her daughter. The Russian Army was encamped for nearly a week, unable to make any progress against the Finnish artillery. She had parked the dray behind the cook's bunker to speed the transfer of food. During this time, Anna and her children made more money than Razan had earned in a year. Eventually, the porcine cook, Mamish, a Circassian, began to exhaust his food supplies, which were slow to arrive. When he had nothing to trade, Anna abandoned his cot. He tried to charm her with stories about his home on the Black Sea, but she wanted material satisfaction not words. From either sexual frustration or a feeling of betrayal, he sought to avenge himself by seducing Natasha, whom he had lured to his bunker one night with the promise of piroshki.

Years later, Anna was still imagining the scene that Natasha described. Lowering her head and ducking into the half-buried bunker, Natasha had said, "They smell divine. How did you manage? Mother told me that you had no more cooking dough."

"For you, I have."

Mamish pulled up a chair, and she sat at his small folding table, savoring the food.

"You are not eating?"

"I had just enough left for you."

"How kind."

His ragged laugh put her on edge. "In this hellish world, everything has its price."

"Meaning?"

"You owe me for the piroshki."

She reached into a pocket of the overalls she had taken to wearing. "How much?"

"A kiss, a hug, and a roll in my rug."

Natasha paused, threw some rubles on the table, and darted for the door. But just as she opened it and screamed, Mamish, the Circassian, fat of face but fleet of foot, overtook her. The rest of the story, Anna knew all too well. Mamish slammed the door but not before Natasha's cry was heard by her brothers. Dimitri grabbed his pistol and entered the bunker just as Mamish was tearing her clothes. Putting the pistol to Mamish's head, he told him to stop. But the foolish cook, now enraged, swung a heavy arm around and caught Dimitri in the face. Dimitri staggered backward. As the cook advanced on him, Dimitri raised the pistol. Mamish stopped. But a second later, as if convinced the man wouldn't shoot, Mamish threw himself at Dimitri. It took only one shot to the face, and Mamish lay dead at Dimitri's feet. A minute or two later, Russian soldiers appeared in the bunker. On seeing Natasha disrobed, they averted their eyes as she dressed; then they led Dimitri away. The next morning, the Russian general in charge of the small regiment applied the coup de grâce to the back of Dimitri's head after three soldiers had served as a firing squad. Anna, needing to be restrained, screamed imprecations.

She blamed herself and took no comfort in the fact that Dimitri had killed the cook. "Mamish was a cur," she told the general and, ever enterprising, extolled the virtues of her own cooking and volunteered herself as his replacement. The general, who had briefly served in the White Army before changing sides, was not a bad sort and felt sorry the military manual had required him to order her son's death. In return, he made Anna the head cook for the regiment, and two days later, when the troops were resupplied, he congratulated himself, as he polished off a plate of her pirogies.

"But tell me," he asked Anna, "what became of your son's service pistol? One moment, he had the gun in hand, and the next, it was gone. Do you have it? His brother or sister? We can't seem to find it."

"I know nothing of pistols and guns and knives and such things. I mind my own business."

The general let the subject drop because the next day, the ragtag regiment broke their encampment and slowly moved forward under the protection of Russian planes bombing Finnish emplacements. Natasha replaced Dimitri in harness and helped Gregori pull the dray. But two days later, she vanished. Anna thought she must have found a favorite among the men and run off, deserting for Finland. Without Natasha's help to pull the dray, Anna joined Gregori and took up the harness. Now she had three jobs: pulling the dray, peddling her goods, and cooking for the regiment. One evening, as she was bending over a stew pot, the general came up behind her and gently placed a hand on her shoulder. She immediately thought, "Not again!" But the general had no such intentions. He asked her to sit down; he had something to tell her. She joined him at the very table where Natasha had enjoyed piroshki.

"We have found the pistol," he said somberly.

"The pistol?" said Anna, who had already forgotten.

"Your son's."

"Dimitri's?"

He slid it across the table. "Yes. I thought you might want to keep it . . . in these perilous times." He paused. "It was found in the woods by the men who resupplied us. On their way back, they discovered it . . . next to a body."

"A body?"

"Your daughter's."

When Anna awoke, she found herself on a cot in a temporary medical tent, with the gun holstered at her feet. Heavily sedated, she was told she had passed out in the company of the general, who had been tight lipped about the cause and would say only, "It's a personal matter." A temporary cook had taken her place, and Gregori was left to haul the dray by himself. Eventually, the regiment had approached Sortavala, where the fighting was fierce. The Russians tried to dig trenches in the frozen ground but finally gave the task up as impossible. Instead, the soldiers felled trees and made rough shelters, one of which housed Anna and Gregori.

And here they stayed, listening to the screaming shells overhead until one day, a soldier in a Finnish uniform burst into their shelter and cried, "We have an opening!" Gregori, thinking the regiment was being overrun by the enemy and their lives were in danger, grabbed his brother's pistol and killed the man, only to discover a short while later he had shot a Russian spy in a Finnish uniform. Thinking of his brother and certain the same fate awaited him, Gregori panicked and fled into the woods. Anna never saw him again.

Although the Russian regiment, following orders, retreated, she insisted on staying with her goods. Harnessing the dray to her waist, she slowly pulled it north until she spotted a Finnish patrol that took her and the dray to Sortavala. When questioned about her role in the regiment, she told a heartrending story about the death of her children and insisted that she had only one goal in mind: to escape. Fortunately, one of the officers remarked she was not the first to cross into Finnish territory that day. Anxiously, she asked for details. It was only after the officer made a call to Helsinki that she learned Razan and Yelena had reached safety and were being housed north of the city, in an area mostly free of Soviet bombs. The officer then ordered her to leave on the next truck for the capital. But she refused. The whole of her inventory, her life goods, she cried, were in the dray.

"It could be a matter of life or death," said the officer.

"So is my wagon. With it, I can support myself; without it, I have nothing."

"Your husband is proving useful to the government. He and your daughter are being generously cared for. I urge you to join them."

"And who will make use of the goods in my dray?"

"The soldiers," said the officer. "Isn't that what you'd want?"

Anna felt morally trapped. How could she ask the very people who had saved her husband and daughter to purchase her wares? But on the other hand, she knew their value, and if she could sell them, she would earn, in addition to the many rubles she had stored in her footlocker, Finnish currency, markka and penni. She had nothing to lose by trying her luck; or might she lose the goodwill of the officer and have to haul her wagon by foot to Helsinki? Every cell in her body contained the memory of her childhood poverty, but Razan and Yelena were her wealth.

"Is there no way," she asked, "to put the dray in the truck?"

"No room."

"These goods might help relieve the rationing in Helsinki."

"More so here on the front," said the officer. "Our men have little in the way of food and money. Just look around."

Anna could not deny the condition of the ragged Finnish soldiers, so she settled on what she considered a fair compromise: The officer would give her a signed statement, confirming her material losses. All her adult life she had equated money and self-preservation, a not unreasonable nexus, and though she sometimes regretted choosing money over morals, she knew that she was not alone. The Soviets talked a good game about sharing the wealth, but in the countryside, she had noticed that the rich ate and dressed differently from the poor; and in Moscow, some traveled in chauffeured cars, and some walked. Only a fool would voluntarily relinquish his holdings and expect nothing in return. And she was no fool.

Even her own family was not exempt from her divided feelings. She well remembered leaving Brovensk and having to decide which belongings to sell and which to take. Once the decision was made and she had sold most of her furniture, Razan had suggested that she give the money to Pavel, since they would be well cared for in Moscow. At first, she thought he was teasing; then, she thought he was mad. "My possessions!" Razan had replied, "Charity begins at home."

She had scoffed at the very idea of Razan quoting the Bible and had said, "Yes, with me!" But in the end, she had given Pavel the money.

On reaching Helsinki, the truck driver called his dispatch officer for instructions. The reply came back: "Take them to the front steps of the Parliament Building, Eduskuntatalo. Her husband and daughter will be inside waiting for her." Northwest of the main post office, the driver stopped. Anna thanked him and leaped out to greet Razan and Yelena, racing down the steps of the building. The driver put her bags at the curb and left. In the winter cold, the family's entangled arms formed a cocoon, and they sank to the pavement, as love leaked out of their eyes. Razan handed her a gift: a broadtail coat with a mandarin collar in fox. But happiness often companions with pain. When Yelena asked about her dearest Natasha and kind Dimitri—the child had never felt close to Gregori—Anna attributed all of their deaths to bombs and artillery shells. Had someone pointed out the connection between her dray and the fate of her children, she would have called them contemptible Bolsheviks. In her mind, she had been a courageous mother, caring and protective. No, they had died from the hateful war and the greediness of nations claiming as much land as their armies could conquer. She had tried only to do what was best for her family: to keep them wealthy enough to live free of the hunger and sweat of the poor.

That evening, at Anna's request, the family attended the Uspenski Orthodox Church. Inside the redbrick building, the family stood at the back, admiring the largest Orthodox cathedral in Western Europe. Anna requested a few minutes for herself and made her way to the altar, where she genuflected before an icon sprinkled with gold dust, "Mother and Child." After crossing herself, she stood and kissed the icon. Then she dropped a few coins in the donation box, lit four candles, and prayed that her children and Yuri be received into heaven. Razan whispered to Yelena to say a prayer in Uzbek for the souls of the dead, and he silently did the same in Hebrew. When Anna returned, she buried her face in Razan's chest and quietly sobbed. He gently stroked her hair, still lustrous, though much grayer than it was before Solovki. No one spoke in the tram on the way back to the government-owned apartment assigned to Razan. During his family's absence, when he was not meeting with the intelligence service, he had consoled himself by decorating the walls of the apartment with reproductions of bucolic country scenes; and of course, he included Yelena's paintings, except for Stalin's iconic mustache.

Weeks later, Razan tried yet again to explain the events in the cinema. But he found Anna's questions as difficult to answer as those of the Finnish secret service.

"I know it sounds crazy," he said in the muted voice that he had acquired from living for so many years in the Soviet Union, "but I swear: I slit his throat." Anna sympathized with his recent misery without actually expressing agreement. "You must believe me, because if I killed an innocent man, he was no doubt forced, on pain of death, to play the role of Stalin."

She looked at him lovingly but not as she had when they lived in Brovensk. "Better," she said, "that we listen to the radio," and turned it on. The Finnish Orchestra was playing the Brahms cello concerto.

They listened in silence, holding hands, until Razan rose to answer a knock at the door. His neighbor, a Russian exile whose family estate had been looted, and the library burned, excitedly asked, "Did you hear?"

"We are listening to the Brahms."

"Me, too. But a special announcement. From the Politburo. Stalin has declared that 'a son does not answer for his father.'"

"Taras, what are you talking about?"

"Stalin just said, on the radio, the purges must end and the country needs to be united. They quoted him in Russian: 'A son does not answer for his father.' It no longer matters if your parents were kulaks or priests or merchants or Jews or Tsarist officers. All is forgiven. He's put forth a new policy. Who knows his motives? First he signs a peace pact with Germany, and now with his own people."

"Four years ago, in 1935, December, I think it was, he made the same declaration, and look what followed."

Taras nodded and crossed the hall to his apartment. While latching the door, Razan noticed that his hand shook. He had become an observer of his own failing health, standing outside of himself and chronicling his progressive decay. Is this my reward, he thought, for knowing about great crimes and, though hating them, continuing to work in the Kremlin? He ran his hand through his hair and paused to view its perfect whiteness in the entry hall mirror. His pale blue eyes brightened, elated by what they saw: Stalin slumped in his favorite cinema chair, his head bowed, and a trickle of blood tracing the cut made by Razan's Damascene razor. "I waited three years too long," he said to the mirror. Stalin's head slowly rose and turned to face the barber. His neck was unscathed and on his lap rested Razan's matryoshka doll. "Konspiratsia . . . the virus of the age," muttered Stalin. "I knew it was only a matter of time before you too caught the virus."

Anna called to him. "Are you talking to me?"

Razan returned to the sitting room. Without any preamble or qualifying expressions, he calmly said, "I was talking to Stalin."

She consoled him and said that with rest he'd recover. But her expression belied her words. The first time he'd told her about the murder—their reunion night—she had pressed her hands in prayer, kissed Razan, and said, "If only it were true." When he insisted then, like now, that it was, she had quoted an old proverb, "Believe nothing and be on your guard against everything."

The radio concert continued, but Razan's attention was elsewhere. Anna leaned over and kissed his head.

"Who was that at the door?" she asked.

He nearly said Stalin.

"You look," remarked Anna, "as if you've just seen a ghost." At that moment, the barber devoutly wished he could escape from the konspiratsia tunnel, where life and lies were one, and ride his train of memories to a place of cure and absolution for having served as Stalin's barber.

FINIS

RAZAN'S LIST

Number of suicides and unexplained deaths: unknown

ARRESTS, 1936

Klavdiya Vasilyevna Generalograva: Ter-Vaganyan's wife

EXECUTIONS, 1936

Bakayev, Ivan: Expelled as an oppositionist, he was at one time the Leningrad security police chief and a member of the Central Control Commission.

Kamenev, Lev Borisovich: Briefly the nominal head of the Soviet state (1917) and
a founding member (1919) and later chairman (1923–1924) of the ruling Politburo. Shortly after his death, his first wife, Olga, Trotsky's sister, and his
second wife, Tatiana Glebova, were shot.

Smirnov, Ivan Nikitich: A former Trotskyite who publicly insisted that Stalin resign
as secretary-general, he headed the Commissariat for Heavy Industry until
his arrest as an oppositionist.

Ter-Vaganyan: one of the original Bolsheviks; a noted intellectual

ARRESTS, 1937

Svanidze, Alexander Semyonovich: brother of Stalin's first wife
Svanidze, Mariko: sister of Stalin's first wife

EXECUTIONS, 1937

Agranov, Yakov: worked for the secret police, controlling intellectuals and liquidat-
ing "enemies of the people"

Bakayev's wife, Anna Petrovna Kostina: a party member since 1917

Bzhishkyan, Gayk (or Gaya or Gai): Armenian Soviet military commander in the Russian Civil War and Polish-Soviet War; accused of terrorism

Enukidze, Avel: one of the original Bolsheviks and, once, a member of the Soviet Central Committee

Goloded, N. M.: Belorussian accused of being a National Fascist and supporting the White Russians

Mironov, L. G.: served in the secret police under Yagoda

Molchanov, G. A.: As head of the Secret Political Department, he investigated the so-called Trotsky-Zinoviev conspiracy.

Mrachkovsky's brother and nephew: arrested as unreliable

NKVD agents: thousands

Pauker, Karl: Chief of security, he was a former hairdresser at the Budapest Operetta and briefly served as Stalin's barber.

Prokofiev, G. E.: Former assistant people's commissar and Yagoda's second secretary in the secret police, he was arrested as a rightist.

Shanin, Lev: disagreed with Stalin about agricultural policies

Smirnova, Roza and Olga: Ivan Smirnov's wife and daughter

Sulimov, Daniil: a former member of the Soviet Central Committee

Zinoviev's son, Stepan Radomyslsky: Stalin hated his father.

EXECUTIONS, 1938

Aitakov, Nedirbai: a Turkmen and a leading Bolshevik figure in the early Soviet period

Bukharin, Nikolai: A leading Moscow Bolshevik and a member of the Central Committee, he and Stalin clashed often, especially over his insistence that agricultural collectivism proceed gradually.

Chertok, I. I.: Chief subordinate to Karl Pauker in the NKVD and principal interrogator of Kamenev, whom he mercilessly bullied. When the police came for him, he threw himself from his office window.

Erbanov, M. I.: first secretary of the Buryat-Mongol Communist Party

Ikramov, Akmail: Former first secretary of the Uzbekistan Central Committee. An internationalist, he once telephoned Stalin to defend a colleague, a call that earned Koba's wrath.

Kamenev's son, Yuri: killed just before his seventeenth birthday

Khodzhayev, Fayzulla: Uzbek who was one of the chairmen of the USSR Central Executive Committee until the Uzbek Party was purged

Krylenko, Nikolai: the people's commissar of justice who signed innumerable death warrants

Musabekov, Gazanfar: a member of the Soviet Central Executive Committee, representing Azerbaijan

Rakhimbayev, Abdullo: chairman of the Council of People's Commissars, Tajik Soviet socialist republic

Redens, Stanislav Frantsevich: married to the sister of Stalin's second wife

Smirnov, A. P.: In the early years, he successfully opposed Stalin's insistence on executing putative conspirators.

Unshlikht, I. S.: One of the original Bolsheviks, he worked in the war ministry and as a GPU leader fighting against Chechen nationalists.

Yagoda, Genrikh: Head of the NKVD and, from 1934 to 1936, director of Soviet internal affairs and border guards, he organized the interrogations for the first Moscow Show Trial.

EXECUTIONS, 1939

Akulov, A. I.: procurator-general who often issued arrest warrants

Berman, Matvei: OGPU deputy chairman; in charge of the Gulag

Chubar, Vlas: a Ukrainian Politburo leader who begged Stalin, without effect, to send food during the great famine

Frinovsky, Mikhail: Ezhov's police deputy, privy to state secrets

Kamenev's elder son, Alexander: Stalin hated Kamenev.

Radek, Karl: A journalist, he advised Stalin on German politics in the 1930s, served two times on the Central Committee, and helped write the 1936 Soviet Constitution. Accused of treason, he died in a camp.

ANNA'S NOTES

TERMS

bolshaya zona: (the big prison zone) or the world outside the camps
bushlat: a long-sleeved, cotton padded jacket worn by prisoners
Christ's followers: religious ones
deshovka: whore, a name given to virtually all the women
dokhodyaga: a person close to death
dry bath: a search
Ivan: a pigeon, a fall guy, a sap
ment: a jailer
Nasedka: a prisoner who worms from his or her roommate information upon which the authorities can act
pachan: the leader of a criminal gang
parasha: the pail for natural necessities; the toilet
popka: a parrot; an informing jailer
stone sacks: the niches hewn out of the monastery walls that unruly zeks were shoved into, making movement of any kind impossible
stukachi: informers
tufta: deception; getting credit for work not done
urki: criminal prisoners who love to hear stories

IDIOMS

The bear roared: the signal to begin working
The dove cooed: the signal to stop working

"I'll make you suck the snot out of dead men!": a threat made at the daily roll call for any infraction

shitting into someone's head: brainwashing

to receive seven kopeks of lead: to be shot

to sit down on a needle: to become a drug addict

GLOSSARY

au contraire: to the contrary
babushkas: shawls; often used to designate old women
beliy grib: white mushroom
biscotti: biscuits
blat: the informal exchange of favors, bribes, payoffs; pull, influence
burqa: an enveloping outer garment worn by women in some Islamic traditions
chadra: head scarf
chai: tea
cherkeskas: Circassian coats, with wide sleeves, that reach to the floor; they resemble burqas, except that they are designed for men.
chistka: purge
cit: citizen
cittadini: citizens
cordon sanitaire: (French) a barrier restraining free movement of people or goods, so as to keep a disease, infection, or some other contagion from spreading from one locality into another
das Ekel: Literally, the word means grouch.
davening: praying
Deus vobiscum: God be with you.
ebreo/a: Hebrew
etta govnaw: Go take a shit for yourself.
Extreme Unction: the anointing of the sick
Fasci Italiani di Combattimento: Italian League of Combat

frum: kosher

genug: enough

govnaw: shit

horribili dictu: as horrible as it is to relate

ichkari: The enclosed women's quarters of a Muslim house; from the outside, it is impossible to see the women inside, though they can look outside.

incroyable: incredible

kvas: A fermented drink made from rye, barley, rye bread, and other ingredients; often flavored, it is not strong.

kvell: to exclaim or feel good about the achievements of a family member or a friend

le brouillon: (French) first draft

mensch: a man who is honorable, decent, and responsible; a man who exhibits strength of character

naches or **nachas:** joy

nepman: a merchant who buys and sells for profit; a capitalist

NKVD: The initials stand for People's Commissariat for Internal Affairs.

Novecento: nineteen hundred

oblast: geographical region

obnovlentsy: church reformers

perlustration: the opening of other people's mail for the purpose of spying

poste restante: general delivery; a service where the post office holds mail until the recipient calls for it

Pravda: truth, the title of a Russian newspaper

predatel: traitor

Qur'an: Koran, the holy book of Islam

sans: (French) without

schmuck: Yiddish pejorative for a penis

shpik: spy

shtiklech: customs, habits, peculiarities

stopiatnitsa: a person who was not allowed to stay in Moscow; specifically, a person who had to live at least 62.14 miles outside the city

Talmud: The collection of writings constituting the Jewish civil and religious law; it consists of two parts, the Mishna (text) and the Gemara (commentary), but the term is sometimes restricted to the Gemara.

Topolino: little mouse; the smallest car that Fiat made

tovarishch: comrade

traif: forbidden food

Vozhd: Leader

Wehrmacht: literally "defense power"; the name of the unified armed forces of Germany from 1935 to 1945